Desert Winds

Desert Winds

Chesterman

CONTENTS

PROLOG

The wind never stopped.

It hissed across the desert floor, dragging ribbons of sand through the stary light until the landscape seemed alive, shifting and breathing beneath the heaven's glow. The night was empty except for the dark figure moving through it, head bowed against the gale, every step measured and deliberate.

His clothes flapped in the relentless wind. Sand scraped across his boots and stung his face, but he never slowed. The lights of the distant industrial complex shimmered on the horizon, pale islands in a sea of darkness.

After nearly an hour of silent progress, a chain-link fence emerged from the gloom.

The figure crouched low and glanced along its length. Nothing moved. No headlights. No voices. Only the constant moan of the wind threading through the metal mesh.

From a pocket, he drew a pair of heavy cutters.

The jaws bit into the wire with muted metallic snaps, one link after another. He worked quickly, carefully supporting the mesh to keep it from rattling. Within moments, a ragged opening hung loose enough for a man to squeeze through.

He dropped to his stomach and wriggled into the gap but was stopped by the snag from his protective vest. He twisted and pulled until the vest was freed then dragged himself across the sand until he emerged on the opposite side. Rising immediately, he slipped the cutters away and broke into a run.

The empty lot stretched between him and a massive factory building, its blank walls climbing into the darkness like a cliff. Pools of yellow security lights left long shadows between lonely trailers and loading bays, but the broad expanse itself appeared deserted.

His footsteps on the asphalt were drowned by the roaring wind.

Reaching the building, he pressed himself flat against the cold concrete and listened.

Nothing.

Only the wind.

He eased his head around the corner, preparing to move again.

A distant crack split the night.

For the briefest instant he seemed merely startled, as if trying to understand what he'd heard. Then the force struck his chest with brutal finality, driving him backward against the wall.

His breath vanished.

He looked down to see a dark stain spreading across his vest, almost black in the yellow security lighting.

His knees buckled. He slid down the concrete until he sat awkwardly on the ground, one hand pressed uselessly against the wound, and a sharp metallic tang filled his mouth. Its finish was salty warm then sickly sweet.

The desert wind swept past him as relentlessly as before, lifting dust into the air and carrying it through the hole he'd cut in the fence.

Far away, beyond sight in the darkness, silence reclaimed the night.

The figure's hand fell limp.

Within moments, there was no movement at all.

Wednesday Night, Thursday Early Morning

Mateo and Sheldon snaked their way between the long industrial warehouse buildings in a late model white panel van. The van had no markings or logos on either side making it indistinguishable from any of the thousands of white vans in the Coachella Valley. Mateo drove towards the back of the building complex on this moonless night through the north side parking lot. The north entrance was much narrower than the lot on the south side and required him to maneuver around several planters, two parked customer cars from Aaron's Smog and Tune, a large dumpster, and four service trucks from Polar Air Conditioning, the business adjacent to the crematory, but it was still the safest way to go because several of the security lights mounted on the roof were out on the north side. As he weaved his way through the narrow drive, the wind blew the loose roof flashing on the building, and it rippled and scratched in the wind, yearning for its freedom.

The noise sent shivers down Sheldon's spine, afraid they would be seen at any moment. For him, the whole complex seemed to take on an anthropomorphic quality, threatening to reveal what they were about to do. He felt queasy but knew Mateo would be angered if he said anything more. He took deep breaths until the nauseousness passed.

It wasn't the fact there was a dead body in the back of the van that concerned him. Heck, Sheldon had been around lots of dead bodies, but never riding around in a panel van in the middle of the night with one, or without the proper paperwork from the hospital, the police, the next of kin. That's the thing that made him anxious, or was it full blown fear, and he questioned once again how he ever got roped into this. He thought this may be illegal, but after pointing this out to Mateo for the third time, Mateo blew a fuse. Cussed and yelled at him followed by threats. Sheldon thought the dead guy in the back made the threat even more real than anything he had said in the past.

Just behind the windowless double doors at the back of the van, the body rested quietly in an industrial sized black plastic trash bag. Sheldon kept taking quick glances looking for movement, signs of life, as Mateo drove. *Maybe he's not be dead. Maybe he's only unconscious, or maybe there's no real body back there. Afterall, it's in a black plastic bag. You can't see through those.* But he wasn't about to ask Mateo again, not after his blowup. He glanced back again. No movement. No sound. he thought, how paradoxical. Even with the wind roaring from the outside combined with all the twists and turns Mateo made, the body seemed to rest quite peacefully now, even if it had been brutally murdered only hours ago.

Once Mateo reached the end of the complex, he saw the two twelve-foot industrial metal doors of the crematory and backed the van to the first one. They resembled a rolltop desk with a series of flexible metal slats from bottom to top, and each had its own padlock at the bottom. He thought again about others he might have gotten to go with him on this little field trip, as he called it, but he came to the same conclusion. It had to be Sheldon, no one else but Sheldon. He had the key, and he knew how to operate the equipment.

At 33 years old, Mateo Rivera was six feet and weighed a toned two hundred twenty pounds packaged in a perfect V posture. His dark complexion, classic Roman nose and black shoulder length hair pulled back into a ponytail contrasted his clean-shaven face and pockmarked cheeks; scars left from his teenage years. His eyes were dark and projected a sense of mystery, but his behavior said he was a no nonsense professional. Women found him alluring but men were often intimidated by him.

Tonight, he was dressed in black jeans, black long sleeve sweater, black shoes, and black leather gloves rested on the console of the van.

"Sheldon, get that door unlocked!" Mateo barked. Sheldon smiled as he opened the van door. Why did I ever agree to do this, anyway, thought Sheldon.

At twenty-two years old, Sheldon Goodman stood at five feet, ten inches and weighed a slim one hundred forty pounds with scruffy wind-blown brown hair that covered his ears and touched his collar. His brown eyes were perched above high cheekbones. He wore a charcoal gray hoodie with an Under Armor logo, jeans, and worn tennis shoes.

Sheldon was quiet and seemed hesitant as he stepped out of the van and braced himself as a gust swept through the parking lot causing him to stumble. He squinted to keep the blowing sand from his eyes as a tumbleweed rolled across the lot then eddied in the corner of the cinderblock wall that surrounded the complex. Once he regained his footing, he pulled a key out of his pocket and opened the padlock, lifted the door then shimmied through the opening. Once inside, Sheldon found the looped chain that ran from the bottom of the door to its top where it looped around a pulley system. He pulled on the chain and opened the door to its full height. The door rattled as it ascended, and the wind whistled through the opening. Sheldon shivered at the sound.

"You wanna just unload him here and carry him in?" squealed Sheldon attempting to be heard above the sound of the wind.

"No. I'm gonna back the van in, and we'll unload once you shut the fucking door," Mateo responded, frustrated that Sheldon couldn't have thought this on his own. This would keep any prying eyes from their work.

"Hey, that's a good idea. That way we won't need to carry him so far," unaware of Mateo's frustration.

Mateo backed the van in on the gray cement floor while Sheldon shut the door, and it rattled as it closed. The cremation room was a large open room, longer than it was wide, consisting of three windowless gray cinderblock walls. The fourth back wall was textured sheetrock and painted desert sand with a solid metal door in the middle also of desert sand. There were two reefers pushed against the left wall, and a furnace stood against the right wall. The far-left corner held a break area.

As Mateo stepped out of the van, Sheldon started to show him around. "The two reefers are where the bodies are kept. See the green lights above the doors? I always check the lights when I come in. If they're green, the reefers are cooling. If they're red then they're too warm, but I never saw them red when I was here."

******

Sheldon had worked at the crematory, but was let go a few weeks ago. His six-month employment had ended in disaster with talk of a lawsuit and possible criminal charges. It wasn't his inaccurate paperwork or the one time he fell asleep while operating the Cremator. Heck, the thing operated itself once you started it. It had more to do with the mix-up of Mrs. Greenbaum's body with Angela Lopez.

Angela was an older woman with no family and a local church had paid for the cremation. Mrs. Ethel Greenbaum came from a well-to-do family with extensive children and grandchildren. After all, ashes are ashes, once they're cremated, who's gonna know?! The thing that couldn't be explained away was the fact that Mrs. Greenbaum was scheduled to be cremated on Friday not Tuesday. Sheldon had mistakenly stuck Angela Lopez's ashes in the urn that the Greenbaum's ordered, tagged it and completed the paperwork on Tuesday. Who would have thought that on Thursday someone from the family wanted to view Mrs. Greenbaum one last time before her scheduled barbequing... and there she was, still laying in the reefer while Sheldon held the tagged Ethel Greenbaum urn in one hand trying to convince the group that the body in the reefer was some Hispanic woman named Angela Lopez. Needless to say, that was Sheldon's last day working at the crematory, but he did keep the padlock key.

It wasn't that Sheldon was incompetent, it was because of his lack of sleep. He was out most nights doing runs for Mateo. After working all day at the crematory then catching a few hours of sleep before meeting Mateo at the casino and driving all over the valley with pickups and deliveries with those black Timberline backpacks, he never got enough sleep to be at his best when he came to work at the crematory in the morning. It eventually cost him the job.

******

Sheldon looked at Mateo and pointed to the cremating furnace positioned midway along the right wall and stopped mid step. "Look here. That's the cremator!"

Sheldon had always considered the cremator as a sacred apparatus, initially much like the altar at a church, a communion wafer, or communion wine. Later, he came to believe this machine possessed supernatural capabilities of transporting the deceased to their final resting place through some mystical means. The noises it made during each cremation reminded him of a rhythmic heartbeat, the fans and burners representing its breath and soul. The mouth of the beast consisted of a wide door in the center, and above the door to the right and left were indicator lights that made up its eyes. Now he stood with Mateo facing this sacred beast once again.

Mateo looked at his watch then said, "Sheldon, there's no time for this! Let's unload the fucking body and get the thing in the furnace." He didn't need a tour of the place. He needed to get this job done and out of there before it was light and before workers came to the surrounding businesses. Sheldon smiled, but thought, this is the last time I do anything for Mateo.

Sheldon opened the van doors then Mateo helped him lift the body in its black industrial plastic bag onto the dolly.

"We just wheel it over and throw it in, right?" Mateo asked.

Sheldon, feeling like the expert on cremations, responded as matter of fact as he could, "We first gotta weigh him so I know how to set the cremator. We usually put the bodies in one of those cardboard boxes over in the corner and store them before we put 'em in."

"Fuck that! We'd have to take it out of the bag. Too messy. We'll just throw it in, bag and all," said Mateo.

"I dunno. That's how we always did it when I worked here."

We're not taking it out of the bag!" Mateo now insistent to get the cremation started. "There'd be blood, brains, and who knows what else leaking out of it to deal with. The bag stays closed!"

"I guess I could set the casket type on the cremator for a body bag. That should be okay," He became anxious about this change in protocol. Then Sheldon smiled again, thinking, I'm the one who knows how to do this. Where does he get off telling me how to cremate a body! This is the absolute last time....

"Wheel it over to the scale and get this damn thing started," Mateo insisted. He was nervous and wanted to move things along.

Once weighed, Sheldon wheeled the body in its plastic bag to the door of the furnace. Mateo grabbed the door handle thinking they could just throw it in but Sheldon stopped him.

"Wait! I have to turn the thing on and get it warmed up first. Once it's at 1,450 degrees, then we put him in."

"Let it warm up with in the furnace! We need to get this done in a hurry," replied Mateo.

"That's not the way we did it when I worked here. I think it'll create smoke, and who knows what else." Sheldon replied then smiled, ...the absolute last time!

Ignoring Sheldon's advice, Mateo threw open the door of the furnace and ordered Sheldon to help him load the body. Sheldon did as he was told then Mateo shut the door.

Sheldon headed towards the company office through the door on the back wall, "I gotta get an ID number and password to start the cremator. They keep them written on a clipboard behind the counter."

Moments later, he reappeared making a bee line to the cremator's control panel. He punched a few buttons, then the cremator came to life. Lights began flashing, and several fan motors began turning, then Mateo heard the sound of several burners firing up as the cremator happily started its run cycle. He began to relax, and Sheldon listened to the familiar rhythmic sound of the cremator's heartbeat and for an instant he stood alone, just him and the sacred cremator doing its spiritual work.

He looked at the control panel and read the remaining time. Proudly, he announced, "One hour and fifty-three minutes, and it'll be done." Moving to the table on the far side of the room, Sheldon grabbed a deck of cards from the book shelves. "What about a game of cards while we wait?"

"Poker. Five card stud. Nothing wild. You got cash? It's no fun if we're not playing for anything."

"Just a second," and Sheldon disappeared back into the office. Moments later he returned with a can of change. "They keep this around for the vending machines at the front of the complex." Sheldon began to separate the change into equal piles.

Mateo rolled his eyes, "We're playing for change!? I haven't done that since grade school."

"Hey, I'm poor, remember."

Shaking his head, Mateo shuffled the deck. "Ante's five cents."

While they played, Sheldon thought about tonight's events and all the night work he had been doing for Mateo, and he became anxious again. For Sheldon, anxiety was connected to a feeling of worthlessness that he hated. Anxiety was the horse, and worthlessness was the cart that followed. He appreciated the help Mateo had given in the beginning, but as their relationship progressed, he wanted out. He wanted to be done with all of these deliveries and favors. "Mateo, I'm not sure what we're doing tonight is legal, and I don't want to go to jail."

"Shit, Sheldon. We're not doing a damn thing wrong," insisted Mateo. "It's not like you killed the guy. And you don't know how he fucking died anyway. I never told you. For all you know, he could have passed away from natural causes, and we're just helping a family in need. A poor family that has no money to take care of their loved one. Don't jump to fucking conclusions!

Sheldon grimaced, "No, but I don't want to end up in jail either."

"It's a dead body that's being cremated in a business that does this all the time. No fucking law is being broken! Would you feel better about it if I made the dead guy's family pay us for the cremation? Just make sure you keep your mouth shut, and everything'll be fine."

Changing the subject, and his tone Mateo said, "There may be an opening at the casino in about two weeks. I got a guy that plans to move up north so his spot will be open when he does."

"You know this is at least the fourth time you've said this or something like it to me, 'a position is about to open'." Mateo seemed to bring this up every time Sheldon was feeling like he needed to end things with him.

Mateo raised his voice, "You callin me a lair?" Now more calm, more business-like, "Shit happened outside of my control the other times. This time it's for sure. I do the hiring on this one so it's definitely yours. A six-figure income in three years! You'd like that now, wouldn't you? And no more of these little evening field trips once you're hired. Isn't that what you're complaining about? You can wait two, maybe three weeks, right?"

Sheldon didn't answer. He had sworn to himself this would be the last time... the last time he would do anything more for Mateo. And that meant no casino job. He would not apply even if it actually opened up. No six-figure income in three years, even if it were actually true. That old feeling of worthlessness began to rise inside him, and he hated that feeling, but he hated the road he was following, the one Mateo was leading him down.

"Sheldon, two, maybe three weeks. You can wait, right?" Mateo said again, insisting on an answer.

He did not want a confrontation with Mateo. Sheldon always bent to his will when confronted. "Yea, I guess I can wait." He knew this would avoid a conflict.

******

Mateo could convince Sheldon of almost anything, but that was because of their history. They had met at Witch's Brew Coffee and More, the only coffee shop in Desert Hot Springs. Sheldon had just started working part-time, and he was making drink orders when Mateo strutted through the front door just after 6:30 pm. He wore expensive designer clothes and looked like he had just stepped out of a GQ Magazine. The coffee shop didn't get people dressed like Mateo and was a sharp contrast to the city's reputation of gang violence, drugs, prostitution, and the downtown area littered with low-income and government subsidized housing. The million-dollar homes that surrounded the northern hillside did little to change this reputation.

Mateo ordered an espresso then sat down in a pillowed leather chair near the counter to wait for his drink. He studied closely as Sheldon prepared the order and met him at the pickup area as Sheldon started to call out the completed order.

"Thanks. That's mine," he said, reaching out with two hands to carefully take it from Sheldon. "I was watching you as you made my drink. You've got a real knack for this."

"Thanks," replied Sheldon, embarrassed.

"You just started working here, right?"

Sheldon was surprised because this well-dressed successful man was taking notice of him. He was a nobody, as insignificant as an ant on the sidewalk to this guy, yet he knew something about him. "Yea. I just started. It's only part-time for now. How'd you know?"

"I come here a lot, and you're a new face. What's your name?"

"Sheldon, Sheldon Goodman," he replied.

"Well, Congrats, Sheldon Goodman, on doing an excellent job." Mateo smiled a confident smile, then before he sat back down said, "Thank you for the drink," and left a ten-dollar tip.

At 6:50 pm Sheldon moved to the dining area to clean in preparation for closing. Mateo sipped his drink and continued to study Sheldon as he cleaned. At 7 pm the manager put a closed sign in the window and held the door open for Sheldon who was done for the evening. Mateo followed him out.

"Hey Sheldon," called Mateo. "Wait up a second, I wanted to talk with you." He stopped and turned to face Mateo confused.

"You live close by? I noticed you weren't headed to the parking lot so I thought you lived close if you're walking."

"No, it's about a mile away towards the mountain, and I don't own a car. I'm just staying with a friend right now until I can get my own place. It's a studio and there're three of us."

"Wow! Those are some great friends to let you stay in a studio with three people."

"Only one's a friend. That's Mic. The other guy gave me two weeks to get out. I don't know how I'm gonna get enough money in two weeks to move out."

"You got a plan?"

"Not really. I've mostly been living with other people and moving from one side of the valley to the other. Guess I'll do that, maybe go back to Indio."

"Let me give you a ride home. I go that way myself so it's not out of the way. My car's right over here."

Mateo led Sheldon to his dark blue Mercedes AMG then sat in the car and talked for some time. Sheldon told Mateo about growing up with his addict mother who had gotten into a church operated drug rehabilitation program then abandoned him leaving him at fifteen to be raised by the church. Mateo listened intently, complimenting Sheldon on his strength of character, his courage, and his choices, saying anyone else in his situation would be in prison by now.

Sheldon found it easy to talk with this man he had just met. Mateo seemed to see something in him that Sheldon couldn't. When Mateo praised him, he felt good about himself. Mateo made him feel intelligent, successful, and powerful; being victorious over the circumstances he had faced in life at such a young age. Most of his life experiences made him feel like the world thought he was worthless, but Mateo didn't.

And that feeling projected itself from Mateo to Sheldon. The more they talked the more he beamed with confidence and pride with what he had already overcome in his life. Mateo finally drove him to the apartment, and as he stepped out of the car, Mateo gave him his business card.

"I need help with some things around my house, Sheldon. I was hoping you could come work for me when you're not at the coffee shop. And I'll make sure I pay you enough so you can get your own place by that two-week deadline."

Sheldon read the card, Desert Winds Casino, Assistant Director of Security. Sheldon called Mateo the next day.

Mateo kept Sheldon busy during the next few days doing odd jobs around his house. He would leave the key under the mat, and Sheldon would work doing whatever was on the list that Mateo left for him. After three days, he earned enough money to get his own studio apartment and did just that. He knew Mateo was paying him much more than his work was worth. He didn't know why but was grateful.

Sheldon would come over when Mateo was at home just to hang out when he wasn't working. They would shoot pool in the patio sunroom, swim in the infinity pool, and barbeque on the patio. This is when Mateo asked him if he could help a few evenings a week with some casino business. Because he was the Assistant Director of Security at the casino, he did some confidential business "off books" from time to time and needed someone he could trust to help him. Sheldon beamed when Mateo asked. Mateo was someone who really believed in him, and that gave him confidence. Sheldon smiled and told Mateo he would help him with anything he needed. Sheldon trusted Mateo.

"Sheldon, I need you for tomorrow night. It's a very important business meeting, and I need you to work as my chauffeur. Can you do that for me?"

Sheldon hesitated, "I can drive, but I don't have a license. Will that be a problem?"

Mateo smiled a confident smile, "For what we'll be doing, it'll be fine. But next week let's work on getting you a license."

"But I don't have a car,"

"That's okay. You can use mine, and I'll help you study for the driving test."

Sheldon was dumbfounded. Why was this guy, this successful, rich businessman taking such an interest in him. "Thank you, Mateo."

"Let's meet at 9 pm at Witch's Brew tomorrow night."

That evening after they got into Mateo's car with Sheldon behind the wheel, Mateo opened the glove box and brought out a Glock 19 in a leather clip holster. As the chauffeur for these "business meetings" Sheldon would also be security. After all, Mateo was a security officer for the casino and these evening "business meetings" were with some shady people. Sometimes seeing security at a meeting kept people from losing their temper or acting like a fool. Tonight's meeting place would be outside in the back of the casino parking lot, and Mateo said he could legally authorize him to have the sidearm. The area did not have cameras and limited lighting so when Mateo got out of the car, Sheldon was to step out of the car too, then shut the door, and stand at the car watching Mateo and anyone else he was meeting. He needed to ensure the Glock 19 was clearly seen on his belt.

Sheldon had never handled a gun before and was uncomfortable with the weapon. Mateo listened to his concerns then told him that as a man, and Sheldon was clearly a young man going somewhere, that it was important to adjust to unexpected situations with confidence, not fear. Mateo could get anyone at the casino to do this for him, after all, he was the Assistant Director of Security. He wanted Sheldon to do it for training purposes. Sheldon was unaware, but Mateo was grooming him for something more. Mateo decided he would start taking Sheldon out to a gun range to get used to handling firearms.

Feeling better after Mateo's explanation and Mateo's unwavering trust in him, he swallowed hard then clipped on the Glock 19. The engine of the Mercedes AMG roared to life when Sheldon pressed the start button, and they pulled out of the parking lot heading west to Desert Winds Casino.

Mateo held true to his promise and took Sheldon to the gun range once a week, and he also helped him get his driver's license using his Mecedes for the driving test. Sheldon passed and Mateo took him out to celebrate by getting him his own Glock 19 and a car. The car was used, small, and inexpensive, but it was a car.

Now that Sheldon had his own car, Mateo wanted him to make some evening pickups and deliveries. He would pick up and deliver backpacks to and from various locations in the valley, always black in color and always Timberline. Initially it was one or two backpacks per week, but it quickly escalated, and now he was required to drive to Riverside, San Bernardino, Los Angeles and San Diego regularly. Several times he made trips to Calexico, the border town with Mexicali. Mateo told him it was confidential casino work and to never look in the back-packs. Sheldon complied and never opened a backpack. He was happy for the money and being able to help someone he respected, but even-tually he questioned the legality of it all. When he was promoted to full-time at the coffee shop, it conflicted with his work for Mateo so he found the job at Desert Valley Cremations. He hoped he could do both, but eventually was fired and now was back at Witch's Brew.

He had trusted Mateo, blind loyalty, a soldier obeying the orders of his commanding officer without question, but no longer did he trust Mateo. When he was fired, Sheldon swore to himself this would be the last time... the last time he would do anything more for Mateo. This was the first time Sheldon thought this... but it would not be the last. Mateo held a power over Sheldon, and regardless of how hard he tried, he just couldn't say no. Whenever he thought about refusing or tried to make an excuse, that old feeling of worthlessness would rise inside him, and he hated that feeling. This is why Sheldon, once again, ended up here tonight doing something he really didn't want to do.

******

Two hours and ten minutes later, Sheldon opened the cremator door and was greeted by a swoosh of hot air while the cremator's ticking sounds indicated it continued to cool. Mateo had been worked up for the last twenty minutes asking why they needed to wait for it to cool, but the rush of hair-singeing hot air answered his question. Sheldon put on some work gloves, grabbed the cleanout tool hanging on a hook next to the door, and brushed the ashes into a pan after smashing several larger chunks of bone that had not completely deteriorated. Mateo handed Sheldon the old Hills Brothers coffee can he had brought, and Sheldon dumped the remains into the can then put on the plastic lid. The can heated up quickly so Sheldon wrapped it with a towel he found lying on one of the chairs and handed it to Mateo, smiling as he gave it to him. Never again, he thought.

The morning light slowly seeped from behind the eastern mountains as the sky started its metamorphosis from black to navy, purple, orange, yellow, then blue. It was spring, the air was cool, and filled with the smell of fresh sage. Birds chirped welcoming the new day. By noon it would be 95 degrees and the birds would be gone, but now, the desert seemed alive, friendly, and inviting. Mateo and Sheldon, who were snaking their way out through the parking lot of the industrial park, had completed their job. The lot was just as empty as they found it when they arrived but the strong winds had subsided. They always did in the early morning hours this time of year, but they would be back by the afternoon. Tired and ready for sleep, they turned south onto the road heading towards Interstate 10 where 18 wheelers were just starting their day, their trailer lights of red and amber creating a captivating line of color through the desert valley floor down the artery that runs between the San Gorgonio and San Jacinto mountains to Riverside, Los Angeles, and beyond.

******

The desert winds had always existed here in the Coachella Valley. They soughed across the valley floor long before any indigenous person marked the smooth desert sand with their print. She surveyed the length and breadth of her kingdom with each gust from her lungs. She sighed as early visitors from all directions of the country arrived to experience the valley's healing mineral waters. She howled when Capone and others brought gaming and crime to her virgin sands but swished through the parties of the Rat pack in the 60s. She whistled as casinos rose from the valley floor. Hotels, restaurants, bars and people came to her kingdom, people with their actions and their secrets coveting her kingdom for themselves. She reminded them it was her domain whenever the temperature changed, and it would always be her realm long after the last building turned to dust. But she did keep their secrets. She always kept them. Well, until now.

3

Thursday Early Morning

It was almost 2:30 am when Officer Armando Martinez pulled his cruiser onto the Denny's parking lot just off Indian Canyon Road radioing dispatch code 10-7, out of service, for his usual early morning break. At 34 years old, Armando had been a deputy sheriff for six years with Riverside County, an extensive county covering 7,303 square miles which included large cities as well as unincorporated areas and all of the Coachella Valley. He had always worked the Coachella Valley where he was born and grew up. Armando was called by friends and family, Mando, getting the nickname when he was two years old by his grandfather who was also named Armando. This made clear whose attention a family member wanted when they addressed Armando. Calling Mando, Junior, just didn't fit since his father was named Ezekiel, and Armando the second sounded too formal. Mando stood at six feet and a beefy 220 pounds with a barrel chest. His hair was cut short in a military style, and his face was shaved clean conforming to police standards. His dark brown eyes were framed by an olive complexion. When he smiled, his eyes lit up, and Mando smiled more than he frowned. He had a quality about him that made people comfortable, and it was this quality that instinctively allowed him to walk into a volatile situation and immediately de-escalate those in conflict. The academy gave de-escalation training classes, but Mando had a natural ability for this that transcended his training. This quality came in handy regularly and because backup could be up to twenty minutes away, it had saved him from physical confrontations on many occasions.

Mando parked, locked his cruiser, and walked across the wind-swept parking lot and into the restaurant breathing in the aroma of hot coffee that saturated the air. He needed a cup or two before he finished his shift. This particular Denny's was located at the far southwest corner of his patrol area right off the I-10 Interstate, and Mando made a point of taking his break there when he worked nights.

Mando was working the Desert Hot Springs area. Twelve hours on, twelve hours off, three days a week. Due to the city's budgetary constraints, this year the city contracted with the county to handle all of its public safety needs. It was cheaper for the city to rent from the county than have its own dedicated police force. The county would provide three officers each evening and four officers on Friday and Saturday evenings as well as several officers during the day. While the city's official name is Desert Hot Springs, locals use the abbreviation, DHS. However, if you say DHS to a tourist, they would think you're talking about the Department of Homeland Security which would always be confusing when a local was giving directions to one of the many tourists visiting the Coachella Valley.

After reaching the cash register, Mando turned left and sat down at his usual table where he could keep an eye on his cruiser. The parking lot was well lit so he had a direct view of it through the big picture windows that lined the front of the restaurant. The waitress walked to the table, coffee pot in one hand with saucer and mug in the other.

"Officer Martinez, good to see you tonight. Do you want your usual?"

"Evening, Maria. Yes, I do. You're a godsend! I really need this tonight in order to finish my shift."

"Sounds like you've been busy tonight. All those criminals been keepin you hoppin?" asked Maria while setting down the saucer and mug then filling it to the brim with hot coffee.

"No, just the opposite," Mando responded. "It's been a slow night. Only a few calls and the streets are pretty much dead. I haven't even seen a single crack whore walking Palm Drive tonight. I think that's a first for me since I started working nights here. The weekends keep me awake with all the activity but these weeknights can be slow and the night can just drag on... like tonight. It being the end of the month, people are waiting to get paid so they can hit the streets again, or the bars. Criminals need money too, you know."

Maria laughed, "I suppose they do. You know, I grew up in DHS and I don't remember there being the gangs, drugs, assaults, robberies, and break-ins that we have now. Maybe I was just too young to know all this was going on."

Maria was a short, round Hispanic woman in her early sixties. Her eyes were dark and her dimples shone when she smiled. Her hair, once flaxen, was now dull and streaked with gray and pinned up off her shoulders. She was dressed in a Denny's uniform and wore what once were white tennis shoes, now more gray than white from being used as her only comfortable work shoes.

While Mando didn't know her history, he guessed hers was common to Hispanic families throughout the Coachella Valley. She probably had a brood of children and later her husband had left her. He could have been an illegal and was deported or he just moved on to other pastures. This was common for any family living just above (or below) the poverty level in the Coachella Valley. So, she worked to support her kids. As they grew, they continued to live at home but worked to help support the family. It's usually the youngest that ends up at the local community college then maybe the state university and eventually works their way out of the cycle of poverty that seems to plague DHS and other impoverished cities in the Valley. Growing up in Cathedral City, Mando knew families that perpetuated this cycle of poverty, each generation repeating the cycle from the previous. A family lives with hunger, poor health, and living conditions. This keeps them from seeking education, and the family pressures them to work rather than go to college or even finish high school. This creates a lack of opportunity that in turn keeps them at low-income jobs. When they have kids, the cycle repeats for the next generation. Mando's parents had broken this cycle for his family. He was the youngest of three siblings, and his parents worked in the healthcare industry, his mother a nurse and his father an X-ray technician. He never knew the circumstances that helped them get their education, but as he learned more about this cycle and seeing so many families perpetuating it, he realized how fortunate he was. Mando was a police explorer in high school, then went to college for a criminal justice degree. Eventually, he completed the police academy then was hired on by the Riverside Sheriff's Department.

"No, Maria, crime in DHS and the whole Coachella Valley has gotten worse over the years. And believe it or not, it's really the result of the Los Angeles court system. Young men in and out of the criminal system in Los Angeles are told by the judge when they're released, they can't live in the Los Angeles area because of all the bad influences they have around them so they send them out here to the Coachella Valley. Years ago, we dealt with our own local gangs like Outpost or Dream Homes, but today, thanks to the LA courts, we have the Crips, the Bloods, MS-13, Mexican Mafia, and now the cartels from Mexico have even moved into the area."

"I live up on Miracle Hill. It's not as bad as the numbered streets in the middle of town. Been up there for years, and still living in the home my parents bought when I was young," said Maria. "I'll be right back with your fries."

Mando always ate the seasoned fries with his coffee. He found they soaked up the coffee and were much tastier than regular fries. Something small and saltish in his stomach along with the coffee helped him finish his shift awake and engaged.

Mando took a sip of his coffee and pondered once again about what he thought he saw as he pulled into the Denny's parking lot. Even though it was a moonless night, the sky was crystal clear, the stars twinkling and the tram light was visible from the top of Mount San Jacinto. At night, that tram light was visible to almost half the valley. Mando still wasn't sure of what he saw but it looked like a puff of smoke over the small industrial complex just behind the Denny's building. There's no reason there should be smoke coming from that complex at 2:30 am, and he wanted to dismiss it as nothing, but he just couldn't clear it from his mind. Did he really see smoke or was it a hallucination from being tired and past time for a break? Still, some gut feeling wouldn't let him put it out of his thoughts.

Maria returned with the fries that were steaming from the plate. She sat them down on the table in front of him, "Here you go. Nice and hot. They just came out of the fryer."

"Thanks. They look great," replied Mando, taking another sip of his coffee and deciding he should let the fries cool a bit before popping one into his mouth. Then, pointing north, "By the way, isn't there a crematory in that complex just behind this Denny's?"

"Why, yes… yes, there is. I remember when I first started work here. I thought, Wow, that's really creepy and so close to the restaurant. What next? Will we be serving Soylent Green? Why do you ask?" Maria smiled at her little joke but was sure Officer Martinez was too young to get it. After all, the movie came out in 1973.

Mando felt like he just missed something (Soylent Green? What the hell is that?), ignored it, and asked, "Do you know if they ever work at night, say around 2:30 am?"

"Not that I've ever heard. Again, why do you ask?"

"Just curious," replied Mando, thinking it's better not to say anything. He didn't want to start any rumors and still didn't know if he actually saw anything. He took another sip of coffee, grabbed a fry, blew on it then put it in his mouth and started to chew. Mmmm, seasoned fries. They can't be beat.

After finishing his fries, Mando looked at his watch. He'd been there a full 20 minutes and decided to check out the crematory when he got back to his cruiser. Finishing his second cup, he left money on the table to cover his bill and a nice tip for Maria then headed out. He pulled his jacket around him to block the wind and sand from his body. This time of year, the wind is always bad thought Mando. Once situated in the driver's seat, he started the car and radioed dispatch a 10-8, back in service.

Mando exited the lot and turned north heading to the complex parking lot entrance. Technically, this complex was not his area. It's on the west side of Indian Canyon which is incorporated by Palm Springs. The east side of Indian Canyon is incorporated by DHS. Indian Canyon is the dividing line between the two cities in this part of town. But he is a Riverside County Sheriff and Palm Springs is part of Riverside County so he turned and entered the south parking lot of the complex.

Following protocol, Mando used his spotlight to ensure doors and windows looked secure as he creeped through the lot past each business façade in the front of the complex. Coming around the end of the building, Mando saw the last business was the crematory, but now he didn't see any smoke. He rolled down his window and could hear machinery or maybe a furnace working inside. Driving out through the back of the building onto the north parking lot, he noticed two rollup industrial doors. One had its padlock open and laying on the asphalt.

They must be working there tonight, he thought. Now he was convinced he had seen some smoke, but these furnaces were not supposed to produce any smoke. As Mando thought about it, everything didn't quite add up. Thinking he should investigate further, Mando stopped his cruiser in front of the industrial door that had the open padlock. Just then dispatch called with a 10-16, domestic problem. He was at least 7 minutes away. Mando hit his lights and headed out of the parking lot towards the numbered streets. He would at least log in what he had found before his shift was over.

4

Sheldon

Sheldon grew up in the Coachella Valley. His mother, Naomi Sanchez, bore Sheldon when she was 15 years old. The first few years of his life, they lived from man to man with Naomi always looking to trade up. She was a beautiful woman with blonde hair and slim figure who looked not older, but experienced for her young age. When her first and only husband introduced her to cocaine, she became an addict. Eventually he kicked her out and divorced her, but all this happened when Sheldon was very young and only had faded memories of those days. According to Naomi, her husband had died of an overdose and there were no other relatives.

Needing a way to support herself, Naiomi taught Sheldon how to distract tourists so she could lift their wallets, purses, or other valuables. A cute little 6-year-old boy put tourists at ease and held their attention so she could pick their pockets. She taught him how to do this in stores, hotel lobbies, on Palm Canyon Boulevard and El Paseo Avenue.

They would live out of motels, cheap apartments, or run down trailer parks moving from one end of the valley to the other many times only one step ahead of the law. Naomi spent most everything they stole on her habit so Sheldon grew up with nothing beyond what was furnished where they lived. He often went hungry and rarely attended school, but she did teach him loyalty; loyalty to her, to their little family, and to their lifestyle. Loyalty was more important than the law and keeping his mouth shut about her addiction and how they lived was included as part of being loyal. According to Naomi, attending school could jeopardize his loyalty because he could develop a friendship and inadvertently tell them about their secrets so Sheldon had little schooling.

Eventually, their life of theft became too risky as Naomi's addiction caused her to become careless. She knew she would eventually be caught so she looked for an easier way to get money and support her habit, and Sheldon. This is when she discovered church sponsored drug rehabilitation programs. They were all over the valley. Act like a needy, helpless, and abused single mother trying her best to raise her son, and they would open their doors to her, for a while anyway. But that was good enough. She discovered that she could even get money and drugs from rehab program residents at these church-operated programs. Church run programs were easy targets.

Her final target was the drug rehab program at New Life Empowerment Church. With Sheldon in tow, she attended a service at the church and found it had a two-year drug program. After the service she checked herself into the program, and they moved to the women's home that night.

They were loaded into a church van with five other women ranging in age from mid-fifties to as young as sixteen years old and transported to the women's home where they were assigned a small room that was once a storage closet off the kitchen. It was on the opposite side of the house from the other bedrooms and had been converted to a bedroom consisting of bunk beds, a small desk, and a nightstand. There were no windows and no light in the room except for the small lamp that sat on the desk. The other women lived in two bedrooms each holding four bunk beds. The third bedroom was reserved for the den mother.

The next day, the den mother and the pastor discussed separating them. Sheldon was male, but Naomi insisted that Sheldon, almost fifteen, was too young to be separated from her. After all, they were a family and loyal to each other. Sheldon liked the den mother who had completed the program and was now helping the other women beat their addiction. She encouraged both Sheldon and Naomi which made him feel good about staying in the home. Some of the other homes they had stayed were not supportive or loving. This home gave Sheldon hope that maybe his mom would actually complete the program and make a new life for them.

After two weeks at the women's home, Pastor Alfredo Eminis came over one evening to meet with Sheldon and his mother. The pastor pulled three chairs from the kitchen table, setting two facing each other and the third off to the side. He sat Sheldon's mother in the side chair then he and Sheldon sat in the two remaining chairs.

Sitting across from Sheldon, Pastor Eminis took both Sheldon's hands in his, looked sincerely into his eyes, and with a voice filled with compassion, said, "Sheldon, because you are a young man and not a child, it could appear to some of our parishioners that there may be sinful activities taking place in this home that's been dedicated as a sanctuary for these women who're trying to serve God and overcome their demons."

"As a young man, you have urges just as these women have urges, and with you living here, the church would be allowing all of you to be tempted beyond what you're able to bear. It's a definite appearance of evil, and the church and ministry must shun any appearance of evil. We're all committed to helping these women learn how to walk in victory. We're also committed to giving you a stable, healthy, and Godly living situation. That's why it's in everyone's best interest to have you move to the men's home."

"I don't want you to be used as a tool for Satan to destroy any of our dear sisters in Christ. And I know you don't want Satan to use you to destroy any of them either. I've talked with your mother," Pastor Eminis glanced at Naomi who looked concerned, maybe just slightly scared, but said nothing, "and she agrees with me. So, you and her are going to pack your things, and I'll take you over to the men's home."

With that, the pastor prayed a prayer of submission to the will of God then sent Sheldon and his mother to pack. After packing his few belongings, they said teary good-byes, then Pastor Eminis loaded Sheldon into one of the church's two dilapidated vans and drove the 12 miles to the men's home.

Sheldon was stunned that his mother would allow them to be separated, but he said nothing. After all the moving around the Coachella Valley, her addiction, the thefts, and her talk of loyalty to their family, she was allowing them to be separated. His head hurt, and that familiar feeling of worthlessness began to grow from the ache in the pit of his stomach and to settle somewhere deep inside him.

Sheldon believed his mom's commitment to the program was important, life changing, and thought she was really serious about beating her addiction this time. She was finally doing something to conquer it so Sheldon was determined to support her efforts, especially after Pastor Eminis emphasized how important it was for him to never communicate disappointment, annoyance, or irritation to her. He was to only tell her the uplifting, positive, experiences to his mom as his part of her recovery. If he didn't follow these instructions, it would slow her recovery or cause her to relapse, and he didn't want to be the reason she relapsed.

On the ride to the men's home, Sheldon looked at Pastor Eminis as he drove the van. He was an older man in his mid-fifties, round face, clean shaven with short salt and pepper hair. His shoes were leather and shiny. His tan walking shorts were pressed and creased, and his black Tommy Bahamas shirt held an extensive brightly colored embroidery picture on the back of a beach and beach chairs under the shade of palm trees. He was jovial and sang church choruses as he drove. Sheldon noticed his wedding ring as he tapped it on the steering wheel to the beat of the song he sang, its oversized diamond sparking as the sun shone in through the windshield. They both had their windows rolled down, and the fall desert air breezed through the van. Sheldon admired Pastor Eminis and wished he could maybe be like him someday, happy, confident, successful, secure in who he was, what he was doing, and where he was going.

Looking out the window as the desert landscape passed, they made their way out to an unincorporated area of the Valley where the men's home was located. Sheldon thought he would still see his mom at church services. But there was never any time on Sundays. Both homes had schedules to keep and everyone had chores and duties to complete. They could sit together by special permission during the service and have a few minutes before and after the service to talk, hug, then say another teary good-bye. He saw her a few times while at the church during the week when she would come to clean with the other women from the women's home.

After being there for two months, Sheldon was devastated the night Pastor Eminis came to the men's home driving his brand-new Cadillac Escalade. It was shiny and black and everyone at the men's home gathered round it ogling, like a supermodel had just walked onto the driveway. Pastor Eminis took Sheldon by the hand, led him to the end of the yard where they had some privacy while the other residents continued their ogling. He told Sheldon his mom had run away from the women's home and they did not know where she had gone. She had relapsed (Pastor Eminis used the word backslidden) and started using again. When they confronted her, she ran. Pastor Eminis promised Sheldon they would look for her and assured him they would find her and bring her back. He told Sheldon several times that no one can rely on people. They will always let you down. God is trustworthy, and because he was a servant of God, he was also trustworthy. "God will never let you down or abandon you, Sheldon," Pastor Eminis said. "And I won't either."

The next few Sunday sermons Pastor Eminis gave were along this same theme. Sheldon wondered if it was for his benefit. The next few years while Sheldon was there, he regularly asked Pastor Eminis about his mom, had he heard anything or found her. The pastor always told him that there had been no word, but trust in God. She's in his hands, and if his faith was strong enough, God would bring her back. Sheldon felt the familiar feeling of worthlessness again whenever the pastor predicated her return on his faith. I'm worthless to God and my mom, thought Sheldon.

The men's home functioned much like the women's home but with four bedrooms. There were ten men living there aged from mid-sixties to sixteen years old. Sheldon was the youngest as he had just turned fifteen. The sixteen-year-old was Michael Montague who went by Mic. He had been living on the streets when the church found him and took him in. During the week Mic and Sheldon would be loaded into the men's home van with the rest of the men and driven to the church. This was the second of two dilapidated old vehicles each seating fourteen people. It ran but the AC had broken long ago, and they were told the church did not have the money to fix it. There were no markings or logos on the outside of the van beyond the random scratches, paint chips, small dents, and oxidation.

Because he and Mic were the only ones who were required by the state to be in school, they attended the church's private school five days a week. He and Mic were the only two students. They would go to a smaller room in the back of the church for their private school while everyone else went to work for a landscaping contractor who was a member of the church. He put all the men from the men's home to work during the week mowing lawns, trimming hedges and trees, raking, and disposing of dead clippings. He paid the church a fee for each worker which gave him cheap labor. The church used the money to support the homes and the church, and the men doing the work never saw any of it. Both Sheldon and Mic thought the church was taking advantage of the men in the home and had made a commitment to each other never to work like that.

The church's school program lacked supervision, and the two boys would be alone in the room most of the day. They were given self-instructional material to read and study. Once they completed the packet and scored it with provided score keys, they would take the test on the packet. They had no one to monitor testing so Mic showed Sheldon how to use the instructional packets to complete the tests. They called it open book tests. Wow, it was an easy A grade for Sheldon, but even with using the instructional packets, Mic struggled to pass the tests.

Sheldon excelled with the work and earned merits for the amount of work he would complete at the end of the week, but Mic struggled and often got demerits for his lack of production. This was per the merit/demerit system the pastor had instituted for the men's home. Once all the requirements were completed for graduation, the church would issue an actual diploma recognized by the state since all of the proper paperwork for the school had been filed with the state Department of Education years ago. Sheldon finished and got his high school diploma just before he turned eighteen. Mic, however, was not as successful. The den father told him that once he turned eighteen, that he would be going to work with the other men doing landscaping, no more school. When Mic turned eighteen, he left the men's home to look for a job and a place to live. Sheldon left the next year and roamed the Coachella Valley living mostly with friends, acquaintances, or co-workers. He went from one part-time job to another. Eventually he found Mic who was working full-time at Witch's Brew Coffee and More in Desert Hot Springs. With Mic's help, Witch's Brew hired Sheldon part-time. Now he had a job as a barista and saved everything he made to get his own place. His second evening on the job was when he met Mateo, Mateo Rivera.

5

Thursday Morning

It was just before 8 am when Joe Conti parked in the front parking lot on the south side of the industrial complex. He and hurried across the throughway to the business he and his wife, Toni, started almost four years ago. The complex resembled a strip mall on the south side with storefronts designed in cookie cutter fashion. Coachella Valley Transportation and Cremations was painted on the glass door. The crematory was the last business at the end of the complex.

Joe unlocked the door and walked into the office. The morning sun shone through the glass lighting up the small lobby area. There were three desks set in a horseshoe formation, Toni's on the left, the reception desk center, and Joe's on the right. The back wall held the company name and logo. The door to the right led to the conference room, and behind the conference room was the door to the crematorium where dead bodies were stored in cold reefers and cremations were carried out.

At five feet, eleven inches, Joe had turned forty last month. Toni and the other staff at his birthday party teased him about his extra weight and growing stomach. Joe hated getting older. He had worked construction in the past, but now had a sedentary job. His six pack was turning into a keg; hair had stopped growing where it should (or at least thinned) and started growing where it shouldn't. On weekends he would spend extra time in front of the bathroom mirror plucking ear and nose hairs. When he was younger, he could eat anything and never gained weight. Now, he was sure he would gain five pounds just looking at one of Toni's homemade dishes of lasagna, spaghetti, or ravioli.

His dark eyes and sharp facial features were starting to look fatty from the age. His dad eventually got those bags under his eyes and large jowls to accompany his brow wrinkles. Joe resembled his dad, and the family often compared baby pictures saying they could be twins. Joe suspected age would eventually do the same to him as it did to his dad.

The office opened at 9 am, 9-5 Monday thru Friday, all painted on the side glass panel next to the door, and included the business cell number for 24-hour service. Joe arrived early because he was a morning person and usually got to the office around 8 am. It gave him some personal time to organize and prepare for his day. Connie and Juan were also bringing in a body for storage. He didn't need to be there for this as the business was set up so the on-call crew could make night deliveries without the office being manned. They would enter on the north side of the building, unlock one of two industrial doors on that side of the building, unload their body in a reefer, then put the paperwork in the office updating the reefer storage clipboard with the name, date, time, and reefer storage location of the body.

Connie Asghar and Juan Lopez made a great team. They were both in their early twenties, were professional and reliable. These traits were essential in a business where employees work independently. Connie, who was finishing her second year at the local community college studying psychology, was the lead on the team. She was always empathic and caring when interacting with clients. Juan, who Joe had trained when he first started, rounded out the team. While Connie spoke with the clients, Juan would unload the gurney from the van with an empty body bag, take it to the body and get the deceased ready to load. Once loaded, they would transport the body back to the office and store the deceased in the reefers. They picked up from other funeral homes that contracted with Joe for cremating as many did not have this service in-house. They picked up from the morgue at all three of the hospitals in the Coachella Valley, and they picked up at private residences. Many of these pickups were transported to their business while others went to different locations.

Joe walked to his desk and moved the mouse to wake up his computer but was interrupted by his cell phone. The name, Connie, appeared in the caller ID window. "Hey, Connie. What's up?"

"We're five minutes out. Are you at the office yet?"

"Yup, I just got here. The back doors are still locked so you can open 'em when you get here," said Joe as he grabbed the reefer storage clipboard that hung next to the cremator clipboard looking for empty shelves. "Put the body in reefer two, shelf eight."

"You got it. Will the coffee be ready when we get there? I've been looking forward to a cup for the last twenty minutes."

"I'll get right on it."

Great! We'll see ya in a few," replied Connie as she ended the call.

Joe headed to the conference room to start the coffee. As it was started brewing, Joe heard Connie and Juan open the 12-foot industrial door, so he entered the back room where they were parking.

"Hey, boss. You got the coffee ready? Cuz I need a cup. Juan, you want a cup too?"

"Sure," said Juan, as he opened the van's back door and got the gurney ready. "Connie, you wanna help me first?" Connie got to one side of the gurney while Juan on the opposite lifted the gurney out of the van, and wheeled it to reefer number two.

Connie Asghar stood five feet seven inches tall. Her dark shoulder length auburn hair that framed her round face was pulled back into a ponytail complimenting her olive complexion. Her face was plain with soft features but her eyes sparkled revealing a uniquely caring personality. She was Native American, a member of the Tranquilo Band of the Mission Indians, an indigenous people who lived in the Coachella Valley long before any white settlers had ever touched the virgin valley floor with their wagon wheels, ox carts, or discovered the medicinal properties of the many hot springs throughout the Valley. Her uncle, Fredrick Asghar, was on the tribal council and a receiver of the monies the tribe makes from its casino and other business interests. Only those on the tribal council have access to these monies. The rest of the tribe must fend for themselves. Many live in poverty on the reservation while others, like Connie and her family, moved off the reservation and live and work in the Coachella Valley. It's the tribal council that makes all the business and economic decisions for the tribe. Tribal positions are passed down by bloodline. Connie was not in that specific bloodline. Her uncle's first born, if he ever had children, would be the next in line for his position. Positions can be held for life, but the older council members usually choose to retire and pass the seat to the next in line. They've already made their fortunes, and now it will be their first born's turn to do so. Fred had been on the council for five years and was just elected Tribal Chairman.

"How was everything on the pickup?" asked Joe.

"Smooth," replied Connie. "It was a private residence in the Las Palmas area. I talked to the daughter. She was very nice, but grieving."

Juan looked in the reefer, smiled, then looked at Connie, "Connie, there's already a body on shelf eight."

Joe interrupted, "That's the number I got off the clipboard. Connie, let me check it again," as he headed back to the office. Joe quickly returned knowing what had happened.

"Put this one on shelf ten. The body you brought in earlier last night didn't get put on the clipboard. The paperwork's in the in-basket so I updated the clipboard." Said Joe.

Connie turned to Juan and smiled. "Someone, and I'm not mentioning any names, Juan, forgot to update the clipboard when they put the paperwork in the basket last night."

"Guess that was me," Juan said sheepishly realizing it was his mistake. Then quickly added, "Good thing Joe's got our back." They both entered the reefer and unloaded the body to shelf ten.

Once the body was stowed on shelf ten, Connie and Juan headed for the conference room for a cup of coffee. Connie handed Juan the paperwork for the office in-basket then grabbed a Styrofoam cup and pored the hot liquid. When the front office door burst open, she was startled and almost spilled her coffee. Toni Conti bustled through the door, using her shoulder to push it open as she cradled a box of donuts with both hands.

"Anyone interested in donuts?" she said as she walked into the conference room setting the box on the table. "But no one touch the apple fritter. I got that especially for Joe."

"Mmm, breakfast of champions," said Juan as he opened up the box of donuts and grabbed a jelly filled. Connie, right behind him, grabbed an old-fashioned and took a bite. Once they had made their selection, Joe took his apple fritter. He loved apple fritters and was glad Toni remembered when she picked up the donuts. She must have forgotten about their conversation last night about eating healthier, but right now, he didn't care. There was an apple fritter with his name on it.

"Hey, Toni, I thought we were going to start eating healthier," said Joe through a mouthful of apple fritter.

"I bought these for the staff, not us."

"What about the apple fritter?" asked Joe, smiling as he took another bite.

"Well, next time I get donuts I just won't think about you then," now defensive, but she still had a glimmer in her eye and a slight smile.

Joe, not knowing if she was serious or just giving him a hard time, didn't want this to be his last apple fritter. He sat the apple fritter down, took Toni by both arms and in his most melodramatic voice pleaded, "I'm sorry. I didn't know what I was thinking. All that sugar went to my head and made me crazy! Please don't forget about me when you get donuts. I don't want this to be my last apple fritter!"

Juan and Connie busted up laughing, and Juan, who had been in mid-sip, wiped hot coffee splash from his face with a napkin. Toni smiled. Her eyes danced and her cheeks reddened, but she held back any laughter.

"Well, we'll just have to wait and see what happens tomorrow when I get donuts. Joe, what's on your agenda for today?"

"I've got two cremations, and I'm interviewing for that open position this afternoon," said Joe as the office phone started ringing.

Toni went back into the office, turned the sign in the window from closed to open, then answered the call, "Coachella Valley Transportation and Cremations. This is Toni. How may I help you?"

Joe was sure that was a call for transportation. Who knows. They may get a cremation out of It or a full funeral service as well. Those additional services beyond the transportation really did help with the bills and payroll.

Joe headed to the back deciding he should get the cremator up and running so he could start the cremations he had scheduled. It takes a few minutes to get the furnace up to operating temperature so he always starts the cremator before getting the body and doing the paperwork. Joe walked to the front of the cremator and opened the door. Even though the furnace is cleaned after each cremation, Joe always checked it before starting the unit. Peering inside, Joe did his inspection looking for any damage to the inside of the unit and for cleanliness.

"Well, that's strange," he stated, bewildered as he noticed a small object in the back corner. It was eight feet from the front of the unit and could easily be missed if one was not careful and thorough. Joe grabbed the six-foot cleanout tool and used it to reach to the back corner and shook his head. How could he have missed this last night when he cleaned after the last cremation. He wasn't overly tired, and he is a man that pays attention to detail. He swept this little unwelcome guest towards the front and grabbed it.

The cremator doesn't turn the whole body into a fine powder. This is the first of a three-step process. Once the cremation is complete. The remains are swept into a funnel in the front of the unit then caught in a bucket container at the bottom of the unit. There are always small chunks, usually bone, that will go down the funnel into the bucket. The second step is to take the bucket over to the counter and pour everything into a large plastic container. Using a powerful handheld magnet, the remains are stirred to collect any metal. After this, they are placed into a tumbler that turns the remains into a fine powder.

Once Joe got this little visitor to the front, he put on gloves then picked it up and examined it. "Well, hello there, little guy. Just what are you anyway?"

The piece was round about a quarter of an inch in diameter and over one inch in length with a dulled point at one end, flattened somewhat. The other end was flat. The heat scoring on its surface indicated it may have gone through a cremation cycle.

Thinking aloud, "This looks like a bullet, but bullets are usually made out of lead... and lead would melt in the furnace." But this bullet was made out of a much harder material than lead. Could it be steel? Some bullets will have a copper jacket on them, but inside the copper jacket, lead is still used. And copper would also melt in the furnace. He wasn't sure if bullets were made with other metals for special uses.

"So, how'd you get in my furnace anyway?" asked Joe to the bullet. He hung up the cleanout tool, then, with his new little friend in hand, walked back to the office where Toni was giving Connie and Juan final instructions on a pickup. Joe took a seat at his desk and waited for Toni to finish and the crew to leave.

Once he and Toni were alone, he asked, "Hey, Toni, of the last, say five cremations we've done, has anyone been a murder victim? Maybe shot to death?"

"No, all of them died from natural causes. You know, that's a really strange question. Just why are you asking me that anyway?" Toni puzzled.

"Well, because I just found this in the furnace," as he held up the bullet between his thumb and forefinger. "I have no idea how it got there. But it looks like a bullet to me."

"Whoa, a bullet!? It can't be. Let me see it," Toni stood and crossed the office to where Joe was standing and snatched the round from him. She held it up just as Joe had held it and examined the bullet in the morning light. "Did you miss this yesterday when you last cleaned the unit?"

"I don't think so," said Joe. "I don't think it was in there. But the bigger question is what the hell is a bullet doing in our cremator? Do you think Connie and Juan are messing with me? They were on call last night, and they put a body in the reefer earlier in the evening."

"I don't think they'd do that. They mess around with each other, not with us. That's just not consistent with our relationship with them. Plus, it'd be very unprofessional. And they're just not that when it comes to the job." Toni continued to ponder about how a bullet might have gotten into the furnace. "And it doesn't look in very good shape," holding the bullet up again for Joe to see. "Do you think it went through a cremation cycle?"

"I thought it did. Which means it had to have been in the furnace yesterday before the last cremation. But it couldn't have been. I always clean the unit out between cremations... and I'm thorough. I wouldn't have missed it."

"Where was it in the cremator? If it was in a back corner, it'd be hard to see."

"It was in a back corner, but it wasn't hard to see. The thing is a different color than the furnace floor so it stuck out like a sore thumb. I opened the furnace door and the thing was almost yelling for my attention, 'Here I am, look at me!'"

Joe continued to think, now worried. "Maybe we ought to just toss it and not say anything. You know. No harm, no fowl."

"Let's just hang on to it for now," replied Toni, and pondered the best course of action. "I'll put it away, and we'll keep this between ourselves. If nothing comes of it, then no big deal. If it does become an issue, then we'll have it if we need it." Toni took an envelope from the stationary drawer, put the bullet in it, sealed the envelope, then put it in the back of her top desk drawer and locked it. Joe was satisfied with this and went back to the cremator carefully reexamining it before firing it up for the first cremation of the day.

When Joe and Toni developed processes for the business, they created checks and balances so things would not accidentally be missed and that no one person could transport or cremate on their own without others knowing or being involved with the process. While Joe worked off the cremation clipboard for cremations, the official document was on Toni's computer. She would print out a new list each morning for the clipboard then as cremations came in during the day, Toni would update the computer list but her or Joe would hand write the information on the clipboard. The clipboard lists were kept on the clipboard but were taken at the end of each week, reviewed with the corresponding electronic document then filed.

Toni printed the current list for the cremation clipboard and put it on the top of yesterday's list. She would normally rehang it for Joe to pick up when he was ready to start his cremations, but today she decided to compare the list from yesterday's cremations. She was still mystified about the bullet Joe had found and was searching for some answer to where it might have come from.

First, she noticed a name on the clipboard list that had been entered in but did not appear on her electronic list. There was a location, both reefer and shelf number, of where the body had been stored, and there was also a time of day when the cremation was started. It was printed so anyone could have done it. She compared the location on this clipboard with the reefer storage clipboard and discovered no body had been stored at that location.

Taking the clipboard with her, Toni hurried to the back room where Joe was getting ready for the day's cremations. "Joe, take a look at this. Something doesn't make sense here. Someone entered in this cremation on the clipboard but we have no record of this person at all. It's not on my electronic list, and there was wasn't anyone in the reefer at that location. I doublechecked it with the reefer storage list. It's just a first name. No last name. It looks like the name is Mateo."

"Hmmm, that's strange. That's not me. I write the names." said Joe. "Do you recognize it?"

"No, I don't. I'm gonna check the reefer just in case there's a body there," replied Toni as she opened the reefer door and walked in. Moments later, she exited the reefer, "No body there. Can you compare the case numbers on the cremator with our records, Joe?"

"Good idea," said Joe as he turned off the cremator and went back into the office to print spreadsheets from the computer for comparison. He spent the next 45 minutes spread out at the conference table comparing each case from the cremator's electronic files to the spreadsheets he had printed out from the office computer. He checked names, genders, weights, days and times, along with case numbers for each body. Joe was sure they hadn't made any mistakes. Still his heart raced as he worked. Some bodies are stored for other funeral homes as storage is often in short supply. he charges storage fees and will pick up and deliver for the funeral home for an additional service fee. He hoped they had not cremated a body from another funeral home. And if they did, what happened to the ashes, and what would they tell the other funeral home?

After completing his work, Joe gathered up all his printouts and went back to the office to talk with Toni who had been busy sending out their second crew. This crew would pick up four bodies from the local hospital and deliver them to UCLA's Medical School. These bodies are donated for science by the family or are unidentified bodies the state donates for medical training. Once at the Medical School, the crew will set them up for the medical students on flat stainless-steel tables. Because of traffic, the crew would be out the whole day.

"Toni, I think I've figured out what happened."

"Okay. Tell me what you've found. I've been worrying about this all morning," replied Toni.

"Someone came in last night and ran the cremator through a cremation cycle. I am assuming there was a body in the furnace, but I don't know for sure. I only know there was a bullet in there. Whoever did it had to be aware of some of our processes. They knew how we use the clipboard to track cremations and where to find the codes. They knew how to run the cremator, and they knew our reefer storage location system. Apparently, this Mateo, no last name, was cremated in a body bag.

He was male and weighed 220 pounds. The cremation took place at 2:15 am according to the cremator records. His cause of death may have been by shooting since I found that bullet."

"They also knew how to get in and out of the building without breaking any locks," added Toni.

"Shit, what the hell are we gonna do with this, Toni? And who do you think did it?" asked Joe, thinking more out loud than expecting an answer.

"We need to think about this for a while before we do anything. I don't want any bad publicity. It could hurt the business and we've just gotten ourselves into a place where we have a solid business stream, money coming in, and good employees. I don't want us to overreact then be sorry for what we did. We need to just think about this for a while before we do anything."

"I think we change the locks and contact an alarm system company today. Then I'll stay here at night until the alarm system is up and running. We could also change our night procedure for the back doors. We use the indoor locks and the crews will need to open up the office door to unlock 'em." Joe was thinking out loud again.

"I don't think having them go through the front door is a good idea," said Toni still processing possibilities in her head. "We'd have to give everyone keys to the front door. The door between the conference room and the back is a solid metal door. What if we lock it, alarm it, and put in a night paperwork drop box on the wall next to the door? If the back doors are alarmed, then we should still be able to use the padlocks on the doors and maintain security. I'd feel better if no one but you and I had access to the office because of this."

"And what about the bullet? And the extra cremation?" asked Joe.

"Let's just keep all that quiet for now and keep thinking about it. I don't want us to do something stupid because we didn't take the time to think it through. Does that sound okay?"

"Yup, that sounds okay for now. You know we may need to go to the police about this before it's all over."

Toni was clearly the best person between them to handle issues that required critical thinking skills on the fly. Through the years Joe had learned this and knew it was in their best interests to listen to Toni right now. There'd be time to talk more about it, and he knew from past experiences with Toni, the best option seemed to present itself if they gave it some time. After all, it was her education, experience, and knowledge that allowed them to open the transportation business then to expand it, opening the crematory. It was his skills and expertise in managing crews and the hands-on responsibilities that made the day-to-day operations successful and profitable. Also, Toni could get really pissed off if she felt like Joe wasn't treating her as an equal or listening to her when things like this came up. He had once heard that anyone could do 90% of a big executive's job, but the executive got paid the big bucks because of the 10% that no one else could do. Toni was better at that 10%.

"Yup, we might need to go to the police," said Toni. "Or maybe they'll come to us first. I think I'd like that better if I had a choice. It would allow us to play dumb. Let's just keep quiet about everything right now. I'm sure the right opportunity will present itself, and we'll recognize it when it does."

"So, who do you think did it," asked Joe again. "You think it was someone on one of our crews?"

"I don't think so. These are all good reliable people. Most of them are like family. I trust everyone we have. By the way, you can't say anything to anyone on our crews either." Toni didn't want Joe to get lost in conversation while working with others and forget little things like keeping this a secret.

"I know. I won't say anything," agreeing with Toni. "And that includes everyone who works here. I think you're right about our crews. I trust our people too. Then who?"

Hesitating, Toni finally said, "Sheldon. Who else could it be?"

Toni liked Sheldon when they first hired him over six months ago now. She thought with Sheldon working here, she could help him become a productive member of the community and improve who he was as a young man. He seemed honest but naive needing direct instruction even for the simplest of tasks. Everything was new to him, but he was a hard worker, picked up on routines and processes quickly, and showed a sincere desire to learn. Joe was training him to do cremations and pickups when the crews needed help. She had encouraged Sheldon to start the local community college and get an education, but Sheldon lacked the confidence to start and even seemed afraid to attend.

******

Just before Sheldon turned 18 and still living at the church men's home, Pastor Eminis called him to his office for a talk. Sheldon sat in the chair facing his desk. The Chair was low and Sheldon's chin only came to the top of his desk making him feel more inadequate than he normally felt.

Pastor Eminis entered his office, shut the door, and made his way around his desk. As he sat in his chair, he said, "Sheldon, congratulations on completing your high school requirements. We'll have to throw a party at the men's home for you and make an announcement in church on Sunday. It's quite an accomplishment."

"Thank you, Pastor."

"Now let's discuss the next step for Sheldon Goodman. What does God have in store for him?" said Pastor Eminis, confident.

"Well, I've always wanted to help people, and I thought that becoming a nurse would be my next step. Desert Valley Community College has a program."

"No, no, no, Sheldon. This would never be God's will for you," reproved Pastor Eminis. "Don't you know by now that Satan's knowledge will destroy you and rip the salivation that you've found at New Life Empowerment Church? We showed you the way. You must not deviate from that path or your soul will be destroyed."

Sheldon sat and thought about what Pastor Eminis said. He had always wanted to help others and wanted to become a nurse since he was little. "Can't Christians be nurses?"

"Well, yes, they can, but God's revealed a different pathway for you. When Christians try to go their own way, they always fail. You don't want to fail, do you, Sheldon?"

"No, I don't, but I want to be able to help others too. Can't I do that and serve God too?" he asked.

"Yes, you can, and you should. That's exactly what God has revealed to me for your future, Sheldon. Don't you want to know what God wants for your future?" Pastor Eminis began to press Sheldon, leading him in the conversation.

"Yes, Pastor. I really want to know my future."

"Here it is in a nutshell. This is what God revealed to me as I lay prostrate just this morning seeking His will for your future. Did you know I've been praying for His revelation for you for over a month now. I've fasted and stayed until the wee morning hours praying for Him to tell me. I've lost so much sleep and denied myself many regular meals for you, Sheldon. You don't know how much I've sacrificed for you. But I have because I love you, Sheldon. Because you are part of the church. Because you are important to me."

Pastor Eminis held a long pause to let everything he said sink in. None of this was actually true, but he had discovered that if he prefaced what he was about to say with this type of dialog, it would be readily accepted.

"God wants you to stay at the men's home, complete our two year Den Father Training Program then become the men's home den father and teach others to walk in victory. This is a high calling, a noble calling that few people receive, but this is what God wants you to do."

Sheldon thought about this. Helping others was what he wanted, but he didn't have any desire to help addicts learn how to overcome their addiction. Even though his mother was an addict, he wanted to work with people that were not addicts, people who already had some basic success in living – people that were not addicts.

"So, I'd just be in training, taking classes and other instruction for two years?"

"Well, no. Not exactly. You'd be working with the men doing land-scaping during the day, and doing training on the weekends and in the evening. God expects you to be submissive both physically, emotionally, and spiritually," replied Pastor Eminis.

After a long pause, "May I think and pray on that, Pastor Eminis?"

"Certainly, you may, Sheldon. But this is God's will so your time of decision is about you submitting to the will of God. You take the time you need, then come and tell me you're ready to follow God's will."

Sheldon never talked to Pastor Eminis again about his future, but he did leave when he turned 18. Before he left, Pastor Eminis told Sheldon that because of his background, he would lose his salvation if he worked in the secular world. Going to college would destroy his faith, and his only hope of staying saved was to stay in the men's home and work there, eventually becoming the den father. He left anyway.

Sheldon roamed the Coachella Valley for the next few years living mostly with friends, acquaintances, or co-workers. He went from one part-time job to another but held a few full-time jobs for short periods before some life emergency disrupted it.

******

After several months at Coachella Valley Cremations, Sheldon started having trouble coming to work on time. He seemed to be tired, unable to focus, and started making mistakes or overlooking things. Sheldon said he just had trouble sleeping, but Joe was concerned and thought there was more to it. If he was staying out most nights rather than in bed sleeping, then just what was he doing? Joe was familiar with addictive behavior from managing construction crews and recognized signs.

Sheldon became more inaccurate with the required paperwork, for-got or made mistakes with tasks he had been doing since his first day, and was easily distracted. He'd go from the back room to the office and get sidetracked. Toni found paperwork left by the donuts or coffee-maker, in the bathroom, and once in the reefer. Joe even had to wake him up when he fell asleep during a cremation. That was the first time

Joe talked with Toni about letting Sheldon go. Toni, who had decided to make Sheldon her personal project, wanted Joe to give him a bit longer. She promised to talk with Sheldon and get him back on track. Much to Joe's frustration, he agreed knowing he may be sorry for not putting his foot down and firing Sheldon right then.

The day Sheldon mixed up cremations was the last straw. The cremations were done correctly but on the wrong days. Sheldon had mismarked remains and put these remains in an urn reserved for another client. That was the day Joe let Sheldon go. Toni was disappointed but decided never again would she try to interfere between Joe and an employee... even an employee that tugged on her heartstrings. Joe wasn't sure he believed her even though he appreciated the apology.

******

"I thought it had to be Sheldon too," said Joe. "I never knew what he did with his padlock keys. He always told me he sat them down in the conference room and they disappeared. I just didn't think about those keys until about five minutes ago. We still have his contact information. Maybe we should get ahold of him."

"That's an idea. But let's keep thinking about our options before we do anything. The longer we wait the more options will present themselves. Just like that one." Toni moved to her computer and opened a web browser.

"I'm gonna start contacting alarm companies then I'm going out to get new padlocks," she said. "I'm also going to contact a locksmith and have the front door locks changed. I know the crew doesn't have a key to the front, but I don't want to take any chances. When the locksmith gets here, we can ask him about the back doors."

"Don't get padlocks yet. Wait until the locksmith gets here. We may go a different route after talking with him." Joe knew that motors could be installed on these doors making them electric, opening, closing, and locking. They would be opened by remote over a secured frequency or keypad and this was considered some of the safest and most secure technology on today's market. He hoped the cost would not be prohibitive.

"I've got to start these cremations. I'm already two hours behind. Between the cremations and the interview this afternoon, I'll be tied up here all day. Are you interested in pizza for lunch? They deliver, and I don't think either of us are getting out of the office."

"No pizza! We both made a commitment to eating healthier. We can order Subway, and I'll run over and pick them up," replied Toni.

"Hey, who brought the donuts this morning?"

"Okay, so I forgot and wanted to do something nice for you, and I know you love apple fritters. But I don't think eating pizza fixes that."

"Okay, Subway it is. But I'm getting a footlong Hot Sicilian just for me."

"You always did like hot Italians," replied Toni, who was full blooded Italian.

"You mean you or the sandwich?" Joe teased.

Toni smiled, "Both, me and the sandwich."

Joe laughed, "Baby, you know me so well."

The rest of the morning and afternoon was uneventful. Toni made an appointment for tomorrow morning with Desert Alarms between calls for three pickups for transportation. Two of them would be cremations and full memorial services for the deceased. Toni had contracted with several churches in the valley for memorial services so she called and scheduled them in with the church's administrative assistants. The locksmith showed up about two pm, rekeyed the lock on the front door, installed a locking door knob on the back door to the crematorium and storage area, then gave them new padlocks for the back door with five sets of keys. Only Toni and Joe would have keys to the front door and the door from the conference room to the back. Joe got to work on his cremations while calling people he knew from working construction about installing electric motor and lock systems on the back doors.

At 4:30 pm Toni noticed a police cruiser in the parking lot. It drove past the front door then parked in a stall facing the cinderblock wall. Toni watched as the officer exited the car, walked to their door, and entered the lobby area facing the reception desk. Curious, Toni moved from her desk and stood behind the reception desk directly facing the officer. His name badge listed his first initial and last name, A. Martinez.

6

Thursday Afternoon

"Good afternoon, ma'am. I'm Officer Martinez. How are you today?"

"I'm doing well. I'm Toni Conti. My husband and I own Coachella Valley Transportation and Cremations. How can I help you?"

Mando looked directly at Toni watching for any reaction as he began to speak, looking for any tell that may give him more information than anything she may say. "I was patrolling last night and noticed some activity from this complex. This was about 2:30 am. Were you here doing business during that time?"

Toni froze for a split second, her eyes opening, but no other facial expression, she hoped. Mando, however, knew from her reaction she knew something. Something that she was uncomfortable talking with him about.

"Well, Mrs. Conti, was there something going on here last night?"

"Yes, there was some work going on early this morning, around 2:15 am is when it started. Why do you ask?"

Mando perceived Toni was being evasive, but she had at least been truthful about the business working that early in the morning.

"I cruised through the parking lot and noticed something was going on in the back. Were you cremating bodies that early in the morning?"

"Well, we had the equipment running, but it doesn't mean we were cremating anyone. You know this is sensitive equipment and sometimes it has to be checked and calibrated. We can't do that without running it through a cremation cycle."

"So, you were calibrating your equipment at 2:30 in the morning? Is that correct?"

"Just why are you asking this?" Toni slightly agitated. She didn't want to lie, but she was not yet ready to come clean with everything she knew. Not yet anyway.

"Do you burn anything in the furnace when you calibrate your equipment?" Mando pressed.

"No, when we calibrate, the cycle is run with an empty furnace," less defensive now. She didn't actually say they were calibrating it, so it wasn't a lie. He was just assuming that.

"Your stack was producing smoke last night, so there had to be something is the furnace. This means you were not calibrating it. Crematoriums are not supposed to produce smoke. They should run clean. You have your license so you know the ordnances that dictate this. So, why were you cremating at 2:30 am, and why was your equipment producing smoke?"

Toni paused, a long pause. "Let me get my husband, Joe. He's in the back right now." Picking up her cell phone, Toni called Joe. "Joe, there's a police officer here in the office asking about last night. Could you come to the office so we can talk with him together?" Toni hit the end button, turned back to Officer Martinez, and said, "Joe will be right here."

Moments later, Joe appeared through the door that led back to the crematorium. He walked through the conference room and into the office. "Hi, I'm Joe Conti," extending his hand to Officer Martinez who gave Joe a firm handshake.

"Maybe we should go into the conference room," stated Toni. "We can sit there, and it'll be more comfortable." As Officer Martinez and Joe went to the conference room, Joe gave Toni a serious look. She returned it with a confident one, chin up, strong, in control. That made Joe feel better, but not by much. Toni moved to her desk, retrieved the sealed envelope containing the bullet, then followed Joe and Officer Martinez into the conference room.

Officer Martinez sat in a chair on one side of the long table with his notepad and pen in front of him. Toni or Joe both moved to the opposite side and sat across the table from Officer Martinez.

Toni handed Officer Martinez the sealed envelope. "Open it up."

Mando felt something hard and round as he tore open the envelope and poured its contents into his left hand. Examining the object, he held it between his forefinger and thumb, spun it around several times with the fingers of his other hand, then sat it down on the table by the flat end, its dulled point facing skyward. "This is a round, from a large weapon. Maybe a .45 but smaller than a 9-millimeter. But it's not made of lead. Most likely steel or steel alloy, which means it's an armor piercing round. Looks like it's been laying in the desert for quite some time. What's this have to do with last night?"

"I found that in the furnace this morning. I have no idea how it got there. It looks like it was out in the desert because I think it went through a cremation cycle," Joe and Toni exchanged glances.

Mando took some notes then said, "This could have been fired out of an AR-15. They fire a 5.56 by 45 mm round. But you need a special license to buy an armor piercing round. They're encased in a copper jacket and this would be the hardened projectile within that casing that pierces the armor. The copper jacket is shed when it hits the armor and what you see here," holding up the bullet once again, "is what penetrates the armor and goes into the target. The copper casing is added to protect the barrel and rifling. The penetrator," noting the bullet in front of him, "without the casing would damage them."

Toni said, "We checked our records this morning and the furnace was run last night. We didn't do it. We were closed. We didn't know if the cycle was run with an empty furnace or not. We only knew it was run. If you saw smoke from our stack last night..."

Joe interrupted, "Smoke?! You saw smoke coming from the stack? Then there had to be a body in there."

Toni, gave Joe a look that told him he had said too much then continued, "There had to be something in the furnace. We don't know what it was, maybe a body, or maybe something else. Whoever did it, ran the cycle without letting the furnace warm up first. That's why you saw the smoke."

Mando, thought for a minute. If there was a body, then who was it? Just how did they die, and was law enforcement notified? Was the bullet connected to their death? If it was still in the body when it was cremated, that would explain how it got in the furnace. His questions on the armor piercing itself was a completely different topic that he would need to think about later. "I'd like to keep the bullet."

"Sure," replied Joe. "But I had a question about it. What happened to the copper casing? I should have found the copper in the furnace. It should have melted and turned back into a solid as it cooled, maybe even reattaching itself to the bullet."

Mando thought for a moment, then replied, "It most likely is still stuck in the armor this bullet penetrated." Then turning back to Toni, "Do you have any idea who might have run the furnace?"

Toni was quick to respond, "No we don't. We trust our employees and they are beyond reproach." Joe was still thinking about what Officer Martinez had just said. What is this armor that the bullet pierced? Body armor? Then we would certainly be talking about a murder, and the murderer cremated the body in their furnace early that morning.

Joe added, "And none of them know enough of our cremation procedures to get the thing going anyway."

"I want you to think about who might have done it, and I'll be back in a day or two to get your list of possibilities," stated Mando. As of now, he wasn't sure if any law had actually been broken. After making another note, he asked, "What steps have you taken to secure your business to prevent this from happening again?"

"We're installing an alarm system tomorrow, and we've already had the locks changed," replied Toni.

"And I'm looking into adding an electric door system that opens, closes, locks, and unlocks the back doors. It's the most secure system on the market right now." Added Joe.

Mando took another note, then got up. "Thank you for your time, Mr. and Mrs. Conti," shaking their hands. "I'll be back in a day or two."

"Thank you. Have a wonderful day," Toni said as Officer Martinez turned, exited through the front door and headed to his cruiser. Toni and Joe watched as he backed out and finally drove out of the parking lot.

Joe looked at Toni, "Shit! Do you think we're in trouble?"

"I don't think we are. Not yet anyway. We didn't do anything wrong, and he doesn't even know if any law's been broken."

"Why didn't you give him Sheldon's name when he asked who we thought might have done it?"

"Why didn't you?" retorted Toni. "You could have easily done it as me."

"Well, first I don't know that he actually did it. And second, I don't know if any laws were broken. I'm feeling more like this is something that's handled in-house. It's not a police matter for us."

Toni agreed with Joe that they would keep Sheldon's name out of it. At least for now. Toni was thinking more and more that they would need to find Sheldon and talk with him, and soon.

******

Sheldon slept through the afternoon before getting up. When he first got home, it was early morning. The sun was up as he walked from his car to his rented studio apartment on 5th Street. While advertised as a studio apartment when he saw the ad, it was actually a small trailer in a rundown mobile home park made up of three alleys that dead ended halfway between 5th and 6th Streets. Each alley in the park was paved fifty years ago, but today the pavement was broken, potholed, and in places packed dirt and sand. Each alley was lined with tamarisk trees that provided shade throughout the park helping to cool trailers in the hot summer mornings and evenings. During the day the sun would heat the trailer roofs like a broiler cooking a steak in an oven. Tamarisk needles littered the alleys, parking spots, the tops of trailers parked cars, and spilled out onto 5th Street. Piles of them would stack up in the curbing gutter as cars cruised down the street and the trailing gusts blew them to the curb.

Sheldon took a shower, trying to wash off the dirt from last night's field trip with Mateo. He took a total of three showers before he gave up and crawled into bed still feeling dirty. At 1:15 pm he got up, relieved he had gotten the day off from work. He had traded with another coworker at Witch's Brew before he met up with Mateo. He once again played back last night's call from Mateo that ended in the field trip as Mateo had called it. Mateo said he needed help with something of great importance, and Sheldon was the only person who could help him. He refused to say more but insisted he bring the padlock key for the crematory.

"Get in, and I'll fill you in while we drive. We're going on a little field trip tonight," insisted Mateo. Sheldon hopped in while Mateo started the van and headed towards the crematory.

"So, what's the field trip?" asked Sheldon.

Mateo was deadpan. "There's a dead body in back, and we're gonna cremate him."

"Holy shit! Are you kidding?!" cried Sheldon.

"Hell no! It's no joke. That's our little field trip tonight," Mateo very matter of fact now.

"No way!" Sheldon's heart began to race, adrenaline began to flow, and he felt dizzy.

Mateo was calm while Sheldon freaked out. "Think of it as just a field trip. You know how to do this. You have the key. You've done it before. And I need the help. Field trips in school were fun, right. Let's have some fucking fun with it."

"I don't think I can," Sheldon said as his heart began to slow, and he was able to think again.

"Sheldon, you don't get to just walk away from this without ending up like the guy in back." You know the old saying, 'In for a penny, in for a pound.' And with everything you've done for me, and what I've done for you, you're in way fucking deep."

"Did you kill the guy?" asked Sheldon, deciding he didn't really want an answer to that question just after he asked it.

"Don't worry about what happened to him. Not a part of our field trip. He actually died of natural causes. Too much lead in his system." Mateo laughed at that.

After taking one more shower, he made breakfast then got ready to leave. He planned to stop at Witch's Brew on his way out of DHS for a cup of coffee. Just one cup then he would head out to the college. On his way out the door, he grabbed the Glock 19 Mateo had given him and tossed it in the dumpster as he made his way to his car.

As he drove, Sheldon thought about Toni Conti, and how she insisted that he start college. This was the bright spot in the six months he had worked at the crematory. Feeling like he was part of a family was the other bright spot. He looked forward to coming to work because of the people. Toni kept telling Sheldon he needed to go to college. Connie Asghar, had been going and encouraged him to start college too, but trying to fill out the applications made his head hurt so he never finished them. One afternoon, Connie took Sheldon to a computer and helped him complete them. He never would have done it without her help.

Next, he thought about how Mateo demanding he work all night for him most weekdays and how he was so tiered that he kept making mistakes at the crematory. The lack of sleep affected Sheldon's performance so much that Joe had to let him go. Joe was nice about firing him. Toni must have felt even worse than he did being the nurturer she was. He went back to work at Witch's Brew after that.

His mom, Naomi Sanchez, would be so proud of him if she knew he was starting college. He still missed her and wondered where she was and what she was doing. Her maiden name was Goodman and this Sanchez guy that she married was her first and only marriage. Sheldon was too young to remember much about him beyond loud arguments. He was the one who first introduced his mom to crystal meth.

Maybe he'd try to look up Pastor Eminis once he was done at the college. Maybe the pastor had heard from his mother after Sheldon left the men's home. Who knows, maybe she's back at the women's home now, trying to get clean again. Sheldon's heart leaped at that thought, then he sped up wanting to get things done as quickly as he could.

******

It was 3:30 pm when Mateo pulled into the parking lot at Desert Winds Casino. The casino was owned and operated by the Tranquilo Band of the Mission Indians and only one of several business ventures that earned the Tribal Council income. He drove to the back and found his reserved spot behind the Indian Tribal Council building. Looking through the windshield of his Mercedes AMG, the sign, RESERVED, Assistant Director of Security, stared back at him. A sense of pride welled up inside him every time he read it. He deserved the title. The executive staff recognized his skills and abilities and had given him the right position. He loved starting his day reading that sign because it reminded him not only of his importance to the casino, but also who he was... someone special, above the riff raff of people who came to the casino to give their money away or all the little people living in DHS apartments or shanty homes that made the vista his home overlooked.

Mateo grew up in DHS with three families living in the same house, his grandparents, his parents with their two children (Mateo and his sister), and his aunt with her three kids. The father of his aunt's kids had left her long ago. Mateo wasn't interested in school but did graduate after some brief run-ins with the law that didn't produce any record. After high school he joined the Marines and went to boot camp in San Diego. After boot camp he applied for and was accepted to the Force Reconnaissance asset. This asset conducts deep operations all over the world with training at Camp Pendleton. This is the Marine equivalent to the Navy Seal training, but tougher. More like Navy Seal training on steroids. Some of the training took place at Army and Navy facilities since this part of the training was the same. When receiving his parachutist badge, he and every other Marine had the badge hammered to their chest through their shirt, the two pins on each side of the badge drawing blood. It was custom and culture for all Marines, and only

Marines, to receive the badge in this manner. Other specialized schools were elective, and could be chosen or ignored. They included Combatant Diver Course, Survival, Evasion, Resistance and Escape School, Army Airborne School, Army Ranger School, Special Operations Training Group Schools that included sniper training, Recon and Surveillance Leaders Course, Pathfinder Course, Military Free Fall School, Mountain Leaders Course, Reconnaissance Team Leader Course, Scout/Sniper Team Leader Course, Methods of Entry/Breacher, Joint Terminal Attack Controller, and High-Risk Personnel Course. Mateo took none of these.

Upon graduation he was ordered to the First Recon Battalion on Camp Pendleton. From Camp Pendleton, this battalion sends teams to Central and South America on Black Operations. These clandestine activities often resulted in upheaval of governments, destruction of cocaine fields and deaths of cartel drug lords. It also included intelligence gathering. Mateo was a member of one team that went to the jungles of Columbia for three weeks. After that, he was assigned to the office supporting the paymaster officer ensuring leave and earning statements were correct. He also helped in procurement filling out forms to order clothing, equipment, weapons, and ammo. He even worked for a very short time in scheduling training for the battalion. But he never again went on another mission, either in country or out of country. He had heard many of the confidential stories of Marines that went on those clandestine missions, and he was quick to repeat them at local bars after a few drinks. He was always the center of those stories and his embellishment of them sounded more like a new Rambo movie.

Working the relationships he had developed with some of the officers, Mateo was finally reassigned to the Force Recon Training Command where he trained other Marines who had been accepted into the program. He kept a photo album of some of the classes he trained, but most of the photos were of him demonstrating a dangerous maneuver, self-defense technique, firing some of the heavy weapons, and biting off the head of a snake or the occasional frog. He had been on active duty for six years and re-upped for another six. But after getting drunk and punching out some loudmouth captain at a local bar for calling him a liar, he was court Marshaled then discharged.

Mateo moved back home and applied for a security position at several of the casinos in the Coachella Valley. Desert Winds Casino was the first to offer him a position so he took it. He studied how they ran security and made extensive notes on what they did. Eventually the opportunity presented itself and Mateo spoke to the executive staff emphasizing security protocol shortcomings along with his glorious history as a Marine Recon Ranger. By now, his military stories had become so ingrained that he no longer knew where reality ended and fantasy began. For Mateo, it was all true. The executive staff had him present to the tribal council at their monthly meeting, and the next day the tribal council cleaned house, firing many of their top security officers and executives. After that the Chief Executive Officer, Dr. Reginald Martin, came to Mateo and offered him the job of Assistant Director of Security. Mateo quickly settled into the job, made few changes, but became the security guru of the corporation.

Mateo rode to the third floor that held the executive suites. His office was on the third floor which held the offices of the executive staff and the two top security positions, the Director of Security and the Assistant Director of Security. The Tribal Council hired the Chief Executive Officer over twelve years ago, Dr. Reginald Martin. Dr. Martin had built his executive staff and hired his top security officers putting together a team of professionals. Security had been a mess in the past, but since his promotion, the team was now solid, no weak links.

He stepped from the elevator into the third floor waiting area. The Administrative Assistant sat at her desk facing the elevator. Mateo always referred to her as a secretary. The floor was covered in emerald green carpet, and the four padded leather chairs, all tan, complimented the Native American artwork on the right wall. The left wall was all windows from floor to ceiling allowing visitors and staff an inspirational view of the Native American Desert Gardens on that side of the building.

Charlotte Finney looked up from her desk when Mateo stepped into the waiting area. She looked only at his eyes hoping he would meet her gaze. When he did, she smiled, and Mateo smiled back. Mateo liked what he saw. He always did, but until now, had only flirted with her. Their eyes locked on each other's as he walked towards her desk. Twenty-six-year-old Charlotte was five feet three inches with thick flowing red hair running six inches down her back. She had a milky white complexion, and green eyes that would slightly close when she smiled. Mateo began to salivate as he looked at Charlotte. She was sexy, but when she smiled, she was almost irresistible. He noticed her red lipstick matched her long neatly manicured nails. Her light green silk short-sleeve blouse was low-cut revealing ample cleavage, and a small diamond pendant dangled just above hanging from a delicate chain around her neck. The pendant was complemented by matching earrings, and when they sparkled under the recessed office lighting, Mateo's mouth filled with saliva.

"Mateo! Good afternoon. I didn't think you'd be in today," said Charlotte making no real effort to hide her excitement.

Mateo stopped on the side of her desk so he could get a full view of Charlotte, head to toe, without the desk obstructing his view. Now more saliva. Mateo swore she didn't have more than one ounce of fat on her fit, hourglass body. "How's my favorite secretary! Yup, I've been working nights all this week. I should be back on a day schedule next week, but when the unexpected happens I have to be flexible. This is more of a 24/7 position not a 9 to 5 one," feeling quite important and just a little full of himself.

Charlotte and Mateo had been going back and forth with flirty banter for several months now. He wasn't sure who started it, but he did find it fun and arousing. Mateo had practiced the don't shit where you eat maxim since he first started working at the casino, but holding this powerful position made him feel like the old hard and fast rules didn't really apply to him anymore.

Smiling again and giving Mateo a slight come hither look, she cooed, "Well, I'm glad you made it. It's what I look forward to the most."

"So, what you're saying is I'm the one person that makes your day." Mateo held a finger to his temple, then bent down resting his other hand on the edge of her desk giving her a devilish grin and whispered, "Hmmm, I think... I like that."

Charlotte's eyes danced as she clasped his hand with hers, held it firmly, and whispered back, "And I like it too. But do I make yours?"

Mateo straightened up and Charlotte released his hand. Mateo smiled knowing he now controlled the conversation and stated in an almost joking manner, "Sounds like inquiring minds want to know."

Charlotte liked where the conversation had been going until now. She felt the shift and decided to use a different strategy to regain control. She stood and moved close to Mateo, their bodies almost touching as her breasts gently pressed against his chest. Her smile was replaced with a serious expression. Then she whispered, "Yes, Mateo. Yes, I do. Do you look forward to seeing me?" pressing him for an answer.

Mateo thought for a moment about how to answer, quickly discarding several options until just the right response popped into his head. He would surely keep control of the conversation with it. He smiled with his best mischievous little boy smile and whispered back, "I'd look forward to seeing you on a lounger around my pool with a cocktail in your hand."

Charlotte smiled a pleasing smile and whispered, "Anything else?"

"No, just the cocktail," said Mateo, now loud enough that if anyone else had been in the waiting area they would have heard. He used his best devilish smile as he said it.

Charlotte realized he continued to control the conversation, but she didn't mind because it was in the direction she wanted it to go. "Oh my, that might be fun."

"It just might be, but right now, I'm going to my office. Work is calling," responded Mateo ending the flirtation and sounding more professional.

As he turned and started down the hall towards his office, Charlotte called down the hall, "Hmmm, maybe I'll call after you've finished your call with work." She laughed at her double entendre and hoped Mateo got the double meaning.

Mateo called over his shoulder, "Oh, Baby, you can call me anytime."

He unlocked his office door, stepped in, and examined his office. Mateo was always suspicious that someone may have been in his office when he was out so he began his routine systematic examination of his desk, chair, and computer then sat down behind his glass desk supported by a chrome framework. Two leather chairs were stationed in front of the desk and a small computer desk sat to one side holding a screen, keyboard and mousepad while the tower lived somewhere inside. Behind him sat a large oak credenza that hid a bar. One wall was tinted glass from floor to ceiling revealing a view of the Native American Desert Gardens. The desert sand walls held various native American scenes and complemented the emerald green curtains and carpet.

Security responsibilities were split between the Director and Assistant Director of Security, both reporting directly to the Chief Executive Officer, Dr. Martin. The director was responsible for all security at the casino and its peripheral businesses. This included the four onsite restaurants, the bowling alley, the event venue, the parking structure, and public safety in these areas. Mateo was responsible for security at the building called The Factory.

The Factory was 45,000 square feet of industrial space built at the foothills as far away from the interstate as possible. It was two miles from the casino on reservation land, painted desert sand, rectangular, and windowless. It had a large paved yard area that was circumferenced by cyclone fencing topped with razor wire. The Factory sat in the center. A guard shack stood at the gate and was manned twenty-four hours a day. Each door entrance had its own spot light. The back of the building had three docking areas for large trucks to back and load. Security cameras circled the building covering not only the building but the parking area as well. The topography of the desert floor made it extremely difficult to see from the interstate at night even with all the lighting, and it was almost impossible to see in daylight hours. Employees at The Factory were required to pass a strict background check before being hired. They were required to show their photo employee badges and driver's license at the guard shack before they were allowed to enter for their shift.

The inside of The Factory held cutting edge security features. Each door had a keypad that required the employee's special pass code to open it. The computer area also had laser sensors to detect movement added to its already keypad requirement. There were cameras at every door recording at all times. One security guard patrolled the building's hallways and manned the security office. He was also connected to the guard shack by radio. The bathrooms were the only place in the building that didn't require a passcode and didn't have security cameras.

Because Mateo was solely responsible for security at The Factory, he didn't always keep regular hours. Duties at The Factory often required him to be out nights, sometimes all night and to travel throughout the valley at times going to Riverside, San Diego or Los Angeles. Since grooming Sheldon, Mateo farmed out many of these trips to him. For political reasons, he was in his Tribal Council office as much as he could because maintaining good relationships with the other executives and the Tribal Council would keep him from getting fired, like the guy he replaced. He always made sure they knew how important his work was, that he was the expert in his field, and he kept The Factory safe and secure so it could continue to do its work and make money for the tribe. Actually, for the previous two years, The Factory had been netting 25% more annual income for the tribe than the casino and its peripheral businesses combined. Mateo took credit for this at every tribal council meeting as he shared these numbers with the council members.

Mateo woke up his computer and started looking at emails when he was startled by a knock on the door. Dr. Reginald Martin stood in the doorway. He was in his late fifties, six feet, with a pudgy build. His stomach and love handles hung slightly over his belt as he supported himself on legs that still reflected the stamina from earlier years. His full head of hair was silver and if it had thinned any over the years, it was undetectable. He had a full graying beard that he kept neat and trim. His blue eyes were warm and inviting, but also penetrating giving a hint of the nature and spirit of the man. Doc, as he was called, always gave his undivided attention to people listening with a keen ear and quickly read people understanding their strengths, weaknesses, and character. He wore thousand-dollar Dior Tailored Chinos made of black wool and mohair, eight-hundred-dollar Dior white cotton poplin shirt with the Dior emblem embroidered on the collar. The top button was unbuttoned and the sleeves had been rolled up making himself comfortable as he worked throughout the day. He must have left his sport jacket on the back of his office chair as Mateo had never seen him without it on or nearby. Doc rarely wore a tie but always kept several in his office that he put on for meetings.

******

Doctor Reginald Martin held a doctorate degree in maybe philosophy, psychology, or sociology. No one was really sure, and he never displayed any of his degrees in framed document holders on his wall like most people that held a post graduate degree. If asked about his education, he always said the education mattered least, it was people that mattered most.

Mateo appreciated Dr. Martin's approachable style as did the rest of the office and the six-member Tribal Council. The office staff quickly accepted and respected him as the new boss when he was first hired. Then he gracefully maneuvered through the political landmines that were part and parcel of his position as CEO of a multimillion-dollar organization. Within a month he had won over every member of the Tribal Council who controlled all the businesses of the tribe. But now no one would never know it as they put their entire trust in Dr. Martin. In the years since his hire, revenues increased every year to their delight.

Previously, Dr. Martin worked for the government in Central and South America before being hired by Desert Winds Casino as their CEO. He had been assigned various positions at different embassies, first Mexico, then Argentina, and finally Columbia. After that his work history was nonexistent for over five years. The current rumor around the casino was that he moved from the State Department to the Central Intelligence Agency and had been working undercover during those five years. Some whispered that he was a spy for the government while others simply referred to him as the company spook. He never discussed his past experiences, what he did for the government, or where he was those missing five years, so others speculated. And his silence only added fuel to the rumor mill.

When he first took the job as CEO, everyone called him Dr. Martin. After discovering his love of weapons, two of the Tribal Council members, James Thunderhawk and KJ Howahkan, decided to take him out into the canyons on the reservation to shoot. As they first climbed into KJ's four-wheel drive pickup, James noticed Dr. Martin was wearing new Doc Marten boots. Thinking it funny that Doctor Martin would be wearing Doc Martens, he started calling him Doc Martin. KJ laughed then followed suit. The title stuck and more people around the office started using this title as well. Eventually someone shorted in to just Doc which quickly caught on. Now he was known simply by the nickname Doc.

******

"I didn't expect you today. I hope you slept a few hours before coming in, anyway," said Doc.

"I wanted to catch up on emails and messages. You know how quickly they can build up, even if you're out only a day."

"Yes, I understand, but I want to make sure you get the rest you need. After all, it was a big night last night. Lots of things happened, but if you work at night, you recuperate during the day. Make sure you take care of yourself, body, soul, and spirit. They're all connected and if one's ignored it hurts the other two."

Moving on to the reason Doc was in Mateo's office, he said, "I've got one thing I need done tonight, just one. I was hoping you might be able to do it for me."

Mateo knew that this was actually an order. Doc put his orders in the form of a request, but you would always happily say yes. That is, if you still wanted your job. "No problem. I would love to help out."

"Great! This one will have more money than the usual deliveries, and you need to be the one to take it. They already know you so they'll be comfortable with you making the delivery. We don't want to make them nervous. The pick up will be in the safe in the executive suite at The Factory. I'm not comfortable with having security hold it at the gate for this one, so keep it confidential. Your delivery instructions will be in the envelope with the backpack and it will be ready by 9 pm. It's the only thing that needs to be done tonight."

Thinking about the timing, Mateo said, "I think I'll run home before I go out to The Factory to get the bag, but I'll make sure I'm there by 9 pm."

"Great," replied Doc. "You'll be going out of town so don't be late."

The Factory was originally built through the efforts of Doc and approved by the Tribal Council the second year of Doc's tenure as CEO. The building was divided into six specific departments. First, it held an indoor gun range that ran the length of the building. Targets could be set at multiple distances by selecting a desired distance on the computer screen after a target was attached to a clip that hung from an electronically operated cable system. It reminded Mateo of the Tramway where cable cars hung from a cable that took its occupants from the desert floor to the top of Mount San Jacinto.

Second, was the weapon and ammunition development department where engineers worked to modify and create new military weapons for use in the field. While many of their designs were for infantry, others were more powerful, designed as anti-aircraft and antitank weapons. This department also worked on development of specialized ammunition that included rounds that could pierce the armor plating on various vehicles or rounds that would explode on impact. By the time Mateo started working as Assistant Director of Security, The Factory had extensive government contracts with the Pentagon as well as several countries to the south.

The third area was the executive offices suite that included an office for Doc and Mateo as well as the director of each corresponding department. There was a full weight room, shower, and lounge area as well. Mateo and Doc spent little time at these offices as it was politically prudent to be seen in the Tribal Council building during working hours.

The fourth section was brand new and was still waiting for final approval from the Tribal Council before work officially began. This was the Computer Software Development Department. Doc had already courted government contracts with several nations and was waiting for final approval.

The fifth section was the computer room. It was one hundred feet long and fifty feet wide. Every inch of the place was filled with computers and switching systems all mounted in racks that created narrow isles the length of the room. They were all high tech, brand new, and top of the line. These were industrial mainframes not personal towers. The cooling system in the building was industrial with overpowered AC units and fans. All of the computers ran twenty-four hours a day nonstop. This section was also brand new and constructed at the same time as the Computer Software Development Department. The computer room ran on its own proprietary system from the Computer Software Development Department and had a firewall that kept ever other system on the reservation from accessing it, even security. The computer room was already up and running, doing its own thing. What that was, Mateo didn't know, but he did keep it secure. And this is where Doc had insisted on putting the laser movement detectors.

"Tonight's errand will complete our preparations for the Tribal Council meeting tomorrow. Have you looked over the agenda yet?" asked Doc.

"No, not yet. Has it been emailed?"

"Yes, it was sent out yesterday." Mateo turned back to his computer scrolling through his emails from yesterday looking for the subject line, "Tribal Council Meeting Agenda". He found it and double-clicked to open it.

"Print it out and take it with you before you leave the office. I don't perceive the council members will have questions for you regarding security, but you must be ready in case they do. My computer expert will also be at the meeting to handle any questions they might have for him. Once they approve the proposed plan, we can move forward."

Mateo looked over the agenda and saw the item that concerned Doc, Approval of Proposed Software Development Plan (Appendix C). The complete plan was listed in the back of the agenda, Appendix C. The Tribal Council members originally got the plan almost a year ago. It had gone through several changes based on council member concerns and government agency requirements and counter proposals. This was the final draft, and all council members that would be present at tomorrow's meeting had privately confirmed to Doc they would be voting to move forward.

"Can they approve the plan if one of the council members is missing? Don't they need everyone there?" asked Mateo.

"All they need is a quorum. As long as four of the six members are there, they'll have a quorum and can conduct business."

7

Thursday Afternoon

Sheldon pulled into the parking lot at Desert Valley Community College and parked in a stall marked Visitor Parking. He left his windows open only a crack before getting out and heading towards the campus. The day was hot, and Sheldon felt beads of sweat under his hair and t-shirt as he hesitantly made his way to the campus directory. He had no idea where counselors were and hoped he could find them listed on the directory. He wore shorts and sandals, and was glad he did due to the heat. Sheldon stopped when he reached the directory and stared at the monument before him. The directory was a flat map of the campus about ten feet high mounted on two pillars that resembled palm trees. He studied the map looking for a title or symbol for counselors. There was nothing on the legend and nothing on the map that said counselors. This was his first time on campus, and he felt lost, a very small fish in a very big pond. He gazed up at the map before him, but it refused to reveal its secret, the location of the counselors. He felt defeated, powerless against this maze of buildings, classrooms, and students coming and going, everyone busy knowing exactly where they were going, what they were doing, and what they needed to accomplish. They didn't need the directory, but he did, and it was useless to him. It was as if the thing spoke a foreign language that he couldn't understand. Why did he think he could ever go to college much less finish a degree. He couldn't even find his way around.

"Sheldon!" a voice called from across the courtyard that led deeper into the campus. The directory stood at its entrance, and this was as far as Sheldon was able to make himself go. "Sheldon!" the voice calling again. It was a woman's voice. Sheldon looked up. She was making a bee line towards the directory, no, towards him. It was Connie Asghar. She waived as she approached. They had worked together at the crematory before he was fired, and Connie was the one who helped him fill out the applications for college.

Sheldon took a deep breath, relieved. He was just about to give up, turn around and walk back to his car. He thought Connie would help him, and his confidence returned. He waved, "Hi, Connie. Whatcha up to?"

As Connie reached Sheldon, she said, "I was at the bookstore getting books for summer. I'm so glad you're here. I was afraid after you left the crematory, you wouldn't follow through. Good for you! So, what are you doing?"

"I'm, ah, going to see a counselor, I think. That's what someone at work said I should do anyway."

"Where are you working now? Oh, and by the way, I'm sorry things didn't work out at the crematory. I really liked seeing you when I did my drops. You're a smart guy. You're gonna do well wherever you are." Connie spoke in a quick allegro fashion. Sheldon decided to wait until she was done feeling like she had just asked him three questions in rapid fire succession.

"I'm back at Witch's Brew. But now, it's full-time. The day shift. Yea, I didn't do so well at Coachella Valley Cremations. Thanks for saying that."

"No worries. I meant it. Do you know where counselors are?" she asked, empathic.

"I'm not sure. Really glad you showed up. Could you help me with this?" Sheldon, apprehensive.

"Yup," replied Connie with a smile. "Counselors are in Student Services," pointing to the building on the directory, then pointing across the courtyard, "It's right over there. Second floor on your left. Look for the sign that says Counseling, then sign in at the counter.

Sheldon thought, Maybe I can do this.

"I'm so glad you're here. You won't be sorry." Connie exuded confidence in him as she spoke and made him feel confident.

"Thanks. I hope I can. I wasn't so good in high school."

"But this is different, and so are you. You're not the same person you were in high school. And this is not high school. Instructors will help you, and there's free tutoring available. And the staff are really helpful too. You can do it. I know you can," encouraged Connie.

"Wish I felt as great about it as you. I don't even know what to take, when to take them or how long a class is. And how am I gonna fit it in with work?" said Sheldon, overwhelmed at the thought of trying to schedule and navigate multiple responsibilities. He could do one thing at a time, but the idea of multitasking seemed incomprehensible.

"Talk with a counselor. They'll make it all clear for you. I gotta go. Juan's waiting for me in the van."

"You're out for a pickup?" asked Sheldon.

"Yup. Since we were in the area, I swung by to get books. It only took a minute, but Juan's been waiting for me. Hey, let's keep in touch." Connie grabbed a business card from her pocket and started writing on the back. "I wanna hear about what classes and what instructors you'll be taking." She gave him the card with the back side up, "Sheldon, it was really nice to see you again." Pointing to the back of the card, "That's my cell number. Bye," Connie waved and smiled again as she hurried towards the parking lot.

Sheldon watched Connie until she disappeared behind a line of parked cars. He liked Connie but felt like she was way out of his league. He was sure she came from a nice family with both parents who went to church on Sundays and always ate dinner together while each shared their day's activities. They must have celebrated birthdays together, took yearly vacations together, and their home was always filled with love and acceptance. A regular Leave it to Beaver Cleaver family. She was going to college. She was responsible and successful. He was none of those things. There was nothing he could offer her in a relationship. He could find no reason why she would be interested in him. Connie had always been sweet, talkative, and showed real interest in him whenever they had talked. She even took time out to help him fill out the college applications online. He remembered how her hair smelled when they sat close, both looking at the laptop screen, her hair brushing against his ear and side of his face. His heart began to race as he relived the moment. Then he remembered last night. The cremation with Mateo. Thoughts of Connie dissipated like morning mist in a gust of wind. I'm such a fuck up, he thought, but he put her card in his wallet.

******

Sheldon left the counseling center and headed to his car. The counselor helped him register for two classes that both met on Wednesdays, his day off. He had never imagined that he would ever be able to go to college, but now he was excited and felt empowered. He was going to be a real college student. As he drove, Sheldon's thoughts wandered back to his mom. How proud she would be of him being an official college student. He decided he would definitely stop by the women's home before he headed home. The feeling of euphoria and empowerment lingered from his meeting, and he thought, what if my mom is there? She could be. Maybe I haven't heard anything from her because no one from the church knew how to get in touch with me. His mom wouldn't just walk away from him or her opportunity to change her life for the better, would she? He knew completing a drug rehabilitation program, any drug rehabilitation program would be difficult, but even if she had quit, she would never have left Sheldon alone. Maybe she thought he had better care at the men's home than what she could provide. So, she just left him. No, she was his mother and there is no stronger bond than a mother and her son. At least it used to be that way.

The next question he pondered was this. Did she still love him? If she just ran out on him, did that mean she stopped loving him? Or did it mean she loved him enough to let him go and allow him to grow in a healthy environment, a home without drugs. He thought about all the stupid things he had done, stupid decisions, stupid actions, stupid behavior. Maybe that was why she left him. Maybe she stopped loving him because he was a fuck up. No! He refused to believe that. He had his own place now. Yes, it was just a studio apartment. Okay, just a small trailer. But he had a job, and now he was a college student. He could make the rent, and living there with his mom would be better than many of the places he had lived with her while growing up. He decided on the drive over to the women's home; he would look for her. He would find her. And he would not give up until he had brought her back to his little studio apartment, and she could live there with him.

Sheldon parked on the street in an older residential area where the women's home was located. As Sheldon walked to the front door, he noticed how immaculate the planters looked. Tightly trimmed hedges, manicured bushes, and new flowers bloomed showing vibrant desert colors. Yellows, oranges, and reds mixed with plump green leaves decorated the old home. It was painted white with light blue trim. The front windows were covered with light cream-colored curtains to block the afternoon sun. The front yard was covered in gray rock, a typical desert landscape. Sheldon noted the men's home had been doing a good job with the landscaping.

He opened the front door and walked into the living room. It was a community area so both men and women from the church would walk in without knocking. Just like they lived there. The back areas, bedrooms, kitchen, and bathrooms were all private areas, and men were not allowed. As he stepped in, he saw two women sitting on the couch. Tweedledee and Tweedledum he thought. They looked up and froze. Their eyes wide and mouths open. On the coffee table in front of them rested a Ziplock sandwich bag filled with buds. Tweedledee held a pipe that she was refilling, the ashes from the previous load sat on a paper towel in front of her. Tweedledum had been watching her refill the pipe. Both looked to be about thirty years old. They were slim, both with thin brown hair that looked to be about the same length. Tweedledee wore it down, the tangles reaching midway down her back. Tweedledum wore it up with a large plastic hair clip. Their facial features were slight, small noses and thin lips. No makeup. Both wore tank tops and no bras. The tank tops were faded from multiple washings. They may have been hand-me-downs that the home gave them when they first moved in. Tweedledee in faded green and Tweedledum in faded and stained yellow. Tweedledee could have used a bra. She was well endowed. It didn't matter with Tweedledum. She was as flat as a board. Each wore old faded jean shorts, maybe wrangler brand, but not designer. Their feet were bare.

They knew they were caught in the act when they saw Sheldon come through the door. Various forms of punishments quickly ran through their minds, then possible explanations of why it wasn't their pot or their fault that they were sitting in the living room getting stoned.

Tweedledee stopped loading the pipe mid-load, and asked, "Who are you?"

"I'm no one from the church."

Relieved, Tweedledee finished reloading the pipe, "You wanna hit?" Holding the pipe up in one hand and a lighter in the other.

"No thanks." Sheldon had seen so many lives controlled or destroyed by drug abuse and addiction, that he had made a decision never to touch it. When people turn twenty-one, they usually go out to the bar and party with their friends, celebrating their coming of age. They can now legally frequent bars and drink alcohol. Not Sheldon. No drugs and no alcohol for him. When he was at the men's home it was easy because Pastor Eminis taught that drinking was a sin and drinkers were going to hell along with smokers and drug abusers. Salvation meant abstinence from these things. Sheldon's convictions about drug and alcohol use were no longer religious convictions. It had to do with healthy life choices and his understanding that he may have an addictive personality.

Tweedledum chirped, "Well, I'll take a hit. Gimme that pipe." She grabbed both pipe and lighter from Tweedledee, put it to her lips, lit the bowl, took a deep breath, then held it for several seconds. Handing the pipe and lighter back to Tweedledee, she began to cough. Smoke exited her mouth and nostrils in force then floated about her head as it slowly dissipated into the air. She coughed again, twice, three times, then a fourth before she caught her breath. Tweedledee leaned towards her to breathe in the still THC charged vapors that swirled around Tweedledum's head.

"Is the den mother around," asked Sheldon.

"You think we'd be doing this if she was!" Tweedledee said as she lit the bowl and took a hit.

"No, I don't think so. Do either of you know Naiomi Sanchez?"

Tweedledum said, "No. Never heard of her. How 'bout you?" looking at Tweedledee.

Tweedledee exhaled, pushing smoke out of her lungs through her mouth and nostrils like an angry bull pawing the ground. Smoke rose and circled her head as she released the last bit into the air. Tweedledee did not cough. "No, never heard of her either. Did she stay here before?"

Ignoring her question, Sheldon asked, "So where's everyone, anyway?"

"They're at the church right now. We've all been at a women's retreat with the church for the last three days. We came over early to get the place cleaned up for the women when they're done at church."

"And they trust you?" asked Sheldon, now surprised.

Tweedledum became agitated. "Hey, we're about to graduate, just finishing our second year. Why wouldn't they trust us? We're overcomers!" she said proudly.

Sheldon shook his head. Unbelievable, he thought. "Mind if I go to the kitchen and look around?"

"Help yourself," said Tweedledee who had passed the pipe to Tweedledum who was just about to take another hit.

Sheldon walked into the kitchen then to the back hallway that led outside to the back yard. The door to the bedroom his mom stayed in was in this hallway, just off the kitchen. He had slept in the top bunk for two weeks before he was taken to the men's home. He didn't know if she had been moved to one of the bedrooms after he left, or if she continued to live in that bedroom. It's been a few years, he thought. But what if there was some clue left somewhere in the room that would lead him to his mother. Maybe there was something left, something overlooked when it was cleaned, that could explain why she left without him and had never contacted him again. Maybe Pastor Eminis knew something. He wasn't here, and the bedroom was. With trepidation, Sheldon slowly opened the door. It creaked as he stepped inside.

The windowless room was dark except for the ambient light shining from the kitchen behind him. Sheldon's body cast a long shadow through the doorway and onto the hard linoleum floor. He saw the shapes of objects but they were difficult to make out and appeared in black and white. He stepped to the side after entering the room allowing more light to enter. Now things became clearer. The shapes turned into objects, and colors appeared that were only mists of grays and blacks before. He could make out the bunk beds, the desk and the lamp. He turned it on. Sheldon remembered the room from the two weeks he had stayed there. He remembered the poster on the wall. Two sets of footprints walking in the sand. He remembered the twelve-step poster on the adjacent wall that the homes taught their residents. The familiarity made him feel almost at home for an instant.

Sheldon didn't know what he was looking for or even if he could find anything. Maybe something that said his mom had been there, that she existed, that his memories were not some fantasy, dream, or nightmare. Maybe, if he turned around, she'd be standing there in the doorway with open arms. How could she just leave and never contact him again? A stream of emotions passed through him. Anger, hurt, rejection, loneliness. He questioned whether she left because he was a fuck up, or if it was some other reason. He determined, once again, that he would not blame himself. But he did, almost every time he thought about her.

Sheldon looked at the desk then at the dresser. The dresser must have been added later. He remembered he and his mom using the desk for their clothes. Using the desk drawers and folding items that didn't fit in neat piles and stacked on the desk. He started there, opening the top drawer and almost could not believe what he saw. Right there, carved in the top of the wooden drawer front was a name. Naomi Sanchez, and a date followed it. When the drawer was closed, the desk top had hidden the carving from view. When it was opened, it was plain to see. He thought the date was the day they had moved into the home. Or maybe the date of when he was sent to the men's home. Or could it have been the date his mom had left the home on one of her binges, never to return. He wasn't sure. It was so long ago. He ran his finger over the carving. Followed each line of her name. The myriad of emotions that had been swimming in his head now slowed down to a small eddy of current, the loneliness and desire for his mom rising to the surface. Sheldon's eyes began to well up. A tear ran down his cheek. He wiped it with the back of his hand thinking, I will not cry. I will not cry. He turned away now facing the bunk beds to regain his composure.

The top mattress of the bunk had been stripped, and the mattress lay bare. Its fabric displayed small blue and white stripes running the length of the mattress. The pattern broken by the occasional button. Several buttons were missing from age and wear and left an odd random pattern on the mattress. He noticed several circular stains, maybe older than he was, scarred the fabric's lined design of colors. His eyes moved to the bottom bunk. There were sheets and a light blanket on the bed. They were crumpled. No one had slept in the bed since it was last made, but it looked like someone had been laying, or maybe sleeping on the top of the covers and blanket. They were in disarray and whoever it was had slept restless. Very restless. Maybe Tweedledee or Tweedledum had taken a nap back here earlier.

Sheldon turned back towards the desk. He wanted to finish examining it. He opened the rest of the drawers but they were all empty. Then he pulled out the drawers and looked at the bottom of each, remembering he had once seen an envelope taped to the bottom of a drawer in a James Bond movie. Nothing. He looked at the trash can in the corner. James Bond had found clues in the trash can, but Sheldon was looking for clues from years ago. There would be nothing there now, but he did notice something else. It was sitting on the floor next to the trash can wedged between it and the end of the desk. It was black and looked like it was made of cloth. He picked it up and examined it.

"Wow! Where did this come from?" Sheldon questioned, aloud. It was a black Timberline backpack. His thoughts went back to all the pickups and deliveries he had done for Mateo, always a black Timberline backpack. It must just be a coincidence. Walmart must sell these by the hundreds. There was something in the backpack. He opened it and found two sets of handcuffs with keys. He didn't know if they were police issue, but he could tell by the feel of them, they were strong.

Before leaving he searched the rest of the room. The only other thing he found were two lengths of old rope, about six feet each. He could tell they had been used in the past. They were twisted and knotted. He put them in the backpack. When he walked out of the room into the kitchen, he had the backpack over his shoulder, the metal jingled inside as he walked and headed to the living room.

Tweedledee and Tweedledum were still there, on the couch, quite toasted by now. "So, is anyone staying in the back room there?" They were whispering and giggling with each other and had not heard him. He said it again, this time louder and more forceful.

Tweedledee responded, "Hey, you don't have to yell!" Tweedledum grabbed Tweedledee's shoulder, whispered in her ear, and started to giggle. Tweedledee looked at her and started to giggle too. Giggle quickly turned into laughter. Both women were too stoned to control themselves and laughing too hard to care. In unison, both of them fell on the floor between the couch and the coffee table, laughing uncontrollably.

Sheldon shook his head, walked to the couch until he was standing directly over them thinking what could I say to get their attention. "The den mother just pulled up in the driveway," he shouted. This brought both women back to reality, and they stopped laughing, quickly got up, and reset themselves on the couch. Tweedledee took the baggie of buds and put it between her cleavage. Tweedledum put the lighter in her pocket and started fanning the air with her hand.

"Shit! We're gonna be in so much trouble," Tweedledee said. Tweedledum looked at her and laughed. Tweedledee looked back at her and started laughing again. They both ended up back on the floor between the couch and coffee table continuing to laugh.

"Is anyone staying in the back room?" asked Sheldon one more time. This time he was more direct, enunciating each syllable.

Tweedledee stopped laughing long enough to answer him this time. "Yea, Cindy had been staying there. I don't know what happened to her. She was there when we left for the retreat."

"Cindy's gone. I miss her. Maybe she found our stash and absconded with it," chimed in Tweedledum. "Ya know, that's what cops tell you when you get out of jail. They make everyone that's released that month go to a meeting, and they tell you, if you start using again, don't abscond, don't abscond, don't abscond. I didn't know what abscond meant. I had to ask the guy sitting next to me." Tweedledee laughed with delight. "What a funny word, abscond." She said abscond several more times in a sing-song manner then both women started laughing again and ended up, once again, on the floor. This time they were flat on their back gazing at the ceiling and laughing hysterically.

Sheldon walked out the front door to his car. He threw the backpack into the passenger seat, started the car, and headed to his apartment. He was hungry and wanted some dinner.

8 |

Thursday Evening

Mateo arrived home at 4:45 pm. His pickup time was 9 pm so his plan was to make some dinner, take a short nap then dress and head out to arrive at the factory by 9 pm. At 5:30 pm his cell phone chirped. He looked at the caller ID and didn't recognize the number. He thought to let it just go to voicemail but after the fourth ring decided to answer it. Hitting the answer button Mateo said, "Hello."

"Hey there. I'm glad I caught you," a woman's voice responded. He knew immediately who it was, Charlotte Finney.

"Hey Charlotte, what's wrong?" Mateo inquired not knowing exactly why she was calling.

"Nothing's wrong. I said I was going to call you after work. Remember?" replied Charlotte. Her voice was sultry and brought back their flirty conversation from the morning. He hadn't thought anymore about it since he'd left her desk.

"Yes, I do remember. Sounds like you're driving. Are you headed home from work?" Mateo asked. He still hadn't decided how he wanted this conversation to go.

"Yup, but rather than head to my apartment, I thought I could pick up a pizza and take it up to your place."

"Hmmm, that sounds nice. But what could I have after the pizza, you know, for dessert?" asked Mateo, beginning to flirt again.

"Well, I could pick up something sweet too. That is, if I'm not sweet enough for you."

"Oh, Baby! You're plenty sweet for me," Mateo smiling. "But I don't really eat pizza. Stop at McAllister's Deli and get me a large Southwest Chicken and Avocado deli sandwich."

"Okay. I'll be there as soon as I can."

"You know where I live?" asked Mateo

"Yup, I've got the address."

"I'll leave the door unlocked. Just come right in. I'm gonna jump in the shower so I might still be in the back when you get here," replied Mateo.

Mateo ended the call and thought, this is what all the flirting at the office today led to. He contemplated how he wanted his time with her to go. He still didn't think dating a coworker was a good idea, but he also felt it was inevitable the two of them should get together. He continued to ponder the potential pros and cons as he took a quick shower and got ready for the evening.

Mateo walked from the master bedroom through the living room and stood in the sunroom looking out the windows in a southeast direction at the valley below. He marveled at the beauty of the desert landscape, especially at this time of day. The sun was low casting long shadows of huge rocks, mesquite, tamarisk, palm, and date trees. The sand, almost white, carpeted the valley floor and was dappled with smaller vegetation. Dust clouds could be seen on the valley floor far below his vantage point. The winds would blow until early morning. The temperature had reached over ninety during the day but now had dipped back into the eighties as the sun dropped behind the mountain. The horizon burned yellow then faded into a cornucopia of colors, orange, red, and finally purple. From his place on the mountain, DHS lay before him, behind that was Interstate 10, then the western side of Palm Springs backdropped by the San Jacinto mountains. The occasional golf course broke the stream of tans and grays with its vibrant green fairways and deep green manicured putting greens. They jumped out from the landscape like a macaw taking flight from the tropical forest, its bright red, green, and yellow feathers hidden from sight until it cleared the branch on which it was perched. The desert, and especially the Coachella Valley, had its own beauty, unique from anywhere else on earth, and Mateo felt this place, with all of its tourism, expansion and growth, would always be home to him.

He was still standing in the sunroom soaking in the desert beauty when Charlotte opened the front door and stepped into the entryway. She held a bag with the McAllister's logo in one hand and her purse in the other. Mateo's hair was no longer in a ponytail but hung to his shoulders. It was still slightly wet from his shower and appeared shiny and silky. It hung loose around his face. He wore jeans and a white form fitting t-shirt that snugged his V-shaped body.

Mateo turned and smiled. "Come over here," he said more as a command than a request.

Charlotte held the McAllister's bag out to Mateo but kept one eye on the magnificent view of the valley as she walked into the sunroom. Mateo took the bag from her as she stopped in front of him.

"That's a beautiful view. It's breathtaking," she said.

"Yes, it is," replied Mateo as he looked in the bag and saw two sandwiches and two lava cakes. "Are both of these sandwiches for me?" he asked, teasing her now.

"No, silly. The other one's for me. You only asked for one, and I got you the large. And two lava cakes for dessert."

"So, you didn't think you were sweet enough for me and got a backup?" Mateo said, starting to flirt again.

"Hey I'm plenty sweet, and I don't need any backup," said Charlotte emphatically.

Mateo smiled. "Well, we'll just have to see about that."

Charlotte smiled a sexy smile but didn't say anything. Mateo watched her eyes slightly close as she smiled, but now noticed very slight dimples in her cheeks. He had never noticed them before. He had always looked at her green eyes. They were captivating and demanded his complete attention.

He directed her to the bar table in the middle of the kitchen. The home was designed with an open floor plan so the view of the valley and the late afternoon light spilled into the kitchen and living room from the sunroom. Charlotte began preparing the sandwiches as Mateo opened the refrigerator and took out a beer.

"You want one?" asked Mateo, holding up a beer bottle.

"Sure. A nice cold beer would be perfect."

Mateo opened both bottles, sat them on the table then sat next to Charlotte so they both faced the sunroom windows.

Mateo said, "I love this view. That's why I bought the house. Well, that and the pool."

"Oh, that's an infinity pool!" Charlotte said, surprised. "I didn't realize that until just now. It looks like you could swim right into the sky."

For the next several minutes Mateo and Charlotte concentrated on their food and beer. Once they finished, Mateo got both of them a second beer before moving to the couch in the living room. Charlotte took both lava cakes from the McAllister's bag and sat them on the coffee table in front of Mateo.

"Charlotte, I didn't say anything earlier, but I'm working tonight so I can't hang here for long."

"Wow, you really work all the time, don't you?" replied Charlotte.

"It's a 24/7 job. Not like you. At five you go home and leave it all. I can't do that."

Charlotte looked down at the lava cakes and asked, "Do we have time to eat our dessert?"

"That's too sweet for me. I don't really eat much sugar."

Charlotte thought for a second then gave him her naughty girl smile. Next, she leaned close to him, putting one arm on his shoulder and said, "Well, maybe I have something else that would satisfy your sweet tooth."

Mateo took her shoulders in both hands and kept her from moving closer to him. "Charlotte, I've always had a policy of not dating coworkers. You know the old saying. Don't shit where you eat."

Surprised, Charlotte said, "But coworkers date all the time. People meet at work, date, fall in love, get married. It's really the place people meet. Well, that and the internet."

Mateo wanted her but also wanted to protect himself and his job. "If we do this, you need to know that after a while I'm going to break things off. You need to be okay with that. And not cause a scene or be angry with me about it."

Charlotte thought about this for a few moments then said. "Then you need to promise me not to date anyone else while we're going out, and you'll tell me before you see anyone else."

"Sure," replied Mateo without hesitation. He really didn't think this through. He just wanted her so he said what he thought she wanted to hear.

"Then I'm okay with it."

Mateo knew she was agreeing to something she would not be okay with. He had told women this in the past, but when he had ended the relationship, they were always upset. Women thought they controlled things and could change a man. Change his feelings, his character, his thoughts. They would emasculate him to get their way if he would let them. He never let them.

Mateo took Charlotte in his arms and kissed her hard. He heard her catch her breath as she wrapped her arms around his neck, tilted her head, and kissed him back.

They made love on the couch with Mateo playing the dominant. His nature was to enthrall then to ravish his partner, and Charlotte responded just the way he wanted. When she started to moan, he put a firm hand around her milky white neck now hot and clammy from all their exertion. She stretched her arms above her head, yielding in complete submission to him, and squealed.

When he was done, he got up, his body covered in misted sweat while beads ran down each side of his face, from hairline to jawbone. He walked back to the sunroom, grabbing a hand towel from the pool table railing and wiped his face. Looking out the sunroom windows,

Mateo saw it was now dark. The sun had set behind the mountains, but the lights from the garden planters around the infinity pool shone through the sunroom windows illuminating the living room enough to see her. She had watched him walk from the couch. He knew the look. She liked what she saw and had just experienced. And why not, thought Mateo. He was handsome, successful, and full of machismo which was an aphrodisiac in itself. Any woman should be honored to have his attention or to be chosen to be his plaything for the evening. When Mateo was with a woman, he didn't make love to them. He consumed them, like an animal that caught its prey and was now feasting on its prize.

"Come here," Mateo ordered.

Charlotte hadn't taken her eyes off him but hesitated, then smiling, responded, "Yes, sir," using her most submissive voice. She got up and walked over to him while Mateo took a hair band from the pool table and pulled his hair back into a ponytail. Then opened the slider that led to the infinity pool.

"Get in the pool," was the next order.

Smiling her response, "Yes, sir," she walked through the slider into the desert night air and crossed the cement. It must be in the mid-eighties by now, thought Mateo, the perfect temperature for an evening swim. She slowly stepped down the three steps into the infinity pool. The pool was made so that each of the opposite sides were three feet deep but the middle sloped to five feet. She swam across underwater surfacing on the other side, her red hair now straight and clinging to the middle of her wet back. She turned and watched Mateo grab two towels from the rack and set them on the pool side before entering the pool. He looked at Charlotte standing at the opposite end of the pool in three feet of water that reached just past her waist. Her wet shoulders and breasts glistened in the surrounding light from the moon, stars, and landscape lighting then danced on her skin as she moved while her diamond pendant and earrings twinkled like stars. He swam to her just as she had crossed moments before.

Coming close to her, they both became aroused once again. "Turn around," he ordered. Saying nothing, she complied. Now they both were looking at the valley below. The lights of DHS shown outlining the gingham patterned streets. They watched the cars on the interstate creating white and red lines moving in opposite directions. The lights of Palm Springs shone against the base of the San Jacinto mountains, and the tram light at the top of the mountain winked at the beauty of the valley below. This is how he had her for the second time.

Once he was done, Mateo crossed the pool, got out and turned on the pool shower waiting for it to warm. Now satisfied, he was ready to move on with his evening agenda.

He removed his hair band and turned on the shower. "It's been over an hour. I've got to get ready. Get out of the pool."

For Mateo, sex was an activity, like working out at the gym, playing a game of tennis, or shooting at the range. He enjoyed it like any other activity, and having the right woman was much like using the right sized weight, having the right racket, or having the right weapon.

Charlotte swam to the other side and up the steps following Mateo's track to the shower. Mateo adjusted the temperature and rinsed off. "It's still early, we could sit and talk more?" she asked hopefully.

Not looking at her, Mateo responded. "Can't. Gotta get ready for work. I'm already running late." Finishing with the shower, he grabbed his towel. "It's all yours," as he dried and headed toward the house.

Charlotte was disappointed. She had hoped to spend most the evening with Mateo since things were going so well. Maybe he'd be okay with her staying here until he got back. She stepped in the shower and started to ask. "Mateo?"

"Your clothes are by the sofa," was the last thing he said as he disappeared through the slider and into the house.

Fifteen minutes later Mateo walked out of the hall from his bedroom into the living room. Charlotte sat on the couch, now fully clothed. Fuck, thought Mateo. Am I gonna have a problem getting her out of my house? "Hey, you're still here. I'm glad you didn't leave yet."

She turned towards Mateo, a downhearted look on her face. "Mateo?" she said, "I was thinking that maybe I could just...."

Mateo cut her off mid-sentence, stood her up, took both shoulders in his hands, looked her straight in the eye, and using his most compassionate voice, said, "Baby, I've got to go to work. I'm already running late, but I want to see you again, when I have more time to give you. Would you like that?"

Hopeful now, "How is this weekend?"

"Baby, I don't know. I'll need to check my calendar at work first, and then see what's happening with my mom. Did you know she's got Parkinsons, and when I'm not at work, I'm taking care of her? I was supposed to be there with her when you called tonight. I'll have to smooth it over with the family tomorrow as it stands now." This was a lie but worked well for him in the past, and it was designed to make her feel guilty for taking as much of his time as she already had. While saying this he started walking her towards the front door and then out to her car.

Surprised, "Parkinsons! Oh, no I didn't." Charlotte had no idea what Parkinsons was but didn't want Mateo to think she was uninformed.

"You've got everything, keys, purse?"

"Yes, I think so," as she reached for the car door. Mateo beat her to it and opened it wide.

"We'll talk tomorrow and set something up," he reassured her, but breathed a sigh of relief when he saw her taillights crawl down the hill and out of sight. Shit, that took forever, he thought.

******

It was 9:10 pm when Mateo arrived at The Factory's guard shack and entrance gate. The night guard checked his ID before opening the gate as per protocol. He drove to the back of the building, parked, and entered his security code at the back entrance then beelined to the executive suites and the large free standing safe that sat in the back corner. He opened the safe and found a black Timberline backpack with an envelope perched on top with his name printed in all capital black ink, MA-TEO. He opened the envelope and read the instructions. He was to go to the Mission Inn Hotel and Spa in Riverside. Once there, he was to find The Presidential Lounge. His contact would be sitting at the far end of the bar. He would be expected at 10:30 pm and if there were any problems, if he had been followed, or if anything seemed out of place or compromised in any way, he was to say, "The weather in Palm Spring was shit yesterday." If he was confident that it was safe, he was to say "It's clear tonight. Nice weather." If the contact agreed that it was safe, he would confirm the weather was nice. Only after that would the drop-off be made. He rolled his eyes. This was classic spook dialog. Mateo read through it several times then grabbed a lighter from the desk next to the safe, lit the instructions and put it in the ashtray to burn.

Once at his car, he threw the backpack on the floor of the front seat, pressed the start button on his Mercedes AMG, backed out of the parking space, and headed to Interstate 10 that would take him to The Mission Inn.

Mateo's thoughts began to wander as he drove. Why had Doc farmed out this hit anyway? It was dangerous to bring more people into their affairs. Why didn't Doc trust him? He had experience with wet work as a Marine in Force Recon. He had infiltrated foreign governments, assassinated corrupt dignitaries, burned acres of cocaine fields after slitting the throats of drug lords running multimillion dollar cartels. He'd be a fucking hero if it weren't for the fact that all of these were clandestine operations. No one could ever know about them, especially the public and the media. Mateo had never done any of these things, but he had told so many stories that he no longer realized they were just that, stories that other Marines coming back from the field had shared over drinks at the Staff NCO Club on base, or his additional fabrications that dramatized his stories often times beyond belief.

Doc must have some hidden agenda of his own. If this were true, he could not trust Doc. It must be true since Doc brought in this guy, this washed-up spook, and without consulting Mateo. Doc informed Mateo that this guy was coming to take care of a few things. Mateo decided he would need to keep an eye on Doc. He has shown by his actions that he can no longer be trusted.

Mateo thought about this ex-spook that Doc brought in. He went by the name Mulder, just Mulder. Mateo thought he must be an X-File junkie. Mulder was the guy he was to deliver payment for services rendered. He remembered meeting him the other evening at The Ridgeview Bar and Grill, an upscale bar in La Quinta built on the side of a rock wall overlooking the central Coachella Valley. He was plain looking, smaller than Mateo in every way, and uglier. He obviously spent no time at the gym, and Mateo was sure he would have flunked out of Marine Corps bootcamp much less trying to handle the rigors of Force Recon training. He was a scab, and Mateo decided he could take him in a fist fight, a knife fight, or draw down on him, and kill him if the need arose. What if he walked into the bar, shot this ex-spook in the head, and calmly walked out? He'd never be caught. He was just a stranger in a strange town, in a strange bar one quiet night. He put that thought to bed, but it came back several times before he arrived at The Mission Inn.

Finally, Mateo thought about Sheldon and last night's cremation. Sheldon had really stepped up and was becoming a reliable foot soldier. There was no job for him at The Factory or the casino. And if he ever applied, Mateo would make sure he would not be hired on the casino side. With all of the things Sheldon had helped with, Mateo could not allow him anymore contact with others in the organization. To maintain confidentiality, people could only know about their piece of the puzzle and no one else's piece. People and organizations are taken down when their people know too much about the business. Mateo would never let this happen and decided Sheldon was in for life as part of the network he was building. Sheldon was his first soldier, and Mateo had brought him in and trained him. Mateo realized he would need to pay Sheldon a regular salary so he could drop his other job and give Mateo all of his time whenever he was called. He would talk with Doc about it, creating a no-show position at The Factory for Sheldon. If Doc balked at this request, then he would know for sure Doc had a hidden agenda that was working against Mateo.

He pressed down on the accelerator focusing his rising anger through his foot to the gas pedal then resetting his speed to eighty-five miles an hour once the needle covered its mark. He needed a drink and wanted to be there now.

******

Mateo swaggered into The Presidential Lounge at 10:38 pm with his Glock 19 clipped to his belt, the black Timberline backpack slung over his left shoulder. He knew being late would irritate Mulder. The Glock was under his sport jacket and hidden from direct view unless his arms swung excessively while he walked which slid the bottom of his sport jacket back just a bit revealing his belt and the weapon if he were not careful. But someone would have to be staring at his belt at just the right time to notice it and see it was a pistol. It could easily be mistaken for a cell phone.

He walked past the bar tables in the guest area noticing several couples, men trying to convince their date to come home and sleep with them, the lame sons of bitches. He looked the length of the bar and at the end saw his contact, Mulder. What a fucking asshole this guy was. He was slumping at the bar with both elbows leaning forward over a drink. Probably some fruity little sissy ass drink for this sissy asshole. With all of his experience in Central and South America killing cartel lords and corrupt government officials, he could have done the killing himself. He resented Doc farming the hit to outsiders. Mateo walked to the end of the bar seething, a futile attempt to keep his emotions in check as the alcohol worked against him. He had arrived early and guzzled down two Old Fashioneds in the California Lounge before his meeting. The thought of Mulder and Doc's obvious mistrust and lack of confidence in him consumed him. Mulder had been the trigger man, but Mateo was only the bag man. His anger swelled while the liquor suppressed his ability to keep it in check.

Standing at the corner of the bar in The Presidential Lounge, he strutted to the far end like a rooster strutting towards its opponent in a cock fighting ring then sat down next to his contact. He tried once again to sooth his anger that was directed toward Mulder, this one-time government spook most likely, a washed-up has-been that Doc knew from his time with the agency. He probably begged Doc for the job, the lowlife scab.

Mateo did not look at his contact but looked directly forward across the bar to the top shelf where the most expensive liquors were kept and snarled, "I just drove up from The Valley. The sky's clear tonight. Nice weather." He almost chocked on each syllable thinking this was a stupid little game.

Mulder, showing no emotion, stated in a thick Brooklynese accent, "Yea, the weather's been nice all day."

Mateo disliked Mulder when he first met him at the restaurant with Doc Martin. He was east coast and Mateo was west coast. Mulder sprinkled the evening's conversation with diatribes of California and commendations of the east coast and the New England states. The only good thing about the meeting was that Mulder's Brooklynese was so think Mateo sometimes couldn't understand what he was saying.

Mateo looked left and stared directly into the eyes of his contact, Mateo's eyes windowing the anger he was feeling at the moment. This was the man that murdered three people last night. Mateo had cleaned up one of the bodies, but the other two still lay where they were murdered, and this man did nothing to take care of that. Anger continued to rise, and Mateo put his hand on the grip of his Glock 19 strapped to his waist. He thought, This is no one special. I'm better than him. I could draw my weapon, shoot him in the head, and casually walk out of this bar. No one would know who I was, and he'd be dead. He's a fucking asshole, a nobody.

His contact's eyes narrowed. His face became deadpan and intense. Then Mulder placed his hand under his coat, held it there, and said in his Brooklyn accent, "You have something for me, right? That's why you were sent? To deliver a package? Is it the backpack on your shoulder?"

This shook Mateo from his thoughts and brought him back to the present, but he kept his eyes on the eyes of the man on the barstool next to him. He removed his hand from his weapon and moved it to the backpack's strap on his shoulder. He removed the backpack, dropped it to the floor, and said in disgust, "Here it is."

The contact kept his eyes focused on Mateo as he stood then bent down to the floor and retrieved the backpack. He felt the weight. "This is all of it?"

"That's it," replied Mateo, maintaining eye contact.

Mulder got up from the barstool, left a ten-dollar tip under the glass of his half-finished drink and walked out of the bar. All the while keeping his eye on Mateo. Once he was gone, Mateo's anger receded, and he ordered another drink, another Old Fashioned and asked the bartender to also put a shot of Fireball in the cocktail. When the bartender returned with the drink, the Fireball was in a separate shot glass. Mateo poured the Fireball into the Old Fashioned and took a sip. He stayed there for the next hour and had two more drinks before he left.

9

Friday

At 10:30 am Mateo walked out his front door dressed in sweats, tank top, and tennis shoes. He headed straight to the non-attached garage where he always parked his car. He noticed the winds had already started to pick up, and from his driveway view, he could see dust clouds forming on the valley floor. The winds were insignificant on the side of the hills in the morning, but by late afternoon, even the hills would not be spared from the effects of the wind. Wind gusts would reach seventy miles an hour or more in the spring and fall on the valley floor, but on the hills, they rarely reached twenty miles an hour.

Mateo pressed the open button on his cell phone app, and the garage door started its ascent. He stopped at the trunk of his car, sat his workout bag on the ground but kept the garment bag suspended over his shoulder by its hanger. Inside was his suit – slacks, matching jacket, collared shirt and tie. He pressed the trunk release button on the back of the car, and the trunk lid latch popped then the lid slowly rose to its fully open position. Mateo picked up the workout bag and placed it in the trunk. He planned to work out at The Factory before changing into his suit for the Tribal Council meeting.

As he sat the workout bag in the center of the trunk's carpeted floor, he noticed a kitchen sized plastic trash bag in the right corner of the trunk. While kitchen trash bags are normally white, this one was black and was industrial strength. Feeling frustrated, he thought, I'm gonna need to take care of that later. It was Friday, and he had moved the bag from the white van to his trunk after he and Sheldon finished their field trip. He smiled thinking he had been quite creative in giving it that name. Field Trip. A fun adventure and learning experience. Mateo had already scattered the ashes from Wednesday night. He had held the coffee can out the van window as he drove and slowly poured them out as he traveled down I-10 towards the reservation. The wind caught the tiny particles and scattered them in a million directions. The few chunks that were left were light and were also carried on the wings of that same wind. This black plastic bag sitting in his trunk was the only evidence left to destroy. There was no rush. He would do it in the next few days but needed to think about the best way to dispose of it before he did. It was going to be more difficult since the bag's contents could not be destroyed by fire. Mateo took the bag out of the trunk and put it on the garage shelf before he closed the trunk lid and hung his suit in the back seat. After that, he slid behind the wheel, pressed the start button, and the six hundred horsepower Mercedes AMG roared to life. He backed out of the garage and headed to work.

Mateo would need to discuss with Doc about creating the no show position for Sheldon. If Doc refused to create this position for Mateo… well, Mateo thought he would wait and see before going down that road. On the drive he replayed last night's confrontation with Doc's ex-spook at The Mission Inn for the third time. That ex-spook had circled his thoughts as he went to sleep last night, like vultures circling overhead and caused a restless sleep.

******

It was 1:30 pm when Mateo parked his car and walked to the Tribal Council building. He entered his security code then rode the elevator to the third floor. He had worked out at The Factory's weight room, showered, did some work in his office there, then put on his suit in preparation for the 3 pm Tribal Council meeting.

"Good afternoon, Mr. Rivera." Charlotte's sultry voice filled the empty waiting area as Mateo stepped off the elevator. It brought back vivid mental pictures of last night's frolic at his place. She smiled a seductive smile, her red lipstick contrasting her milky white skin and complimenting her vibrant red hair. Her eyes conveyed a come-hither look. She wore the same diamond necklace and earrings as yesterday, and last night. They were the only things she never removed.

"Hey, Charlotte. Could you get me a cup of coffee?" Mateo said, smiling as he met her eyes then quickly looking down the hall and past her desk. He brisked through the waiting area wanting to get to his office to avoid any comments from Charlotte about last night.

As Mateo passed her desk, Charlotte smiled her most seductive smile yet. "Yes, sir," emphasizing the word 'sir'.

He thought again of last night with her as he headed down the hall to his office. Not looking back, he replied, "I'll be in my office."

It was a full five minutes before Charlotte arrived with a steaming cup of coffee. She held the cream-colored mug with the Tranquilo Band of the Mission Indians logo with both hands. "Here's your coffee," then sat the hot mug on the corner of his desk. "I was thinking I could stop by and pick up some deli sandwiches after work. Then take it up to your place."

Mateo looked away from his computer screen and turned towards Charlotte. He had been researching information on cyber-attacks and keeping business networks safe. He could talk instinctively regarding physical security, the fences, lighting, cameras, security codes. But he often felt insecure when it came to cyber security. This was a new field that grew with the internet. His knowledge had grown with it, but the field changed so quickly that he often felt like he was one step behind. He wanted all his ducks in a row if he were called on during the Tribal Council meeting.

He placed his hand gently on Charlotte's hand that had remained on his desk when she sat the coffee mug down. He fixed his eyes on hers. In his sincerest tone he could muster, he said, "I can't tonight, and not this weekend. I'll be with my mom. The rest of the family is going out of town, so I have the duty." This was a lie, but he didn't want to see her again, or not this soon anyway. He'd already scratched his itch with her. His excuse would keep her hopeful and happy. If he told her what he was really thinking, it was sure to cause a scene.

Charlotte frowned in disappointment, then hopeful, "Well, maybe we could make a date for next week then?"

"I'm not gonna be able to schedule anything that far out, sorry. Let's talk next week. Hey, I gotta get ready for this meeting. I'll be fucked if I don't get this prep work done."

Charlotte's expression changed to something that could be interpreted as downhearted, "Okay, I'll leave you to it." A moment later she smiled again, but this time with a mischievous expression on her face, "I really had fun last night."

"Yup, me too," replied Mateo then he turned back to his computer screen. Charlotte left his office back to her desk.

******

Mateo needed a break after thirty minutes, so he picked up the phone and buzzed Doc's office on the intercommunications system. After three rings, Doc picked up. "Hello sir. Are you prepared for the Tribal Council meeting at 3 pm?" Doc's voice, upbeat and cheery.

"Yes, sir, I am. But I had another issue I wanted to talk with you about."

"What is it, Mateo?" Doc still sounding cheery but now also sincere like a counselor to his patient or a parent to a child with a problem.

"It's one of those face-to-face subjects." This was their code for a confidential subject that pertained specifically to The Factory. The Factory had legitimate income producing businesses that the Tribal Council knew about and approved. These were discussed regularly in and out of the office. The code told Doc that Mateo wanted to talk about the illegitimate activities at The Factory that only he and Doc knew about. And it was only he and Doc that profited from them.

"It shouldn't take more than a few minutes. I hoped you had time now before the meeting," Mateo now hopeful. He tried not to cuss around the office and especially with Doc. Doc considered it unprofessional, and Doc was so urbane.

"I always have time for you, Mateo. Let me come to your office. I'll be right over." Doc still sounded warm and friendly. His voice was filled with confidence. Confidence in Mateo. This was Doc's way, his way with everyone.

Three minutes later, Doc walked through Mateo's office door. "Woah, you look great! That's a nice suit," Doc sounded quite impressed. Doc wore a suit that cost maybe three times as much as Mateo's, but Doc would never tell you that. It was Doc's way.

"Thanks," replied Mateo as Doc shut the door and took a seat in the first of the two padded tan leather chairs that faced Mateo's desk.

Now, becoming more serious and business-like, "So, Mateo, what is it?" Doc got right down to business. There wasn't much time before the Tribal Council meeting, and Mateo thought Doc may be feeling the time crunch.

"I've been training, no, more like grooming, someone for some time now in our confidential work." Mateo was referring to Sheldon. This was not completely new information for Doc, but he thought Mateo had been doing all of the pickups and deliveries bringing Sheldon along from time to time on the bigger jobs. Mateo spent the next few minutes explaining to Doc that while the training started there, Mateo had advanced it, and Sheldon had grown into a real "standup" guy. He thought using the term "standup guy" would impress Doc. Doc listened with intensity but kept a concerned composure. Doc seemed more concerned than impressed with Mateo's brief history of Sheldon's training. That's when he finally told Doc how they disposed of the body, by cremation, and Sheldon was invaluable in this. Doc's look of concern changed to bewilderment, then amusement.

"You cremated him?" Doc now almost laughing and shaking his head still in near disbelief.

"Yup, and the ashes were blown from one side of the valley to the other," Mateo stated this with pride.

"Look, Doc, our confidential business interests have taken off, and I don't got the time to keep up with it. I need someone else. This guy's both groomed into the culture and trained in the job. But he needs to make a salary so he doesn't work somewhere else. Another job conflicts working for us and maybe undermine loyalty over time. We need to create a no-show job at The Factory that I'll hire him for. It keeps him loyal and committed to us while he continues to do what I trained him to do. And it keeps him separated from anyone here at the reservation."

******

Mateo was referring to all of the drops and deliveries Sheldon had made using the black Timberline backpacks. When The Factory was first constructed, its purpose was for arms and ammunition. Doc used his government contacts and secured contracts to supply government agencies with specialized weapons and ammunition. The agency then asked Doc if The Factory could develop other ammunition that was not available and specialized weapons to shoot the ammunition. They submitted their specifications to Doc who insisted on a government contract which included monies for development with no guarantee of success. The Tribal Council approved it, and signed the contract. He hired two engineers, one for ammunition development, and one for arms development. The range was installed for testing small arms and ammunition while the bigger weapons systems were tested in the gorges between the hill's fingers behind The Factory. The engineers were successful in development (the tribe submitting a patent on the ideas) and several government agencies had annual contracts for purchase. These were the legal activities of The Factory that produced income for the Tribe.

Eventually, the Agency wanted to supply "freedom fighters' with the newest weapons and ammunition focusing on the western hemisphere, Central and South America, but wanted the reservation to sell directly to them, keeping the Agency from being the middleman. Freedom fighters were the Agency's name for terrorists that accepted U.S. monies, supplies, and influence. Their political leanings were not taken into account, but only their loyalties to the Agency and the U.S. government. Doc felt the Tribal Council would never approve, so he made an "off books" agreement and pocketed the payment for himself giving Mateo a 20% cut. Mateo originally wanted a 50% split but Doc was only offering 10%. The final arrangement was 80% to Doc and 20% to Mateo who did all the physical work once Doc finalized the arrangements.

One day, while Mateo was in Doc's office discussing an off-books shipment, Doc said, "Did you know that in 2022 the ATF identified almost 16,000 firearms crossing the U.S. border going to Mexico?"

Surprised, Mateo said, "Holy Sh..!" stopping himself mid-sentence. "That's a lot of weapons."

"That's only what they were able to count. It's actually estimated that about half a million firearms illegally cross the border every year. That's what they can count plus what they're unable to count."

"Wow! Too bad we can't profit from some of that," Mateo said, now even more surprised by the numbers.

Doc grinned like a Cheshire cat then said, "The southern border in the U.S. only cares about drugs entering the U.S. but no one really watches firearms going out to Mexico so the cartels capitalize on this. That's where we could make some big money as long as The Factory can handle the volume, and you can keep everything secure."

"No need to worry about security. No one can do it better than me. But don't the cartels already have established suppliers?" questioned Mateo.

"They do, but things happen so they're always looking for new opportunities."

"Like what we do at The Factory?" Mateo smiled because he now understood what Doc was thinking.

"Exactly," replied Doc as another smile slowly came to his lips. "And we would be relatively safe from ever being shut down."

This became the second illegal activity of The Factory. Doc had the cartel contacts through his buddies from the Agency, and he told Mateo to hire more employees at The Factory creating two shifts, a day crew and a night crew.

Doc and Mateo split 80% of these profits at the negotiated percentages. Doc insisted 20% went back into the legal contracts to pad the profit margins keeping the Tribal Council from growing suspicious. Doc established the relationships and agreements while Mateo would handle the deliveries.

Southern California and Coachella Valley gangs were small-time operations compared to the cartels, but Mateo wanted to sell to them as well. Growing up in the Valley, he had the contacts for these gangs. Unfortunately, Doc would not approve selling to them so Mateo sold to them on his own without Doc's knowledge. This became the third illegal activity of The Factory. Mateo made agreements with the gangs and would keep 100% of the payments.

Delivery to the cartels and the Agency contracts often included a cargo van or a box delivery truck filled to the brim with product. A few times they loaded up 18-wheelers from the loading dock in back of The Factory. There would be a flurry of deliveries and pickups before the final products were set, paid for, and the delivery made. Payments and product samples for the illegal activities were always made in black Timberline backpacks. Mateo's gang deliveries were small-time by comparison. Everything was put in black Timberline backpacks, both guns and payments. These were the deliveries Mateo had Sheldon do but would also include Sheldon on the larger deliveries to the cartels. The Agency would send trucks directly to The Factory for loading.

Mateo had approached Doc about manufacturing drugs at The Factory, but Doc had refused. He said it was just too dangerous to be in competition with the cartels who were already buying their weapons and ammunition. Mateo showed him the kind of money they could make marketing only to local gangs in the Coachella Valley, but Doc hated drugs and wanted nothing to do with it. He liked the cartels that made them because they purchased the weapons. Doc was a gun guy, not a drug guy, and buying guns forgave making drugs in his mind.

It was Mateo that started expansion to other areas unbeknownst to Doc. The local gangs Doc knew nothing about, nor did he know that

Mateo had started trading crystal meth and heroin from the cartels for guns then reselling it to the local gangs for distribution. This was pure profit for Mateo. As his side business grew, Sheldon became a real asset. Doc might have gotten wind of his secret operations if Mateo had to do all the work himself.

******

Doc reflected on Mateo's proposal of a no-show job for Sheldon pondering need, setup, costs, and potential consequences with potential rewards. "Hmmm, that sounds interesting. Let me think on it and get back to you. I'm sure I'll have a question or two," sounding upbeat and positive. That was Doc's way.

"Sounds good. I'll be waiting to hear back."

Doc rose from the leather padded chair, "I have to finish what I was doing for the Tribal Council meeting, but we also have to discuss the software development proposal later. And remember, the computer room is part of the proposal for the computer lab."

Mateo responded, "Hey, I've got a question about that. The lab has a completely separate proprietary system from the computer room. There's been no work in the lab cuz we're waiting for approval from the Tribal Council. But those computers in the computer room are running twenty-four hours a day. Just what are they doin?"

A look of anger flashed over Doc's face then quickly became deadpan. "Both are part of the proposal. We can't have one without the other. They are intrinsically connected. This is what the proposal says. No work has begun on the proposal because it has yet to be approved. That is what you say. Got it?"

Mateo's eyes narrowed, and he took a long pause before responding. "Yea, I got it," then turned away from Doc and back at his computer monitor. He felt his anger start to rise but quickly suppressed it. Mateo hated being told what to do, especially when anyone, including Doc, was trying to manipulate him when he fully knew Doc was not being honest.

"Great," Doc smiling again and sounding cheery and upbeat. "I'll see you at the meeting." Doc turned and left, and Mateo sat the next few minutes rethinking what had just happened and what it might mean, especially for him. He questioned why Doc had to think about his proposal. Why couldn't he have just said yes right then? Then he thought more about the computer room. Mateo's suspicion of Doc grew.

It was 2:50 pm when Mateo put his computer to sleep, exited his office, and walked towards the elevator. As he approached Charlotte's desk, she turned hearing feet on the carpet and smiled, meeting his eyes. "Going to the Tribal Council meeting now?"

"Yup, then gone for the weekend," replied Mateo, attempting to sound more professional than personal.

"Well, have a great weekend, and I hope your mom's better by Monday."

Mateo entered the elevator and punched the button with the glowing number two. The second floor held the Tribal Council member offices, their administrative assistant, and the Tribal Council meeting chamber that took most of the floor's square footage. Mateo stepped out of the elevator into a waiting area similar to the third floor. Ethel Barend the secretary, as Mateo called her, sat behind her desk in front of the hallway that began after the waiting area. It led to the council chambers with council member offices on each side of the hall. Three on the left, and three on the right.

"Good afternoon, Mr. Rivera. Have you got your agenda?" Ethel asked with a smile as she looked up from her keyboard and monitor. Ethel was in her late fifties, with short bluish hair. She visited the salon once a week to keep her hair looking like cotton candy on a stick. She wore a bright multicolored blouse that reached her neck and a black skirt that extended past her knees. A heavy gold necklace with a different colored stone in each link hung loosely around her neck, her bracelet matched the necklace. The look was old and gaudy. She was slim with an oval face and delicate features. Bifocal glasses rested on her nose slightly higher than where she wore them when she wasn't typing.

"Hi, Ethel. Yup, I have it. Printed it out yesterday."

"Great! They're about ready to start, so you better hurry on back."

Mateo looked at the time on his cell phone. He still had nine minutes, but this was typical of Ethel. She believed in the old Vince Lombardi clock. If you're not ten minutes early, you're late.

Mateo ambled down the hallway noting which council member was still in their office. Two of them were, and the door was closed on the other four offices. He noted that Fredrick Asghar's office door was closed. He stopped and tried the knob. It was locked, which meant no one was there, especially Fred. When he reached the council chambers, he followed the wall to his left and took his usual seat on the front row to the far left, the aisle chair to the left of Doc. Bud Wackenhut, the Director of Security for the casino, sat to the right of Doc's empty chair. Mateo had always thought Bud got into security work because of his last name. Bud was never related to George Wackenhut, the man who started the Wackenhut Corporation, but Bud never volunteered that information. One would have to ask him, and Bud liked letting people think he was related to George and connected to the corporation.

Mateo and Bud exchanged hello nods as Mateo sat down. The council chamber was a large square room with elevated council desks in the front arranged in a semicircle. A large wooden tribal seal hung centered on the wall behind the desks. The desks were connected, looking more like one large table made of hardwood and stained golden oak that matched the seal. There were eight people sitting in folding chairs in the audience area that held maybe thirty people maximum. Doc was talking with James Thunderhawk, the vice chair. James was sitting and Doc was standing over his right shoulder, reading glasses dangling from his nose as he pointed at an item on the agenda. Ted Alexander was seated beside James Thunderhawk at his desk. Ted's nametag held his name and indicated he was a council member. Presently, the last three councilmembers, Kenneth "KJ" Howahkan, Brian Deere, and Michael Hensley, strode in and took their seats at their corresponding desks. The Tribal Chairman's position was equivalent to the Tribal Chief in days gone by. The Bureau of Indian Affairs had brought more structure, organization, and title changes long ago. Fredrick Asghar was the Tribal Chairman, and his desk sat empty. It was 3 pm, and the meeting was ready to begin.

James Thunderhawk pounded the gavel bringing the meeting to order as Doc took his regular seat between Mateo and Bud.

"Our Tribal Chairman, Fredrick Asghar, seems to be missing, so I'll get the meeting started. Before we begin, has anyone heard from Fred? Does anyone know where he's at?"

Several heads moved side to side while others shrugged their shoulders. Several bent and whispered into the ear of the person next to them.

"Ethel," Ethel Barend the Tribal Council Administrative Assistant was now standing in the back of the room. "Would you find out where Fred is? Is he running late?" James instructed Ethel who turned and marched down the hall to her desk.

With that, the meeting began. James Thunderhawk conducted the meeting in the best Robert's Rules of Order that he knew, which was substandard at best. He had only won this position two months ago. In spite of his lack of experience, he was still able to move the meeting along, following the agenda that Ethel had prepared.

While the six Tribal Council positions were passed to the firstborn male of each family, the positions of Tribal Chairman and Vice Chair were elected from the six councilmembers by the tribe's members on a four-year cycle. These two positions were highly coveted because they held most of the decision-making power, and they received a higher percentage of the net income the tribe brought in through its businesses and holdings. Elections were held two months ago, so Fred and James had only held their positions for just over one month. Fred ran on the slogan "Transparency for the Tribe" capitalizing on rumors about embezzlement from tribal income that was generated by its holdings. The tribe's holdings were the Desert Winds Casino and The Factory. The Tribal Council had been slow on diverting income for improvements to the reservation so residents began saying someone must be embezzling money. The council members lived in extravagant million-dollar homes off the reservation while living conditions on the reservation were impoverished. Roads needed paving, the tribal school needed repair, basic services were not always reliable and homes were shanties. Tribal Council members always intended to help with these, but were slow to divert the funds going into their private accounts rather than the reservation accounts for improvements. Fred Asghar focused his campaign on the tribe's frustration and anger, promising to make changes and bring real transparency to the tribe regarding business practices and finances. His message caught on and caused quite a stir. Several fights broke out between factions, and tribal police, in fear of a riot on election day, were out in force. Once the elections were over, everything went back to normal. Now tribal council meetings were quiet and few people attended.

Once Fred was elected Tribal Chairman, he demanded to tour The Factory, demanded to look at the books, accounting ledgers, income, assets, and contracts. Mateo and Doc put him off as long as they could before they had to allow him some access. Doc knew it was only a matter of time before Fred uncovered their clandestine operations. This meant Mateo's secret activities unknown to Doc might also be uncovered. Two days later, Mateo was sitting at the Ridgeview Bar and Grille with Doc who introduced him to Mulder, the ex-spook.

"We're now at Action Item five, Approval of Computer Software Development Proposal," James Thunderhawk's voice filled the room as the rest of the council members looked at their agenda. The eight audience members perked up in their seats being stirred out of their daydreaming. They were interested in this item.

"The full proposal is found in Appendix C in the back of your packet," James notified the group. People turned to Appendix C while council members perused the agenda packet with reading glasses perched on their noses. The information in the agenda packet had been available for almost nine months and had gone through several changes. This was the final draft and would be voted on for approval.

"I motion we approve the proposal as submitted," Ted Alexander declared. His legal name was Theodore, but he went by Ted. Ted was in quotes on his nameplate between Theodore and Alexander.

"I second that," councilmember Michael Hensley chimed in.

"Is there any discussion?" asked James Thunderhawk.

"Have government contracts been secured yet?" asked Council Member Brian Deere.

"I can speak to that," Doc quickly stood and addressed the tribal council. "One contract from a confidential government agency has been submitted to the tribe. I could reveal the specific agency in closed session. If the council approves the proposal today, I would have the contract on your desks by Monday for your signatures. The first year we'll receive a significant amount for development. Once implemented, we would bill for service fees beginning the second year. Service fees are estimated to be very profitable. Also, there would be a purchase fee for units sold beginning the second year. As purchases increase, so would service fee income. The contract would run for three years and then be renegotiated. There will be a significant number of other organizations, both foreign and domestic that will be interested once developed. I could reveal specific dollar amounts in closed session."

An audience member raised their hand and Thunderhawk recognized him, giving him permission to speak. "Now just what is this computer program supposed to do? And hasn't some other company got programs to do it, like Microsoft or Apple?"

Doc addressed the question. "That's a good question, Chad." Chad smiled feeling special that Doc knew his name. "Currently there is no software available that does what the agency is requesting." Doc smiled a thoughtful smile communicating he thought the audience member's question was right on. It was his way. "They've asked us to develop software specifically for prosecutorial Information Management with powerful cross-referencing and reporting abilities. They've also requested that it can easily be adopted to manage other information databases in both the public and private sector."

"I'm not sure what all that means. I'm not a computer geek," replied Chad.

"Basically, it means once the tribe develops it, we will own the most sophisticated software of its kind. Think of it as the tribe becoming the Microsoft of the database world," Doc proudly exclaimed.

Chad smiled from ear to ear than sat down. He was satisfied.

A second audience member raised her hand, and James Thunderhawk acknowledged her to speak.

"How much money from this here proposal will go to the reservation for improvements? We need the school roof fixed or maybe a whole new school building. And the roads…"

James Thunderhawk cut her off, "You're right. All this needs to be done, and the new income we receive will help do all those things."

"But how much!" the audience member becoming insistent.

"Well, the exact amount would be decided by the Tribal Council in closed session. I couldn't even guess until that happens."

"So much for transparency!" she said in frustration. Then sat down and folded her arms over her chest.

There was little more discussion after this and no questions about security. Mateo was glad and thought about getting out of the monkey suit he was wearing as soon as he could. His shirt collar was biting into his neck and his tie felt tighter than when he came down in the elevator just before the meeting. The Tribal Council approved the proposal unanimously and moved on to the next action item.

The computer development proposal all seemed on the up and up, but Mateo knew Doc. There had to be something he was hiding. Some way he would be making money that the Tribal Council would be oblivious to. Mateo kept everything at The Factory secure so he thought he should get a cut of anything that went on there. Doc was up to something, but he hadn't yet figured it out. He thought the key might be the computer room with all those computers. Doc had to have spent several million dollars to build it and it had been running for several weeks now. Approval for the proposal that included the expenditures was only given today. This meant Doc spent the money before approval. That was a gutsy move, even for Doc.

As soon as the meeting adjourned, Ethel hurried up to James Thunderhawk who still sat at his raised desk. "Jim, I've tried several numbers and haven't been able to get a hold of Fred."

"You tried his cell, right?"

"It went right to voicemail. He never turns that thing off. I think we need to send someone out to check on him," Ethel said, concerned and somewhat frenzied.

"I think we should too. His place is out in the sticks. An unincorporated area. Let's wait on calling the sheriff. I'll go out and check on him as soon as I wrap up here. I hope he didn't fall off his horse or one of his toys out there and hurt himself. He's got about fifty acres or more."

Ethel click-clacked back to her desk still fretting over Fred while James Thunderhawk told the other councilmembers he was going out to Fred's place to check on him. Fredrick Asghar was in his late thirties and single. He lived alone on a large ranch between Palm Springs and Banning. He owned several horses and toys for men, a motocross motorcycle, two quads, and an old Willy's Jeep that he turned into a rock crawler. The Jeep conversion was his newest and favorite toy. He loved tooling around the desert hills or rock crawling up in Joshua Tree National Park. All the council members agreed that he could have crashed on any one of his toys or his horse got spooked and threw him. He could be stranded on his desert ranch unable to call for help. They all decided to load up into councilman Kenneth "KJ" Howahkan's Chevy crew cab and head out to Fred's place. They would have to finish up with questions, paperwork, and lock up their offices first.

Mateo stood up from his chair and turned to leave the meeting while Doc headed up to the councilmember's desks for more discussion. About what, Mateo didn't know. He was still simmering over Doc's probable plans to cut him out of income he was entitled to over this computer deal.

As he turned, Bud Wackenhut grabbed his arm. Bud, the Director of Security for the casino, was in his late thirties. He was prior military, Army, and was a military police officer, then moving to intelligence before leaving the Army and entering the private sector. He kept the short military buzz, and looked like a G.I. Joe doll; lantern jaw, broad face with a defined jawline. He was built like G.I. Joe too, not lean, but sinewy and beefy.

"Hey, Mateo. How's things?"

"Hey Bud. They're, good. What's up," Mateo responded knowing Bud had something important to say. He never talked to Mateo unless he had something important.

"I got a small group of high rollers in suite two. It's the four-bedroom suite with four guys. They're down from New York and will be in their room tomorrow night at twelve midnight."

Mateo knew the suite. It was used for families but more often for groups of men coming out to gamble. Men coming to party were influenced by the movie "The Hangover," older guys trying to relive their youth now that they had made their fortune and had the resources.

"Yea, so what do they want?"

"You know what they want. That's why I'm talkin to you." Bud said, sounding slightly perturbed. This was the primary reason Bud talked with Mateo. Bud didn't feel like he needed to give all the details and Mateo should just know what it was about.

The casino had special agents that catered to the high rollers. They would comp them rooms, meals, concert tickets, even bowling if they wanted to bowl, and the casino limo would transport them to and from the airport. If a guest deposited $50,000 before or upon arrival, they received high roller status and were required to gamble during their stay. When they checked out, they received back the balance of the $50,000 with the stay comped by the casino. If they were a big winner, they got back their winnings plus the initial $50,000. If they were a loser (as most of them were) they got back the balance from the $50,000. Most received enough back to buy lunch at McDonalds. Some didn't even get that much back.

Some of these gentlemen would discreetly let their high roller agent know they preferred some adult entertainment. This could mean a pole dancer/stripper in the room, but it usually meant hooker. The agent would speak to Bud, who in turn would speak to Mateo who had grown up in the valley and had these kinds of connections. Bud was not comfortable with this arrangement and thought the casino should stop the practice. But Doc had insisted that Bud facilitate it for the business. The casino not only had to compete with the other casinos in the valley, but also Las Vegas that was just over three hours away. Bud made himself feel better about the practice by refusing to tell Mateo what was needed, just the number of men, the room or suite they were staying in, and the time and day. Bud expected Mateo to infer the rest. Which Mateo did, but he did like watching Bud squirm when he played dumb.

"I can make that happen, Bud. Usual payment arrangements?" Mateo responded.

Bud opened his satchel and slipped him a large manila envelope. To anyone still lingering in the room, it would be assumed normal casino security paperwork. Later, once Mateo was back in his office, he opened the envelope and found $4,000 in cash. This meant four women would knock on the door of suite two at twelve midnight tomorrow night and stay for one hour. He would get things set up after he left the reservation.

Mateo looked out the window from his office and saw the Tribal Council members pile into KJ Howahkan's four-wheel-drive crew cab Chevrolet. He knew where they were headed, to Fred Asghar's place. He also knew what they would find because he had paid Mulder and had picked up the other body just off the security road that circled The Factory. But he couldn't think about that right now. It was Friday afternoon. The council meeting was done, and he had some work to do. He locked his office and hurried down the hall towards the elevator.

"Good night, Mateo. If you need any help with your mom, let me know. I'm not busy this weekend," Charlotte said, talking loud and fast to ensure he heard her as he strode by her desk.

"Oh, thanks, but I think I'll be fine. Good night." Mateo stepped into the elevator with a black Timberline backpack over his shoulder and the doors shut. Once in the parking lot, he pulled out his cell and called Sheldon. No answer again. When he heard the voicemail message, he hung up. This was his third call to Sheldon who always picked up. Mateo was frustrated and angry. He got in his car and peeled out towards the Coachella Valley.

Mateo exited the the interstate in an unincorporated area in the Coachella Valley which often meant high crime and little police presence. He turned off pavement after two miles and onto an unpaved road of hard dirt and sand. The road was narrow but just wide enough for two cars to pass in opposite directions. This was considered an unpaved county road, and as he drove, he passed homes on both the right and left side. After clearing the completed homes, he continued for another mile and a half before coming to a gated Spanish style complex on his right. The complex stood alone in the middle of the desert. The gate and fence facing the road was black ornamental and broken into sections by cinderblock pillars that were stuccoed peach. Each held a black Spanish style light fixture mounted to the top. Behind the fencing were rows of queen palms paralleling the fencing. The driveway was a half-circle with closed electric gates on each end. The driveway was lined with queen palms on each side and three lemon trees grew in the center of the half circle. There was a gravel road off to the left of the driveway disappearing as it continued around the back. The peach stuccoed home was long and low but the center entrance rose six feet above the rest of the structure resembling the center of a kingly crown. The rest of the complex resembled desert gardens with gravel walkways snaking between planters filled with palm trees, and date trees and other flowering desert plants.

Mateo pressed the call button on his steering wheel and said, "Call Hector." His cell phone sprang to life and started ringing through the Mercedes speaker system.

After the third ring Hector picked up, "This is Hector."

"This is Mateo. I'm at the gate."

"Just a sec."

Moments later, the gate in front of his car began to open. Mateo pulled onto the driveway as the gate closed behind him and parked in front of the house. He exited his Mercedes AMG after he scooped the backpack from the floor then walked to the door's ascending three steps and rang the bell.

Moments later, Hector opened the door, and Mateo walked in with Hector closing the door behind him. Hector was five feet ten inches and at least three hundred pounds. His face was round with portly features. His black hair was clean and cut short and reminded Mateo of Bud Wackenhut's hair, an Army cut. He wore a black AC/DC tee shirt, black shorts that hung below his knees and sandals.

"Hector! You son of a bitch! You're lookin' good, my man!" Mateo said as they bro shook with the right hand and hugged with the left. Mateo had difficulty getting his arm around Hector's overweight body. They had known each other since high school. Mateo enlisted in the Marine corps after high school, and Hector got involved with a little bit of everything, developing relationships throughout the Coachella Valley. Hector was one of those guys that you naturally liked and trusted. Hector bought, sold, and helped transport drugs, fenced stolen goods and jewelry, connected stolen cars to buyers, and facilitated many other illegal business activities, always taking a cut for his services. He was a hustler, a buyer and seller, he worked the angles to create win-win opportunities. However, if a competitor disappeared (and it did happen), and if their body turned up murdered, dismembered, beheaded or just dry bones in the desert, Hector was never involved. He had people for that. The rumors motivated others to always deal honestly with Hector.

Most recently, he was meeting the needs of lonely men, horny men, who were looking for companionship. Some would call him a pimp, but Hector didn't like the name. He saw himself more as a businessman, a broker of goods and services.

"Hey, Mateo. You got some business for me don't you! Nothin' else would get you down my road in that Mercedes." Hector laughed because he knew how annoyed Mateo was having to drive down that unpaved road.

Nodding, Mateo said, "Your fucking road! I hate your fucking road. You need to pave that thing."

"The county owns it, not me. Let them pave it."

Now moving on to why he was there, "I need four young ladies tomorrow night at the casino hotel. The details are in the backpack."

Mateo wished he could have sent Sheldon to do this delivery, but Sheldon wasn't answering his phone. He hated Hector's road. Mateo had called Sheldon again from his car on the way over but still didn't get an answer. He handed Hector the black Timberline backpack. It included the details Mateo had typed up and printed out in his office before he left, and $2,400 dollars. He paid Hector $600 for each girl and he kept $400. A finder's fee he called it. They sat and chatted for a while over Coronas before Mateo left, leaving the same way he came.

Driving home Mateo thought about Doc again. He thought he had now figured it out. Doc was keeping him in his own little cell allowing Mateo to know only enough to do his security job. Doc was moving forward with some other lucrative plans, and he was cutting Mateo out of it. He would need to do something about it. But what? That would take more thought. But first, he would find out what that computer room was doing. They hadn't even started development on the software and that room was running hot, fans and AC units running all day and night to keep them cool. He was going to be cut out of money for the software development and was being cut out of whatever was happening in that computer room. He would find out, then decide what to do with Doc.

Mateo had been home for twenty minutes when his cell phone rang. It was Ethel Barend.

"Mateo, I just got a call from James Thunderhawk. I don't know if you know, but he and the rest of the Tribal Council went over to Fred's house to check on him after the meeting. You won't believe what they found. Jim asked me to notify you since you're our Assistant Director of Security."

"Did they find Fred?" Mateo asked, already knowing the answer.

"No, Fred wasn't there but Fred's girlfriend and her brother were. And they were dead! Shot right out in the backyard of Fred's place! Jim's already called the police, but I don't know what we're going to do. We have an empty Tribal Chairman seat, and Fred didn't have any kids," Ethel now thought of the Tribal Council and if there were rules that addressed this situation. Ethel was like that. She hid from the horror of the murder with her work.

10

Monday

Joe went to his recent call list, scrolled down until he found the number and selected it. The cell phone immediately dialed the number. "Hey, Sam. Did you find anything out yet?"

Sam was Joe's construction contact that was a possibility for motorizing the twelve-foot industrial doors. "Good news, my friend! My contact says you can have them at the price you offered."

Sam's contact had recently been hired to refurbish a building and had taken two electric door systems out of it. The company that planned to wall in the existing door openings. He was willing to sell them at a fraction of the cost for new ones.

"Fantastic! Where do I pick 'em up?"

"My warehouse. I'll have them there, and make the check out to me."

"To you? So, I'm buying 'em from you?" asked Joe surprised.

"Yup, the amount includes my finder's fee."

"Finder's fee? You're charging me a finder's fee?"

"Of course, I am. You know how it works."

"We're friends, Sam. And you're still charging me a finder's fee?" Joe beginning to plead.

"How many times did you charge me a finder's fee in the past? You want me to remind you, cuz I still remember..."

Joe cut Sam off, "Okay, okay! I hear ya. I'll be out there Wednesday afternoon to pick it all up. Thanks, Sam. I appreciate you for helping me with this."

"No problem. See ya Wednesday," Sam replied as he ended the call.

Joe put his cell back into his belt clip then checked the cremator. It was late morning, and Joe was glad he and Toni had completed all of the items they identified to keep the business secure. The locks had been changed on Thursday, and the alarm system was installed on Saturday. Joe had created a drop box for paperwork, and all that was left was the electric motor system for the industrial doors.

He looked at the cremator control panel. It was twenty minutes from finishing its cycle then it would need to cool. He took the cell back out of its clip and called Toni who was in the office. It was easier than running back into the office.

Toni answered, "What's up, Sweetie?"

Joe loved it when Toni used endearing names even after all the years they had been married. "I got the electric door system set. I'm gonna run down to Indio Wednesday afternoon and pick it up. Can you put that on my calendar?" Joe, with Toni's input and control of his calendar, had Monday and Tuesday all scheduled. His first opportunity would be Wednesday afternoon. The interview to fill the open position last week didn't go well. Okay, the guy never showed. That wasn't uncommon when they hired. Most people thought this was a creepy business, but he and Toni thought the deceased should be treated with respect and dignity. This is what they tried to emphasize, but the general population just thought creepy.

Connie was only working part-time this week so Joe would need to fill in for her as well. She was finishing her second year at the community college and this was finals week. He and Toni, especially Toni, insisted on being flexible when it came to employee education. It meant more work for them, but Toni said it was worth it to see young people making something of themselves.

"I can put it on your calendar, but let me ask you a question first."

"Shoot." Joe knew what was coming. They already had several discussions about used equipment versus new.

"If the equipment is just like new, then why is Sam selling it to you so cheap?"

"Two reasons. First, the new owners of the building don't want any of the old equipment that's being pulled out. So, it didn't cost Sam's contact anything. Second, Sam picked it up and hauled it off for the guy so he didn't have to figure out where to store it, how to get it there, who would take it, and how he might sell it. It's convenient for him so he's not asking a lot. He may not even know how much a system like that costs. Who knows, the guy may have just given it to Sam."

She thought more about it, then asked her next question. "And you can install it? We won't have to pay someone to come out and put it in? There're no hidden costs?"

"That's right. No hidden costs." Now acting offended, "And why do you even question my installation abilities. All the years I worked construction. I know a few things."

Toni laughed, "Yes, I know. I just want to make sure we're not overlooking anything. With the new locks, alarm system, and now this, payroll will be tight. I don't want any surprises."

Joe planned to do the prep work for installation the next three days after he got the equipment. He hoped to get all the prep work done by Friday so he could do the actual installation over the weekend. He knew there would be some additional costs, metal framing for mounting, conduit, and wiring, along with some other incidentals. It would be nominal compared to the equipment. Toni would balk when he brought her the receipts from Home Depot, but sometimes it's just better to ask for forgiveness than permission. This was one of those times. She must be under real pressure to make payroll.

******

Joe heard a van pull up outside then someone opening the new padlock that was installed last week on one of the twelve-foot doors. As the door opened, he saw Juan Lopez and then Connie Asghar backing the van into the building. They had just come from John F. Kennedy Hospital (JFK) in Indio. Toni had called Connie this morning before her shift started and instructed her and Juan to do the pickup before they came in.

Juan opened the van's back door, and they both unloaded the body of Margaret Olson, a 73-year-old woman who passed from colon cancer. Joe noticed they were both quiet. Connie looked almost sullen. He had never seen her like this before, even with the pressure from finals in previous semesters, she had always been upbeat.

"Morning, you two. Everything go okay at JFK?" asked Joe.

"Yup, it went fine," replied Juan. Then to Connie, "I'll get the reefer storage number from the office," as he headed towards the door leading to the office through the conference room.

"Don't forget to log it on the clipboard," reminded Connie then she sat down on a chair in the break area.

Joe sat down on the empty chair across the table from Connie. "There's coffee and donuts in the conference room. Why don't you go get some, and I'll help Juan with Margaret."

"Thanks," replied Connie, now sounding more upbeat. "Think I'll do that."

As she got up, Joe, trying to make her laugh, remarked, "But there's no apple fritter for me today. I may have eaten my last one." Connie smiled but didn't respond.

As Juan returned, Joe said, "Juan, I'll help you with Margaret Olson. Connie's gonna grab some coffee and a donut."

"Great. She goes in reefer one, shelf four." And they both headed to the gurney to put Margaret into cold storage.

"So, what's goin' on with Connie? You two didn't get into an argument or anything did you?" questioned Joe.

Surprised, Juan replied, "You didn't catch the news this weekend?"

Joe opened the reefer door, and he and Juan wheeled the gurney into the reefer. "No. Toni and I were here working all weekend."

"Man, then you missed it! There were two murders at her uncle's ranch, and the uncle is nowhere to be found. I think the uncle did it and hightailed it out of state, " remarked Juan as they each grabbed one end of the body bag and laid Margaret on shelf four.

Joe was shocked. He couldn't believe what he had just heard. "You didn't say that to Connie, did you? Accusing her uncle of murder would really piss her off. Hell, it'd piss anybody off."

"Not on your life. I'm no fool. The police updated the family on Sunday, so Connie knows a little bit more than what's been on the news. But from what I saw, I still think the uncle did it."

They wheeled the gurney out of the reefer and Juan shut the door. As Juan started to load the gurney in the back of the van, Joe hurried to the office. As he entered the conference room, he saw Connie sitting at the long side of the conference table, coffee in one hand and donut sitting on a napkin in front of her. She was staring into her donut deep in thought.

"Toni," yelled Joe. "Come in here for a minute." Connie didn't move, didn't look up. She kept staring at her donut seemingly searching for answers in its center.

"What's up?" asked Toni as she walked into the conference room from the office. She stopped mid stride when she saw Connie. Then she came around to Connie's side of the table and stroked her hair. "Baby girl, what's wrong?"

Connie's eyes began to well as she continued to look down at the donut in front of her. Then she started to sob. Toni put her arm around Connie's shoulder, and Joe put a napkin in front of her thinking she might want it for the tears. After a few moments, her sobbing subsided, then she picked up the napkin and daubed at her eyes and cheeks. Toni sat down in the chair next to her sitting sideways so she faced Connie. Then took Connie by both shoulders making her sit up, turn, and face Toni.

Toni repeated herself but more forceful, "Baby girl, what's the matter?"

Connie, now more composed and ready to talk, began to sputter out her story. "My uncle's missing and Vanessa Orosco, his girlfriend, and her brother, Jamie, were murdered at the ranch."

Toni sat back. She was stunned.

"I rode horses and quads with them and Uncle Fred out at the ranch. I knew 'em! We had a barbeque together too. She was the nicest person. I don't know why anyone would want to hurt her... or her brother!" She stopped her story to pat her eyes again, then continued.

"The police came by the house on Sunday with new information. We're the closest relatives here in the valley so they've been sharing what they find. They said the evidence indicated that Uncle Fred wasn't there or wasn't hurt there. It was only Vanessa and Jamie. Maybe he ran off before the shooting began and is hiding somewhere. That's what we think right now. Maybe Uncle Fred will call us. Let us know he's safe. We think he might be hiding on the reservation. It'd be a safe place, and he knows the area."

"I'm so sorry, Connie. How's Maria holding up?" Connie's mom, Maria, was married to Frank Asghar, her first husband. He passed away from a car accident when Connie was only six years old. Her Uncle Fred became a substitute for her father.

"She's doing better than me. She says to look at the positives right now. Uncle Fred must be alive because he wasn't there. She says we should focus on that right now and wait to hear from him or more information from the police. It makes me feel better if I do that."

"Well, that sounds like good advice. She's right. You don't know very much yet, and who knows, you may hear from him before the end of the day," Toni, sounding positive.

Connie wiped her eyes one last time, then used the napkin to blow her nose. "Thank you, Toni. I love you guys," Connie said as she stood and gave Toni a long hug.

"We love you too, Baby girl. Let us know if there's anything we can do. We want to help in any way we can," said Toni as she released Connie.

Joe chimed in, "Yup, Connie, anything we can do to help. We're there." He had been feeling like more of a spectator and wanted to interject anything to be part of the conversation.

"Thank you, all of you," as Connie looked around the room meeting everyone's eyes. "I've got finals to study for." She started to gather her donut and coffee.

"I'm covering your shift for the rest of the day," reminded Joe.

Toni gave Joe and Juan their next transport, and they piled in the van with Connie. Connie brought the van home last night so Joe needed to drop her off on their way out of town.

******

After Connie was out of the van, Juan asked, "So do you really think Connie's uncle is still alive? And do you think he might be the killer? I've seen lots of crime shows. It's always the spouse or the boyfriend that does it."

Joe pondered his questions for a moment. "I think you gotta take it one step at a time. Now just what do we know? We know two people were murdered. Do you know how they were murdered?"

"Yup, the news said they were shot."

Joe replied, "I was afraid to ask Connie. I didn't want to upset her any more than she already was. So, we know two people were shot. We know that no one else was hurt at the ranch other than those two people. We are assuming the police have already ruled out Connie's uncle because they are sharing information with the family and are not accusing the uncle."

"But can we trust the police to be telling her the truth?" asked Juan, skeptical.

"I think so. They're not lying to coerce a confession out of Connie and her family. If the uncle were a suspect, the police would have pressed them more than what Connie indicated. The three scenarios I can think of are, first, that the uncle wasn't there or escaped before the killing. The second is that he was kidnapped and is being held against his will somewhere. The third is that he was killed somewhere else, and they haven't found his body yet."

"I hadn't thought of that. I only thought he might really be the murderer," Juan considering Joe's three scenarios.

"I think the police have ruled that out for now anyway, so it wasn't one of my scenarios," Joe now being strictly matter-of-fact. "And don't mention any of those scenarios to Connie."

"No, I won't. Not any of the ones that have her uncle kidnaped or dead anyway."

They hurried to the hospital morgue and then back to the crematory so Joe could get back to work on his cremation list. Once finished, he could check it off his "To Do" list that Toni kept up for him along with his calendar.

11

Monday

Mateo had wanted a quiet weekend where he could relax, unwind, and process the week's events and the tension from the tribal council meeting, but that was not what he got. The disposal of Fred's body went well, and he had paid off Mulder for Doc, but he knew there would be some kind of police investigation over the murders. Feeling anxious, Mateo replayed picking up Fred's body and asked himself if he had left any evidence by mistake. He had done this at least ten times since loading the body but still felt uneasy. The only thing left was the plastic bag in his garage holding the blood-soaked bulletproof vest Fred was wearing when Mulder had shot him. He would dispose of it in the next few days, but there were more pressing matters to focus on first. After all, investigators would not be looking around The Factory's perimeter fencing, and the first good rain would wash away any traces of anyone ever being out there. Nor would anyone be coming to his home to search it.

The Tribal Police wouldn't have any involvement beyond coordination with the Riverside County Sheriff's Office. Since the murders took place at Fred's house off the reservation, Riverside would have jurisdiction. They might want to question people on the executive floor as well as the rest of the Tribal Council members. Who knows, maybe the FBI would get involved before it was all over. Then there was the Bureau of Indian Affairs. They might also want some involvement but none of these groups worked well together. Coordination always disintegrated into protection of turf, competition to outdo the other agencies, refusal to share information, and finally a disintegration of any coordinated effort. With a cluster fuck like that, they couldn't solve anything.

Next, The Factory had several large orders for weapons and ammunition to fulfill next week. Two were contracts with the Agency that Doc had established and one clandestine order for the Sinaloa Cartel. He would be at The Factory all week finalizing these orders and handling the logistics. This would give him ample time to search offices and files to discover Doc's real plans with the computer room and the computer lab. He was convinced Doc wanted to keep him uninformed. He didn't approve the position for Sheldon, and Doc was ripping him off from secret income with the computer room and the lab. Just who did Doc think he was, anyway? Just because he held the CEO position didn't mean he controlled all the illegal activities at The Factory. The Factory was Mateo's turf, his responsibility, and he controlled it... according to Mateo anyway.

Finally, there was Sheldon. Mateo had called him several times but it went straight to voicemail. He wanted to check on Sheldon, to gauge his emotions and thought processes. Cremating a body was a step beyond what he had ever demanded from him. He was still a kid, easily manipulated in so many ways, but he may still have some old-fashioned ideas of right and wrong. All of these thoughts played in his head and haunted a restless sleep so when he headed to work Monday morning, he was in a foul mood and was glad to be going to The Factory this week. He was in no mood to play politics.

******

Mateo spent his first two hours at The Factory reviewing product inventory and factory line run orders to be sure he had all the weapons and ammunition he needed to fulfill the Agency orders and ensured the orders would be completed prior to the pickup/delivery dates. Next, he began to work on the logistics, the size and number of trucks needed, when they would arrive and back onto the loading docks, the number of staff needed to move and load the product, then when they would arrive at their destination. Finally, he would have to arrange for payment. The

Agency orders were easy. Everything was electronic and payment was directly deposited into the tribal accounts.

The Sinaloa Cartel was more complicated. This one would be done at night, and payment would be done at the delivery site and always in cash. Mateo always used Sheldon for these deliveries. Sheldon would drive Mateo's Mercedes leading the delivery vehicle to the site then acting as security while Mateo arranged the trade. The site locations were never the same, but always in places where prying eyes could not see. They had met in the desert, on uninhabited ranch land, highway rest stops, and even unused warehouses. What didn't change were the people. Dealing with the same people built a feeling of trust on both sides.

At 10 am the Cisco phone on his office desk rang. The caller ID said Charlotte Finney. "Hey, Charlotte," said Mateo as he picked up the phone.

"Good morning, Mr. Rivera," said Charlotte.

"Good morning yourself, Beautiful."

"How was your weekend? And how's your mom doing?"

"My weekend was shit," replied Mateo, not going into any detail.

"I'm sorry. Well, I hope your week is better. Hey, did you hear about Fred Asghar and the murders?"

"I'm the director of security. I knew about it on Friday," said Mateo, sounding arrogant.

"Yup, I guess that makes sense. They'd notify you as soon as they found out."

Duh, he thought but didn't respond.

"Well, Doc asked me to call you. The police are here, and they're starting to interview people."

Surprised, Mateo said, "Really? What the fuck for?"

"I dunno. They're investigating, and I guess they think they may be able to get some leads and figure out where Fred is. That's my guess, anyway."

"Well, that's a waste of fucking time. The murders took place off the reservation and the people that were killed weren't even part of the tribe," replied Mateo feeling anxious now. "The tribe had nothing to do with it."

"Hey, don't shoot the messenger," replied Charlotte.

"Sorry. Not your fault. It pisses me off they're here asking questions. It'll be a dead end, a waste of time, while the fuck that did the murders gets away. Law enforcement in Riverside County can be so fucking stupid."

"There's a special agent from the FBI here too."

Mateo hesitated. "Oh, yea?"

"Yup."

"Then they're just as fucking stupid," responded Mateo very matter of fact.

"Doc says, he's scheduled an interview for you at 3 pm today. He says he wants you back here by 2 pm to review with him before you go for your interview."

"Really," saying this more as a statement than a question. "Well, that's just what I need. Another fucking thing on my plate when I've got all this other important shit to take care of. It'll be such a fucking waste of time. Hell, you know as much as I do. Maybe you should go in my place."

"I'm sorry, Mateo. You're right. It isn't fair for you to get pulled away from the things you've got to do this week for this interview. But the boss and the police are requiring it. Who knows. Maybe it won't be a complete waste of time. Maybe they might find a lead or two before they leave. What do you want me to do?"

Charlotte's response made Mateo feel somewhat better. "I guess nothing. Tell Doc I'll be in his office by 2 pm."

Mateo ended the call then sat behind his desk for the next few minutes thinking. He was surprised they would be interviewing at the reservation so quickly. What did they already know and what brought them here so fast? Mateo's anxiety rose as he sat and thought. He reminded himself, I'm in control of my destiny, then took a break to clear his mind.

*****

At 1:56 Mateo exited the elevator and walked toward Charlotte's desk. She looked up and smiled seeing Mateo.

"Hi, Mateo. I see you made it. I'll let Doc know you're here."

Charlotte picked up the Cisco phone and buzzed Doc's office. "Hi, Doc. Mr. Rivera's here for your 2 pm appointment. Yes, I will. Thank you," then hung up.

"Doc says to go right in. And don't worry about it. It'll be fine, and you'll get everything done this week," Charlotte said, hoping to reassure him.

As Mateo passed Charlotte's desk and headed down the hall to Doc's office, he said, "Yup, it will." He said this with confidence, but he still felt conflicted.

Doc stood and greeted Mateo, having him sit in a chair at his desk and got straight to his agenda skipping any pleasantries. This was the first time Mateo could remember Doc doing this.

"You are going to be meeting with a Riverside County detective and an FBI special agent. Their names are," Doc stopped to look at a paper that contained the names, "Detective Bill Sullivan and Special Agent Tony Rossi. They're here to get background information on Fred Asghar. As of now, they believe he's only missing. They've not said anything about the possibility of Fred actually being the murderer, nor have they said anything about Fred being murdered."

"Why do they need to interview me?"

"They're interviewing all of the executives and the rest of the tribal council. We are cooperating because we have nothing to hide. And we want them to know that."

"That makes sense."

"Some of their questions will be about the recent elections and especially Fred's campaign slogan, Transparency for the Tribe. They wanna make sure there's no cover up here at the reservation. No fraud, embezzlement, or other illegal activity. However, anything we do at The Factory is confidential. We have contracts with governmental agencies that require confidentiality. You may refer them to those government agencies for specifics since we are not allowed to give out that information. Mention the Agency if you need to but remind them all tribal council members sign these contracts so everything is transparent."

"I see," said Mateo. This was exactly why Fred had been murdered. His anxiety began to rise.

Doc continued, "We work for the Tribal Council. They are able to look at everything we do. Our books and ledgers are always open to them or anyone they may hire to examine them. This includes the casino and The Factory."

Mateo kept a secret ledger for The Factory that only Doc and he knew about. The tribal council had access to the falsified ledger. Mateo would say these things even without Doc's instruction, but he realized this was a critical juncture in their operation. One wrong word, one inconsistent gesture or look could mean potential ruin of everything he and Doc had built.

Doc paused and studied Mateo. Then he opened a desk drawer and withdrew a prescription bottle. He opened the bottle and took out two pills. "Here, take these. They'll calm you down," said Doc as he handed them to Mateo.

"What's this?" asked Mateo.

"Something to calm you down. So, you can focus and get through this interview without screwing anything up."

"I'm okay."

"No, you're not. That's why I'm meeting with you now. So, we can go over everything and make sure you're calm and focused." Mateo took the pills and swallowed them.

Doc got up and walked to the office sitting area. "Come over here, sit down in the chair, and use the recliner to put your feet up." Mateo followed Doc and did as requested while Doc took a seat on the sofa.

"I'm going to take you through some relaxation exercises to help you with the interview." For the next fifteen minutes Doc led Mateo in several visualization and breathing exercises. After that, Mateo felt quite calm and confident. He didn't know if it was the effect of the pills, the calming exercises, or both.

"Now I'm going to ask you some questions like I'm that FBI agent interviewing you. I'm going to listen to your answers, but I'll be paying more attention to your voice and your nonverbal cues, how you sit in your chair, what you do with your hands and legs, your facial expressions, how long it takes you to answer."

Mateo put the recliner to the upright position, and for the rest of their hour, Doc grilled him with questions pointing out different nonverbal cues that could indicate deception.

******

It was almost 7 pm when Mateo finally made it home. His interview with the FBI agent and the Riverside County detective lasted 45 minutes and went smoothly. But then, he knew it would and decided his meeting with Doc was more of a waste of time than the interview. He went back to The Factory after that to finish his work for the day then headed home. Charlotte had called him at 5 pm on his cell phone. After three rings he decided to pick up and told her he would be working late. She sympathized with him which he appreciated then cut the call short to get back to work.

On his way home he tried to call Sheldon two more times but the calls continued to go to voicemail. He fumed as he drove. Of the things Mateo hated most, the two biggest were other people thinking they had authority over him or welded more power and control than he did. That detective and FBI agent fell into this category, and so did Doc. The other was people not jumping to his commands. Right now, that was Sheldon. For Mateo, all relationships were one up or one down. He was always the one up guy, the one who held more power and control. And if he wasn't he would work, or manipulate, until he was. And if he couldn't, he always cut off the relationship forcing them to submit to his will or forever be out of his life.

12

Tuesday

At 5:26 am Sheldon, wearing the company polo shirt, pulled into the parking lot at Witch's Brew. Michelle Archuleta, the store manager, had promoted him to shift manager, and he was to start training with her. Mic, the previous shift manager, had left to work in construction. He was Sheldon's friend from the men's home and had originally gotten him the job at Witch's Brew. As Sheldon reached the door, Michelle, in her Witch's Brew cap and apron, saw him and let him in. She was a brunette who stood at five feet, four inches with hair that reached midway between her shoulder blades. She always wore it in a pony tail threaded through the size adjustment hole on the back of her Witch's Brew cap. In her thirties, she was married with one little girl who started kindergarten last year. She still carried the leftover weight gain from her pregnancy.

"Welcome to your first day of shift manager training," Michelle cheery. She must be a morning person, he thought.

"Thanks," replied Sheldon. "I'm used to rolling in just before 6 am. Getting here at 5:30 was harder than I thought."

"You'll get used to it, believe me. Let's get started. 6 am comes quick, and we have a lot to cover before the crew gets here for opening."

The coffee shop was set up in two large open rooms. The front door spilled into the first room facing the L-shaped bar and cashier. The coffee paraphernalia was to the left. Once ready, the order could be picked up on the right side of the bar. The condiment area was located at the end of the bar and offered lids, stir straws, napkins, half and half, sugar with various sugar substitutes, and heat protector sleeves. Thick padded couches and chairs filled this room with corresponding coffee and end tables. The second room was to the right of this room and set up as a study room with long tables, hard chairs, and electrical outlets along the walls. A long table was positioned in the center of the room and had a power strip mounted into the middle and ran the table's length. It also had two conversational areas with pillowed chairs and round coffee tables.

Michelle and Sheldon quickly finished their prep work as the other baristas and cashiers arrived. Sheldon's coworkers congratulated him on the promotion as they arrived then got prepared for the morning rush. Customers had already lined up at the door, and the drive thru had four cars waiting for the 6 am opening. When Sheldon unlocked the door, the small line of customers filed in and the line continued to grow as commuters started their day with a hot brew from Witch's Brew. The bakery showed up at 6:15 am with their fresh pastries and an apology for running late. Sheldon gave the invoice to Michelle who showed him where the completed check was kept and gave it to Sheldon. Once the bakery staff finished loading the display case with their fresh pastries, Sheldon handed them the check.

******

At 8:50 am after the morning rush had died and Sheldon inspected the customer areas for cleanliness, sending baristas out to clean, straighten and restock, he noticed Connie Asghar getting out of her car and heading to Witch's Brew. She carried a green backpack and a thick textbook under her arm, her head was down, her hair up, and her gait made her look as though she was tired. Sheldon knew she was there to study. Witch's Brew had students coming to study regularly. He could tell when mid-terms or finals were about to be given because the back study room would have students trickling through all day and evening. There were already five students there so the college must be getting ready for finals. Students would order coffee when they first arrived then meander to the back room where they would set up camp. Laptops, books, notepads, pens, and highlighters would be spread across the tables as students quietly worked. Some came in pairs or groups and would quiz each other. They would study for hours making use of the free Wi-Fi and refills to keep them engaged with their work. The morning's pastry delivery would be gone by late afternoon as they got hungry.

"Hi Sheldon," Connie said, smiling when she looked up and saw him. She wasn't wearing any make up and wore a tee shirt, shorts, and flip flops. Sheldon thought she must have worked last night and now needed to study. It was typical of college students burning the candle at both ends. He had never seen her without makeup but still thought she was attractive.

"You gettin ready for finals?" asked Sheldon.

"Yup, I am. You know next semester you'll be doing this," reminded Connie.

"Lookin' forward to it," he said, sarcastically, then "You must have worked last night."

"I wasn't working, but I was up most the night," Connie frowned and looked slightly distressed.

"How come? What's goin' on?" Sheldon, emphatic.

Connie hesitated, then blurted out, "Oh, Sheldon, my uncle's missing. He just got elected Tribal Chairman but missed the meeting on Friday. They went out to his place to look for him and found Vanessa, his girlfriend, and Jamie, her brother, murdered!" Her eyes began to well up, "But they couldn't find Uncle Fred." Connie, now distraught, released a flood of emotions as she said the words. Tears began to trail down her cheeks, and she began to tremble.

Her distress both surprised and frightened him, and he began to feel the same emotions as if they were his own. Sheldon was naturally empathic. He often felt the feelings of others and when he was younger had thought those were his feelings. He was often confused and did not understand why he felt certain ways when this happened. He was only beginning to realize that he had this gift of empathy and compassion.

Sheldon reached out and wrapped his arms around Connie, book, and backpack in an effort to comfort her. Connie buried her face in his shoulder but continued to hold book and backpack with both arms. He didn't know what else to do. In a few moments, Connie regained her composure and Sheldon released the hug and took a step back, his polo shirt wet from her tears.

"What happened? How did they... how were they... what happened?" not sure of the best way to ask the question. He didn't want Connie to start crying again, especially if it was because he said something insensitive. Now he felt awkward.

Quietly now, almost in a whisper, "They were shot."

Sheldon's mind took him back to his field trip with Mateo. He wondered if there might be a connection. His heart began to race and adrenaline started pumping through his veins. He made a quick decision not to think about Mateo or the cremation they had done.

"Connie, I'm sure they'll find him. He'll be alright. After all, he wasn't there," Sheldon reasoned.

Connie sighed, "I hope so." Changing the subject, "I gotta go study. And get a cup of coffee. I really need one."

"You go back and get set up. I'll bring it to you."

"Okay. Thanks. And," hesitating, "thanks for caring. It means a lot."

"No worries. Glad I was here."

Connie moved to the back room, quickly greeted several other students that she knew, then set up her laptop on a table against the wall as far away from the other students as she could. Sheldon thought she must want to be alone.

As she turned on her laptop, Sheldon returned with her coffee.

"How much is it?'

"Don't worry about it. I got it," replied Sheldon as he handed her the cup with the heat protective sleeve.

She met his eyes, "Thank you," she said but didn't look away.

Sheldon held her gaze for a moment, maybe more, then started feeling uncomfortable. His palms started to sweat and his heart throbbed.

"I still have your number. I can call and see how you're doing, if that's okay," he inquired sheepishly.

"That would be great. My last final is Thursday afternoon. I'll have more time after that."

"Great." Sheldon turned and walked back to the counter. He was working and needed to bring his mind and emotions back to the job he was being paid to do.

Thoughts of Mateo and the cremation continued to haunt him intermingled with thoughts of Connie as he worked. He liked her, not because she was gorgeous or sexy, but because of how he felt when he was with her, talking to her. She made him feel confident and secure in himself. She showed real interest in him. She wasn't pretentious but down to earth, real, and didn't play games. What you saw was what you got with her. But there was more to it. It was something on the inside that made her so attractive. He didn't have any other words or ways to express himself about that quality as he thought about it. Then Mateo and the cremation injected itself back into his head like a semi-truck barreling down a steep grade, brakes burned out, and plowing into a long line of slow-moving cars at the bottom. It crashed his thoughts and spread them like the wind. What if it was Connie's uncle? How could he live with that and how would Connie react to that information if it ever got out. Mateo said to keep his mouth shut about it. That seemed like good advice right now.

Sheldon's cell phone vibrated, and he pulled it out of his back pocket and looked at the caller ID. It was Mateo again. Mateo had called Sheldon four times on Saturday and five times on Sunday and several times on Monday. Sheldon had let each call go to voicemail. Mateo only left voicemails on the last two calls. He started to listen to the first message but after a few seconds just deleted it. Sheldon didn't like Mateo's tone, didn't like the way it made him feel, and didn't like that it made him think of the cremation. He deleted the second message without listening to it at all. He was determined to sever his ties with Mateo. He remembered Mateo's threat about ending up dead. A strand of fear ran up his back, like electricity through a wire. His head and face got hot. His heart began to race.

Sheldon spent the rest of the morning focusing on his job. He checked on Connie several times, refilling her coffee twice. Mateo called once more before noon but didn't leave any messages. At noon Connie packed up her laptop, books, and papers and headed out. She stopped by the counter before she left to thank Sheldon again and remind him that her last final was Thursday afternoon. Sheldon hoped the reminder was because she wanted to see him. A date. Sheldon would need to work up the courage to ask her out. But first he would need to figure out where he could take her and what she might like to do. If he made the wrong decision, she would be bored to death and never want to see him again. And the same thing could happen if he said something stupid which was almost sure to happen. Maybe he should just forget the whole thing if he was going to screw it up anyway. At 2:30 pm his shift ended. Mateo had called one more time, and he let it go to voice mail again dismissing Mateo and the cremation from his thoughts. It was getting easier to do.

******

It was 7:30 am when Mateo sat down at his desk at The Factory. He had gotten most of the logistics completed for this week's contracts. He still had a few loose ends with the cartel delivery. The day and time were set, but he still had not gotten the location from his cartel contact. He also had not been able to reach Sheldon who he needed to work security for the delivery. He tired calling but again got his voicemail.

Mateo decided that most of his day would be spent trying to discover Doc's secret plans for the computer lab and the computer room. He knew there wasn't any real connection between them regardless of what Doc said.

At 10 am Mateo received an email from Human Resources. He remembered Doc was to hire two new people for the computer lab and the computer room and wondered if this was information on those hires. He opened the email and saw that it was. Wow, that was a quick hire, he thought. But now would be the perfect time to create that no show position for Sheldon. He decided that another conversation with Doc was in order, but this time he'd be firmer with Doc.

He spent the next two hours building security protocols to allow the two new hires to enter The Factory, their individual offices, and the computer lab and the computer room respectively. Doc had already told him that there would be no cross entry allowed between them. Mateo scoffed to himself as he worked on this and thought, the two being linked or connected my ass. Doc's a fuckin' liar.

At 3 pm Mateo strode past Charlotte's desk and down the hall to his office in the tribal council building. Charlotte had greeted him with a smile and a friendly greeting. He smiled back saying hello, but today there would be no flirting. He had something to discuss with Doc, and his mind was preoccupied with the potential scenarios depending on the outcome of the meeting. If Doc approved Sheldon's new position, then there was only one scenario. He would continue to be Doc's loyal partner in the confidential/illegal businesses they had built at the factory. If Doc refused, then there were several different scenarios. First, he could outright blackmail Doc, but this would put him in jeopardy too. Second, he could leak evidence to the police about Doc's involvement in the murders. Third, he could hunt to discover what Doc was really doing with the computer lab and room at the factory, confront him, and demand his cut. His fourth scenario was more extreme. He could kill Doc and plant evidence tying him to the previous murders.

After entering his office and shutting the door, he checked his desk, computer, and the credenza. Everything seemed in order, so he called Doc who picked up after the third ring.

"Hello, Mateo. What arc you doing here in the office? I thought you'd be tied up at The Factory the rest of the week." Doc was upbeat and cheery.

"I had a few things to take care of here. How did all the interviews go with that FBI geek?"

"Yea, he was kinda different wasn't he. I got several comments about him along those lines from others they interviewed. But everything went well. We may see them back sometime in the future, but I don't think there's anything that came up on their radar."

"I wanted to talk with you for a few minutes. It's one of those face-to-face subjects. Do you have some time?" asked Mateo.

"For you, always," replied Doc. It was his way. "Come on down to my office now."

"I'll be right there." With that, Mateo hung up the receiver, closed and locked his door, and headed to Doc's office. As he entered, Doc rose from his desk and made his way to the sitting area in the front part of the room.

"Here, Mateo, take a seat. You want a drink?"

Mateo sat in one of the two loungers furthest away from the bar. "Yup. Sure would." Doc mixed two Old Fashioneds with Elijah Craig Bourbon Barrel Proof, his favorite bourbon.

He handed one drink to Mateo and held up his glass to toast. "Here's to business."

"To business," replied Mateo and they both took a drink before setting the glasses on their respective coasters.

"Did you get the information from HR on the new hires yet?"

"Yup, I did, and that's what I wanted to discuss," replied Mateo as he picked up his drink and took another sip.

"Yes, Mateo, go ahead," said Doc, also taking a sip.

"With the new hires, this would be the perfect time to also hire for that position we discussed last week. You know. For Sheldon, the one I've been training and grooming him for."

Doc sat back on the sofa and took another sip from his drink. Mateo could tell he was thinking.

He continued, "Business is growing, and if I don't get this kind of help, we're liable to leave our asses hanging in the wind because there's just too much for one person, for me, to do. It's a matter of security, for our protection, and for efficient business. When businesses grow, manpower must grow with them, or it'll kill the growth, maybe even kill the business. You know we need this just as much as me, but you've got so many other things to worry about that it isn't in your face all the time like it is for me."

Mateo took a long sip from his drink while Doc continued to listen, and to think.

Finally, Doc spoke, "What, specifically, do you need him for?"

"This week, I need him to run security for me for the cartel delivery. I use him to deliver samples, finalize our confidential orders, and he's picked up and delivered payments too." Mateo could not tell Doc he used Sheldon for his gang deliveries and payments that Doc was unaware of. This was actually most of the work Sheldon did for Mateo.

"But these are all things you have time to do. As far as security goes, we had security staff at The Factory set up for you to use for the cartel deliveries. You chose to stop using them. Why, I'm not sure. I'm unable to see a need for the position you're asking for." Doc took a long drink finishing his Old Fashioned. Mateo knew Doc was done discussing it, but he wasn't.

"It's too risky to use the security staff for the cartel deliveries. We stay safe by keeping all the different people in the operation uninformed of the other responsibilities. We keep 'em in their own cell of knowledge, just enough to do their job and not enough to expose the system. People working security positions on site shouldn't be doing security off site with the cartel deliveries. They'll know too much and put our operations at risk." Mateo was getting angry now and finished his drink in one big gulp.

"So, you want to bring someone in, someone unknown, unvetted, untested, to expose the whole operation rather than use a Factory security officer who's been vetted, tested, and trusted that only does one thing? From what you've explained to me, the only thing this Sheldon wouldn't know is how we manufacture the weapons or ammunition on an assembly line Hell, he may know it all now. I just can't support that, Mateo."

"He knows nothing important. I've kept him in the dark. But I need this position," spat Mateo, now insistent.

"No, we are not doing the position, and no more using Sheldon. Not for anything." Doc was direct and to the point.

"We've already grown, and I'm having a real staffing issue. It's threatening exposure to the wrong people now." Mateo said this more as a threat than a statement.

"I think we're done talking, Mateo. It's been an enlightening conversation. Thank you for coming in to discuss this with me." Doc stood, walked to the door, and opened it.

Mateo got up, and walked out the open door, his anger burned.

As he passed Charlotte's desk she was surprised and said, "What happened? You don't look happy."

"Not the way I wanted it to go. That's for sure," Mateo said, still angry.

Charlotte had never seen anyone leave Doc's office angry. He was such a nice boss, a nice person. And Mateo was such a professional. What could have happened? She was bewildered.

Now Mateo had an idea. An idea on how to implement one of his scenarios if Doc said no. That's when he stopped, turned back to Charlotte and said, "Hey, I'd like you to come over tomorrow night if that's good for you."

"What about tonight?" asked Charlotte.

"I'm in a fucked-up mood tonight. You wouldn't wanna be around me. Tomorrow would be better. I'd love your company. Actually, I really need your company or I may just go crazy."

Charlotte smiled. "Sure, tomorrow night after work then. You wanna do anything special?"

"What if we do something next time? Tomorrow I really just want to relax at home and talk. I gotta share some stuff with someone before I explode. Could you pick up sandwiches again on your way over?"

"Sure. And hey, don't stress. It'll get better."

"You're right. It will. See ya tomorrow," said Mateo as he turned and headed toward the elevator. He smiled a sinister smile as he stepped in the elevator. On his way home, he tried calling Sheldon, but this time the phone was disconnected.

******

After work Sheldon decided to drive out to the college and get his books for the fall semester. It started in August, and he wanted to be ready. It was still three months away, but he remembered Connie was picking up books for a summer class she planned on taking, and he could get familiar with the campus layout.

He quickly found the bookstore on the directory and trekked across campus towards his destination. There were few students as it was finals week. Students only came to campus for their final or to study. The clerk at the bookstore counter informed him that books for fall would not be available for another month but books for summer classes were available now. Frustrated, he turned and headed back to his car but stopped when his cell phone rang. The caller ID said Mateo so he let it go to voicemail but decided he would get a new cell phone and cell number. If Mateo couldn't call him, he'd eventually just give up and go away. He hoped so anyway.

Sheldon left the campus and drove the two blocks to the Palm Desert Mall. He found a store and after an hour left with a new cell phone and a new number but he had gotten all of his information transferred to the new phone.

******

Sheldon left Palm Desert Mall and headed to New Life Empowerment Church to see Pastor Eminis. Maybe he knew something about his mom. She was the only family he had, and he hadn't seen her in years, not since she had run away from the church's woman's home and from him. It still hurt when he thought about it. He also wanted to ask the pastor about the black Timberline backpack and the things he found in that room. He looked at the time, and it was after 5 pm. No one would be at the church now. He decided to see Pastor Eminis on Wednesday,

Sheldon's day off. He would stop by the church in the morning after the men left for their landscaping jobs.

When Sheldon arrived home, he decided to sit on the metal steps that led to the door and send out his new number. The steps were actually a free-standing metal frame unattached to the ground. It sat on a four-foot by four-foot concrete slab that had been poured for the sole purpose of holding these steps. The complex owner must have poured the slab himself because it was uneven, and the whole metal frame rocked slightly from side to side when climbing the stairs from the shifting weight. The metal frame held three steps with a metal handrail on each side before reaching the square platform that butted against the trailer door. Sheldon grabbed a towel and laid it on the steps before sitting down. The mid-day sun had heated them up, and they were still too hot to sit comfortably. The park was quiet and peaceful in contrast to how his life now felt.

When he saw Connie's name in his contacts, he remembered that he said he would call her. Her last final was Thursday afternoon, and he had Saturday off. Maybe he could ask her out for Saturday? But where would he take her, and what would they do? Sheldon began feeling anxious, and his palms began to sweat. And what if she said no? What if he misunderstood her intentions? And what about her missing uncle? Then he thought, if I keep thinking about the what-ifs, I'll never do it. He pressed her number, and the new cell phone completed the call.

After four rings it went to voicemail. "Hi, ah, Connie, it's me, Sheldon. I just got a new cell phone and changed number. This is my new number." Sheldon read off his new number with area code to make sure she had it. After he hung up, he fretted over all the reasons and scenarios of what it meant that she didn't pick up. Five minutes later his cell phone rang. The caller ID displayed "Connie".

"Hi, Sheldon. I didn't recognize the number so I didn't pick up. What's up?" Connie sounded cheery and upbeat. Sheldon thought that maybe her uncle had been found after all.

"I was calling to see how you were doing. You were worried about your uncle last time I saw you. Any news?"

"No, no news about Uncle Fred yet. The police said there was no evidence of anyone else being hurt at his place. They think he's alive and maybe hiding somewhere. So that's good news. Work and finals keep my mind occupied so I'm not thinking about him all the time."

"Well, if you're not working this Saturday, and need your mind occupied, would you like to go out to the Fun Zone and then get a late lunch after?" asked Sheldon, his heart racing and palms wet with moisture.

The Fun Zone was a six-acre amusement park that had four miniature golf courses, arcade games, laser tag, and a spectacular midway with rides that equaled the biggest Barnum and Bailey circus. They even had a small roller coaster. All the classic midway games were there, and carneys, hawking their prizes to the would-be players passing through the midway, made the atmosphere charged with excitement and expectation. They had three different restaurants, a pizza joint, fast grilled food, and a nicer sit-down restaurant with waitresses that took your order and served your meal. The Fun Zone was always busy on weekends with kids, families, and younger adults.

"That sounds like fun, and yes, I'd love to go."

Wow, she sounds really excited, thought Sheldon. "Okay, I was thinking we could meet at 11 o'clock and head on over. Do you want to meet somewhere or do you want me to pick you up?"

"Oh, could we do it in the evening instead? Say, 7 o'clock, and maybe we can grab some fast-food after?"

"7 pm works for me," replied Sheldon who had been holding his breath.

"You can pick me up. I'll be at my mom's. I'll text you the address." Connie was staying with her mother in DHS since the disappearance of her uncle.

"I gotta get back to studying for finals, but I'm glad you called and for the date on Saturday."

"No problem," replied Sheldon. Each said their good byes then he heard the call end on Connie's end of the line.

13

Wednesday

Tuesday had been busy day for the crematory. Joe still needed to hire someone for his open position, and he had to fill in for Connie who was only working part-time for the rest of the week since she was studying for finals. It was another late day for them working until 9 pm. Toni was happy that more work came in than was expected so she wasn't stressing as much over making payroll, but both of them didn't like working this late. It was the plight of the small business owner.

Joe had scheduled to pick up the electric door system on Wednesday afternoon so after working through lunch, he picked up a check from Toni, hopped in the van, and headed to Indio. He swung by fast food on the way and grabbed a quick bite.

As Toni finished some paperwork and took another bite of pizza that she had ordered earlier, she noticed a police cruiser park in the stall across from the office door. As the officer exited his cruiser and trekked across the lot, she recognized him as the officer that was here the previous week, Officer A. Martinez.

"Good afternoon, Officer Martinez. Hope you're having a great day," Toni greeted him with a smile as she stood behind the reception desk with her paper plate still holding the second slice.

"Yes, ma'am, it's a good day. I see I've caught you during your lunch. My apologies,"

"No worries," replied Toni, "I'm just grabbing a bite between my paperwork. Would you like a slice? There's still half a meat lovers left in the conference room."

"That's very thoughtful of you, Mrs. Conti, but I've already had lunch. I'm actually here to discuss the bullet you found in your furnace last week. I said I'd be back at that time, and you were to give me names of possible susp..." now changing the word. "...people who might have gotten into your back room. Just what have you come up with for me?"

"Hmmm, I really haven't had any time to work on a list of possibilities. We've been so busy with the new alarm system, new locks, and my husband's picking up an electric door system for the big industrial doors even as we speak,"

"Mrs. Conti, there's been some new information about the bullet you found. And it's quite serious. Let's sit down and I'll fill you in." Mando knew she was making excuses. Could she be involved, or was she covering for someone? If she knew how serious this was, and her whole business could be implicated, she might tell all she knew. If she continued her evasiveness, then he could only conclude she and the business were involved.

They entered the conference room and sat on opposite sides of the table. Toni moved the pizza to the far end so it didn't sit between them. The lid was closed, but the rich smell of pepperoni, sausage, cheeses, and garlic still filled the air.

"What exactly is all this about? It was really just a foreign piece of metal we found in the furnace."

"It's actually much more than that," replied Mando. I told you and your husband last week that it was an armor piercing round, a bullet that cannot be purchased on the open market. A special license is needed for anyone to buy a bullet like this. Our lab analyzed the makeup of the bullet to determine what materials and amounts of those materials were used. We can identify the manufacturer through this analysis because each manufacturer uses slightly different materials or different percentages of these materials. We found there is no manufacturer in the U.S. or abroad that produces an armor piercing round with these specifications. It's quite unique."

Mando let this information sink in before continuing, but before he could start on his next topic, they heard one of the industrial doors open in the back.

"That must be Joe," Toni quickly interjected. "Let me get him before we continue." Toni jumped up and opened the door to the back room. Joe was backing the van into the building, getting ready to unload the equipment he'd just purchased.

As he turned off the engine and exited the van, Joe saw Toni standing at the conference room door. "Hey, Baby, I got it, and it looks in great shape! We got such a deal," excited about the purchase. Then he noticed Riverside Deputy Sheriff Armando Martinez standing behind Toni. He shut the industrial door and plodded towards the conference room door, his excitement about the purchase waned when he saw the deputy sheriff.

"So, what's goin on?" asked Joe as they all stepped back into the conference room and resumed their seating arrangements. Joe took the seat next to Toni.

"I was telling your wife that the bullet you found was not made by any known manufacturer. Our lab analyzed the materials in its makeup to determine that."

"Okay, so no big deal, right?" asked Joe.

"Because it's unique with no known manufacturer, it is a big deal, a very big deal," Mando stated in his most serious voice.

"Did you hear about the shooting that took place last week? Two people were shot and killed on a ranch near the Tranquilo Indian Reservation?"

"Yea. Yea, we did," replied Joe, uneasy.

Toni added, "As a matter of fact, one of our transporters is the niece of Fred Asghar, and she's updated us on what the police know so far."

"Then you know they were both shot," Mando said. He knew this was already reported by the news. "When the bullets were recovered and analyzed, we found they matched the bullet you found in your furnace.

The bullets that killed them and the bullet found in your furnace came from the same maker,"

"Whoever shot them must have also used your furnace, and we'll still need to determine how the bullet got in the furnace and what was cremated. This is why it's of critical importance that I get a list of anyone who might have done the cremation and anyone who you would suspect of doing it. If you don't give me any names, then I can only assume both of you are involved in some way. I'll also need a list of all your current and former employees for the last year."

Toni and Joe sat dumbfounded. They were in shock and now realized they were suspects, or at least persons of interest, in the murder investigation.

Mando watched their reactions. They were truly stunned. But were they stunned because they were innocent, and all this had taken them by surprise. Or were they stunned because they hadn't covered their tracks well. They did volunteer the bullet which was the only link to the murders. He had known nothing about the bullet until they brought it out in its sealed envelope and gave it to him. If they hadn't given him the bullet, he wouldn't be sitting across from them at their conference room table now. He felt they did know something. Something they were trying to keep secret.

"When can you have that list for me?" asked Mando after giving them some time for the gravity of the situation to take effect.

"I should be able to get it together for you by tomorrow. Tomorrow, late morning?" Toni replied in a weak voice. "Would that be okay?"

"That'll be fine. And I'll also want a list of people you think might have been able to run your cremator without your knowledge." Mando knew that they could refuse to give any of this information without a warrant, but their desire to cooperate demonstrated their innocence. And, he would have no problem getting a warrant if they refused. The bullet was a powerful piece of evidence linking this business to the murders.

After Officer Martinez left, Joe began to feel his anger rise, "That son of a bitch, Sheldon! I know he had something to do with this."

"We don't know anything yet," insisted Toni. "We need to talk to him," attempting to pacify Joe. She still felt a motherly connection to Sheldon but less now than an hour ago.

"I heard he's working at Witch's Brew. I'm gonna go over there now," Joe stood and headed towards the back where he'd parked the van. "Or after I unload this equipment."

"No, we've got too much to do right now. Plus, you need to cool off before you talk with him. I'll put it on your calendar for tomorrow afternoon."

"No, I'm gonna go now. I don't want to wait," Joe replied, still angry.

"If you go now like this, being all angry, what do you plan to accomplish?"

"I plan to beat the crap out of him. That's what I plan to accomplish!" Joe unleashing the anger he had held while Officer Martinez was still present.

"And what will that accomplish? You may end up in jail. That's no good for us. It's no good for the business. And it's no good for our employees. You need to calm down first and get control. Then we need to have a plan for what we want to accomplish with Sheldon," Toni almost pleaded now.

Joe hesitated. He knew Toni was right but didn't want to admit it. He started to calm down, then replied, "Okay, tomorrow afternoon. Why not morning?"

"I remembered when he worked there before, he worked afternoons and evenings. I figured he'd have the same schedule," explained Toni. This made sense to Joe.

Toni started to work on the list that Officer Martinez had asked for, but she had trouble concentrating. She was not her normal efficient self, and her mind kept wandering back to their conversation with Officer Martinez. Joe went to the back and consumed himself with his work.

This was work that was in his control, and it was calming and refreshing to his soul as he focused on it.

******

It was just past 9 am on Wednesday when Mateo pulled up to the gate of The Factory. He had gone to the gym early that morning hoping to work out some of the frustration he was feeling over work. Gym time always helped with this.

"Good morning, Mr. Rivera," greeted Manuel, the day gate guard. May I see your ID and driver's license?"

Mateo already had them out and handed both to Manuel. "Morning, Manuel. How's it going today?"

Manuel studied both IDs before handing them back to Mateo. "Everything is peaceful today. The night guard said there was a lot of wind last night. I found several lights out along the fence behind the building. I've emailed you the report so you can get maintenance to fix it."

"Shit," replied Mateo. He didn't want anyone back along the fence anytime soon. "I'll look into it, but don't expect them to get to it in the near future. They're short staffed and the casino has priority on maintenance issues over The Factory."

"Yes, sir. But doesn't that create a security risk?"

"It does, but we can only do what we can do. Some things are even outside of my control. Let everyone else know that it'll be a while before it's fixed." Mateo took his IDs and drove through the open gate. He watched it close in his rearview mirror as he drove around the building to his regular parking spot.

Mateo unlocked his office door after checking his mailbox in the mailroom and found an envelope from HR with the badges for the two new hires. He wrote a note to Manuel before stuffing the note inside the envelope and setting it into Manuel's inbox. The note told Manuel to notify him when they arrived, and he would orient them himself. Manuel would activate their badges and explain gate procedures then wait for him to get to the gate.

He spent the day ensuring the offices for the programmer and engineer were all in order. While doing this, Mateo searched everywhere for information about what was really happening at the lab and computer room. He even searched Doc's Factory office but found nothing. It frustrated him but he was also glad Charlotte was coming over tonight. He would recruit her to help in his investigation. He called Sheldon two more times that day, but both said the number was not in service.

******

Sheldon was in high spirits the rest of the evening and Wednesday morning. He had taken steps to separate himself from Mateo, he had asked Connie out, and she accepted. He had a full-time job, and he had a car. He called it his POS car, meaning piece of shit car, but a running POS car none the less. He planned to clean it up Saturday morning remembering the saying, 'You can put lipstick on a pig, but it's still just a pig.' That really applied to his car.

At 9 am he retrieved the black Timberline backpack he had taken from the women's home. He tossed it on the passenger seat of this car then headed out to New Life Empowerment Church and a surprise visit with Pastor Alfredo Eminis. He decided to confront Pastor Eminis about the backpack and its contents even if it had nothing to do with his mom.

Twenty-three minutes later Sheldon pulled into the parking lot of New Life Empowerment Church and parked. Pastor Eminis' brand new Cadillac Escalade was parked in his reserved spot. He got a new one every year. Always the Escalade with all the bells and whistles. The campus consisted of two buildings. The first building held the sanctuary, church offices, prayer rooms, and an elaborate fellowship hall with an adjoining industrial kitchen. The home school that Mic and he attended was run out of the fellowship hall. The second building had two stories and was broken up into various classrooms and larger meeting rooms. The grounds were landscaped in desert landscaping. The planters around the building were immaculate and matched the greenery in the parking lot planters. The men's home maintained these and were as attractive as the buildings. Finished with stucco, each building had slanted tiled roofs, coming to a high-point in the center of the building. The front of the first building sported a large stained glass window depicting Christ on the cross. Light shone through this glass and lit up the sanctuary on Sunday mornings bringing the image to life. Sheldon remembered thinking the image was so life-like that Jesus might jump off the cross and land on the stage in the middle of Pastor Eminis' sermon then lay hands on him. Pastor would then be able to lay hands on the sick and heal them instantly while Jesus kept his palm scared hands resting on the pastor's shoulders. It never did happen, but Sheldon dreamed about it many Sundays.

Sheldon grabbed the backpack as he exited his car and headed to the first building. He felt anxious about confronting the pastor as he entered the building. He would need to pass through the fellowship hall and down another hallway to get to Pastor Eminis' study and office. It was quiet inside, but he heard faint music coming from somewhere down the hall. The fellowship hall was empty, but a bottle of spray cleaner with a wet rag rested on the kitchen counter. There was also a hula hoe leaned up against the counter. Then he heard faint noises coming from the church's main office. Its solid hardwood door located next to the kitchen was closed, but someone was in there. Sheldon walked to the door and swung it open. He stood there for several seconds dumbfounded, not believing what he was seeing. There, leaning in front of the desk was what Sheldon assumed to be some men's home guy who must have abandoned the hula hoe. His long blonde hair was held with a handkerchief tied around his forehead, and he was shirtless. His pants and shorts were down around his ankles. On each side of him was a bare female leg, a right leg on one side and a left leg on the other. Toes were pointing skyward while her feet were level with the guy's shoulders. She must have abandoned the bottle of spray cleaner for a more exciting activity. They had cleared the desk, and the woman lay on her back moaning in ecstasy while the guy grunted.

He stopped mid-grunt, turned, and looked at Sheldon and yelled, "Shut the fucking door!" Sheldon shut the door and turned to find Pastor Eminis.

The door to the pastor's study was shut so Sheldon knocked then opened it. There were ledger sheets and an accounting balance book opened on his desk. As Sheldon walked in, he held the backpack behind him, not wanting the pastor to see it just yet.

Pastor Eminis looked up at Sheldon, reading glasses still perched on his nose, "Sheldon, my boy! Come in, come in. Sit down. It's good to see you."

The office was roomy decorated in various shades of purple. A computer sat on the credenza behind the pastor who sat in a large backed leather chair. The right wall was a large bookshelf from floor to ceiling. It ran almost the complete depth of the office. It was filled with books and the occasional Christian themed nicknack. The front of the office was designed as a parlor area. There was a small couch, coffee and end tables that sat on a shag throw rug. Sheldon sat down in a chair in front of the pastor's desk moving the backpack to the floor next to the chair.

"I haven't seen you in church for some time. But we have wayward sheep all over the valley. They come, they go, but eventually they all come back. Is that why you're here?"

Sheldon didn't say a word. His anxiety had turned to anger as his heart raced. Adrenaline coursed through his veins. He stared at Pastor Eminis trying to contain the rage that seemed to come from nowhere. Sheldon threw the backpack on the desk and stared at the pastor. His eyes filled with rage, "I'm here because of this." He didn't shout, but his voice filled the room with sound and emotion spilling out into the hall.

Sheldon stood, grabbed the backpack, pulled out the handcuffs and rope, and threw them on top of the backpack. "I'm here because of this!" Sheldon's eyes burned into Pastor Eminis'.

The pastor stared at the backpack, handcuffs, and rope that lay in front of him covering his ledgers and account book. His hands were spread on the edge of his desk as he leaned forward, frozen like a statue out of time.

"Where's my mom?" demanded Sheldon, his eyes welling up. Then louder, "What happened to her!"

The pastor, now beginning to move like the Wizard of Oz's tin man who finally received oil in his joints, removed his reading glasses but still stared down at his desk. Then he blubbered, "I've never seen these things before. I don't know where they came from." Looking up at Sheldon and finally meeting his stare, "Just what are you accusing me of, anyway?"

"Where's my mom! What happened to her!" Sheldon wailed as tears streamed down his cheeks.

"I'm the man of God! I'm righteous. Holy! How dare you accuse me of vile sinful acts! You're a devil! A devil, I say!" Pastor Eminis yelled so loud that the couple Sheldon met in the church office came running down the hall and burst into the study. Sheldon was glad they had gotten back into their clothes.

"Pastor, this dude causin' ya trouble?" the guy asked in a southern drawl.

"Brother Peter, thank God you're here!" Pastor Eminis now relieved since reinforcements had arrived. "This backslidden sinner has lost his mind and is threatening to kill me!" Pastor Eminis started collecting the backpack and reinserting its contents.

"You fucking liar!" roared Sheldon as he stood and tried to grab the backpack away from the pastor.

"Get y'all's hands off a dat, an git outta here," demanded Peter, his drawl becoming more apparent.

Peter grabbed Sheldon by the shoulders as the backpack slipped from his fingertips and threw him into the hall. Sheldon's shoulder bounced off the wall then he hit the floor. Peter stepped out of the office and picked Sheldon up by the arms and pushed him down the hallway. Pushed him again, then again moving towards the door with each push. Sheldon stumbled with the force but didn't fall down again.

Once out of the pastor's earshot, Peter said, "Ya fuckin loser. Get da hail outta here! And if'n ya eva come back, I'll beat yo ass. Y'all hear? Asshole!"

With Peter's last push, Sheldon was now out of the building, and he stumbled across the parking lot to his car. Tears streamed down his face. He didn't understand why he had gotten so angry, but he did feel like the pastor knew something about his mother that he refused to tell. He had lied to Peter. Sheldon never threatened him. Why would he say that? Why would he keep the backpack? He wiped the rest of his tears on the bottom of his t-shirt, started his car, and drove back to DHS. When he got home, he was spent so he decided to take a nap. He slept most of the day and didn't get up until early evening. When he woke, he felt alone, defeated, and powerless. He hated that feeling, but he still missed his mom.

******

It was almost 6 pm when Charlotte arrived with a McAllister's Deli bag in hand. Mateo met her at the door. "Hey, Baby. Glad you made it," he said, giving her a hug. She hugged him back as he smelled her hair.

"Mmm, your hair smells nice. I didn't notice it the other night, but I remember your perfume."

Charlotte beamed, "So, you approve?"

"Yes, I do."

Mateo closed the door and led Charlotte to the couch. "Let's eat over here. It's more comfortable. Wanna beer?"

"That would be great," replied Charlotte as she took the sandwiches out of the bag and unwrapped them on the coffee table. Mateo got two bottles out of the refrigerator, opened them, and sat down beside Charlotte on the couch.

Charlotte was wearing a light peach short sleeve blouse and white form fitting dress slacks. The blouse was low cut and directed his eyes to her cleavage. She still wore the necklace and earrings she had worn the last time she was there. Mateo was surprised how quickly his frustrations from the confrontations of the day melted away with her just sitting there on the couch.

Mateo picked up his sandwich and took a bite. It was a large Southwest Chicken and Avocado. "Wow," he said after swallowing his first bite. "You remembered what I like."

"Are you surprised?"

"Yup, a little. I never would have remembered."

"Well, I pay attention to the little things. That's how you know you're important to someone. When they remember the little things." After a few more bites and a few sips of beer, Charlotte asked, "So just what did happen with you and Doc?"

Mateo swallowed the bite of sandwich in his mouth then took a drink of his beer. He turned to face Charlotte and said, "I really don't know how much I should tell you, Charlotte. What I know, and what I've been asked to do could be dangerous... even deadly. If I told you... you could be in danger too."

"What are you talking about, Mateo? What did Doc ask you to do anyway?"

Mateo hesitated, a long pause for effect, then said, "Doc didn't ask me to do anything."

"Well then who asked you to do something, and just what did they want you to do?"

"You know the FBI interviewed the tribal council members and all the executives, right?" Charlotte nodded.

"Did they interview you?" asked Mateo. If she had been interviewed by the FBI then he would need to change his game plan somewhat.

"No, only the executive staff on our floor."

"Well, they asked me questions about the new developments at The Factory. You know, the computer lab and the computer room."

"Okay, so it sounds like they were just getting background information."

Mateo hesitated again then began his story, "They contacted me again after all the interviews were done. Here at my home! They just showed up at the door. No phone call, no scheduling of any kind of meeting. They just showed up."

She put down what was left of her sandwich and sat straight up. "Really! What did they want?"

"They told me I impressed them with my interview, and being a security director (Mateo intentionally left out the word assistant in the title) they felt I was one of them. You know, an enforcer of the law, like a cop, but with more responsibility."

Charlotte sat wide-eyed, holding on to every word.

"There are some things they told me that I can't tell you. It'd be just too fucking dangerous, and I don't want to put you in any danger." He reached out and held her forearm firm with his hand and paused like that for a few moments while their eyes met. Then he let go and went back to his story.

"Basically, they think the new computer room and lab have something to do with Fred's death...." Mateo stopped speaking for a moment then corrected himself, "I mean disappearance."

Charlotte, shocked, asked, "Do they think he's dead?"

"They didn't say anything about it, but come on, Charlotte. It's been a week since he went missing, and no one's heard anything from him. What do you think?"

He watched Charlotte ponder it seeing her expression change from shock to sadness. She never responded, but that was okay. He wanted to continue spinning his tale.

"So, they had more questions about the fucking lab and the computer room. I couldn't answer any of 'em because I didn't know anything. Doc's kept everything under wraps. Do you know I know everything about every department at The Factory except the new computer lab and room?"

"Well, that must be what you and Doc were arguing about," replied Charlotte.

"Yup, it was, but let me get back to the FBI here at my house. We'll get to what happened with Doc in a minute. The FBI asked me if I could dig up information for them. You know, find out exactly what was going on there. I've looked through every fucking room at The Factory and found nothing. Not a damn thing! I got info on every program all organized, cataloged, and filed, but nothing on the computers. It's fucking strange. And just why do you think that is, Charlotte?"

Mateo looked directly at her waiting for her to respond. Finally, Charlotte said, "It sounds like someone wants to keep it a secret."

"That's exactly what the FBI said. They asked me to get as much information on the lab and computer room but do it confidentially. They don't want anyone to know, especially anyone on the tribal council or who works for the tribal council."

"Then you're like a confidential informant for the FBI, helping them get information to solve the murders?"

"No, Charlotte. A CI is a civilian that the FBI uses. I'm like an undercover agent for the FBI. I'm part of law enforcement." He paused, then said, "I shouldn't even be telling you any of this. But I trust you. I know you won't betray that trust."

Charlotte thought about this as Mateo watched her. When she smiled, he knew she would do what he was going to ask her before the morning.

"Today, I spoke with Doc about the lab and computer room. I got new hires coming tomorrow and need more information in order to do my job... and to pass along to the FBI. But Doc refused to give me a fucking thing! He knows I can't properly establish security protocols for these people or secure their offices or the lab and computer room without more information. And he fucking refused."

"I remember Fred was wanting more information about The Factory before he disappeared," she interjected. "Do you think he was asking about the same thing?"

"I know he was, Charlotte. I was ready to give him a tour of The Factory, but Doc kept putting it off. Then he disappeared."

Charlotte thought some more then asked, "You don't think Doc had anything to do with Fred and the murders, do you?"

"Hell no," he replied. "But Doc has all these connections with Agency folk, ex-Agency people, corrupt military and government officials from South America, and even cartel connections. Any one of those could be responsible. They may be setting Doc up for the murders."

"Doc's gotta have the information the FBI wants somewhere in his office. I've looked everywhere else, but I've got no fucking way to get into his office to look around."

Mateo put his head in his hands and bent forward towards his lap. "I feel so fucking helpless right now. I'm letting the FBI down when they were counting on me. And if this thing isn't solved, I know it'll be my fault... because no one could get into that office."

Charlotte leaned over to him and put her arm around his neck to comfort him then kissed his neck. He turned his head and kissed her back. After a few minutes he stood up and led her to the bedroom. Mateo mentioned several more times that night about how bad he felt because he couldn't get the information from Doc's office for the FBI, but he never asked her to spy for him.

******

"I've gotta get going," said Charlotte as she walked out of the bathroom into the bedroom. She had gotten dressed but still needed to retrieve her shoes and purse from the living room. "It's 6:10. I'm already late."

Mateo rolled over to face her. "Glad you're looking forward to work. At least one of us is."

"You know, Mateo, I have keys to Doc's office. I go in there all the time when he's gone. I'm the administrative assistant. I practically run the whole office."

Mateo was tempted to tell her she was only a secretary but stopped himself and said, "I couldn't ask you to help me with this, Charlotte. I just couldn't."

"Well, you don't have to. I'll just do it. And no one will know. I'm in there all the time so I can do a little snooping." With that Charlotte turned and walked out of the bedroom. Moments later Mateo heard the front door shut then a car start and drive off. Mateo smiled and thought, this is going to be much easier than I thought. I didn't even have to ask her.

14

Thursday and Friday

At 9:30 am Mateo's Cisco phone rang. He was away from his office at The Factory supervising the packing for his delivery to the Sinaloa Cartel so he missed the call. The delivery was to take place tomorrow night in Calexico. The cartel owned an old warehouse just outside of town and that would be the delivery location. It would be almost three hours each way so Mateo knew it would take him all night, but the money he would make was more than worth it. He listened to the voicemail after he returned to his office. The new hires were at the gate so he headed out the back entrance to his golf cart and drove to the gate.

As he pulled the cart up next to the guard shack and got out, Mateo could see Manuel had completed his part of the orientation with the two newbies, and each was wearing their badge.

Mateo greeted them with a smile. "Welcome to The Factory. I'm Mateo Rivera, the Director of Security here." Mateo read their badges. Mike Riggs was the programmer. He was in his late forties and had balding brown hair with a bad combover. His dark rim glasses sat high on his nose and his beer belly formed a round hump under his long sleeve button down shirt that tucked into brown wool slacks.

Jim Coleman, the engineer, was younger, maybe late twenties or early thirties. He was tall and slim with curly red hair, light complexion with a blanket of freckles across his nose. He wore an untucked blue polo shirt with black designer jeans. Jim had been the engineer Doc originally brought in to set up the computer room. Jim showed up every evening for two weeks with a crew of five other technicians to get the room up and running. HR had never known about them, and Mateo thought Doc was paying them with his own money, proceeds from their confidential activities at The Factory. Jim's previous work was clandestine so Mateo pretended he was meeting Jim for the first time. Jim did the same.

They introduced themselves to Mateo shaking hands then parked their cars just inside the gate and piled into the golf cart. For the next forty-five minutes Mateo oriented them to The Factory explaining procedures, protocols, creating individual special passcodes that identified them whenever they entered the building, a department, or their office. He showed them the gym and showers, the gun range, and the lounge area. He finally deposited them each in their own office to settle in. After that Mateo went back to Jim Coleman's office bringing a pad and pen with him.

"Jim, it's good to have you officially on board. And now that it's official, I need a little more information about the computer room. Have you got a few minutes right now?"

"Sure do. What do you need?"

"First, I need to know about power requirements. Currently we are wired to handle all the computers in the computer room. Do you see this as sufficient or do you predict that we may need more power in the future."

"That's a funny question for a security guy. Why do you need to know that?"

"Was it not explained to you that I run everything here at The Factory. It starts with me, and it ends with me. Who do you think gave the final approval for your hire anyway!" Mateo thought this young guy was naive and could be easily intimidated.

Jim leaned forward in his chair and studied Mateo. Jim was not intimidated. "You'll need to talk with Doc about anything I do here. If Doc wants me to give you any information, he can tell me."

Making a feeble attempt to hide his anger, Mateo stood and left Jim's office. He reassured himself knowing Charlotte would be searching Doc's office. She was sure to find the information he needed.

******

Thursday afternoon Joe drove to Witch's Brew to confront Sheldon. Twenty minutes later he was back because Sheldon was already gone for the day. Joe had at least gotten his schedule. Joe told Toni who quickly responded by saying she had a new idea about confronting Sheldon and shared it with Joe.

"I think I should be the one to see Sheldon. I have a better relationship with him so he'll be more willing to talk with me," Toni reasoned.

"No, I'm gonna talk with him. He's put our business at risk and pulled us into some murder plot," Joe insisted. Toni continued reasoning with Joe, and after twenty minutes, Joe finally acquiesced. He was still angry with Sheldon and wanted an opportunity to let him know but agreed it would be better if Toni went.

Three minutes later, Officer Martinez stood in the office lobby asking for his list. Joe had gone to the back before he arrived, and Toni thought it would be better if Joe wasn't there. He would get angry all over again when she was just starting to feel like she had some control back.

Toni handed Officer Martinez the list in a sealed business envelope. He opened it and looked it over. It contained two names only; Joe and Toni Conti. He had already notified Detective Bill Sullivan, and the detective had authorized him to follow up with getting the list since he had made the initial contact and established a rapport. He and the detective were expecting a list naming anyone that may have operated the furnace. Not this.

"This is not what I asked for. I need the names of all your current and former employees and any others you think might be involved?"

Toni paused then said, "Officer Martinez, these people are like family to us. I don't want to give you names of people that have no involvement. It could destroy our relationships with these people. And we love and care about them very much. We've invested in the lives of many of them," Toni now being honest and sincere.

Mando replied very matter of fact, "But this is a murder investigation. At least two people have lost their lives. You want to hinder the investigation?"

"No, I don't want to hinder anything," Toni said respectfully and in a submissive voice. "But I don't want these people brought into something they have no part in, like Joe and I have. Can we make a deal about this?" Toni asked, hoping there would be some wiggle room.

"What kind of a deal?" asked Mando.

"I want to do some of my own investigation into our people first, and I will have that list for you late Friday afternoon."

"So, you want to warn potential suspects before the police can question them." It was a statement, not a question.

Toni argued her position attempting to convince the officer. "Look, these people trust me. They'll talk to me. They may not say anything to the police. I've built trusting relationships with them. They'll talk honestly with me. You can't make the same claim, can you?"

Mando thought about it. She might be able to get information that he couldn't. He did use informants in other cases to help gather information, and this could be one of those times. "Okay, Friday afternoon. I'll be back then. But, if you don't have a list for me, we'll be talking more about it at my place of business, not yours. Understood?"

"Yes, understood. And thank you," said Toni, relieved the officer had agreed.

"I'll see you at 4 pm on Friday. Have a good rest of your day, Mrs. Conti." Mando turned and exited through the front door, and drove out of the parking lot.

Toni's racing heart began to settle as she sat down at her desk. She would need to talk with Sheldon tomorrow before Officer Martinez returned. Toni only told Joe that Officer Martinez had picked up the list and not that it contained only two names or the deal she had made with the officer.

******

Friday

Today was Friday and he was feeling more like his old self again. He refused to think about his confrontation with Pastor Eminis, and working helped keep his mind off it. Things were going smoothly at the coffee shop. He had not seen Connie since Monday. If she had come back to study, it was after his shift ended. This afternoon, Sheldon counted twelve students in the back studying. He also had not seen or heard anything from Mateo since he changed his cell number. He hoped Mateo had finally given up, and now the cremation felt more like a bad dream. A feeling of excitement stayed with him as he thought about Saturday and Connie. He had been afraid to call it a date, even to himself until this morning. He didn't want to jinx the day. But now he felt more confident about the date feeling more confident and self-assured.

Johnny, one of the baristas on the late shift, had just arrived. Today Sheldon had assigned him the cash register.

"Hey, Sheldon," called Johnny as he put on his apron, wrapping the ties around his waist and bringing them to the front where he tied it.

"You got everything you need?" asked Sheldon.

"Yup, I do," as he signed his money count log and put his tray into the cash register. He handed the signed money log to Sheldon who would file it in the office. "Some guy came by last night looking for you."

Sheldon's heart stopped, "Did you get a name?" thinking it must be Mateo, but hoping it wasn't. It couldn't have been Mic. Johnny knew Mic.

"No, he didn't leave a name."

"Well, what did he look like?" asked Sheldon.

"I dunno. I guess under six feet, kinda stocky. Dark complexion, maybe Hispanic. You know him?"

Shit, it had to be Mateo. "That could be almost anyone. So, I might know him. Ya got any more details?" replied Sheldon now feeling a little sick and beginning to panic. He hoped it didn't show, then turned to walk to the back office. He needed to file Johnny's cash log, but more importantly, he needed to be alone for a few minutes to think.

"Sorry, no other details, bro." Johnny finished preparing the cash register and watched as a customer entered and walked towards him, gazing at the menu above his head. "Welcome to Witch's Brew! How may I help you?" Johnny engaged the customer with a smile.

Sheldon sat down at the desk in the back office. He reassessed his actions. He had refused to take calls from Mateo. He had gotten a new phone number so Mateo could no longer call him. Shouldn't that communicate to Mateo that he was done? Sheldon hated conflict and would do most anything to avoid it, especially conflict with Mateo. He hadn't told Mateo that he was done, and he didn't want a confrontation because he knew Mateo would be mad. But how mad would Mateo be? Mad enough to yell and cuss him out? Mad enough to get physical, beat him up, put him in the hospital, break a bone or two? Mad enough to do something worse? Shoot him? Slash him? Strangle him? He had already threatened him about the possibility of ending up like the person they cremated. Sheldon hoped and prayed it wasn't Connie's uncle, Fredrick Asghar. But what could he do?

Maybe if he paid him back for the POS car, with interest, Mateo would be appeased. Maybe he could move out of the area, quit his job, load his car up with everything he owned, and head somewhere out of the valley. Someplace Mateo could never find him. The more he thought the more confused and panic stricken he became. His head began to swirl.

"Sheldon, everything okay?" It was Michelle Archuleta's voice.

Sheldon snapped back to reality, "Oh, yea, I'm fine. Just a few things on my mind."

"Johnny's got a question about the register. I told him you'd be right out to help him. Since you're new to the shift manager position, I want to establish with everyone they come to you for questions, not me."

Sheldon got up and started towards the door, "Thanks. I'll see what he needs."

It was 2:30 pm and Sheldon was done with work for the day. He hurried to his car, getting the key from his pocket as he walked. He found the key and inserted it in the door lock when a white panel van pulled up and parked in the stall next to him. He stopped dead in his tracks as he looked through the passenger window to the driver on the other side of the van. Adrenaline began to flow through his veins. His heart began to race. He couldn't think and looked around the parking lot thinking he could run, but his feet seemed to be welded to the asphalt. He was frozen in place. The driver shut down the engine, then stepped out of the van and walked around it to Sheldon's side. The driver was now facing Sheldon. Three feet from his face.

******

On Friday Toni closed the office at 2 pm and drove to Witch's Brew. She spied Sheldon's car parked under a Tamarisk tree then parked on the far side of the lot where she had a direct line of sight. The day was hot so she kept the engine running and the air conditioning on. Toni had arrived fifteen minutes early, and she nervously waited and watched for Sheldon. When she saw Sheldon walk out the front door of Witch's Brew and cross the parking, she put the van in drive and pulled into the stall next to Sheldon on his driver's side. She killed the engine, got out, and walked around the van. Now she stood face to face with Sheldon.

"Hi Sheldon, back at Witch's Brew I see," Toni said, breaking the ice. Sheldon looked unraveled.

After a long pause Sheldon replied, "Yea, full time now."

"Do you know how bad I felt when we had to let you go?" asked Toni. "I know you were trying hard and didn't want to let us down."

Sheldon cautiously said, "Yea, I'm really sorry about that. I was doing some odd jobs at night, and it just got in the way."

"Well, since you're working full time, I hope you're not still trying to work nights too."

"No, not anymore. I let that job go," Sheldon now feeling more comfortable. Maybe they didn't know.

"Well, I'm glad you're doing well. I really want to see you be a success. You have so much potential."

"Thanks, I'm trying. Hey, I even signed up at the community college. Starting this fall."

"Good for you. You won't regret it. Hey, do you remember Connie Asghar? She's a transporter for the business."

"Yea, I remember Connie," Sheldon was wary.

"Well, her uncle's missing, and two people were murdered out at his place last week," Toni said.

"Yea, I heard about it on the news," Sheldon, defensive. His heart began to pound.

"They were both shot with a unique armor piercing bullet. Did you know that?"

"No, I didn't. Where did you hear that?"

"From a police officer that came by the crematory. And here's the strange thing. We found a bullet in our furnace that matched the same bullets that killed those two people. What do you think of that?"

There was a long awkward pause. It was awkward for Sheldon anyway. "I dunno. What'd the police say."

"They said the murders and the bullet had to be connected."

"Wow!" Sheldon began to feel nauseous.

Toni continued, "And here's another strange thing. The cremator was used early Thursday morning at 2:15 am. Someone ran it through a cremation cycle. What do you think of that?"

Sheldon didn't respond. He couldn't respond. He stood in front of Toni wanting to run, but his feet were cemented to the pavement.

"Sheldon, I don't know what happened, and I don't know what you were involved in, but I think it had something to do with your late-night odd jobs. You said you were done with those. I hope so. But here's my problem. That police officer is coming back this afternoon and wants me to tell them who I think ran our furnace. What am I supposed to tell him? Sheldon, take a breath, look at me, and help me with this."

The color had drained from Sheldon's face, and his hands and knees began to shake.

"Sheldon, I'm afraid too. The officer thinks the business might be involved with the murders. That means, they think Joe and I might be involved. I think you got sucked into something way over your head. I don't think you had anything to do with the murders, but..." Toni paused, "I do think you know something about the cremation on Thursday morning."

Finally, Sheldon stammered, "I don't know what to say."

"Did Mateo have something to do with it?" asked Toni. She remembered the name entered on the cremation clipboard.

Sheldon cringed, forgetting he had written Mateo's name on the clipboard.

"You're afraid of Mateo, aren't you?"

A long pause, then, "Yea," Sheldon hung his head and gaped at the ground, then just stared.

"And you want to do the right thing, but you're afraid, aren't you."

Another long pause, then, "Yea," Sheldon's head still down his eyes now focusing on his own shoes.

"Sheldon, will you let me help you with this? We can figure this out together."

"I dunno. I'm gonna need time to think." He didn't look up.

"Okay, how much time do you need?"

Sheldon looked up at Toni's face. "I dunno."

"Today's Friday. Let's give you the weekend, and you come to our place for dinner on Monday night, 6 pm. When was the last time you had a home cooked meal, Sheldon? I'll get Joe to barbeque steaks. We'll put baked potatoes and corn on the cob with it. Maybe some apple pie for dessert. We'll have plenty of time to talk and figure things out. And you won't need to do it alone." Toni let Sheldon think for a few seconds then pressed him for an answer. "Can we do that, Sheldon? Treat you to a nice home cooked meal while we figure out what to do, together?"

"Okay," Sheldon said, still hesitant, "Monday 6 pm, you said?" Sheldon had been to their house before. Toni and Joe would throw parties for all the employees from time to time, and Sheldon had attended one of them.

"Great," Toni said with a smile, "Is your cell number still the same?"

"No, I got a new number." Sheldon gave Toni his new number then Toni gave him a big long hug before they parted ways.

******

Toni pulled into the empty parking stall across from Coachella Valley Cremations. She felt good about her confrontation with Sheldon and wanted to share the conversation with Joe. She unlocked the door and went to the back where Joe was working. The furnace was just completing its run cycle as Joe looked up from its control screen.

"Hey, Baby, how'd it go?" Joe hoping to hear good news.

"I think it went as well as it could," replied Toni. "He didn't admit to anything, but he looked guilty as hell. He's gonna come to dinner on Monday night, and we can talk more then."

"You've got to be kidding!" Joe, surprised and angry once more. "That little shit breaks into our business and uses our equipment to dispose of a body, and we're gonna feed him dinner? Have you lost your mind!" said Joe, his anger grew with every word.

"Joe!" Toni raised her voice attempting to quell Joe's anger so he would listen to her. "Sheldon is a scared kid that doesn't know what to do. He's caught up in something much bigger than himself. I think he may even be afraid for his life. He needs help, Joe. He needs people he can trust to give him that help."

"And we're supposed to be those people?" Joe started to calm down a bit.

"Who else has he got, Joe? He came into our lives for a reason, and we both saw his potential when he first started working here, right?" It was more of a rhetorical question, and Joe didn't respond. But he was listening now.

Toni continued, "We're the ones in the position to help him figure this out, and we can do that Monday night."

"Shit, Toni, you act like he's our kid or something." Joe realized he was going to lose this argument.

"We've always treated our employees kinda like family. Let's not change that now."

"But he doesn't work here anymore, remember. I fired him." Joe hoped Toni couldn't counter this point.

"Yes, but he's still intertwined with us. We still have a responsibility to teach him, help him, and guide him. Just because he's not working for us now doesn't mean he's out of our lives," Toni was insistent.

Joe shook his head. Damn her. She always wanted to bring the strays home to nursemaid, but he heard her tone. He knew the discussion was over.

Joe hesitated then shrugged his shoulders, "I'm so angry with that guy."

Toni knew Joe had acquiesced and replied, "Joe, anger is a poor teacher."

"Shit, Toni," Joe paused as his anger subsided. "Okay, I'll work on it. I've got til Monday night to cool off. Maybe I won't strangle him by then."

"I love you, Joe Conti. You're a good man," Toni replied with sincerity as she grabbed Joe's arm, embraced him, and kissed him. Joe kissed her back then turned and went back to work not saying a word. Toni could get him to agree with most anything he thought.

******

Toni went back to work on payroll and other paperwork. She was consumed with this and didn't realize Riverside Deputy Sheriff Armando Martinez had arrived until he walked into the lobby. It was 3:58 pm.

"Good afternoon, Deputy Martinez. I was expecting you."

Mando reached across the desk and shook Toni's hand. "Mrs. Conti, I've come to get more information from you regarding who might have used your crematory." No pleasantries today.

Toni hesitated, "Yes. I've done some investigating and found out who did it. I'm going to meet with him again Monday evening, and I'll have more information for you then." Toni hoped this would appease the deputy and wait until after her meeting with Sheldon.

"Mrs. Conti, that's not what we agreed to. I'll need this gentleman's name now," Mando insisted.

"I don't want anyone talking to him before Monday. If the police start nosing around, it'll spook him and then he may not say anything. So, you'll need to wait. I'll give you the name after that along with whatever I find out," Toni now adamant.

Mando studied Toni for just a moment. He looked at her face and her body stance. Both indicated she had dug in her heels and was determined to keep the information she had to herself. Finally, Mando said, "Mrs. Conti, I'll need you to come to the station to answer some more questions."

"I don't think so. Come back on Tuesday, and we can talk more."

"That wasn't a request, Mrs. Conti. There're more questions you'll need to answer, and this is not the place to ask them or for you to answer them. You'll need to get in your car now, and follow me to the station. Do you understand?"

"No, I'm not." Toni became agitated at his demand thinking it was foolish and way out of line. "You'll just have to wait or forget about any help from me."

"Mrs. Conti, you may willingly follow me to the station, or I can arrest you, handcuff you, and drive you to the station in the back of my cruiser. Now just how do you want to go?"

Toni, hated being forced to give up the name until she was ready, but decided she should tell the officer now to keep from being taken to jail. "Okay, okay, it was Sheldon Goodman. And I can give you his contact information if you absolutely need to have it."

"Thank you, but you'll still need to come to the station... now."

Surprised and irritated with Officer Martinez, "Whaddaya mean? I gave you the name. I don't need to go anywhere with you."

"I appreciate the name," Mando continued, still even tempered, "but there's still more questions to be answered. We'll need to do that at the station."

"And just what questions are these? I've already told you everything I know. I don't see why you can't ask more questions right here. And I gave you the name you wanted," Toni now getting worried, "I told you everything you wanted to know."

"Yes, ma'am, you did. But I said there were other questions to be answered and the station is the place to do it. Now just how do you want to get there? Voluntarily or under arrest and in handcuffs?"

Toni stared at Deputy Sheriff Martinez, confused and angry. There didn't seem to be a way out of it. The officer was firm. After several moments, Toni broke her gaze and finally said, "Well, just a minute. I've gotta let my husband know then lock up the office."

Toni fished her cell phone from her purse and called Joe who was in the back working. "Hey, Toni." Joe's voice sounded a bit more upbeat than before.

"Joe, I've got to run out for a while so I'm locking up the office."

"Now? Can't it wait until we close?"

"No it can't. I'm going to the police station. They want to ask me some more questions and didn't want to do it here."

Joe's heart stopped. They must have gone back to suspecting him and Toni. Would they arrest her after she arrived or arrest her after hours of questioning then come looking for him? This had turned into such a mess. "They... ah... okay. I'll be finished at 5 pm and go there. It's the DHS station, right?"

Toni turned to Deputy Sheriff Martinez, "Are we going to the DHS station?"

"Yup, the DHS station," Mando replied.

"That's it. The DHS station. Love you, Joe." Toni ended the call, snatched her purse from the desk and walked out of the office to the van locking the office door behind her. She still couldn't believe this was happening.

15

Friday

Toni parked in the front lot of the DHS police station designated for customers. Customers might not be the correct term. Maybe suspects, perpetrators, or the falsely accused might be more appropriate. Would she be driving home after this or would be there for an extended stay? Her heart raced and her palms sweat as she walked into the bluish gray lobby area and to the customer counter.

"Hi, I'm Toni Conti," she stated as she walked to the open window. "Deputy Sheriff Martinez asked me to come down."

The female clerk didn't look away from her computer screen as she responded, "When you hear the buzz, open the door on your right, then turn left going to the end of the hall. Once there, make a right turn and enter interview room one, on your left. They'll be waiting for you there."

They? What did she mean by they? Would there be more people than just Deputy Martinez? Toni's anxiety level rose could not remember the clerk's directions. Then she heard the door buzz so she opened it and stepped through. She wandered down the hallway and found the interview rooms. Each side of the hallway had three doors. Above each door was a sign, Interview One through Interview Six. Odd numbers on the left. Even numbers on the right. Toni entered the room with the Interview One sign.

The pictureless walls in Interview One were cinderblock and painted institutional gray. It was a large room, and a desk and chair sat in the left corner. Several files lay on the desktop, papers sticking out in random

| 173 |

fashion. A round table sat in the right corner with four chairs evenly spaced. Two men filled the far two chairs against the walls. Both wore ties. One looked mid-thirties, clean shaven with a blonde military cut. He was maybe six feet and round. His face was round, his chest barreled, his stomach hid what must have been a six pack fifteen years ago, now hidden by home cooked meals, hours of watching sports, and no gym membership. He wore a badge clipped to his belt, on the opposite side was his sidearm.

"Hello, Mrs. Conti. I'm Riverside County Detective Bill Sullivan." He stood with outstretched hand. Toni reached and shook. Detective Sullivan wore gray wool slacks, a pastel orange shirt with a matching patterned tie. His smile was warm and welcoming.

"Nice to meet you," Toni said timidly.

The other man looked late-fifties and was tall and thin. He wore wire rimmed glasses the style that would look at home on the face of a conservative university professor. He was clean shaven with a black balding pate. He kept his Brylcreem saturated horseshoe patterned hair high and tight. His pants were black. His shirt was light gray. A solid red tie was the only thing that brought color into his outfit. A black suitcoat hung on the back of his chair, and a file lay on the table in front of him. There was no badge clipped to his belt but he did have a pistol nestled in his shoulder holster.

"I'm Special Agent Tony Rossi with the FBI," Rossi stated as he held out a leather wallet displaying a badge and FBI identification. He didn't get up nor did he offer his hand to shake. He reeked of cigarette smoke and his teeth were coffee stained yellow. "Take a seat here," stated Rossi as he pointed to the seat directly across from him.

"I thought I would be talking to Deputy Sheriff Martinez," Toni inquired feeling intimidated.

"Deputy Martinez will be along shortly. He's already filled us in. We'll wait for him before we start," replied Detective Sullivan. "Would you like some water or coffee?"

"No thank you."

Moments later, Deputy Martinez entered the interview room, closed the door, and sat in the last empty seat to her left.

Special Agent Rossi started, "Okay, let's begin." He picked up the file in front of him and perused one of the documents. "A bullet was found in your cremator that matched the bullets from the murders. Is that correct?"

"My husband found it, and Deputy Martinez told me it matched bullets from the murders," replied Toni. She felt like Special Agent Rossi had just accused her of something by his tone. For her, this quickly turned into an interrogation. "We gave it to Deputy Martinez. You'd know nothing about it if we didn't volunteer this information. We've got nothing to hide,"

"Then why are you being so defensive?" asked Rossi as he looked up from his file and stared into Toni's eyes creating an awkward moment of silence.

"Because I feel like you're accusing me of being involved with all of this," Toni replied, her voice raising. "And we're not!"

"We're not accusing you of anything," Detective Sullivan broke into the conversation, his voice calm and regular in cadence. "But this bullet is a lead we've gotta follow. We're wanting to get as much information as we can. It may lead us to the killer and the discovery of what happened to Mr. Asghar."

Rossi gave Sullivan a sharp glare. He was not happy with what Sullivan had said. Rossi had been pressuring Toni, but Sullivan's response brought her some relief. Rossi quickly followed up. "Mrs. Conti, you and your husband are persons of interest right now. As we continue to investigate, you certainly may become suspects. Your business is connected to these murders. It's a small business so you must know when and who runs the cremator."

"They've already reviewed things at their business," interrupted Mando. "They believe it was a former employee, Mr. Sheldon Goodman." Is that right, Mrs. Conti?"

Relieved now and feeling like Officer Martinez was on her side, she replied, "Yes, that's right. He's a young guy and naive. He's easily influenced but has a good heart. I think he was manipulated in some way and got into something way over his head."

The conversation went for the next hour and covered everything Toni knew about the bullet and Sheldon. Martinez came to Toni's rescue three more times before the interview was over. She thought at least he knew she was innocent of anything, and she was only trying to help.

"We'll need to question this Goodman kid," Special Agent Rossi said as the meeting was coming to a close.

Toni, after spending more than an hour with these three officers, was no longer intimidated and stated, "No, you don't want to do that. He'll just clam up, and you won't get any information out of him."

Rossi with disdain said, "So, you think we should not question the next lead in our investigation because he's a scared naive kid?"

"I'm saying in order to get the information you want, you need to let someone that knows him, someone he trusts, to talk with him," Toni now resolute.

"There's over fifty years of experience in questioning suspects and investigating crimes in this room. Do you really think you're better than us at doing our job?" Rossi stated. Anger began to build.

Toni shot back, "Information gathering is based on relationships. I have the relationship with Sheldon, not you. He'll be willing to talk with me. He won't say a word to you. I know him. I know how he'll react if you try the same tactics with him as you've done with me," Toni now at the same level of anger Rossi was displaying.

"What tactics..." Rossi retorted, his anger building to a crescendo but was cut off.

"Wait a minute, Tony," Detective Sullivan interrupted the exchange and addressed Special Agent Rossi. "What she's describing is becoming a CI for the investigation." Then turning to Toni, "Toni, what you're talking about is working with us as a confidential informant."

Rossi stated. "Bill, we can't do that. Her and her husband may turn out to be the murderers or accessories to the crime. They'd be in the perfect position to derail this whole investigation if we made them Cis."

Rossi's statement scared Toni, and she became visibly shaken. Mando reached out and patted her arm and shook his head while the two men continued their discussion as if Toni was not in the room.

"Gentlemen," Mando finally interjected, "let me take Mrs. Conti to the office area to get some water while you two finish this part of the conversation. Mando stood up and escorted Toni out of Interview One and shut the door.

"Deputy Martinez, do you really think Joe and I might be murderers?" asked Toni. She was still shaken from Rossi's accusation.

"I think you're putting too much credence to a conversation that never should have taken place, especially with you in the room. From what I know, you haven't tried to hide any information, and we'd know nothing about the cremation or bullet if you hadn't given it to us. However, I'm a little uncomfortable with you thinking you're the mother hen for Sheldon Goodman. It creates dual allegiances and could motivate you to hold back information or lie.

Mando let that sink in then continued, "Mrs. Conti, you can trust us to investigate in the right way. We're not looking to burn you, Sheldon Goodman, or any one of your employees. But we do need to investigate, and we'll eventually need to talk with Mr. Goodman without you acting like a protective mother bear."

As they talked, Mando grabbed two bottles of water from the office refrigerator. Rossi and Sullivan continued their conversation in Interview Room One.

"I think she's got a point, Tony," replied Sullivan definitively. "She'll be able to get the information we need to move this part of the investigation along. It'll give us the time we need to continue analyzing the evidence we got from the crime scene. And following up on leads there."

"Well, you're not in charge of this investigation," Rossi replied in a snide voice.

"And neither are you. It's a joint task force. That means you and I work together on this," reminded Sullivan.

Special Agent Tony Rossi was a career FBI agent, hired by the FBI fifteen years ago when the agency experienced a massive retirement, and they were desperate to fill the vacancies it left. He had been a good investigator and an excellent interviewer, but today he was more interested in working four more years before retiring. He was a tired, burned-out special agent looking for the simplest, easiest answers to difficult questions.

"Have you considered the amount of paperwork and time commitment involved in setting up and handling a CI? Have you ever even had a CI?" questioned Rossi to Sullivan. Rossi was correct. Running a CI would require approval, paperwork that included regular reporting, and contact time. It would seriously limit the amount of time they needed to put into the investigation. These were all things Rossi wanted to avoid.

Sullivan replied, "I can do the paperwork and get the approval through my department. And since Mrs. Conti already knows Deputy Sheriff Martinez, I can have him assigned to run that part of our investigation. It's the smart play here, Tony. And it increases our manpower for solving this thing without costing the FBI or the Sheriff's Department any money."

"And I won't need to be involved with it? You and Deputy Martinez can handle it? And all information you get is shared with me?"

"That's exactly what I'm saying," Sullivan responded. Rossi did not have to approve this idea. Sullivan could run with it on his own, but he also knew if they were going to work as a team, he would need to get Rossi's "buy in" on the idea. Without the 'buy in" from Rossi, it would create more friction between them and their two departments.

"Okay, let's bring her back in," said Rossi, now feeling better about the decision.

Sullivan called Toni and Mando back to the interview room. Once there, everyone took their previous seats.

Sullivan looked at Toni and said, "Mrs. Conti, we would like you to work with us as a confidential informant." Rossi kept his nose glued to the file he had been reviewing earlier and didn't look up.

"Before you agree, let me explain exactly what that means. You will be a secret source who, through Deputy Martinez, will supply information on criminal activity to us for this investigation. We expect you to get information from Mr. Goodman regarding the cremation and the murders."

"We always try to keep a CI's identity a secret, but as a CI, you may be required to testify in court. If that happens, your identity would be revealed. In many cases, working as a CI is very dangerous, but in this case, there should be no danger to you or your family as it only extends to gleaning information from Mr. Goodman. Does all this make sense to you?"

Toni thought for a few moments, then said, "Yes, it does."

"Do you agree to work for us as a CI?" asked Sullivan.

"Yes, I do," replied Toni.

Rossi looked up from his file and interrupted, "Well, you don't need me to finish this up." He picked up his file, stood and gathered his suitcoat from the back of his chair. "I'm gonna have a smoke." With that, he removed a pack of Marlboros from this suitcoat pocket and left Interview One.

Sullivan continued, "Give us a few minutes to draw up the paperwork. We'll need your signature on it before you leave," Then turning to Mando, "Deputy Martinez, I'm going to request you be assigned to be Mrs. Conti's contact officer. Do you see any issues with that?"

"I've worked as a contact officer a time or two in the past. That should be fine," replied Mando.

"Get the paperwork together and get it back in here ASAP for Mrs. Conti's signature."

"I'll get the clerk to draw it up now," and Mando left Interview One but returned minutes later with the documents. Toni signed them, followed by Sullivan, and finally Mando.

Next, Sullivan gathered up the signed documents and picked up the files on the desk in the corner. "I'll get this filed and you reassigned," talking to Mando. Then Sullivan left the room leaving Toni and Mando alone.

Mando looked at Toni and asked, "How are you feeling about all of this, and working as a CI?"

"I'm feeling relieved, excited, and intimidated all at the same time, Deputy Martinez."

"Since we'll be working closely for the next week or so, you can call me Mando."

"Mando?" Toni questioned.

Yup, it's a nickname I got when I was young. My family gave it to me. It's short for Armando. I've gone by Mando all my life."

"Okay, Mando it is."

Toni and Mando talked for another twenty minutes covering all the aspects of Toni working as a CI before leaving. She had forgotten that Joe left the crematory at 5 pm and had been waiting in the lobby all this time. As she reentered the lobby through the same buzzing door, Joe jumped from his seat when Toni appeared.

"Toni! Is everything okay? They wouldn't let me back. I've been sitting here for over two hours. What'd they do? Are we okay? They're not arresting us, are they?"

Joe pummeled Toni with questions. He had been worried.

"Everything's gonna be fine," Toni replied calmly. "Let's go get some dinner, and I'll fill you in."

Joe, looking slightly relieved, said, "All right, but everything's okay, right?" He needed to hear it from her lips again.

"Yes, everything's fine. What about Mexican? Pescados?"

"Yup, sounds great," replied Joe who hungry. He hadn't eaten since lunch.

Toni filled Joe in on her meeting with the three men while they sipped margaritas and shared fajitas for two. She had to reassure him several more times that they were no longer suspects and the business was safe.

16

Saturday

Sheldon woke early looking forward to his date with Connie. These pleasant thoughts almost made the events of the previous week seem like a dream. He had never dated anyone like Connie, someone with a good job and a college student. She was smart, independent, and had plans to make something of herself. The more he thought about it, the more he thought maybe he should just cancel the date. It might be better not to go at all than go and do something stupid, something that upset Connie, something that a fuck up would do. He decided he'd just stop thinking all the things that could go wrong and focus on positive scenarios for their date which made him feel much better.

******

Late morning found Mateo lounging by the pool enjoying a bloody Mary. He was up most the night with the delivery in Calexico and was still frustrated that he had to use a guard from The Factory for security. But the delivery was uneventful, and he had left the payment in the safe at The Factory before he came home and went to bed.

As he was enjoyed the morning sun, he thought, I run the fucking Factory. It's under my fucking control. I say what happens there or it doesn't happen. And I get a fucking cut of everything... or I'll shut it down. And, if anyone crosses me, just maybe..., but didn't finish the thought. Taking control of a situation helped Mateo feel better about everything. By controlling something, his destiny was in his hands, not someone else's, and not left to fate. He could make his own future, his own success, and shape his own destiny as long as he controlled it.

He closed his eyes and felt the morning breeze on his face. He took a deep breadth and relaxed, really relaxed. The chirp of his cell phone quickly snapped him back to reality. He grabbed the phone and almost knocked over the bloody mary then looked at the caller ID. It said Alfredo.

"Hey, Freddie. Good morning." said Mateo, answering the call.

"Hello, Mateo. I hope you are having a blessed day," came Pastor Alfredo Eminis' response.

"Yup, I'm great. It's Saturday, and I'm lounging by my pool with a bloody mary."

"Good for you, Mateo. We all need to take time to relax and rejuvenate from our labors. It's how our Creator made us. You work hard. You deserve some time just for you," Pastor Eminis replied.

"And that's just what I'm doing."

With pleasantries out of the way, Pastor Eminis got to the reason for his call. "I was wondering if you had any plans for tonight. I had hoped you were free because we are having a revival service tonight."

"A revival service?" repeated Mateo. "Is it one of those services that goes till all hours of the night?

"Yes, Mateo, it is. Everyone from our women's home will be there for the service. Well, everyone except one of our new women at the home. She's not feeling well so will be unable to attend."

"Oh, that's too bad," replied Mateo.

"She's not yet ready to be in our program, and there's really nothing more we can do for her until she can submit to our program requirements. She has no family or friends so if we let her go, she'd be right back out on the street."

"Yup, Freddie. I know you get those sometimes. So, whaddya want from me?" asked Mateo.

"Could you swing by the house and pick her up?" asked Pastor Eminis. "She'll go to Hector per our usual arrangement."

Alfredo Eminis and Hector knew each other since Hector was a boy. Back then, Alfredo went by the nickname Freddie and was part of the local gang culture. Freddie was charismatic and quickly became the leader of one of the local gangs in Indio. Being arrested and in and out of jail never hurt his leadership position in the gang. He would direct them from jail through his lieutenants, oftentimes talking in code by phone. His last time in jail, Freddie got religion. When he got out, his charisma naturally drew people to him as he gave testimonies about his conversion. That's when he discovered offerings, and found he could make as much or even more money than through his previous illegal gang activities. So, Freddie started a church and was now Pastor Alfredo Eminis. He and Hector maintained a close friendship even after his conversion, and when Hector opened his brothel, he approached Freddie offering him a business proposition.

Southern California is a top destination for human trafficking which is the world's fastest growing criminal enterprise. When Hector learned it was a $150 billion-a-year profit industry, he decided to expand his business interests to get a piece of that pie. But for Hector, it wasn't just about sex trafficking. The illegals he dealt with could also be sold for domestic work since they did not have passports, so he established a network with other traffickers from Los Angeles, San Diego, Phoenix, Albuquerque, and eventually San Francisco and Sacramento. He sold most of them into this network, which required a constant stream of new targets. That's when he reached out to his old friend, Pastor Alfredo Eminis.

Hector offered Freddie a substantive fee for young girls and women who had no family ties, like most drug addicts. Initially, Freddie refused to be a part of this operation, but when the state threatened to take his church and his home for unpaid back taxes, Freddie decided to take Hector up on his offer justifying it by saying there were people looking out for them so they weren't alone out on the streets. The Greek philosopher Simonides once wrote that even the gods are persuaded by necessity. Freddie writhed under the pressure of necessity. Now taxes were all up to date, Freddie bought a new home in an upscale Rancho Mirage neighborhood, and bought a new Cadillac every year. The only thing Freddie insisted on was a middle man to pick up the girls and deliver the payments, and both of them agreed Mateo would be acceptable for this task.

Mateo quickly rethought his schedule for this evening. He would need to go to two places tonight to deliver guns. The backpacks and arrangements had already been made, but these would be later in the evening. He could do the pickup for Freddie, drop off the girl at Hector's then do his other runs. "Yes, sir. I'd be happy to do that. She'll be out of it when I pick her up, right?"

"Yes, Mateo. She should be able to walk with help but won't give you any trouble."

"I'll be there between nine and ten tonight," replied Mateo.

"And my payment will be in the box on Sunday?" asked Freddie.

Mateo would get payment from Hector when he dropped off the girl then, after taking his cut, go to the post office and put it in the rented box that only he and Freddie had a key. This arrangement kept Freddie from any direct contact with Hector.

Mateo tried to call Sheldon again hoping his phone would be back on. He'd get Sheldon to do the other two runs tonight. That is, after he chewed his ass good for being so irresponsible. But he got the out of service message.

"I'm gonna teach that asshole a fucking lesson!" Mateo bellowed. His voice echoed off the walls of his patio and the surrounding rock hills.

******

Sheldon pulled onto the street and headed for the ATM to get some cash. He did not have a credit card and didn't know if he would even qualify for one. His mom had used his social security number to open up several credit card accounts when he was young. She maxed out every card then never paid a cent on them. He thought his credit was still shot today from what she did back then so he never bothered to apply.

He pulled up to the address Connie gave him at 6:56 pm. Early, but not too early. The two-car driveway had one car, Connie's car, parked in it so he parked next to hers, killed the engine, then got out and walked up the walkway to the front door. The home was an older home of tan stucco with beautiful desert landscaping and had brown security bars on the windows and the front door.

He stopped in front of the security screen door and looked at the doorbell just to the right of the door. Butterflies were bouncing off the sides of his stomach as he reached up and pressed the bell. He heard the bell ring then somewhere in the house dogs began to bark.

When the door opened, Connie stood behind the security screen door, "Hey Sheldon, come on in and meet my mom." Connie was smiling and hugged Sheldon as he entered. Her hair was down and smelled of flowers, lilacs or rose, and maybe a slightly citrusy aroma. He wasn't sure, but he liked it. Connie wore a plain pastel pink t-shirt except the material was silky, not cotton, tan walking shorts and sandals complimented by a small necklace, pendant, and matching ear ring studs. She took his hand and walked him into the living room where Connie's mom sat in a lounger with a book in her hands. Someone had escorted the dogs to a room in the back, and he could still hear them bark randomly before quieting down.

"Mom, this is Sheldon," said Connie as she introduced him. "We worked together for a while, and he's going to start taking classes at the college this fall."

Sheldon stepped forward and held out his hand. Connie's mom didn't get up, but took his hand and shook it saying, "Sheldon, it's nice to meet you. I'm sorry for not getting up. I was out working in the yard and now my back hurts horribly."

"No worries Mrs. Asghar. Your yard is beautiful," replied Sheldon.

"Call me Maria. Mrs. Asghar was my mother-in-law."

"Oh, Sorry," feeling like he'd just committed a faux pas. "Maria."

"I'm just glad I don't work tonight. I'd never make it through my shift."

"You work nights? Where at?" inquired Sheldon.

"I work the graveyard shift at Denny's on Indian Canyon," Maria said smiling. She liked her job and was good at it. Her tips would verify that. "Well, I'll be there for six more months anyway.

"Mom turns sixty-two in six months then she plans to retire," interjected Connie. "She'll be able to collect social security then."

"Now Connie, it's never polite to tell a woman's age, especially mine!" Maria gave Connie a stern look then smiled. "What if I told the whole world how old you are? How would you like that?"

"It wouldn't bother me, Mom. I'm not old," replied Connie, smiling back at her mom.

"Are you calling me old!" Maria raised her voice but still smiled. "You're not so big that I can't take a switch to you!"

Connie looked at her mom like an educated professor lecturing her students, "I'm calling you wise, Mom. And to look at you, no one would think you were over fifty."

"I thought you were about forty-five," interjected Sheldon, still not sure if they were teasing each other or if they were serious.

"Connie, I like this young man!" Maria responded. "Maybe he and I should be the ones going out tonight."

"I'll see if he has a friend for you. Maybe we can double date next time," Connie said laughing as Maria joined in. Sheldon was now sure they were just teasing each other. And it was a good thing too because he didn't know anyone that he could fix Maria up with.

"Hey Sheldon, we ought to get going before it gets any later," Connie said, then she took him by the hand and led him out the front door. "Don't forget to lock the door after us, Mom."

They got into Sheldon's car and he backed out of the driveway heading to The Fun Zone.

Connie broke the silence while Sheldon drove. "Thanks for coming in and meeting my mom,"

"No problem. You two seem like you have a great relationship," Sheldon said, still considering how they could joke with each other. He and his mom had never done that, and it was not something he had seen in parent-child relationships so it made him uncomfortable, not knowing how to evaluate it.

"Yup, my mom's great. Even with Uncle Fred's disappearance, she's been strong for me, helping me not to overreact and reminding me that we don't know anything yet. I just wish he would call us so we know he's all right." Connie's mood changed from upbeat to worrisome which made Sheldon feel awkward.

"Hey, how good are you at miniature golf?" he asked, changing the subject.

"I'm the best! Why, you think you'll beat me?" Connie sounding upbeat and looked at Sheldon with a competitive twinkle in her eye.

"I dunno. I haven't played very much, but I'm a quick learner. So, we'll just have to wait and see," He hadn't considered Connie to be some professional miniature golf player, which is what she sounded like to him. He'd only played a few times and didn't want to look stupid if he didn't play well.

"No, I'm not actually that good. I think it's really more about just having some fun, right?" replied Connie realizing Sheldon was feeling somewhat insecure about an all-out competition.

"Yup, that's right. Plus, you may be able to teach me a thing or two about the game," said Sheldon, now feeling more comfortable.

******

They arrived at The Fun Zone, parked and walked through the building to the back where the miniature golf counter was located and decided to play Egyptian themed course. It had pyramids, fake camels, a sphynx, and of course palm trees. Sheldon discovered he was decent at miniature golf. After nine holes, he was four strokes ahead of Connie. That's when Connie started knocking his ball out of play with her ball. This usually lined up Connie's ball with the hole giving her a short putt. If it didn't, she would use a foot to move her ball into a better position when Sheldon wasn't looking. She would smile and laugh every time it worked to her advantage. Sheldon didn't mind, and he didn't reciprocate. He was having fun.

"Okay, I have our total scores. You wanna see who won?" asked Sheldon as he finished adding up the final scores on the scorecard.

"Yup, let's see those scores," replied Connie as she moved close to Sheldon, and they looked at the card together. Sheldon smelled Connie's hair again, and a volt of electricity shot through him.

"I won by three strokes," announced Connie quite proudly.

"Yea, but you cheated," replied Sheldon, smiling and turning to look at Connie, the scent of her hair filling his nostrils.

Connie turned, now looking at Sheldon but didn't move away. Their faces were only inches apart. "Hey, all's fair in love and war."

"Really? Well, is this love, or war?" asked Sheldon, his heart beginning to race.

"I dunno. Guess we'll need to wait and see." Then Connie took Sheldon's shoulder in one hand, pulled him to her, and gave him a kiss on the lips. After that she moved away and headed back into the building. "Come on, let's ride the go-karts!"

Sheldon stood there for just a moment not knowing what to do. He was pleasantly surprised. Then he hurried to catch up to Connie who grabbed his hand as they walked.

Connie held onto Sheldon's arm while they waited in line to be led to their assigned go-kart. "Thank you for taking me out tonight, Sheldon. I really needed this. I had finals at college all week then working whenever I wasn't studying really had me wound up. Then on top of all that, we had Uncle Fred missing, and I don't want to even think about Vanessa and Jamie. It's still hard to believe they were murdered at his place. Did you know I knew them? I was at my Uncle Fred's place all the time. I've had dinner with them and rode horses with them out there. I still can't imagine who would want to hurt 'em."

Sheldon didn't want to talk about the murders and especially her Uncle Fred. But he felt the emotion in Connie's voice. "I'm so sorry for everything you and your family are going through right now. I can't imagine what it must feel like. It seems like you and your mom are handling it well anyways."

"Mom's great. If not for her, I'd be a mess. The police told us there's no indication Uncle Fred was hurt on the property, so they think he must be in hiding somewhere, for now anyways. But I can think of other scenarios that might be likely as well, and I don't like any of them. He could have been kidnaped, or taken then killed somewhere else, or even ran out into the desert, got lost or hurt, and died somewhere out there. Mom and I think it might have something to do with his election as tribal chairman. He had just been elected before all this happened."

Sheldon stopped Connie, saying, "You know, it might be better for you if you just thought about the positive scenarios right now. That gives hope, and hope is a powerful thing. It can change lives, and work miracles." Sheldon put his arms around Connie and gave her a hug.

Connie hugged him back, "You're right, and that's what Mom keeps saying. Which is why I moved back into her house for a while. Mom and I talked about it earlier today, and she thought it would help her deal with all of this too. I don't think I'll give up my apartment."

The go-kart line began to move and they turned and kept pace with it. When they got to the front, the go-kart attendant took Connie and put her in a go-kart near the front. Sheldon noticed he was about their age, and he was very talkative with Connie. Then he returned and took Sheldon to his go-kart, several karts behind Connie. Sheldon started devising a plan to pass the karts in front of him so he could catch up to Connie once they got on the track.

Before the group was released onto the track, instructions came over the loudspeaker to all the drivers. It was the typical instructions, don't ram into other go-karts, if other karts are stopped, slow down and steer away from them, if you're involved in a wreck, wait for an attendant to come and separate the karts, stay in your kart at all times, and the follow all instructions. Anyone not following these instructions would be removed from the track. After that, the two lines of karts started to move onto the track.

After they entered the track, Sheldon worked to catch up to Connie, avoiding other karts while trying to pass. After a few laps she slowed down to let him catch up, then stayed beside him urging him to race her. Sheldon floored it and started moving ahead of her. He had the inside track on the course so he knew he would pass her. That's when Connie steered into his rear wheels spinning Sheldon around. Now Sheldon sat pinned between Connie's kart and the tire barrier facing the opposite direction. Three more karts crashed into the back of them before the attendant came to separate the karts. The attendant was the same guy that put Connie and him into their karts.

As he approached, Connie looked at the attendant and cried, "That guy there rammed right into me and made me crash!" pointing to Sheldon as she addressed the attendant.

Perplexed, Sheldon held up his hands saying, "Hey, I didn't do anything. It was her!"

The attendant looked at Connie, then looked at Sheldon. Finally, he pointed to Sheldon and commanded, "You! Out. You're off the track." Then he separated the karts and pointed Sheldon to the exit.

Sheldon drove to the exit but still couldn't believe what happened. He was upset at the attendant for believing Connie and kicking him off the track and frustrated that Connie had done this. Accused of something he didn't do. And accused by the person who caused it all, Connie. He didn't know quite how to feel as he got out of the kart and watched as Connie continued to drive around the track.

When the allotted track time was finally over, all the karts headed for the exit to the pit area and their drivers exited their karts. Connie got out of her kart and walked towards Sheldon smiling and giggling. Her eyes beamed like a naughty little girl that had just gotten away with something.

"I can't believe it! You got me kicked off the course for something you did!" cried Sheldon who was not angry but still surprised and was also wondering about why Connie did it.

Connie, smiling mischievously, didn't say a word as she walked up to him. She put her arms around Sheldon and kissed him. This time it was much longer and Sheldon kissed her back. Sheldon quickly forgot the go-kart incident. During the embrace, Sheldon noticed the same attendant who kicked him out. He was walking towards Connie but stopped dead in his tracks when she kissed him. Sheldon thought, yea he knows he's been set up by this woman and kicked me out for nothing. The kiss made the whole event worthwhile.

******

"Hey, let's get something to eat." Sheldon said as they separated from the embrace. "The restaurants won't be open all night."

"Yea, I'm hungry. Which one you want to eat at?" she asked.

"How about The Peppermill?" There were three restaurants in The Fun Zone, and the nicest one was The Peppermill..

"The Peppermill sounds great," replied Connie.

Once seated Connie asked the server, "Could I get a glass of your house red wine?"

"And I'll take a cola," said Sheldon.

"Very good," replied the waiter as he wrote on his pad. "I'll be right back with your drinks."

After the waiter left, Connie asked Sheldon, "You don't drink do you?"

"No. No, I don't," replied Sheldon. "Growing up, my mom was an addict, and I not only saw how drugs can destroy lives, I lived it. I decided long ago, no drugs of any kind. Including nicotine and alcohol."

"Well, good for you." Connie looked uncomfortable now that Sheldon told her that he didn't drink. "Are you okay with me having a glass of wine?"

"Sure. This is my commitment, not yours. And it's not like I'm tempted to drink if I'm with someone who's drinking. I just prefer other things to drink. That's all. Are you okay with me not having a glass of wine?"

"Well, sure. Why wouldn't I be?" Connie responded.

"Same with me." They smiled at each other just as the waiter returned with a house red for Connie and a glass of cola for Sheldon setting the drinks down in front of them then took their orders.

"How's your wine," Sheldon asked Connie.

"It's good. How's your cola?" she asked smiling.

"It's great. A very good year for cola," replied Sheldon, returning Connie's smile. "So, you had fun getting me kicked off the race track?" asked Sheldon, now deciding to tease Connie about it.

"Connie smiled that mischievous smile and said, "Yes. Yes, I did. I couldn't believe that attendant believed me."

"He believed you cuz you're hot," stated Sheldon very matter of fact.

Connie laughed, "So, you think I'm hot, do you?"

Sheldon was glad it was dark. He could feel his face turning red. "Yea, I kinda do."

Connie smiled and was slightly embarrassed because she always thought she was plain looking. It was nice to be with someone who thought she was hot.

She took another sip of her wine, saying, "So just what was it like growing up? I always thought people had pretty much the same experience as I had. But as I got older, I realized that wasn't true. I'm sure yours was much different from mine."

Sheldon hesitated, "I'm sure it was. We moved a lot. One year I lived in six different places between Indio and DHS. And that doesn't include the few weeks we ended up living in our car."

"Wow, I can't imagine what that would be like."

Sheldon told Connie about his mom, the moves, rarely being in school, not having friends because of all the moving around, and how he ended up at the men's home of the New Life Empowerment Church. The hardest thing to tell her was that his mom left the woman's home, and he has never heard from her since. His eyes filled with tears as he told her. She grabbed his hand from across the table and held it until his eyes cleared. The waiter reappeared with their food. He brought Sheldon a refill, and Connie asked for a second glass of wine. The conversation stopped as they both started eating.

As they were finishing their meal, Connie said, "I just can't believe your mom left you there and never contacted you again."

"Well, there's something strange about that. I haven't told you that part yet. Our food came, and I was hungry."

"Then just what's the strange part you haven't told me about?" asked Connie. She had stopped eating and was looking directly at Sheldon.

"I went over to the women's home the other day just to see if anyone had heard anything. I went to my mom's old room to look around even though it's been years since she was there. It was a private room and my mom and I were there for two weeks before they split us up and moved me to the men's home."

"That's just crazy! You two should have been kept together," Connie sounded agitated now. "What'd your mom say about it? Didn't she put up a fuss about splitting you up?"

Sheldon hesitated, finally saying, "Apparently, the pastor had already talked with her about it, and she didn't say anything. I always thought from the look on her face that she felt bad about it. And that was her room for the next two months until she left... disappeared...," shrugging his shoulders, "was gone."

"What do you mean, disappeared... gone? You think something might have happened to her?"

"Well, here's the strange part. When I was over, a woman named Cindy had been staying in that room but had disappeared.

"What do you mean, disappeared?"

"Two of the women in the home told me she was staying there but was now gone, and they didn't know what happened to her. There were no clothes or any personal items in the room, so I'm sure she was no longer there. I found a black Timberline backpack in the room. It had two sets of handcuffs in it. I also found two pieces of rope about this long." Sheldon held up his hands and stretched them as far apart as he could. "I could tell they had been used to tie something up."

"But now I'm getting to the really strange part," stated Sheldon.

"Stranger than this? Do you know what this sounds like to me, Sheldon."

Sheldon stopped her. "Wait until I tell you the rest. Then let's talk about what it sounds like. I took all the things I found over to the church and asked the pastor about it. I showed him everything, the backpack, the handcuffs, and the rope. He accused me of threatening to kill him and had one of the guys from the men's home throw me out of the church."

"He did what!" shrieked Connie. People from nearby tables stopped eating, turned and gawked at them. Connie, realized patrons were staring, looked around the room, and said, "Sorry!" Their audience slowly returned back to their meals.

"And the pastor took everything from me."

"And you let him?" she replied.

"I didn't have much of a choice. This guy twice my size grabbed me, threw me out of the pastor's office and then out of the church."

"Sheldon, it sounds to me like this Cindy person and maybe your mom was kidnaped."

"Yea, but we had no money. And I'm sure Cindy, whoever she is, doesn't have any money either. Kidnapping people who have nothing makes no sense."

"Sheldon, there's other reasons why women may be kidnapped. It's called human trafficking or sex trafficking."

Sheldon slowly made the connections and began to understand what Connie was saying. His expression changed to one of horror as the reality of the possibility hit him, and he dropped his head now staring at an empty plate. "Shit! I guess it could be."

"You okay, Sheldon?" she asked.

"Ah, no, not really. Give me just a minute, will you?" Sheldon waited until his stomach settled down before looking up at Connie. "Connie, these are godly people. The whole church and ministry are set up to help others not hurt 'em. I'm not saying they're perfect, but I don't think they're involved in sex trafficking."

"I dunno, Sheldon. That pastor knows something he doesn't want to tell you.

"Connie, do you remember me telling you about the part-time work I was doing when I was working at the crematory?"

"I just remember you telling me you were working part-time at nights but not what you did."

"I would do drop offs and pickups for this guy's business. I drove all over the valley, and even went to L.A. and San Diego a few times. It wasn't hard, but there were so many of them in a night, or so far out of town, it took me most the night. And all of these drop offs and pickups were always with black Timberline backpacks. Always." Could there be some kind of connection he thought.

"Like a night time private courier service? That sounds a little weird. You think there might be some connection between that business and the church?" asked Connie.

"Well, it had occurred to me."

"You can get those backpacks anywhere in the Valley, you know. K-Mart, Walmart, the mall, just about anywhere. Maybe it's more of a co-incidence than anything else."

"You're probably right. Still, I can't get this feeling out of my head."

"And you had no idea what was in the backpacks you were delivering?" Connie now wanted more information.

"I dunno really, but later I suspected it might be something illegal."

"Then you didn't even know if you were breaking the law or not," stated Connie.

"I guess I didn't. I never thought about it. I got to know this guy before I started working for him, and I trusted him. He taught me to drive, helped me get my driver's license, bought me my car, and paid me a lot of money to do a few chores around his house so I could get into my own place"

"Wow! He really did a lot for you. I can see why you trusted him," She pondered why someone would go to so much trouble to help someone they didn't know.

"You're not still working for him, are you?" asked Connie.

"No! I'm done with him, for good," Sheldon responded resolutely. The thought of the cremation popped into Sheldon's head, but he quickly dispensed it.

"Well, who is he anyway? And what's the name of his company?"

"Oh crap!" cried Sheldon looking at his watch. "I've gotta work in the morning. Is it okay if we head back to DHS?" Sheldon didn't want to tell Connie the name or that he was working off books for the casino. Sheldon had thought for some time that most of what he was doing for Mateo had nothing to do with the casino.

"Oh, I'm sorry. Yup, we can go. What time do you have to be at work?" asked Connie.

"I've got to be there by 5:30," replied Sheldon as he looked at the check and left money for the bill and tip on the table.

17

Saturday Evening

It was 9:30 when Mateo crossed the wash between DHS and Cathedral City driving into an area filled with track homes, store fronts, strip malls, gas stations, and car washes. Driving across the wash, the sand had pounded the side of his car and his windshield. Here, however, the blowing sand was almost nonexistent, but not the winds. It whistled between buildings, howled down allies, and rustled around homes blowing loose trash down streets and plastic shopping bags through the air like ghosts haunting the city streets. Mateo rolled his window halfway down to enjoy the now cool and crisp desert air.

Mateo drove past New Life Empowerment Church as he headed to the women's home. The lot was filled with cars and light shone from every window. The service was still going on and would be for some time. Reaching his destination, Mateo backed into the driveway and parked. He opened the front door and called out several times but there was no answer. Several minutes later, he came back out the front door with a young lady. He supported her as she tried to walk. The drugs made her compliant so it was only a matter of navigating her to the car.

As he drove, Mateo thought about how long it would take to get her dropped off and pick up the payment. He had two more gun drops to do tonight and didn't want to be late for the next one. He would need to hurry. Once he reached Thousand Palms, he found Hector's dirt road and turned. All the while Mateo's anger grew. First it was over Sheldon's out of service phone, then Hector's unpaved road, and finally the blowing sand blasting the side of his car.

Mateo called Hector's number when he saw the lights of Hector's compound. After three rings, a voice came over the car stereo system. "Hector's phone," from a voice he didn't recognize.

"This is Mateo," he responded. "I need to talk with Hector."

"He's busy," was the reply.

Mateo exploded. "You fucking asshole, get Hector now! I'm at the gate. Tell Hector it's Mateo."

Moments later Hector came on the line. "Mateo, are you at the gate?"

"Hell yes! And tell your fucking help if he ever does that to me again..."

But Hector interrupted Mateo, "Sorry, Mateo. He's a new guy. I'll talk to him."

"Well, open the fucking gate, and I've got the girl with me."

He drove through the gate and turned left down the gravel road that led to the back and the free-standing structure about fifty feet behind the house. There were fifteen cars parked in it gravel lot. With no security lighting, the building and the parking lot would never be seen from the road. Mateo parked close to the door and kept his lights on.

"Hey, Baby, we're here. Time to wake up," as he shook the girl then picked her up by the arms and shoulders.

"Come on, Baby. Walk with me. You can do it," said Mateo as he put her arm around his neck and supported her body with one hand around her waist.

"Oh, I just wanna go back to sleep," she moaned, still groggy.

"I'm takin' you to a bed where you can sleep so walk with me," commanded Mateo.

She groaned once then began to walk on shaky limbs following Mateo's command. When they reached the front door, he grabbed the handle and pushed.

Minutes later Mateo walked out of The Barn and got into his car with a black Timberline backpack. He opened it, counted out his percentage and put it in his glove box. $1,000 for maybe forty-five minutes of work. Not bad, he thought.

******

Sheldon and Connie walked hand in hand as they headed towards the car. As he pulled out of the parking lot Connie asked, "Can we go by that women's home where your mom stayed? If we have time."

"Sure.' Replied Sheldon. "It's just a block or two out of our way. How come?"

"I'm just curious and wanted to see what it looks like."

Sheldon drove by the church as he headed towards the woman's home. "See the church there on the corner? That's New Life Empowerment Church."

"Why are there so many people there now, and on a Saturday night?" asked Connie.

"They must be having some kind of revival services. Their revival services will go on sometimes until midnight or later."

They turned into an older residential area. Homes were smaller and many were run down. Cars lined each side of the street. As they approached the women's home, Sheldon pointed to the left, "See the house with the flood light on the garage? That's the women's home."

Sheldon slowed so Connie could get a good look at the house. When they got close, he noticed a car in the driveway.

"Well, that's strange," said Sheldon. "They're having revival services at the church so everyone from the home should be there." Then he recognized the car and almost froze and stopped in the middle of the road.

"Wow," said Connie, "that's a Mercedes in the driveway."

Sheldon found his voice and finally responded squeakily, "Yea, it is."

Connie turned and looked at Sheldon, "Hey, are you okay? You look like you did back at the restaurant."

"I'll be fine in a minute," replied Sheldon then pulled into an open parking spot.

Connie reached over and gently laid her hand on Sheldon's arm. Her touch was soft and loving but firm and comforting at the same time.

"Did you recognize the car? Do you know who that was?" Connie gently asked.

Moments of silence lapsed, but Sheldon felt like it was minutes. Then, exhaling, he said, "Ya know that guy I was working for? Well, that was his car."

"Maybe he goes to that church. Is that where you met him?" Connie asked.

"No, I met him at Witch's Brew. And he's no church guy. He wouldn't be caught dead anywhere around a church."

"Could he be dropping off someone in need for the church to help?" asked Connie trying to think of a reason he might be there.

"I don't think so. That doesn't sound like him," replied Sheldon

"Maybe he picked up a hitchhiker and dropped them off."

"He's driving a Mercedes. I don't think Mercedes owners pick up hitchhikers, or none that I know of anyway."

As they watched the Mecedes in the driveway, a man helping a woman exited the front door. He almost carried her as she stumbled on wobbly legs. He took her to the passenger side of the car, put her in the front seat, and buckled her seat belt before rounding the car and settling into the driver's seat.

"She looks really drunk," Connie speculated.

"Or stoned," added Sheldon.

The Mercedes left the driveway and was now headed up the street directly past them. "Here he comes, get down!" insisted Sheldon as he killed the lights. Connie and Sheldon crouched in their seats until the Mercedes had passed.

"Follow him!" cried Connie.

"What!? Are you crazy? I'm not going to follow him." Sheldon began to panic.

"You want to know what he's doing here, right?" asked Connie.

"Yea, but..."

"Then we may be able to figure that out if we know where he's going. Follow him," commanded Connie.

Sheldon pulled into the street but kept his lights off until the Mercedes turned the corner.

They followed for several miles but were separated by a red light. When it turned green, Sheldon sped to catch up looking for the car.

"I don't see him anywhere," said Connie.

"I want to check the road a little farther up. He might have turned off onto a dirt road."

"You know where he's going?"

"I'm not sure, but I made some deliveries out here for him, so I want to check it out."

When they reached the road, Sheldon slowly made the turn. It was well traveled and easy to follow even in the desert night, and Sheldon knew this road. Sand and dust kicked up behind them, and the wind blew sand and small rocks against the side of the car sounding like they were driving through a sand blasting machine.

"I can't believe they actually built houses out here. The road isn't even paved," said Connie, amazed that people would ever want to live this far out of civilization. "I don't think there's anything else out here but desert."

"There's another house further out. It's another mile or two out."

Sheldon continued to drive until lights from the compound appeared in the distance, one light on the top of each pillar facing the road. Flood lights shone from the front of the house onto the circular driveway. Sheldon pointed, "That's where I think he's going."

The moon was almost full and bright enough to cast shadows of the mesquite trees on the desert floor and across the dirt road. "Turn your lights off so they won't see us," she said.

"Good idea.," he replied.

The Mercedes entered the compound slowly driving through the gate then disappeared as it followed the gravel road to the back of the house.

"Move up past the house to the other side. Maybe we can see where he went," she instructed.

Sheldon put the car in gear and moved slowly up the road trying not to kick up more dust than what the wind created. Once they passed the house, they could see Mercedes with it lights still on.

Connie squinted trying to create a mental map of the compound then said, "I can make out part of a building of some kind. It looks like a barn maybe. And look, cars parked in front of it. Something's going on for sure. A meeting, a party, maybe a concert."

"Let's get out of the car and get a closer look." she said, now captivated by the mystery.

"Not with this wind. Plus, it might not be safe. Who knows what could happen if we're caught," replied Sheldon.

"What are they gonna do, shoot us?" she said, sarcastically.

"You don't know this guy and some of the people he hangs with. Plus, I've got to work in the morning. I really need to get home."

Connie sighed a deep sigh. She really wanted to unwind this mystery. She was naturally passionate about things and once she got a hold of something, she put all of her efforts and emotions into it. Reluctantly, she finally said, "Alright, let's get turned around and head back to DHS. But this isn't over. We're gonna find out what's going on with all this."

******

Sunday

It was late morning when Mateo finally crawled out of bed. He sat on the lounger enjoying the morning air as he sipped his coffee and thought about the one thing he needed to accomplish today. That was Sheldon.

It was 12:30 pm when Mateo parked at Witch's Brew and sauntered across the parking lot. He noticed there was no line and only five people in the front dining area, all sitting alone. Three were on cell phones and two were on computers. Sheldon was in the drink prep area talking with an employee, but he went to the register to order keeping an eye on Sheldon.

"Welcome to Witches Brew Coffee," said a pimple-faced kid behind the register. "May I take your order?"

"Give me a grande cappuccino with almond milk," replied Mateo.

Sheldon stopped his conversation and looked towards the register when Mateo ordered.

"That'll be $4.95," said pimple-face as he punched some buttons on the register. Mateo handed him a five-dollar bill and smiled at Sheldon then raised his hand and gestured for Sheldon to come to him using his index finger. Sheldon didn't move.

Mateo studied Sheldon as he stood there then he moved to the drink pickup area. Now he was directly across the counter from Sheldon who still hadn't moved. Mateo gestured for Sheldon to come to him again. This time Sheldon stepped towards the counter.

"Take a break and let's go to the parking lot," demanded Mateo in a low but serious tone.

"Can't," replied Sheldon, almost stuttering. "I'm, ah... I'm the supervisor so I gotta stay here."

Anger flashed across Mateo's face but quickly dissipated. "What time you get off?" he asked.

"I'm... ah... I'm off at 2:30," replied Sheldon.

"I'll see you in the parking lot at 2:30 then." Mateo used his most serious voice and held a deadpan expression on his face except for furrowing his brow. This was Mateo's "go to" look when he wanted to intimidate someone without others in the room knowing. Then he sat down in a large leather padded chair by the window and waited for his cappuccino. Sheldon turned around and went into the back office. Once his drink was ready, Mateo took his time to finish before leaving. Sheldon stayed in the back office the whole 20 minutes Mateo was there.

It was 2:40 pm when Sheldon walked out of Witch's Brew and headed towards his car. The extra ten minutes Mateo had to wait only made him angrier at Sheldon. He had parked next to Sheldon's car and with the air conditioning running. Now he turned off his car, stepped out and watched Sheldon plod across the lot. Sheldon looked up and Mateo held his stare and curled his lip into a subtle snarl as he approached.

When Sheldon was within three feet of Mateo, Mateo demanded, "What the fuck do ya think you're doin'!" then hit Sheldon in the cheek with the back of his hand.

Sheldon stumbled but didn't fall. A tear began to form in the corner of his eye as his cheek became bright red.

"Whaddaya mean?" asked Sheldon rubbing his now tender cheek.

"I've tried to call you all week, but your phone's disconnected. Don't tell me you didn't know."

Sheldon didn't respond but continued rubbing his cheek. He wiped the tear that now trickled from his eye.

Mateo continued, "I don't know what the fuck you're thinkin', but I told you, once you're in, you're in. There's no getting out. You know too much and you've done too much. It's set. Your life is set. It's fixed. It won't change. That's it. You got it?"

Sheldon nodded as he brought his hand from his cheek and crossed his arms.

"Now what about the fucking phone?" Mateo demanded.

"I, ah... got a new contract. They changed my number," Sheldon finally replied.

"Ever think of callin' me with the new number?"

Sheldon paused, then said, "No, uh... sorry."

Disgusted, Mateo retorted, "You're not sorry yet. But if you ever pull this shit again, you can bet your dumb ass you'll be sorry."

"You, my dumb ass soldier, are always on call. You will answer whenever I call. You work for me. Now what's your new number?"

Sheldon didn't respond but stood with arms crossed in front of him and positioned forty-five degrees from facing Mateo.

Mateo paused for a moment then changed his tone. "I'm working on a new salaried position for you. It'll let you quit this job and work for me full time. Another week or two and I'll have it ready."

Hesitant, Sheldon said, "I, ah... still work here at Witch's Brew."

"I just told you, I was taking care of that," stated Mateo now angry again. "Now give me your new number."

Sheldon gave him the new number, and Mateo put it in his phone then called it to make sure it was correct. After that, he left, leaving Sheldon standing in the parking lot.

******

Early Monday

It was just after 1 am when Mando pulled his cruiser into the Denny's parking lot. Sunday nights were always slow and he needed a pick-me-up to get him through the rest of his shift. A coffee and seasoned fries would do the trick. This would be his last shift working nights for a few days. Tomorrow he would start working as Toni Conti's handler. The operation had been set up so quickly that he would not even get a day off between working tonight and starting the undercover operation tomorrow. Another officer would be handling his shifts until he finished this special assignment. Even with the tight schedule, he was excited about it and hoped it would lead to a detective position in the future.

He radioed dispatch and gave them the 10-7 code for Out of Service. As he entered the restaurant, he breathed in the smell of hot coffee and sausage. There were three men sitting at the counter, separated by empty seats. Probably truckers who stopped for coffee and breakfast. They turned turned and glanced his way as he entered, then turned their attention back to their coffee and breakfast plates.

"Good evening, Officer Martinez. How are you tonight?" Maria greeted Mando with a clean cup that sat on a saucer in one hand and a hot pot of coffee in the other. She sat the saucer and cup down in front of him and poured the hot dark liquid into the cup.

"Thank you, Maria. It's just what I needed. It's been slow tonight so the coffee is a lifesaver."

"Would you like seasoned fries with your coffee too?"

"Yes, please," he replied.

Maria wrote down the order then disappeared behind the counter. After that, she returned saying, "Officer Martinez, I don't mean to bother you, but have you got a few minutes to talk?"

They had always chit chatted while Maria worked whenever Mando took a break at Denny's, but this was different. "Sure," he replied, "What's going on?"

Maria took a seat across from the table in his booth. "Officer Martinez, I'm so upset with something my daughter told me last night. I almost can't believe what happened, but she's my daughter so I know she's telling the truth. It's just so disturbing, and I think you should know about it. Something's got to be done."

Mando was intrigued. "Well just what did she tell you?"

"My daughter, Connie, went out on a date Saturday with a young man, Sheldon."

Mando sat straight up when he heard the name. "Do you know Sheldon's last name?"

"No, I don't. I only know his first name, but Connie would know it." Mando took out his notepad and pen, and started taking notes.

Maria related to Mando the story Connie told her when she got home from her date with Sheldon. She told him about a man picking up a girl that was clearly drugged and leaving her at a brothel. She told him about Sheldon's mom disappearing and the backpack, handcuffs, and rope Sheldon had found. She finally insisted that it was a ring for sex trafficking and something needed to be done to stop it. As she talked her voice got louder and she became more animated until the truckers at the bar started noticing. Mando quieted her down several times before she finally finished her story.

Mando asked, "Maria, what is the name of the man they followed?"

"I don't know his name, but I'm sure Connie or Sheldon would know."

"Do you know the name of this church that runs the women's home, and do you have the address to the house?"

Maria, now looking like a daydreaming kid who was just called upon by the teacher for an answer to a question she'd just asked, "No, I don't know anything else. I didn't think you'd ask me any of that. Plus, I don't think Connie knows any of that either. But Sheldon would. And these women are being harmed, kidnaped, and forced into prostitution, and a church is involved. The police need to stop this!"

Mando wanted to downplay this as much as he could. If this was the same Sheldon they were already going after, he didn't want to spook him, and anything he told Maria may get back to him. "Maria, you don't really know for sure if that's what's happening. You and your daughter may be jumping to conclusions. The gentleman they followed may have just been driving a girl home because she couldn't drive herself."

"No, it wasn't!" shrieked Maria, frustrated. "Officer Martinez, the police need to look into this!" Maria was insistent. "I'm officially filing a complaint with you."

Mando patted Maria's arm table while the truck drivers turned again to look at them. "Maria, that's not exactly how it works. If you want to file an official complaint, then you need to go to the Sheriff's Office to do that. I'm taking notes from everything you've told me, and I'll report all of it. It'll go through the regular channels and someone would be assigned to investigate in the next few days. You don't need to go down to the office or file anything because my reporting will get the ball rolling on this quicker than you filing anything."

"Oh, thank you so much!" Maria now relieved and grateful. "I just can't believe anything like this would ever take place in our community. The Valley has changed so much over the years."

"Yes, it has. Now, Maria, you shouldn't say anything about this to either your daughter or Sheldon. Actually, you shouldn't say anything to anyone. There's no telling how quickly information like this can get passed around, and we wouldn't want to tip anyone off before we can investigate, would we."

"I won't say anything to anyone, and thank you for listening to me." Maria stood up and went back towards the kitchen to retrieve Mando's order of seasoned fries that had been sitting under the heat lamp for the last few minutes.

18

Monday

As Mateo stepped out of the elevator into the lobby area, Charlotte looked up from her computer screen and smiled at him.

"Good morning Mr. Rivera."

"Morning Charlotte," acting professional. "Can you bring me a cup of coffee?"

"Yes sir, Mr. Rivera."

Mateo passed her desk and walked down the hall to his office while Charlotte got up to get the requested coffee. He entered his office and did his usual morning examination of desk and computer. Hmmm, that's strange, he thought as he woke up his computer and entered his password. As he checked his email, Charlotte brought his coffee and sat down in a chair after closing the door.

"Has someone been in my office?" Mateo, annoyed.

"I don't think so. Why?"

"My keyboard and mouse aren't where I left them."

"You didn't leave them on your desk?"

Now more annoyed, "Don't be stupid, Charlotte. Of course I left them on my desk. But they've been moved."

"The cleaning crew comes in over the weekend to clean. I'm sure they were in here cleaning. Maybe they moved them. What's the big deal anyways?"

"The big deal is I've got sensitive, confidential shit in my office, in my files, and on my computer. No one should have access to it but me. And the cleaning crew vacuums, empties the trash and dusts everything but my desk. That's how it's always been. Nothing's ever been moved from my desk before."

Charlotte thought he was being paranoid. "Mateo, the whole building's secure. No one could get in the building much less your office without being caught." He made a snarly face but didn't respond.

She said, "I thought I might be able to look around Doc's office sometime today if he's out."

"Hmmm, I've got a meeting invitation from Doc today at 10:30 am. We're meeting at The Factory and it includes the new hires, Mike Riggs and Jim Coleman. Interesting. Doc'll be out of his office so you could do a little snooping for me, and the FBI."

Charlotte smiled, "I'll see what I can find, and we can talk later."

******

Mateo walked into his office at The Factory. This office was larger than the one at the tribal council building and more casual. It had a sitting area that included a bar located in the front section that he passed through before reaching his desk. Mateo thought this would be the meeting where he would get some of his questions answered about the computer room, and the lab. Getting any information from Jim Coleman bombed so he decided to check Mike Riggs background and began his search.

After an hour he discovered that Mike Riggs graduated from M.I.T. with a double major in math and computer science. He went to work there teaching while completing his Ph.D. in computer programming. Upon completion he became a tenured fulltime professor and worked on several research teams developing the ethernet and creating new computing languages that included Fortan and Python as well as research into early AI lab programming. M.I.T. eventually fired him stating that he refused to follow course syllabi, sabotaging research projects, and promoting nonsense theories that were not founded in strict scientific methodology. Next, Mike moved to the desert in New Mexico. There he became immersed in UFO folklore and founded "Encounters of the Fifth Kind", an institute which sought to contact aliens utilizing his knowledge of computers, programming, and telecommunications. The institute became defunct after several lawsuits were filed against it and Mike was arrested several times for instituting public protests that turned violent. Finally, Mike headed back to his hometown of Seatle, Washington. That was where information on Mike Riggs stopped. It was like he had fallen off the planet. No job, no income, no ownership of property, no run-ins with the law. Nothing.

At 10:15 Doc stood at Mateo's office door smiling. "Good morning, Mateo. Are you about ready for our meeting?" Doc seemed to have forgotten all about their previous confrontation, but Mateo knew better. It was Doc's way of leadership, de-escalating and bringing people alongside him building their self-esteem and trust. He had watched Doc work the tribal council members in the same way. He was a master at turning potential confrontations into opportunities to build loyalty.

"Yes, sir. Is there anything specific you want me to cover with our newbies?" Doc stepped through the doorway, walked to Mateo's desk and sat down in a chair directly across from him.

"Yes, there is. I'm sure you went over all this when they first arrived, but you know how confidential our business is here at The Factory, so I want you to emphasize to them again how important it is to keep quiet about anything they'll be working on. Especially Mike Riggs. I don't think there's a better programmer on the planet better than Mike, but he's a unique guy."

"You mean his UFO fetish?"

Doc smiled, "You've already been doing your research I see. That's why you're in charge of security here. You're always one step ahead of everyone when it comes to background checks and security."

Then addressing Mateo's question, "Mike has some quirky ideas, but I'm not worried about that. He's talkative. Get him started talking on a subject, and he doesn't know when to stop. You'll see at our meeting."

"I did have one question about Mike," said Mateo.

"And what's that?"

"What's he been doing since he left New Mexico? He went back to Seattle but there's no information on him for the past few years."

"Hmmm, I'm not sure how much I can tell you, but I do need to give you some background since Mike will be continuing the work he started with the CIA. Incidentally, that's why you couldn't find any information on him after he went back to Seattle. He's been employed by the CIA and moving in and out of the country the past few years."

Mateo heard a door open in the lounge area just outside his office. Doc turned as Mike Riggs and Jim Coleman entered the lounge area from the hallway.

Doc called, "Jim, Mike. We're in Mateo's office. Come on in."

Jim and Mike entered greeting Doc and Mateo.

Doc stood and moved to the sitting area at the front of Mateo's office. "Let's meet right here. Is that okay, Mateo?"

"No problem," said Mateo as they all took seats. Mateo was reminded again at how different these two men were, their ages, looks, culture, and he was sure now even their beliefs. Jim looked like he belonged at Google or Apple, an up-and-coming yuppie executive, while Mike looked more like a nerdy accountant with a missing pocket protector and no fashion sense.

Doc asked Mateo to start the meeting so he covered security, emphasizing confidentiality, and keeping to your own business and no information was ever discussed outside of The Factory, not with friends, relatives, girlfriends, or wives. When he was finished, Mateo turned the meeting back to Doc.

Doc said, "Jim, you have everything you need for the computer room?"

"So far," said Jim, "but after I complete my inventory and run my reports, I may need your help with... accounting and --"

Doc interrupted, "Jim reports directly to me regarding the computer room. Jim, let's talk in your office after the meeting."

"Mike, how 'bout you? You got everything to get started?"

"No, I don't, Doc. I was told the latest version of PROMIS would be here, and I don't see it anywhere," Mike sounding frustrated.

Doc took a deep breath, "Mike, the link to the program should be there. Have you checked your inbox?"

Mike was surprised. "My inbox? Not today. It wasn't there last week."

"Check your inbox after our meeting. It should have been sent over the weekend."

"What's PROMIS?" asked Mateo.

Mike smiled, "PROMIS? It's only the best little database system in the world. Well, it is now since I've been working on it. I didn't create it. God knows I wouldn't have ever taken credit for the mess it was when I first started fixing it. Those idiots at INSLAW first designed it as a case management software system for the U.S. Attorney's offices around the country. But where they got their education to write code's a mystery to me."

"These offices were using antiquated software developed years ago, and each was a closed system. That meant if someone was arrested and prosecuted in New York then moved to California and was arrested, the U.S. Attorney's office in California would have to contact the office in New York in order to get the information about what happened there. But the PROMIS system allows the user in California to see all information on the suspect in every state all at once. It tracks arrests, defendants, charges, cases, attorneys, court events, and even witnesses. All in real time."

"But with my recent upgrades, the system can now be used for the military, government agencies, and even private enterprises. Think of what that means. Say, Iran purchased and used PROMIS for its government employees and military. If the CIA could access it, they'd know who were spies sent to the U.S., or sleeper cells living anywhere in the world, or maybe determine where they were in developing their nuclear program."

"In the private sector, our government could have stopped the housing market crash of 2008 long before it ever started. It would have kept our government from borrowing two trillion dollars from China to prop up our economy to stop a global depression. What we're doing with PROMIS will save lives and money."

Mateo interjected, "And the company is okay with you and... the CIA taking control of it? That doesn't seem like a very good business decision to me." He was now quite impressed with the whole scheme and wondered how Doc was able to get The Factory involved with something this big. Doc gave Mateo a look that said, see what I told you about Mike, then nodded indicating he wanted Mateo to stop him from saying more. Mateo pretended not to notice. He wanted to hear more of what Mike had to say.

Mike continued, "INSLAW. INSLAW's the name of the company, and they're outta business now, or should I say, they no longer run the business. We control the whole damn thing."

Doc said, "This is a joint effort with the CIA. Mike will be working on the PROMIS software to upgrade it."

"Ha!" laughed Mike. "You mean to create a backdoor for the CIA don't you."

Mateo urged him on, "Why does the CIA need a backdoor to the software?"

Doc gave Mateo a hard look this time and communicated, What the hell are you doing? Don't get him started again. But it was too late.

"Shit! I've been all over the world setting up this software to both private and government agencies. Most are friends of the U.S., but some? Not so friendly. Still, they love the software, and because it's through a private company not the U.S. government, they buy it, and I help them get it up and running as the project manager. There are enough programs out there now that the CIA plans to use it to spy on all these agencies that use it. Once I get the backdoor built, updates will go out to all the programs and boom... the CIA can look at everything in those databases and can track anyone through every database from every country or agency that uses PROMIS. It might even eliminate the need for spies."

"Alright, Mike. That's way more information anyone needs to do their job," said Doc, but Mike was on a roll and wasn't ready to quit just yet. It was a topic he loved and lived for, and no one knew more than he did, in this group, anyway.

"And you know how the CIA took over INSLAW? They stopped paying them for all those systems installed in every U.S. Attorney's office in the nation. They withheld the monies until INSLAW was about bankrupted. Then they told the owners, "If we install a new executive board and several administrators, we'll save the company for you." There were only two owners, a husband-and-wife team, and they went for it. But not until the CIA promised regular monthly kickbacks along with lifetime salaries. Now they have these no-show, no-responsibility jobs making bank. They travel the world and own estates in the U.S. and Europe, and even own a luxury yacht and some kind of jet. And all on the CIA's dime."

Mateo interjected, "Don't you mean the American public's dime?"

"Naw, it's the CIA's dime. They have slush funds all over the world that don't come from taxes. Take any large organized crime syndicate, and I'll guarantee you the CIA's making money off 'em. They allow them to work in the U.S. for a fee of course. Then they have their own money-making operations. All off the books."

Mike looked at Jim and asked, "Hey, Jim. You know anything about operations like that?" Jim looked at Doc but didn't respond.

Doc gave Mateo another look, so Mateo decided it was time to intervene. "Mike, you're just a wealth of information, but all this shouldn't be discussed outside The Factory's walls, ever. It really shouldn't be brought up in any meeting either. Not everyone has a need to know, even in our group here."

Mike sat straight up on the sofa, and he opened his eyes wide. "What?! You don't think I can keep a secret? Is that it! If I told you a hundredth of the secrets I know, the CIA would kill you. They trust me. Some little fucking Podunk Indian tribe can trust me too."

Doc quickly interjected, "Now, Mike, it's not that anyone doesn't trust you. I think what Mateo was referring to was his earlier statements about security and a need to know. Our protocol at The Factory is that employees only know enough to do their jobs effectively and there's never any cross sharing of information from one project to another."

Mateo interjected, "That's right. Just one example is when our weapons department finishes a weapons run, they have no idea where or when they're are shipped. They don't know who ordered them, who we're selling them to or how much they're being sold for. They only know what to make and when it must be completed. It's the same with our ammunition department. This protocol has been the key in getting the business we have. You and Jim would never have been hired to do what you're doing now if we didn't have these protocols in place."

Mike calmed, then replied, "I know when to keep my mouth shut, Mattie. I've kept my mouth shut all these years about my work on Project Bluebook and Kona Blue. Kona has more UFO and alien secrets than Bluebook ever did. I'm not telling any of you about that, am I? I know when to keep my mouth shut, Mattie."

"It's Mateo. I don't go by Mattie," trying to hide his anger. No one ever called him Mattie, not to his face anyway. But this was a business meeting, and he realized he needed to act professional, especially in front of Doc.

"It's just that I'm responsible for security, and I take it very seriously. If I need to remind anyone at The Factory about keeping sensitive information confidential, I will. Hell, I even fired one of our gate guards because he didn't check my ID even though he knew exactly who I was. It's procedural, and we all follow our security protocols. I make sure of it."

Doc smiled then added, "Mateo reports to me on security, and I'm a stickler for confidentiality. So, consider anything he has to say on security as coming from me."

After a few moments of silence, Doc looked around then said, "This looks like a good stopping point for our meeting. I'll let you all get back to work. That is except for Jim."

Jim had been sitting quietly listening. Mateo thought he must be wondering who this crazy programmer really was and why Doc had brought him in. Jim and Doc got up and exited the office. Mike stayed for a few moments before getting up off the sofa.

"Hey, I didn't mean anything, Mateo. Let's not get started on the wrong foot here. I'm a professional and keep information confidential. Doc wouldn't have brought me on if he didn't trust me."

"I believe that, Mike. It's just that in any meeting that has more than two people, keep all confidential information, confidential. If it's just you and Doc, or you and me, it's okay. Doc and I know everything that happens here."

Mateo made himself an Old Fashioned, sat back in his chair, and debriefed the meeting in his head. He now knew exactly what was happening with Mike and the computer lab but didn't know Doc's cut from the project. He got a cut from everything. He still didn't know anything about the computer room and thought Jim wouldn't share any information with him. He would check in with Charlotte later today. Maybe she would have the missing information he needed.

He picked up the phone and dialed Charlotte's number. "Hey, Mateo. How's it going at The Factory?"

"We just finished our meeting. Doc's meeting with Jim separately in his office now. I think he'll be headed back up there in just a few minutes. Did you have any luck searching his office?"

"I found some information that I think you'll want to see. I'm not real sure though. Some of it I can't quite understand. Maybe you'll be able to figure it out when you see it."

"I'm gonna be here the rest of the day. I want you to bring everything over to my place after work. We can go through it together then."

******

It was just past 1 pm when Mando pulled into the parking stall just across from Desert Valley Cremations. He got out of his unmarked car carrying a satchel and trekked across the parking lot.

Toni looked up from her computer screen when Mando entered. "Good afternoon, may I help..." but stopped mid-sentence, surprised. "Officer Martinez. I didn't realize it was you. You're not in uniform."

"That's alright. I'm dressed today for our undercover work. Coming here in a police cruiser and in uniform would be like announcing to the whole world we're working together. And you can call me Mando."

While Mando was not in uniform, he wore his clothes like it was a uniform. From his military style haircut, his tightly tucked polo shirt, his pressed jeans, and his aligned belt buckle all said he was connected to some type of military or paramilitary organization.

"That's right," replied Toni. "It's Mando."

"Tonight's the big night for your meeting with Mr. Goodman. How've you been feeling about it?"

"I've had butterflies on and off all day. Mostly I've been busy with office work and it's kept my mind occupied. It's the lulls between the business that I start to think about it. That's when I get the butterflies."

Mando held up the satchel in his hand, "I've got some things for you for tonight's meeting. Can we use your conference room to go over them?"

"Sure," replied Toni as she navigated around the desks and headed towards the conference room with Mando following close behind. "I'll get Joe," she said as she entered the conference room then disappeared through the door leading to the back room where Joe was working. Moments later, she reappeared with Joe close behind.

"Afternoon Officer Martinez," said Joe as he held out his hand.

"Good afternoon, Mr. Conti," replied Mando as he gave Joe's outstretched hand a firm shake. "I've brought some equipment for tonight's meeting. I'll need to instruct you and Toni on setup and use." Mando sat the satchel on the table and opened it revealing its contents.

Mando laid out each item on the table. Joe counted them as Mando did this totaling six items. There was a necklace that held a pendant, a small black box about an inch square and less than half inch in height, a Starbucks Tumbler, a key chain FOB, a pen, and an Apple watch.

Mando began explaining what each item was. "These are all battery powered video cameras that also record audio. We use them in undercover work when we need to have a permanent record of what took place. The battery life varies depending on the item. All of them are also Wi-Fi enabled. This means once connected to your home's Wi-Fi, the video and audio is sent directly to our office where I'll be monitoring and recording."

Toni picked up the necklace and examined it closely then wrinkled her nose. "I'd never wear something like this. It's gaudy, more the style of someone in their seventies."

"That's why I brought several different items. You'll choose two that'll work best for you. So, it sounds like we can eliminate the necklace and pendant."

"We definitely can," said Toni as she put the necklace and pendant back on the table.

"What about the Apple watch?' asked Joe. "It looks just like yours."

Toni picked up the watch and examined it. She took her watch off and put on the one Mando brought. "I feel like I'm in a James Bond movie," she said as she smiled at Joe.

"But the only way you're becoming a Bond girl is if I'm James Bond," winked Joe. "The name's Bond, James Bond."

"Okay, let's get back to the rest of the items," said Mando. "It sounds like the watch will work."

"Yup, I'll take it," Toni, smiling. "What's the little black box, a camera too?" picking up the box.

"That's a small video and audio recording device. It can be hidden most anywhere in a room."

"I like the Starbucks tumbler," said Joe. He picked it up and examined it, taking the lid off and looking inside. "Can I put coffee in here too?"

"You sure can," replied Mando. "If you turn it upside down, you'll notice there's a screen on the bottom with several micro-buttons. You'll use them to connect to your Wi-Fi and to turn it on and off. The camera is hidden in the logo."

Joe examined the label, "Wow, you can't even see it unless you're an inch away." To Toni, "What do you think, Toni? I like the tumbler. Let's take it too."

"How many of these things do we need?" asked Toni not remembering what Mando had said.

"Two will be enough," replied Mando. "That gives us a backup in case anything malfunctions."

"Okay, we'll take these two."

Mando collected the other items and put them back in the satchel then he reviewed with them how to connect to the Wi-Fi and how to turn them on and off. He instructed them to connect to the Wi-Fi as soon as they got home so he could make sure they paired correctly with the recording equipment at the Sheriff's Office he would be monitoring when they met with Sheldon. They were to turn them off after five minutes to conserve the batteries then turn them on when they started questioning Sheldon. This would ensure they could record the whole conversation.

"There's one last thing you'll need to do, Toni," Mando said.

"What's that?"

"I want you to go to the coffee shop now and talk with Sheldon. It's been three days since you set this up, and he may have gotten cold feet since then. Make sure he's still committed to coming over to your house. And if he's not, get him recommitted."

"Hey, that's a good idea," Joe remarked.

Toni thought about it for a moment. Sheldon was confused and wanted help when she saw him on Friday. She was certain he would not have changed his mind. Sheldon was a good kid, but naive and too trusting which made him easy to be manipulated. He'd gotten into something that was way over his head, and he realized he needed help getting out of it.

"Okay, I can do that, but I know Sheldon. He wouldn't have changed his mind. He was glad to have someone he trusted to help him."

"Well, then it should only take you a few minutes, and we'll have verification that he'll be there. Make sure you call me and let me know how it went as soon as you're done." Mando picked up the satchel and stood. "Toni, wait for at least five minutes before you leave. That way no one will see us together if anyone's watching."

"You think people are watching the business?" Joe was surprised.

"It's just a precaution," replied Mando, "Remember, there's been two murders already."

"Or maybe three murders," said Joe.

Mando wrinkled his brow and looked at Joe, "Right now it's a missing person, and let's not jump to conclusions. We should know more after you meet with Sheldon, but until then, let's not start any rumors." Mando shook hands and then headed out the front door. Toni waited until he had left the parking lot before she started a timer on her phone for five minutes.

Joe turned to Toni, "You know when I found the bullet and we figured out it must be Sheldon, I was so angry at him, But now, I'm more worried, and a little scared, for the business... for us. We were just minding our own business, living our lives, and were sucked into the middle of this whole thing."

Toni understood how Joe was feeling. She felt the same. It reminded her of a tornado in the Midwest where she grew up. Clouds appear on the horizon and you look forward to a nice spring shower, but then they turn black and threatening. The winds pick up and become violent while the shower turns to hail. At night, all you see is the lightning flashes and hear the thunder claps against the backdrop of the roaring freight train winds. Then without warning boards and beams begin to creak and moan, windows explode while debris flies around the house and through the broken windows. You pray that the house will stand the pressure and protect you and your loved ones, but you have no guarantees. You are powerless to redirect or stop the destruction. You can only ride it out until it passes hoping and praying, you'll survive. This is how Toni felt, but knew she had to be brave and ride out this storm until they could see the light of day, and pray they would survive.

******

Toni walked into Witch's Brew but didn't see Sheldon. Now she became concerned. What if he called in sick, or quit and left town. She knew he was scared and thought he could run, but where would he go. He's never lived anywhere else, and he didn't even have relatives he could stay with.

She was relieved the place was quiet this time of day with only three people in the front dining area. This would be the perfect time for a quiet conversation with Sheldon since it was not busy.

Toni stepped up to the counter, "Is Sheldon here?" she asked the young man behind the cash register.

"He's in back. I'll get him," said the cashier and he turned and sauntered to the back room stopping to check his hair in the reflection of the stainless-steel espresso machine. Moments later he came back out. "He'll be right out. Would you like to order while you're waiting?"

"Yes, I think I will. Could I have a grande Caramel Macchiato Frappuccino?"

After punching a few buttons on the register, he said, "That's $4.95."

Toni handed him her credit card. He rang it up, and gave her the receipt. She walked over to the closest chair to the pickup side of the counter and sat down, turning her body slightly in the chair so she could see the door to the back room. She was still waiting for Sheldon when her drink was finally ready. She stood and crossed to the counter to collect her drink. That's when Sheldon appeared from the back room. He hesitated then slowly walked towards her in the pickup area. His head was down attempting to keep his face hidden as best he could.

"Sheldon! What happened?" shocked by the bruising around his cheekbone and black eye. She could tell the eye was still puffy.

He stopped three feet from the counter. "I'm off in just a few minutes. Can I meet you in the parking lot?"

"Yea, sure."

"Okay, I'll be right out." He turned and walked into the back room.

She wondered if Sheldon's black eye had anything to do with the cremation or the murders, or was it something else? He could have had some altercation over the weekend that had nothing to do with it. She turned and proceeded out the front door and to Sheldon's car parked under the row of tamarisk trees. The afternoon was hot, and she was glad for the shade of the trees as she sipped her Frappuccino, glad she had gotten an iced drink rather than a hot one. Moments later Sheldon appeared out the front door and lumbered across the parking lot towards his car and Toni, keeping his head down.

"Sheldon, what happened? How'd you get the black eye?" she asked.

Sheldon stared at his shoes, "I dunno."

"Whaddya mean you don't know. It's your eye. You gotta know."

Sheldon didn't respond but raised his head to look at her, then looked back at his shoes.

"Does this have something to do with Mateo?" asked Toni.

Sheldon hesitated but didn't look up. "He threatened to kill me! I don't want to do anything with him anymore, but he said I don't have a choice. The only way out was..."

"And that's when he hit you?"

"No, he hit me first."

She didn't want Sheldon to run out on tonight's meeting, but she had lost all certainty that he would show up. She decided to talk with him now but didn't know how this would play out with Mando. She knew she couldn't wait.

"Sheldon, Mateo isn't the last word on this. He can't control you or make decisions for you. And he's not going to do anything else to you. I've got an idea how we can get you out of this and make sure Mateo can't hurt you or anyone else again."

Sheldon looked up at her, and for a moment, a glimmer of hope twinkled, but then dropped his head. "I dunno. I've been so stupid... my whole life feels like this... one stupid decision after another. And I don't know what to do."

"Let's figure this out now. We don't need to wait until tonight. Come ride with me and we'll go to the office and figure it out."

Sheldon lifted his head, and looked around the parking lot with wide eyes. "I dunno. Maybe I should just go home and forget the whole thing."

"There's no one watching us, Sheldon. It's just me and you, here, talking. It's safe, and we'll be able to figure it all out, together. But let's do it in a less conspicuous place. Like the office."

"Joe won't mind me there?"

"Joe won't mind at all. He's worried about you too."

Sheldon looked at his shoes again, but raised his head to look at her when he answered. "Okay, but I can drive my car over."

Even though the drive was only about five minutes, Toni didn't want to take any chances of him changing his mind on the way over. "No, let's ride together. I'll take you back to your car once we figure out what to do. Your car will be fine, and I don't know you're in the best condition to drive right now anyway." Then she added, "Plus, it may not be the best idea to have your car parked in front of the office right now, if you know what I mean."

With some trepidation, Sheldon agreed, and they climbed into the van Toni had driven. Toni put her drink in the cup holder and blasted the air conditioning as the van's interior began to cool from the sun as the heat from the leatherette seats warmed her legs.

19

Monday Afternoon

On the drive over, Sheldon was pensive, contemplating his dilemma. He looked around the van feeling the space familiar from his time working for the Contis. He and Joe had used this van for pickups and deliveries. The time together with Joe in the van led to long and intimate conversations about himself and about Joe. Joe talked about how he and Toni met, how they ended up starting this strange business of transportation then cremations. Sheldon shared growing up with his mom, her addiction, all the moving, and finally the church and the men's home. He had gotten to know Joe, and Joe had gotten to know him. He looked up to Joe, respected him, and Joe had shown real interest in Sheldon's life as well. It had started to feel like he belonged to a family, but that was before he messed up that relationship, and job, with his involvement with Mateo. Now, he blamed himself thinking it was just more evidence that he was always going to be a fuck-up making the wrong decisions.

Sheldon thought about his predicament again. He had thought about it since yesterday when Mateo hit him then threatened him. He hadn't slept well and was distracted at work. His coworkers knew there was something off, and everyone asked about his black eye. He normally would have made a joke about it, but today he didn't feel like being funny. He just said that he didn't want to talk about it so people finally stopped asking. He reviewed his different options. First, he could run, leave the valley and never return. But this was his home, and he really had nowhere to run... no family, and no friends outside of the valley.

Witch's Brew was privately owned, not a chain outfit that he could ask for a transfer to another city. He would have to take what little money he had saved, drive away, and sleep in his car until he found another job. Next, he thought about going to the other side of the valley, maybe Indio, but Mateo would surely find him. Mateo grew up in the valley and knew almost everyone. Finally, he thought about going to the police, but would they believe him? And he'd most likely end up in jail... where Mateo would know exactly where he was. They might even become roomies in jail. Mateo would kill him for sure if he did that. Maybe the police would put him in a witness protection program if he turned state's evidence, but he really didn't know much. Not enough, he thought, to be valuable to the police. He'd decided having Toni help him figure out what to do was his best option.

His biggest fear was Connie, what would she do if she found out what he had done with Mateo. Saturday night with Connie was wonderful, and he didn't want to do anything to mess things up with her. But cremating her dead uncle would probably end any chance of a relationship. Sheldon thought, But I didn't kill him. I didn't even know who it was when Mateo showed up. I'm still not sure who it was. Maybe she'd only be mad for a day or two.

Sheldon examined the office as they entered Coachella Valley Cremations. "Wow, I never thought I'd be back in here."

"Let's go into the conference room. I'll get Joe, and there's donuts and coffee if you want them." Toni exited to the back room where Joe was working leaving Sheldon alone in the conference room.

Toni burst through the conference room door and beelined for Joe as he was at the reefer examining the temperature gauges. "Joe, I've got Sheldon with me, and he's..."

"You what!" cutting her off. "I don't want him anywhere near the business! And we're supposed to meet tonight at the house, not here."

"The situation's changed, Joe. Sheldon's in some real trouble and there were no other options."

"You're damn right he's in real trouble, but bringing him here isn't an option." He steamed.

"No, I mean Mateo got physical with him and threatened to kill him. Joe, he's got a black eye and that side of his face is all puffy and bruised."

"Shit, Toni." Joe shook his head, accepting what he knew was the inevitable. "Okay, let's go hear his story."

Smiling, Toni turned and led as they went back to the conference room.

"Hey, Sheldon," said Joe as he entered the conference room. "Just a second. I've gotta get something from the office," and disappeared through the office door. Joe grabbed the tumbler he'd gotten from Officer Martinez and turned it on. He had connected it to the Wi-Fi at the office earlier making sure he knew how to do it correctly. The screen on the bottom of the tumbler lit up with the Wi-Fi icon indicating it was connected. Joe hoped it would automatically record at the police station then walked back into the conference room and filled the tumbler with hot coffee.

Sheldon related to Toni and Joe his relationship to Mateo in chronological order. Next, he told them about the night he and Mateo came to the crematory and cremated a body and his decision to never work for Mateo again.

Finally, he began to tell them about yesterday when Mateo showed up at Witch's Brew, hit him, and threatened him. As he began, the door to the back room burst open and Connie and Jaun walked into the conference room. They had picked up a body from the hospital that was scheduled for cremation.

"Whoa, what's goin' on?" asked Connie as she felt the heaviness and intensity that permeated the room.

"Hey, Sheldon. You comin' back to work?" asked Juan oblivious that the group had been interrupted from an intense conversation.

Then Connie saw Sheldon's face. She went to him and gently turned his head sideways by his chin, "Ouch! That looks like it really hurt.

What happened, anyway? You didn't have that eye when you dropped me off Saturday."

Joe and Toni looked at each other, then realized Connie and Sheldon were together on Saturday. Sheldon looked at Connie, "I had a run-in with Mateo, you know, the guy we followed on Saturday."

Connie sat down next to Sheldon, took his hand, "I'm so sorry." Then, "That guy needs to be arrested!"

"You two followed Mateo on Saturday?" Joe asked, surprised.

Connie and Sheldon related Saturday's events to Joe and Toni while Juan found a seat at the other end of the table and listened like an audience member in a theater. Connie did more of the talking than Sheldon explaining her suspicion of sex trafficking. Sheldon added details when Connie over summarized, and he also explained how his mother disappeared from the women's home.

After a few minutes, Joe interrupted asking Connie and Juan, "Hey, did you two get Mr. Pacheco in the reefer?"

"I'll take care of it," Jaun jumped to his feet and headed to the back room. "You guys finish talking. I got it."

Connie to Juan, "Thanks."

Everyone was quiet while Juan left the room, then Toni broke the silence, "Sheldon, there IS a way out of this, a way to put Mateo away and you'll never have to worry about him again."

"I just don't see how."

"We get the police involved. They'll make sure Mateo is arrested and put away for good."

Sheldon's eyes opened wide and sat upright in his chair, "But I don't want to go to jail! I'm sure I've broken some kind of laws and that'll mean me going to jail too."

"Well, maybe not," said Toni very matter-of-fact. "Not if you have information the police want."

Sheldon shrugged, "But I don't know anything about the murders or anything else. I don't have anything that'd help them. I'm not even sure Mateo killed anyone."

"Wait a minute!" cried Connie. "Is Mateo connected to the murders and Uncle Fred?" She already thought Sheldon had committed some type of crime working for Mateo but thought it only included the pickups and deliveries he had done. And because he didn't know what he was carrying, thought the police would most likely not bring any charges against him. But now, Connie's eyes narrowed as she realized they knew something she didn't. Her look demanded answers about the murders and the disappearance of her uncle.

Sheldon looked at Toni with wide eyes. He wasn't ready to tell Connie everything. Toni returned his look with one of confidence.

"Connie, Mateo works for the casino, so we think there may be some connection." Toni hoped this would satisfy her for the moment.

Connie shook her head, "But if you think he might've murdered them, you've gotta know more. That man's such an asshole! And I've never even met him."

Toni ignored Connie and continued, "Sheldon, you're in the perfect position to help with their investigation... because you know Mateo... and have worked for him."

"Hey, wait just a minute. You're not asking him to spy on this guy, are you?" Connie was now defensive for Sheldon even though they had followed him the night before. She already figured out what Toni was about to ask him.

"If Sheldon could work for the police as a confidential informant, they might not bring any charges against him. You know, in exchange for help with their investigation."

Sheldon confused, "Yea, but I don't know how to set anything like that up or if they would go for it. If they didn't, I'd be in jail for sure."

"But Joe and I know some people. We could get it set up."

Sheldon thought and a glimmer of hope sparkled. "And you could make sure they didn't know who I was until they guaranteed nothing would happen to me?"

"You mean that they wouldn't arrest you?"

"Yup. That's what I mean."

Connie realized this would not only help the investigation but also help Sheldon. She grasped his forearm, "You gotta do it, Sheldon. It'll be great, and you can be the one to put that guy behind bars."

As they talked, the front door burst open and in walked Riverside County Sheriff Detective Bill Sullivan and Officer Armando "Mando" Martinez. Detective Sullivan was wearing a tie and his badge was clipped to one hip. His service revolver balanced him on the other. Officer Martinez was still in civilian clothes but now also had his badge and service revolver on his belt.

Everyone froze as Detective Sullivan said, "Good afternoon, ladies and gentlemen. I think it's time for us to get involved with this conversation."

Sheldon melted like an ice cream cone on a summer's day. Toni was sitting with her back to the front office and turned when she heard the door open. This was nothing she had expected and didn't think Joe's Starbucks tumbler would be on and sending video to the police station. Joe smiled and slightly raised the tumbler acknowledging he had turned it on. Toni saw it and sneered at Joe. She was angry and felt Joe had betrayed her and Sheldon, but more her.

"Sheldon, we need to ask you a few questions, but we'll need a more controlled environment. Let's go down to the station where we can talk privately." Detective Sullivan watched as Officer Martinez walked around the table and helped Sheldon stand to escort him to the unmarked cruiser they had driven over.

"I'm going with him!" demanded Toni.

"You can talk with him once we're done. Officer Martinez, I'll take him to the car. Maybe you should answer what questions these fine folks have before we leave." Detective Sullivan escorted Sheldon out the front door and to his unmarked car in the parking lot.

******

Joe sat back while Toni pummeled Mando with questions. How much of the conversation did you hear? Was it recorded? Was Sheldon being arrested? How long would they have him? Can we wait at the police station? Will you not arrest him if he helps your investigation? You have to make him a confidential informant, right? Sheldon's a good guy, just a little naive. You can't arrest him just for that! Mando gave no answers to any of Toni's questions only stating they would know more after they interviewed Sheldon.

Connie insisted the church and the women's home were involved with sex trafficking and it was connected to their investigation through Mateo, but Mando said without real evidence there was nothing they could do.

Once Mando left, Toni gave Connie and Juan the paperwork for a pick up at Desert Regional Hospital in Palm Springs. Now alone with Joe, Toni barked, "I can't believe you turned that thing on!" pointing to the tumbler. "How am I supposed to protect Sheldon now? The police have him, and who knows if he'll end up in jail. Damn it, Joe. Why'd you have to do that anyway? That wasn't the plan at all."

"Bringing him here wasn't the plan either."

"I told you it couldn't be helped. It was an emergency."

"Toni, you've always been like this," Joe frustrated.

"Like what?" Toni sounded indignant.

"You wanna take everyone you meet that doesn't have it all together and fix them. I'd be happier if you'd take home stray dogs or birds with broken wings. But this time, it's just too big. There's too much at risk."

"Sheldon's life is at risk, Joe. And I'm well aware of how big this is. There's been three murders, and we've been put right in the middle of it all. We have a responsibility, Joe. A responsibility to Sheldon, and to Connie. And you just threw it all out!" Toni's anger began to rise again.

"Toni, you need to step back for just a minute and get some perspective. You've got yourself so caught up in this thing that you're not looking at the whole picture." Joe thought this might make Toni angrier but decided it must be said.

Toni aggrieved, "I've got plenty of perspective."

"Then let me point out a few things. First, we needed a way to connect Sheldon to the police. They wouldn't have let you continue to work as a CI. You were only a step to Sheldon for them. That's been done. Maybe not the way you planned it or maybe you never planned to let the police talk with Sheldon. I dunno, but they wouldn't have let you do this any longer than this one time."

Toni, pensive now, looked at Joe. He could see she was thinking it over.

"Second, we've helped Connie because she now knows what we've known and the police are one step closer to finding the truth about the murders and Connie's uncle. That helps Connie and the police. Which is why we were doing this in the first place. Right? To help the police with their investigation. Helping Sheldon was a byproduct of that. Important, yes, but it wasn't the original reason."

"Third, and most important, is that we've protected our business, our livelihood, and our freedom. Police thought the business may be involved with all this, and we've taken the business out of their investigation. We've worked so long and hard to get where we are, and it's threatened to destroy us financially and maybe even be arrested and go to jail. We're now clear of all that. I love you, and I love the life we've built together. That's gotta be our first priority."

Toni didn't respond, but Joe noticed she seemed calmer now. "I know you care about Connie and Sheldon. So do I."

Toni looked at Joe and rolled her eyes just like a teenager.

"Okay, I care for Connie. I'm sympathetic towards Sheldon. But you care, so I'll care, because I love you. And I agree, Sheldon's naive and got into something way over his head. But we've done the right thing here. And if it weren't for you, I'm sure Sheldon would be in jail. But you've given him the best chance to work as a CI with the police and maybe stay out of jail. Who knows, he may end up being the link the police need to solve this whole thing, and it'll be a good life lesson for him. That's what you've done for Sheldon."

******

Detective Sullivan and Officer Martinez drove Sheldon to the DHS Police Station and sat him in an interview room. Next, they went to Sullivan's office to discuss their next move. Said Bill Sullivan, "Mando, we need to update Special Agent Rossi on this conversation. This is a solid lead. We can call him now."

Special Agent Rossi's office was over an hour away in Riverside. As Detective Sullivan picked up the receiver on his CISCO phone and dialed Rossi's number, Mando said, "This is a solid lead, Bill. And it connects back to the reservation. I remember Fred Asghar ran on the slogan...," he grabbed the file in front of him and began looking through it to find the notes from Bill's interviews at the tribal council building. "Here it is, 'Transparency for the Tribe" was the slogan. And Mr. Rivera's title is 'Assistant Director of Security'. Didn't he handle security at their, what was it..." looking through the notes again, "a warehouse. But just what do they produce out there?"

Said Bill, "Rossi was supposed to follow up on that. Can you make sure we don't forget to ask him that?"

"Yup, I can."

When the phone rang, Bill punched the button that said speaker and hung up the receiver. Now both men could hear the phone ring. After four rings, FBI Special Agent Tony Rossi answered.

"Special Agent Rossi here."

"Hello Tony. This is Detective Bill Sullivan, and I have Officer Martinez here with me. You're on speaker phone."

"Gentlemen, how's the investigation going on your end?" asked Rossi.

"We have some news from our CI, Toni Conti," said Bill.

"I thought she wasn't meeting the kid... what's his name?"

Said Mando, "Sheldon Goodman."

Continued Rossi, "Yea, that's it. She was gonna meet him tonight, right?"

"The meeting took place earlier. We've actually just come back from meeting with them and have Mr. Goodman here. We'll interview him after this call. But first we wanted to get an update from you," stated Bill.

Said Mando, "You were going to follow up on the building, warehouse, factory, whatever it was that Mr. Mateo Rivera was responsible for. You know, for security."

Rossi hesitated then began, "Yea, nothing really panned out on that. But we've developed a solid working theory of what happened."

Bill and Mando looked at each other surprised, then back to the phone speaker. Why Rossi had not said anything about this before was a mystery to them. "Well, that's great. So, what have you got?"

Rossi began to explain the working theory his FBI team had developed. "This was a crime of passion. The girlfriend," Bill and Mando heard some wrestling of papers, "a Miss Vanessa Orosco, and her brother, Jamie Orosco, were at Mr. Asghar's home. An argument ensued and Mr. Asghar shot and killed both of them and is now on the lamb."

Bill and Mando looked at each other again, surprised. Bill asked, "What's your evidence that led you to this theory?"

"We're still collecting evidence but what we have so far is this. One, Ms. Orosco didn't have a pot to piss in. Neither did her brother. They come from a poor family, or at least lower middle class. They wanted Mr. Asghar to marry her so they could have access to all his money, but he refused. A fight ensued and Mr. Asghar shot them both."

Bill and Mando looked at each other for the third time. This time both gave the other a look that said, 'is this guy crazy?' Bill questioned, "The bullets collected from the murder scene and the crematorium could only have been fired from a long rifle. We were thinking an AR-15. Your theory would assume the shots were taken at a close range and by a handgun."

Rossi retorted, "No! Our theory is that he went inside and got his AR-15 and shot them."

Bill began to press Rossi, "Does he own an AR-15? Is it there or missing? Have you tested for ballistics if you have the weapon?"

Rossi, now defensive, raised his voice, "Hell yes, he owns an AR-15."

"Well, was it at the house," Bill asked again.

Rossi hesitated then responded, "Yes!"

"Then did the ballistics match?" Bill kept an even tone.

Rossi hesitated again, finally, "I can't give you any more information. It's classified."

Bill shocked, "Tony, we're working the case together, remember. It's a joint investigation. You're supposed to be sharing information with us and we share with you."

Said Rossi, "DC's involved with this now. My boss signed off on our theory and limited what information we will share. That's it."

Bill and Mando were now dumbfounded. Why would the FBI's main office in Washington DC be involved with this case anyway. And why would they stop the sharing of information in a joint investigation?

Rossi continued, "So just why did you call? You said you had something from your CI, right?"

Said Bill, "There seems to be a connection between the bullet found in the crematory and the Tribe, specifically that warehouse, or factory, and Mr. Rivera, the Assistant Director of Security."

Rossi now angry and almost yelling, "What the fuck are you talking about! I told you our working theory. You follow that. The reservation, the casino, the tribal council, the warehouse or whatever it is has nothing to do with these murders. You stay away from all of it."

"We have to follow where the evidence leads. We can't ignore solid leads. Any first-year investigator knows that." Bill kept his voice calm and absent of emotion.

Rossi adamant, "Nothing leads to the reservation. I'm ordering you to stay away from everyone who works there."

"Let me remind you this is a joint investigation, and we're supposed to be working together. You're not running this. We have to follow our leads. And what concerns me is that you don't even want to know what we've found, how strong of a lead it may be, or how it makes those connections I just mentioned."

Rossi hesitated again, eventually acquiescing, at least in part, "Okay, just what is the lead you have?"

"We've discovered Mr. Goodman and Mr. Rivera cremated a body at Coachella Valley Cremations which resulted in that bullet being left in the furnace. If our interview with Mr. Goodman goes well, we may have the name of the murderer and the victim."

Rossi became angry again, "The murderer is Fred Asghar! We've already got that name. And there's no real evidence that your bullet is connected to the murders at Mr. Asghar's home. Similar chemical composition means nothing. You're on a fishing expedition. But if you wanna catch that Goodman kid and get him for the murders I'll listen to that. Beyond that, I won't have you fucking around with my case. You stay away from Mr. Rivera. Got it!"

Bill continued in a calm matter-of-fact voice. "Special Agent Rossi, it's the exact chemical composition, not similar. They come from the same manufacturer, and I'll bet they were produced out there at that factory that Mr. Rivera secures. That's where our evidence is leading."

Rossi now livid, "You stay the fuck away from that reservation. I'll be talking with my boss who'll talk with DC. From there your boss will be getting a call from DC. You're in so much shit now, you'll probably lose your job!" Rossi hung up after that.

Stunned from the conversation, Mando asked, "Shit! What do we do, Bill? You think Rossi really has that much power? And why the hell is DC involved with this?"

Bill replied, "We can only follow the leads we've got. If Rossi can actually do what he says, then we've gotta get this solved or at least far enough along to protect us. Let's go interview Mr. Goodman."

******

Mateo finished lunch at Bonzi Bar and Grille and now sat sipping his second Old Fashioned. He took his cell phone and called Sheldon. After four rings it went to voicemail.

"Damn," said Mateo as he hung up. This was his fourth call to Sheldon. That little shit better not be trying to ghost me, he thought. He would need to deal with Sheldon later because he needed to get ready for Charlotte's visit. He finished his drink, paid the bill, and headed to his car.

******

It was late afternoon when Officer Martinez dropped Sheldon in the parking lot of Witch's Brew. Sheldon walked to his car against the warm spring wind that blew bits of sand across the lot. Once inside, he took his phone off silent and looked at the screen. He had one missed call from the crematory, two missed calls from Connie, and four missed calls from Mateo. He also had two voicemails that he decided to listen to later. He pressed Mateo's number on the missed call list, and after a moment he heard Mateo's cell phone ring.

20 ▮

Monday Evening

Charlotte opened Mateo's front door with a large white plastic bag that read Pescado's Fine Mexican Food in red and orange lettering. Mateo was sitting on the sofa.

Mateo startled, he turned and stood, "Hey! Oh, it's you."

"Well, who did you expect?" walking to the pub table in the kitchen and setting down the bag.

Mateo moved to her and she reached her arms around his neck, stood on her toes and gave him a kiss. "Mmm, I've been wanting to do that all day."

"Set the table, and I'll get us some beers," he replied as he pulled away and stepped to the refrigerator. "Plates and silverware are over there," pointing to the cupboard behind him.

He grabbed two bottles, opened them and sat them on the table and took a long swig as he sat and watched Charlotte. He was taken once again by her V-shaped figure. She wore a marigold designer tank top made of mulberry charmeuse silk with a V neck. Her slacks were buff and made of linen that fit snug around her hips but ended in a slight bell bottom by her shoes. She was petite but her arms, shoulders, and legs were toned and strong. Her long red hair brushed her milky white skin as she turned bringing the plates to the table.

"What's wrong?" she asked.

"Nothin', Baby. Nothin' at all. I was just thinkin' how beautiful you are," flashing his best big bad wolf smile.

Charlotte smiled back, and her eyes danced as they met his. "Thank you. That's nice to hear."

"So, what did you find?" asked Mateo as she emptied the Pescado's bag and dished out the food onto their plates.

"I've got pictures on my phone of what I found. Here, take a look." She fished out the phone from her purse, selected the picture icon then handed the phone to him. He scrolled through several of the pictures then emailed them to his printer."

"There. They'll print while we eat. We can look at them once we're finished."

Mateo's cell phone burred. He looked at the caller ID then stood and said, "Shit, I gotta take this. Be right back."

He walked out the slider to the patio as he punched the answer button. "It's about fucking time!" he growled to Sheldon through the cell.

"Sorry," replied Sheldon. "I was tied up and couldn't get back to you till now."

"When I call, you pick up. You excuse yourself from whatever the fuck you're doing and pick up. Got it!" he demanded.

"Okay, I got it."

"You've got four trips tonight. All in the valley. Three are for deliveries, and they'll have the payments. The fourth is just a pickup. I'll meet you at 9 pm in the parking lot with everything. Don't be late."

"Okay, I'll be there."

Mateo ended the call and went back to the kitchen to finish his dinner.

"Who was that?" Charlotte had watched him as he talked, and could tell he was upset.

"Shit, Charlotte. It was the FBI. I've got to meet them tonight at 9 pm. They're not happy I haven't gotten any information for them yet."

"Who are they to be upset with you, anyways," sounding indignant. "Don't they know you're doing them a favor, and they haven't found anything on their own."

"Don't worry about it, Babe. I'll go through the information you got, and I'm sure they'll be happy. I got it handled."

After dinner Mateo gathered up the printed photos and spread them out on the coffee table. Charlotte had taken 18 pictures of paperwork in different files from Doc's office so it was just as good as going through the files himself.

Charlotte sat quietly and watched him organize them. "How come you're separating them into different piles?"

Not looking up from his work, he pointed to the first pile of four pictures. "This deals with the computer lab; what happens and who's involved." Pointing to a sub-pile just below the first, "These two pictures deal with the accounting; money received, where it goes, what it's spent for."

Then he pointed to the next pile of nine pictures. "These pictures deal with the computer room and the sub-pile below it," pointing to that pile, "is the accounting piece for the computer room."

"Can you make out what's happening from the pictures?" she asked.

Mateo relayed to her what he had found out that morning about the computer lab, Mike Riggs, the PROMIS software and INSLAW and how it was connected to the photos. He was surprised at the amount of information he shared with her. He hadn't planned on doing that, but it seemed natural to include her on it now.

"Wow, you analyzed that really quickly. I remember seeing PROMIS and INSLAW, but you've got a whole backstory on it."

"Yup, there was some stuff on the news awhile back when they were almost bankrupt. I remembered some of that. Hey, let me have some time alone with this stuff so I can think. Go practice some billiards or take a swim in the pool while I study this."

Charlotte smiled. "I didn't bring a suit. I'd have to swim in the nude."

Mateo stopped and looked at Charlotte, "Then shoot billiards. I wouldn't be able to concentrate with you naked in my pool."

At 8:30 Mateo gathered up the photos. Charlotte had gotten bored with billiards and was now sitting on a lounger by the pool with a drink in her hand. Mateo opened the slider, "Hey, Baby, I gotta go."

She turned at the sound of the slider opening, drink still in hand, "Okay. You don't think Doc will be in any kind of trouble with all this do you?" She respected and admired Doc, just as most everyone did.

"I don't think so, but I'll know more after this meeting. I just think Doc got the tribe involved with something bigger than what he can handle and doesn't realize it."

"Can I wait here until you get back? I'd like to hear how the meeting went."

He knew she really wanted to spend the night and would use some other excuse to stay. He never wanted a girlfriend, but his feelings for her were stronger than what he intended. He remembered the old saying, "The heart wants what the heart wants." For Mato, for tonight anyway, it was Charlotte. This was getting complicated quickly.

"You just wanna spend the night?"

She smiled and her green eyes twinkled again. He could see it even in the night by the light of the stars, the moon, and the landscape lighting.

"Sure," she answered.

He noticed her dimples again. Subtle, but slight dimples none the less. They were sexy. He questioned why he'd not noticed them before they'd gotten together. Maybe it was because he was now noticing the little things about Charlotte, the subtle things that made her who she was. And it wasn't just her physical features. He was taken with her empathy, her sincerity, and her approachable personality. She was down to earth and easy to trust. Maybe he had underestimated her and was only now beginning to realize who the real Charlotte was?

******

Mateo pulled into Witch's Brew parking lot and parked in the slot next to Sheldon's. As he exited the car and walked to the trunk, Sheldon got out of his car and met him there.

He popped the trunk, grabbed three backpacks, and handed them to Sheldon. "This is product you'll deliver. The instructions are in the bags."

"Why don't we just call them what they are, guns? Why do we always have to say product or delivery? They're guns."

Mateo stopped and stared at Sheldon, then said, "They're weapons, asshole! Never call 'em guns. The Marines taught me a gun is your dick not the weapon you shoot. Got it?"

Said Sheldon, "Yea, I got it."

Mateo got an empty backpack out of the trunk and handed it to Sheldon. "All the money goes in this one, but you won't drop it off to me tonight. You'll hold it, and I'll come by in the morning to pick it up."

"But I'll be working."

"So, you take a break or you give me your keys. Either way works," Mateo now frustrated. "And when you pick up the money from Hector, make sure there's $8,000. He owes me for back deliveries. I don't want you leaving with any less. Got it?"

"I got it. You sound like you expect him to short you."

"Here's a lesson for you to learn. Never do business with friends, and if you do, never cut 'em any slack. If you do, you'll keep their friendship but you'll never get paid. And if you don't, you'll fuck up the friendship, but you'll get your money and probably lose their business."

"Hector's a friend?"

"We'll see if he's still a friend after tonight. $8,000 from him and not a penny less. Now get the hell on the road and get this done!"

Sheldon paused, "Hang on. I got another question."

"Shit! What now?"

"We need to come to terms on what I get for each one of these. You barely pay me enough to cover my gas, much less my time."

"What the fuck are you talking about?! I give you a job and pay you good money for working around my house. I teach you to drive then buy you a car and now you accuse me of ripping you off!"

Sheldon, adamant, "I'm just saying my time is worth money. I do appreciate everything you've done for me, but I'm not gonna work for free. I need to make money too."

Mateo stared at Sheldon and thought this was the first time he'd shown any real backbone. He could slap him down and make him do what he wanted for nothing, or he could barter with him and settle on an agreed amount. If he was going to keep Sheldon around, he'd need to pay him. But after he confronted Doc, the tribe would be paying Sheldon.

"Okay, then let's say $100 for the night."

"Let's say $100 per backpack," he replied, determined. "I got four backpacks so that's $400 for tonight. And if you're getting $8,000 from Hector, you'll never notice the $400 for me."

"So, you want to get paid as piece work rather than a salary?"

Sheldon firm, "Yup."

"Okay, let's do that for now, but when you start getting paid from the tribe, it'll be salary. You'll get a check twice a month, even if you don't make a single trip."

"That'll be fine," replied Sheldon.

As Mateo drove back to the house and back to Charlotte, he smiled and chuckled to himself. Sheldon was turning into a good businessman, learning how to stand up for himself, bartering, and refusing to be pushed around. He thought as he matured, Sheldon would be a real asset.

******

Tuesday Morning

At 6 am Charlotte's cell phone alarm went off playing some Taylor Swift song. Mateo groaned, rolled to the opposite side of the bed and covered his head with a pillow.

"I've gotta go back to my place to get ready for work. Do you mind if I bring some things over and keep them here so I don't have to run back to my apartment in the morning?"

"Shit! You wanna move in?" Mateo's head still covered.

"No silly. I just want to have a few things here so I can leave for work right from here."

Mateo didn't move.

Said Charlotte, "It works to your advantage too."

"How so?"

"Morning sex," she said with a smile.

He moved the pillow and rolled to face her. "Hey, I want you to bring a few things over. I'll make some room for you in the closet and one of my dresser drawers." He reached for her gently wrapping his arm around her waist then pulling her towards him. "Now what about that morning sex?"

She pushed his arm away and got out of bed. "Not this morning. I said I've gotta go get ready for work. I don't have time."

"Damn! You better get that stuff over here pronto. You hear me?"

Charlotte grabbed her clothes and headed towards the bathroom while Mateo lay in bed reliving last night in his head. He had returned to find her in the pool, nude. After that, he insisted she stay the night.

Mateo had discovered the computer room was actually a bitcoin mining activity, and with the amount of hardware they were running, they'd be making millions annually. The monies, after Doc's cut of 35%, went to an Agency slush fund. Doc was also getting a 35% cut from proceeds from all income on the PROMIS software. Once Mike Riggs was done with the initial programming, the Agency would have a backdoor to every government, agency, and business that used the software. That access would also be worth millions to Doc, and he wanted a piece of that action.

******

Sheldon listened to Connie's voicemail. He dreaded calling her back. Things with her had been going well, but now he was afraid he had screwed it all up and cursed Mateo for getting him involved in that cremation. The second voicemail was from Toni.

It was 3 pm when Connie pulled into Sheldon's trailer park and parked her car next to his. He had been keeping an eye out the front window waiting for her. He hastily walked out the door and down the steps but moped as he headed towards Connie. He wanted to avoid the confrontation. He hated confrontations and would usually make the decision that would avoid it. But if there was any way to salvage his relationship with Connie, he'd have to come clean, tell her everything, and hope she would understand.

"Hey, Connie," said Sheldon sheepishly. "We can talk inside if you like."

"Okay," Connie said, and they walked side by side to the trailer without speaking.

As Connie stepped through the open door that Sheldon held, she looked for a place to sit. The trailer was small and truly a studio apartment set up with a small bed, bathroom and kitchenette. They sat in the two chairs that were sandwiched between the bed and kitchenette.

"Wow, your place is really small."

"It's what I can afford right now, but I'm gonna move as soon as I can."

"Sheldon, you know I've been worried sick about Uncle Fred, and sick about the murders. Apparently, you know something because of your work with that guy, Mateo. But you haven't told me anything. Why have you kept it a secret? From me? From the police? What's going on, anyway?"

"I didn't know I knew anything about it all. I mean, I knew something, but I didn't know it was connected to your uncle. I only just discovered it might be. Then I didn't want you to think I was involved with killing anyone. I wasn't involved with any of that! And..." Sheldon stammered, "as I've gotten to know you, I realize you're important to me. I didn't know how to say anything without putting our relationship at risk. So, I hadn't said anything. But even if you never want to see me again, I'll tell you everything I know."

Sheldon related to Connie everything that happened the night of the cremation. He told her how Mateo called it a field trip, how it was only on the way to the crematory that he was told there was a dead body in the back of the van. He told her the bag was never opened so he didn't see who was in the bag, and that Mateo took the ashes with him in a coffee can when they left. Once he was done, he got up and walked to the cupboard above the sink, took out some equipment, and walked back.

"Look at this stuff," holding it out for Connie to examine.

"What's this?" taking the items from him and inspecting them.

"I got it from that detective, Sullivan. I'm supposed to wear this when I meet Mateo."

"You're gonna wear a wire?" she asked as she handed it back to him.

"Yea, it's part of the deal with the cops. If I help 'em they won't arrest me. But if I don't get enough information for them to arrest Mateo, then they'll come after me."

Connie thought about him working undercover for the police then said, "I'm still really pissed at you, ya know."

"I'm sorry, Connie. I know I've made some dumb mistakes, but I'm trying to make things right. I can't change the past, but maybe I can do something to help make up for it now."

"That asshole, Mateo. You think he shot my uncle?"

"I don't think he killed whoever was in the van. I got the feeling he was cleaning stuff up for someone else. And the police aren't ready to say who they think was back there. It may not be your uncle at all."

Connie asked, "When are ya gonna meet the Asshole with all this equipment?"

"I already got something recorded last night. It was more about some deliveries and collecting money for him."

"So, you worked for him last night? I thought you were going to stop that," Connie said, surprised.

"The police told me to keep working for him for now and keep them updated on what he has me do. I'm gonna hang out with him tonight at his place. This'll be my chance to get the information the police want. Connie, to be honest, I'm scared shitless. What happens if he catches me?"

"But you already recorded him last night, and everything went smoothly, right?"

"That was only for a few minutes, and we didn't really talk about the cremation. I'm just worried about it because I'll have to press him for specific information."

"Connie, it feels like all my life I've screwed things up when I had an opportunity to do something right. Maybe the way I grew up didn't help or maybe it determined my destiny. I dunno. I've always felt like I was more than what I have or I've done, but just can't seem to connect to it. Like something keeps getting in my way, throwing me a curve ball, or fumbling right before the goal line. I screwed up my job and relationship with the Contis. I've let everyone down. I let you down."

Sheldon's eyes began to tear. He looked down at his feet. Connie moved to the edge of her chair and put a hand on his knee. "Sheldon, you have your own place, a car, a job as a supervisor, and you're working with the police as a CI. You may be the one to break this case wide open. How can you say you're a failure? You've accomplished a lot more than most people your age, and you've had a lot more hurdles to overcome."

He looked up then wiped away a tear that began to run. "Thanks. I appreciate that."

"What if I help you get ready for tonight. Would you like that?"

"You'd do that?"

"Yes, I would. After all, I want this information too. And it finally lets me feel like I'm doing something to find out what happened to Uncle Fred." For the next hour, they strategized with Connie dubbing Mateo as The Asshole, referring him by his new title for the rest of their time.

As she was leaving, Sheldon asked, "Can you talk to the Conti's for me? I'm so sorry for getting them involved, and I just don't think I can handle another confrontation right now."

"I can, but you need to talk with them yourself. It's not the same coming from me."

"I will. I promise. I just need a day or two. That's all."

"Okay, but I'm gonna tell them you'll be coming to talk with them in person." She paused then said, "I know you'll do great tonight. Let me know what happened as soon as you get home. I don't care what time it is. Call me."

Before she left, she hugged and kissed him on the cheek. Then smiling, said, "By the way, I'm still mad at you."

Wednesday

Mateo sat in the parking lot of the tribal council building. He stared back at the reserved sign with his title, "Assistant Director of Security" thinking how he hated that sign. He had begun to loathe the word Assistant in the title. He thought it was about time he'd moved up to a better title. The word assistant perturbed him, like he was just some flunky taking orders from someone else. He was much more than that. He secured all of The Factory and its departments. He also kept all the secret activities of it protected so both he and Doc could make their fortunes off them, plus his own covert business which was small-time compared to what Doc had set up with the cartels, but it was completely his. He liked the feeling it gave him, complete control, total authority. He answered to no one when it came to it. Well, just as long as Doc didn't find out, but that needed to change, and change it he would. Mateo needed to put one more piece in place before he confronted Doc. That's why he sat in his car waiting for Doc to arrive for work.

He saw Doc's Mercedes round the corner and turn into the parking lot, heading for his reserved stall that was 2 stalls away from his. Mateo exited his car, extracted a brand-new Titleist driver from the back seat, and hung his satchel over his shoulder. This was their newest driver, and Doc had mentioned wanting to get one.

"Good morning, Mateo. What do you have there?"

Mateo stopped next to Doc's trunk as Doc walked over to him. "It's that new driver you were talking about the other day. I remembered you wanted to get one." Mateo held out the driver.

Doc took it from him, "Yup, that's a fine-looking driver. I bet you'll be a terror off the tee box."

"I actually got it for you."

Doc smiled, "Well, what did I do to deserve this?"

"Nothing really. I know there's been some tension at work lately and thought this might smooth it out," Mateo sounded apologetic.

"That's really thoughtful of you, but you didn't need to do this." Doc held the club up examining the head, shaft, and finally the grip. "I'm gonna take this to the driving range tonight."

Doc reached into his pocket for his key fob then stepped towards the trunk of his car. Mateo moved back out of Doc's way while he put his right hand into the satchel that hung on his shoulder. As Doc found his key fob, Mateo found the clone button on the Xhorse key cloning device hidden in his satchel and pushed the button. Doc pushed the trunk button on his key fob, and his trunk lock clicked then the lid rose. Mateo heard a faint beep from the Xhorse key cloning device indicating it had received and copied the signal.

Said Mateo, "I'll see you inside. I've gotta get something from my car," then turned and walked back to his car. Doc put the new driver in his trunk, shut the lid, and headed to the tribal building.

Once inside his car, Mateo removed the Xhorse cloning device from his satchel and grabbed a new key fob he had laying on the console. He set it up to receive a new signal from the Xhorse device then he pressed the clone button. A light flash red on the key fob. After three flashes it stopped indicating it had received the signal. Mateo exited his car, and walked to Doc's car trunk. He pressed the trunk button on the new key fob, and Doc's trunk lock clicked. The trunk lid began to rise, but he stopped it then re-shut the trunk. Smiling to himself, he walked towards the tribal council building.

******

Connie sat in the back room of Witch's Brew immersed in homework for her summer class. She took a sip from her hot coffee and stretched her legs, arms, back, and neck. They were still stiff from a busy night as she and Juan were on call. They had 5 pickups in all at 3 different hospital morgues.

"How's it going?" asked Sheldon and startled Connie who was engrossed in her assignment.

"Hey, Sheldon. I didn't see you come in." She pushed her chair back from the table and stretched.

"That's probably because you're facing the wall." Sheldon smiled.

"Yup. I didn't want any distractions." She looked at the clock display on her computer. It was late morning and Sheldon wasn't in his Witch's Brew uniform. "What are you doing here on your day off?"

"I came to get some coffee before I did anything constructive today."

She smiled, "Well, sit down and keep me company for a few minutes."

"I thought you said you didn't want distractions."

"I need a break. I've gotten to the point where my mind is saturated and everything's just swimming around in there right now. I'm glad everything went well last night, and thanks for calling me when you got home."

"No problem."

"Hey, did you hear anything from the police today? You know about The Asshole, and the women's home." Sheldon stepped around the table and sat in a chair opposite her. She closed the laptop and moved it out of the way.

"Nothing today. I told you they were happy with the recordings, but they refused to do anything about the church. They said we were just jumping to conclusions."

"Sheldon, I still can't believe what happened at that women's home. The more I've thought about it, the more I'm sure the church is running a sex trafficking ring out of that house."

"I don't remember ever seeing anything like that when I was staying there, Connie, but, you're right. Something's going on. And it would explain why my mom disappeared. She would never have left me on her own."

"I don't think I could just sit by and not do anything about it if I were you. Something needs to be done, and it doesn't make any sense the police won't look into it." The more Connie talked the more frustrated she became.

"I wish I could get enough evidence for them to investigate."

Connie looked out into space for a few seconds, thinking. "Or maybe they'll just focus on the murders and not bother looking into it. And, Sheldon, you have a stake in this too since it's where your mother disappeared. Don't you want answers or maybe even find your mother?"

"Well, sure I do, but what can I do about it? I'm not the police. And it's a woman's home so I can't just move in for a few nights and look for evidence." Sheldon lowered his head and thought out loud, "If I were a woman, I'd do just that."

Connie smiled and her eyes twinkled. "I was just thinking. Do you still have the recording equipment the police gave you?"

"No, they took it back. Why?"

"Dammit! That really would've come in handy, but we can do this even without the equipment."

"Do what?" he asked.

"I could go undercover to that women's home to find out what's going on."

"Connie, I couldn't ask you to do that."

"Why not? You did it with The Asshole. Plus, these are church people. What's the worst that could happen? They refuse to pray for me? They kick me out?"

"But I was working with the police. They knew what I was doing. You're talking about doing this by yourself."

"Well, I wouldn't be spying on a criminal. It's church people, remember. And, we could do it together. I'd be undercover, and you'd be my outside contact. You know, my handler. And if we find anything, we take it to the police so they can open up a real investigation and shut the whole thing down."

Sheldon thought but didn't respond.

"Sheldon, you lived with these people for over four years, right? They're harmless. I'll be safe."

"Hey Dude!" came a voice from behind Connie interrupting their conversation. Sheldon looked up to see the person who lived with him at the men's home for 3 of the 4 years he was there, Michael "Mic" Montague.

"Hey Mic," replied Sheldon. "What's up? How's the construction business treating you?"

Mic was tanned from working in the sun. He looked bigger than when Sheldon last saw him. He thought Mic must have put on some muscle with his construction job. His hair was shorter when he last saw Mic too. But his smile and brown eyes were the same.

"Man, you wouldn't believe all the stuff that goes on at the job sites," said Mic as he walked to the table and sat down next to Connie. "Who's this?"

"Oh, sorry. This is Connie. Connie, this is Mic. We were in the men's home together."

"Hi Mic, it's nice to meet you," said Connie. "As a matter of fact, we were just talking about the church and the women's home."

"No shit. They're an interesting bunch over there," replied Mic with a sarcastic laugh.

Connie continued, "That's what we were talking about. Tell me, Mic, did you ever notice anything strange going on while you were there?"

"Sure did, I saw a lot of strange stuff. Why?"

"Like what?" she asked.

Mic leaned in towards Connie meeting her eyes and began. "Did you know the church was making maybe two thousand dollars a month from the state for every person staying in the homes? They'd put everyone on food stamps and others would get added disability, and they'd use some landscaper to work them but they'd never see the money because it went to the church, plus they'd use unemployment insurance to get money from the state too. But they still worked under the table. Man, they've got a real racket going."

"I never saw any of that. Are you sure?" Sheldon, shocked.

That's cuz you're naive, Sheldon," replied Mic.

Defensive now, Sheldon responded, "Hey, I'm not naive. I know you can't always trust people."

Connie said, "Sheldon's sweet and kind. He believes in people, and truly cares about the feelings of others. I think those are all endearing qualities."

"You know there's an easier way to say it, don't you?" said Mic to Connie.

"How's that?"

"He's naive." Mic smiled, then to Sheldon. "Hey, man, I'm just giving you a hard time. Don't be offended."

"I'm okay," replied Sheldon. "I admit, I may be a little too trusting, but I'm working on that."

"Well, I don't want you to change a thing. I like you just the way you are," said Connie to Sheldon as she squeezed his arm.

Mic looked at Connie then to Sheldon. "Oh, I see. You two are an item."

Sheldon's felt his face get hot as Connie said, "We're not an item, whatever that is."

"Naw, something's going on between you too," said Mic.

Sheldon's face began to cool. "Yes, and we're seeing where things might go." He wasn't sure where they stood. After all, it was only one date. He hoped he hadn't overstepped what Connie was feeling.

"That's right," said Connie as she reached across the table and grasped Sheldon's hand, squeezed, and held it for several moments. Then Connie went back to their original topic. "But we were wondering if you'd seen anything like sex trafficking at the women's home."

Mic smiled, "I always suspected it was going on at both the men's and women's homes."

Sheldon aghast, "What are you talking about, Mic? There's no sex trafficking at the men's home. They're men."

"You don't think men get trafficked," replied Mic not a question but a statement. "Remember that little blonde headed and blue-eyed dude? He was eighteen but looked all of twelve. He wasn't there long and one morning he was just gone."

"Yea, but they said he ran away."

"He didn't run away. He told me he liked it at the home and wasn't planning on leaving. Hell, we slept in the same room so I should know. Pastor Eminis took him out during the night when he thought everyone was asleep. I was sure that's what happened to the little guy."

Sheldon and Connie sat in silence trying to digest what Mic had just said. Then Sheldon told Mic, "I just find it difficult to believe all this was going on, and I never saw it."

"That's cuz you're... how did Connie put it?" Mic smiled at Connie then continued, "You're sweet, and believe in people."

"Did you know Sheldon's mom disappeared from the women's home?" she asked Mic.

"Yup, I did. You two think she might have been trafficked?"

Connie felt like a wayward dissident who had just found a cause. "We want to get some evidence for the police so they'll investigate and hopefully shut the place down. I wanna go undercover to the women's home."

"Woah, Dude! Like a real spy? That's awesome!"

"I couldn't stay more than maybe two nights, but I'm sure I could find something by then. Sheldon would be my outside contact, my handler, and make sure I'm safe."

"Hey, I thought we were just talking about it. We hadn't decided on anything yet," Sheldon, surprised.

"No, we were finalizing the details. That's all," Connie, very matter-of-fact.

Said Mic, "Hide a cell phone and keep it with you at all times. They'll take it away if they it."

"And I can't show up at the church because of my run-in with Pastor Eminis," interjected Sheldon.

"Dude! What happened between you and the pastor?" Mic, shocked.

Sheldon filled Mic in on his confrontation with the pastor and even told him about finding people having sex in the church office. Then the three of them developed a plan for Connie's undercover operation.

Once plans were finalized, Sheldon asked Mic, "So you making lots of money working construction?"

"Yup, the money's good, but I'm not gonna stay in it."

"If the money's good, why not?"

"There's way too much drugs on construction sites. Most crews are high half the day, the dealers deliver right to the sites, and supervisors don't care. They just care that the work gets done on time."

"Wow," replied Sheldon, "I never knew. I figured people partied on the weekends but not while they were working."

"That's cuz you're sweet and trusting," said Mic, smiling.

Connie interjected, "You know, Mic, there's a job opening where I work if you're interested."

"Where you work?"

"Coachella Valley Cremations."

"Woah Dude! You cremate dead bodies?"

Connie, annoyed with Mic's tone, said, "No, I transport deceased loved ones so they can be prepared for their final resting place."

"Mic, the business sees what they do as sacred work, honoring the deceased and respecting the loved ones left behind," said Sheldon.

"So, the job opening is transporting the, ah, deceased?"

"No," replied Connie. "It's actually to operate the furnace, handle office paperwork, and there's some transportation when it's busy. The position works directly with the owners."

Sheldon said, "It's the place I worked at for about six months at that position."

"I might go over there and take a look. Where's it at?"

Connie said, "It's behind the Denny's on Indian Avenue, just this side of the I-10 interstate."

Thursday

Mateo called Doc from his office at The Factory, the place he felt more confident, more in control, more powerful. Mateo always thought about relationships as one up or one down. There was always a power struggle for the one up position, but that was about to change, or so he thought.

"Good morning, Mateo," said Doc as he answered after the second ring.

"Good morning, Doc." Mateo sounded formal, and stoic.

"I want to thank you again for that driver. I got a chance to try it out on the driving range, and it's going to add at least twenty yards to my drives."

Ignoring Doc, Mateo said. "There are some important things we need to discuss about the computer lab and computer room. It's one of those face-to-face subjects, but Mulder needs to be at this one." There was a long silence.

"I don't think that's possible, and I'm surprised we're having this conversation over the phone at work," Doc, irritated.

Said Mateo, "So am I, but it seems your actions have demanded it. It would be a shame if the police and the media discovered what really happened to Fred and why."

More silence, then, "Why Mulder? He's not a part of this."

"He's very much a part of it, and that's because of you. You didn't need to bring him in, I could have..." he stopped mid-sentence.

Said Doc, "Okay, but not here. Let's meet tonight at the Ridgeview Bar and Grille. The place the three of us met before. Say 7 pm?"

"Let's make it 9 pm," replied Mateo. He wasn't about to let Doc get control of the conversation now that he finally had it. Demanding a different time told Doc he no longer controlled things.

******

Mateo parked in the Witch's Brew parking lot at 8 pm to meet Sheldon. They were in the back of the lot away from other cars and street traffic, but the it was still light enough to be seen if anyone had wanted to watch them.

Mateo handed Sheldon the key fob, "This is what you'll use to open the trunk. See the trunk button?" pointing to the button with the trunk icon. "That's what you'll push. It's the only button that's programmed so you won't be able to open the doors or start the car." Sheldon took the key fob and looked at it.

"Which button is it? Show it to me," said Mateo.

"This one." Sheldon pointed to the button with the trunk icon.

"Good. Now here's what you'll put in the trunk." Mateo reached into his trunk and pulled out a black industrial plastic bag with his gloved hand. He had wiped down the bag before taking it out of his garage. He thought again how smart he was to keep the bloody vest that Fred had worn when he was shot. If he had destroyed it, there'd be no evidence to plant in Doc's car if Doc was so dumb as to refuse his demands.

"Fuck! Put on the gloves I gave you. Why do ya think I gave 'em to you anyways? You can't get any fingerprints on this or the car. Understand?"

Sheldon grabbed the gloves from his trunk floor where he'd laid them and slipped them on. They were big but he didn't think they'd slip off. He grabbed the bag and put it in his trunk then removed the gloves and placed them next to the bag.

Said Mateo, "Now let's go over it one last time. What time do you pull into the Ridgeview Bar and Grille?"

"9:15 pm."

"And you have the description and plate number of the car, right?"

Sheldon held up the note Mateo had given him, "Yes."

"Then what do you do?" questioned Mateo.

"I keep an eye on the car and wait. If you text me, I put the bag in the trunk. If you don't, then I just sit and wait until whoever owns the car gets in and drives off."

******

At 9:02 Mateo pulled into the parking lot of Ridgeview Bar and Grille. By the time he parked and made his way to the bar, he would be almost ten minutes late. Fashionably late he thought. They'd be waiting for him, communicating again that he was in control. As he parked and made his way to the bar he thought about Sheldon. He'd better not fuck this up. It was too important, and he hadn't thought about a contingency plan if Sheldon bombed. Sheldon had been more responsible as of late, and his heart seemed to be in it now. He thought it may be time to give him more responsibility and trust him more. Tonight, would be the test for him.

Mateo walked up the hill from the parking lot to the stairs that led to the restaurant. The place had a waterfall that began at the top of the stairs and cascaded down large rocks to a small pool where the stairs began. Landscape lighting on the rocks and water drew customer's attention and acted as security lighting. Mateo grabbed the railing as he ascended the stairs so he could keep one eye on the falls as he made his way to the top.

This place was beautiful. Built on the side of a rock formation in such a way that the building looked like the rocks had grown up around it. Landscape lighting lit up the building, rocks, and various palm trees and desert landscaping. He always thought the place could be a fortress with sheer rock walls guarding it from any enemy that might desire to usurp its power and position. Yet, it held the high ground, and would withstand any attack.

Mateo walked into the bar and looked around but didn't see Doc or Mulder. He walked through the bar to the opposite wall where the patio entrance was located, and found them there, sitting at a bar table in the corner of the patio. Both had a half glass of draft beer sitting in front of them, the mug still cold and frosty. The rock wall on his right was lit and made the crevices and shadows from the desert plants dance as he walked to the table. Soft music played through the speakers mounted overhead along the wall opposite of the rocks. Above him was open night sky and twinkling stars. There were only a few people on the patio and all were away from Doc and Mulder. The setup would give them privacy.

"Good evening, gentlemen," said Mateo as he sat down.

"Hello, Mateo," said Doc. Mulder simply acknowledged him with a nod.

"Do you want to order a drink?" asked Doc to Mateo.

"No. Not tonight. I see you two have already started though," Mateo nodded to the two beer mugs on the table.

Said Doc, "They store their mugs in the freezer before serving drafts. Makes the beer taste better." Doc picked up his mug and took a long sip. Mulder watched Doc with one eye and kept the other eye on Mateo.

"So just what is it that we need to discuss?" asked Doc.

Mateo started, "I know you're getting a 35% cut from all the PROMIS software sales, and I know you're getting a 35% cut from the bitcoin mining operation in the computer room. And I know the tribe only sees the income from PROMIS after your cut. And they know nothing about the income from the bitcoin operation. I also know you had Mulder here," nodding towards Mulder, "take out Fred Asghar because he was getting too close to finding out about the Factory's operations. He would have also discovered the clandestine weapons sales if he were allowed to snoop around at The Factory."

Doc glanced at Mulder then back to Mateo, but Mulder never took his eyes off Mateo.

Said Doc, "You're mistaken about much of this, Mateo. Both projects were set up by others, not me. I really have no control over them and don't make any money off them."

Mateo looked Doc square in the eyes and said quietly but forcefully, "And you're a fucking liar." He reached into the inside pocket of his sport jacket and pulled out several pages and laid them on the table in front of Doc. "You recognize these? They're from your files."

Doc picked up the first page and examined it only briefly then quickly looked at Mulder then back to Mateo. "So, you've been in my office, have you? Mulder, tell our friend here what you've found."

Said Mulder to Mateo, "You've been selling weapons to the local gangs here in the Coachella Valley for some time now. You steal the weapons and ammunition from The Factory and sell them. Sometimes you take cocaine or crystal meth in trade then sell the drugs yourself. You make more profit when you do that. And this is not new behavior. You've been doing this for quite some time." When Mulder spoke, Mateo was reminded how much he hated the east coast, especially Mulder and the way New Yorkers sounded.

Mateo, angry now, "Fuck you, Mulder!" He didn't intend to get loud, but others on the patio heard him and several turned and looked in their direction. "Been snoopin' in my office. You had no right."

Said Doc, "And you had no right snooping in mine." He folded up the papers Mateo had given him and put them in his pocket.

Mateo was glad Doc thought it was him. He wanted to keep Charlotte's name out of this confrontation. If Doc thought it was Charlotte, he'd fire her for sure, or maybe worse.

Mateo said, "Let's move on, Doc. Here's what I want. First, I want a 15% cut from the PROMIS sales and a 15% cut from the bitcoin operation. That leaves you with a 20% cut from both. These are activities from The Factory, so I'm entitled to a cut. 15% is fair. Next, I want the job we discussed for Sheldon created and him hired so he can quit his current job and work full time for me. Finally, I want a new title for my position that doesn't have the word "Assistant" in it. I'm not assisting anyone, especially Wackenhut."

Doc didn't blink as Mateo went through his demands. His face was deadpan. "It seems you've thought this through, Mateo."

"I have," Mateo said, defiant.

"I'll need to give this some thought, and I'll need to contact some other people before I can agree to all of this. But what about the sales you've been doing to gangs here in the Valley? Do you plan to stop those?"

"I'm keeping those. Who knows, I may even expand what I'm already doing. Now I need an answer, Doc."

"I can't give you one now. I just told you that."

Mulder interrupted, "Doc, I'm gonna go. We'll need to catch up later." Mulder got up and started to leave, but Mateo stopped him.

"Mulder, if Doc doesn't agree to this, the police and FBI just might find out what you did. You need to tell Doc to take my offer, or both you and him may end up in jail." Mulder looked angry but didn't respond. He turned and left the patio heading to the parking lot.

"Doc, I need an answer now. If it's not yes, then I'll assume it's a no. If you say you'll need time, then I'll assume it's a no. I know too much for you to refuse to play ball with me."

"You're asking for quite a lot, Mateo. Would you settle for something less? Is there room in your mind to negotiate?"

"Doc, this is more than fair. You're still getting the lion's share of everything."

"I'm getting nothing from your secret gun sales," Doc reminded him.

"Would you consider taking a 5% cut rather than 15%?"

Mateo getting frustrated now, "Why are you stalling? You've heard my terms. It's non-negotiable."

"Why are you being so stubborn about this, Mateo? Let's work out a compromise we can both live with."

Mateo thought Doc was just stalling now. But why? What would be the reason to stall? Then he remembered Mulder had left earlier. He took out his phone and texted Sheldon. Now he wanted to stall as well and spent the next ten minutes negotiating. Neither man was willing to agree to any terms so Doc left with the issue unresolved while Mateo moved to the bar and ordered a White Russian. Twenty minutes later he left, walking out with two couples who had finished their dinner and were now headed towards the parking lot. He thought if Mulder was hidden somewhere in the desert with a rifle pointing towards him, he'd never get a clean shot... just as long as he stayed in the middle of these two couples.

As the five of them got to the bottom of the stairs and started down the small hill to the parking lot, a police car pulled into the lot with its wig wag lights flashing. Then two unmarked cruisers from the far end of the lot turned on their lights and drove quickly to the bottom of the hill, screeching to a halt. Two more sheriff cruisers entered the parking lot from Highway 111 behind the first cruiser. Their wig wag light flashing and sirens blaring.

Mateo froze in his tracks as did the other two couples. They were now surrounded by 10 law enforcement officers, four in plain clothes and six in uniform. Their guns were drawn, and they commanded, "This is the Riverside County Sheriff's Department. All of you stop and put your hands high in the air!"

Eight hands immediately went high in the air while Mateo raised his only about shoulder height.

"Ladies, walk towards us but keep your hands in the air. Walk slowly," came the next command.

After the women were separated from the men and were safely in police custody, the next command was, "Mateo Rivera, take one step forward." Mateo hesitated.

"Mateo Rivera, take one step forward, now!" came the command again only more forcefully. He took one step towards the officers who continued to point their weapons at him and the two other men.

The next command, "Mr. Rivera, turn around and walk backwards slowly to the sound of my voice." Mateo complied, turned, and slowly backstepped towards the officers. As he was walking, he noticed one of the other men had soiled himself. Scared the pee right out of him, he thought. Mateo, however, was not scared. He was surprised and angered, but not scared. As he walked, he quickly thought of Doc and Mulder. Did they set this up? No, it couldn't be them. They'd never get local law enforcement involved. And what happened to Sheldon? He was supposed to be putting a little gift into Doc's trunk. Did he get caught and squeal?

"Stop!" came another command. Mateo stopped. "Get down on the ground. Face down with your arms spread away from your body." Mateo obeyed.

Next a swarm of officers jumped him holding him down with their arms, legs, knees and elbows before they twisted his arms behind his back and cuffed him. Next, they got him up off the ground, searched him confiscating his phone wallet and keys then putting him in the back of a police cruiser. Mateo had assessed the officers and noticed all were from the Riverside County Sheriff's Office. No local police and no FBI.

23 |

Friday

At 3:30 am, Officer Mando Martinez and Detective Sullivan stood in the viewing room and watched Mateo through the one-way viewing mirror. Mateo sat at a table facing the mirror dressed in an orange jail-issued jumper. His hair was pulled back into a pony tail, his hands were chained to the table, and he wore white jail issued slippers on his feet. It had taken over two hours to process him into the jail at the Detention Center in Indio, and Sullivan had let him sit in the interview room for another two hours.

Mateo's lawyer was perched on the table next to him with an open briefcase and a file with three pieces of paper laid open in front of them. Martinez and Sullivan knew it was the arrest warrant which was the only paperwork the lawyer had been given. He had showed up about thirty minutes ago, but didn't know anything other than what the arrest warrant stated and what Mateo had related to him. Mateo continued to talk in an animated fashion while they watched.

"I'd sure like to hear what they're saying," Martinez said, breaking the silence.

"We could turn on all this recording equipment, but that'd be a violation of his rights. And I don't want to do anything that might get this case thrown out of court."

"When's Rossi supposed to be here?"

Sullivan looked at his watch, "The person I spoke with said Rossi would be here by 9 am."

"That's almost six hours," replied Martinez. "You gonna keep him in there until then?"

"No. I'll give it another thirty minutes then have him brought back to his holding cell. Then we'll have him up by 7 am, feed him breakfast, then back here by 8 am. He'll sit for another hour or more before Rossi starts his interview. All the waiting should help him talk."

Martinez smiled. He had never been involved with this side of law enforcement. He had always been a patrol officer, but he liked being involved at this level.

"They've got a room in back with racks if you want to get some sleep." Said Sullivan. "I'm gonna go back there in a few minutes."

"That's a good idea. I'm beat."

Sullivan called the night desk sergeant and instructed him to have Mateo moved to his holding cell in thirty minutes then he and Martinez went to find the sleeping area for the detectives.

******

It was 9:45 am when Martinez turned to Sullivan and asked, "So, when do you think Rossi will get here?"

They had gotten to the viewing room at 8:55 am. And Mateo had been there for over an hour. His lawyer hadn't shown up yet, but they expected he had other clients to see and would be notified when the interview was about to begin.

"Who knows. Maybe Rossi stopped off for breakfast," replied Sullivan.

Yea, that's just like the FBI," Martinez disgruntled. "They don't care about anyone else's schedule."

"You're right," Sullivan agreed. "But let's not make waves with him today. We'll need a federal search warrant to search anything on the reservation. So, let's make sure he's on the same page as us."

"I don't see how he couldn't with what we've got." Martinez thought about everything they had on Mateo doing a quick inventory in his head. "We've got the bloody vest, the bullet from the crematory, and the taped conversation between him and our CI, Sheldon Goodman. Seems like a slam dunk to me."

"Me too," replied Sullivan. "But you never know how these FBI guys will evaluate the evidence. And we don't know what evidence they found on the reservation. Let's be cautious and move things along slowly."

As Sullivan finished his sentence, the door to the viewing room burst open and in walked Special Agent Tony Rossi of the FBI along with another FBI Special Agent. He was younger than Rossi, tall and husky. He sported a military high and tight cut and his clean-shaven chin revealed a solid lantern jaw. His blue eyes sparkled as he surveyed the room communicating both wisdom beyond his age and an awareness that Rossi didn't have.

"Hello, gentlemen," Rossi grumbled. "Traffic was backed up half the way here, and it's always twenty degrees hotter whenever I come out. I don't know how any of you can stand living in the desert. This is Special Agent Cliff Callaghan. He'll be working with us."

Martinez wanted to correct Rossi about the benefits of living in the Coachella Valley as compared to Riverside, but decided not to say anything remembering Sullivan's words of caution.

Rossi and Callaghan gazed through the viewing mirror at Mateo and his lawyer who had just arrived. "So, that's the guy?" asked Rossi. "I remember interviewing him on the reservation. Which reminds me. I told both of you to stay away from all these guys on the reservation. The reservation and all the employees were supposed to be the FBI's responsibility. Not yours." Rossi was gruff and seemed irritated.

"Tony, we never perused the reservation or anyone on it. We followed our leads from the crematory. That led us to Mr. Rivera. Everything was in our jurisdiction, here in the Coachella Valley. You wouldn't have us just ignore the bloody vest or the taped conversations between our CI and Mr. Rivera, would you?"

Rossi frowned. "No, but you could have at least contacted me before you made any arrest. My boss chewed me a new one after Washington chewed him a new one. So, none of us are happy about what you've done."

Callaghan stopped Rossi before he said any more. "Tony, why don't we let them tell us exactly what they've got, then we can move forward as a team." Rossi grimaced then changed the subject. "So, when do you expect to get the blood analysis back from the vest?"

"That should be this afternoon or early tomorrow." replied Sullivan, then handed Rossi and Callaghan each a sixteen-page document. "This is the transcript from the recording we made with our CI, Mr. Sheldon Goodman."

Rossi's eyes flashed, "I told you not to do anything with this Goodman guy! He may just turn out to be the murderer, the one who killed all three people and now he's manipulating the two of you into thinking it's..."

Callaghan cut him off, "Now, Tony, let's just listen to what they've got. Remember, we decided we'd come with an open mind and let the evidence speak for itself. Let's sit down and read over the transcript. Then we can ask some questions."

Rossi grimaced again but didn't say anything. They both sat down at the table and spent the next few minutes reading over the transcript of the recording of Sheldon and Mateo's conversations. As Martinez and Sullivan watched them read, they both suspected Rossi's theory of the murders had changed. Last they talked, Rossi thought Fred Asghar was the murderer, and this morning he thought it might be Sheldon Goodman. Now, as he read the transcript, he looked as though he was beginning to believe Mateo Rivera was the murderer.

Callaghan glanced at Rossi then back to the transcript, "Tony, based on this conversation, Mr. Goodman may not be the perpetrator, but it looks like Mr. Rivera used him to dispose of the body."

Rossi screwed up his face at this but never looked away from the transcript. Martinez and Sullivan looked at each other and resisted a smile. They were beginning to like Callaghan.

"Mr. Rivera never admits to shooting any of the victims," Rossi finally stated.

"No, but he alludes to it, and just because he didn't admit it, doesn't mean he's not the killer. He definitely knows more about it than what he said in this conversation. Tony, I think our goal today is to determine if Mr. Rivera was the trigger man. But if he didn't do it, do you think he knows who actually did the murders?" asked Callaghan.

Rossi nodded his head. "That's what we're here to find out," replied Rossi, now starting to act like a team player. "You and I will interview him first, then Sullivan can follow up with anything else he needs."

Callaghan turned to Sullivan and Martinez and asked, "Is that okay with the two of you?"

"That's fine. We'll work on a list of information we need while you and Rossi interview him."

Callaghan and Rossi picked up their paperwork and exited the viewing room. Moments later they entered the interview room, Rossi taking a seat at the table across from Mateo while Callaghan stood off to the side watching.

"Hello, Mr. Rivera," said Rossi as he studied the transcript in front of him. "So, you and Mr. Goodman cremated a body. Just who was it?"

Mateo fixed his eyes on Rossi, "On recommendation of my lawyer, I'm exercising my right to keep silent."

"Well, that's a stupid decision. This is your chance to tell your side of the story; your opportunity to convince us you've done nothing wrong, or you were coerced into doing something you normally wouldn't have done. Or maybe you were just in the wrong place at the wrong time."

Rossi turned to Mateo's lawyer, "Mr...."

"Smythe," replied the lawyer. "Richard Smythe from Foster, Smythe, and Glenn."

Callaghan stepped forward and held out his hand. "Mr. Smythe, it's good to meet you. I'm Special Agent Cliff Callaghan from the FBI, and this is Special Agent Tony Rossi. We're investigating the murders."

"I know what you're investigating, and my client has nothing to say," Smythe cutting Callaghan off.

"It's to his advantage to talk to us now, to help us understand what happened and how he may be involved," replied Callaghan.

For the next two hours, Rossi and Callaghan grilled Mateo taking turns sitting across from him at the table. Rossi played the bad cop while Callaghan played the good cop, which were rolls they naturally fit into because of their personalities. Mateo refused to answer any questions or he would go off on strange tangents about how the government mistreated the indigenous populations in the U.S., how their land was stolen, forced on reservations, treated like animals, allowed to die in long marches like The Trail of Tears. He accused Rossi of attempting to do the same to him.

Mateo, clearly tired and irritated, finally spoke directly at Callaghan ignoring Rossi, "You have no idea what's going on here or who's involved. This goes beyond the Sheriff's Office, and even above the FBI. And if you don't let all this drop, well, let's just say it might not be safe for any of you."

The threat angered Rossi and he spat, "You stupid shit! Your whole conversation with our CI the other night was taped. Everything you said, everything you admitted to, and everything you alluded to is right here, and he threw the transcript in Mateo's face."

Mateo glared at Rossi while Smythe jumped back in his chair then picked up the transcript. "I never got a copy of this."

Rossi let Smythe and Mateo view it just long enough to know it was real then snatched it out of their hands and stated, "It's evidence of the state. You'll get your copy during discovery."

Callaghan shot a quick glare at Rossi then back at the attorney. "I apologize for my partner. He didn't mean to be so brisk, but he's right. This kind of information is released during discovery, not now."

"I need to talk to my client privately. Could you please remove these handcuffs and leave the room for a few minutes? Oh, and turn off the recording equipment too."

"We'll leave the room but he stays cuffed," informed Rossi.

"You uncuff me or I'm not saying shit! You can take me back to my cell now or uncuff me. Your choice." Mateo continued his attempt to stare down Rossi.

""We'll uncuff you," interjected Callaghan. He turned to the mirror behind him and said, "Gentlemen, could you come in and uncuff Mr. Rivera?" Moments later Sullivan entered the room and uncuffed Mateo then all three officers left the room.

Twenty minutes later Mr. Smythe signaled for them to return. Rossi and Callaghan reentered taking their same seats. Moments after they left the viewing room, a clerk came in with a signed search warrant for Mr. Rivera's home. Sullivan and Martinez decided to leave the interview to Rossi and Callaghan to search the home now. They would review the recording later and reinterview Mr. Rivera as they needed. After all, he wasn't going anywhere.

Back in the interview room, Smythe began talking. "My client wants you to know that activities which took place on the reservation and specifically at The Factory were CIA operations and sanctioned by our government. Mr. Rivera does not have authorization to speak to these activities and requests that you release him while you ask the CIA about them."

Rossi and Callaghan looked at each other, nonplussed, then to Smythe. Did Smythe think they were idiots or was he testing them?

Rossi responded matter-of-fact, "That's the deepest pile of bullshit I've heard in a long time." Now he referred to information they had gotten from the taped transcripts, "First, the CIA isn't authorized to operate on U.S. soil. Second, the CIA would not authorize the murder of three people and set your client up to be the fall guy. Third, the CIA wouldn't authorize the sale of weapons to terrorists, drug cartels, or local gangs."

Smythe and Mateo looked at each other. Smythe gave Mateo a look that said they've called our bluff but Mateo still responded, "You have no clue what the CIA is capable of and what it does on U.S. soil."

Rossi smiled. "Mr. Rivera, we have the bloody vest that came from you. When the blood analysis comes back this afternoon, we'll have Fred Asghar's blood on it. We have the bullet that matches the bullets from the murders, and when we search The Factory, we'll find matching bullets where they were manufactured. You are the common denominator. So, here's what'll happen. You'll be convicted of the three murders, but you'll be convicted in federal court, not the state of California. Federal court has the death penalty. You'll be shipped to Leavenworth Federal Prison in Kansas where you'll sit on death row never to see the desert or your loved ones again. Finally, you'll be injected with a chemical that causes paralysis. You'll be able to feel, hear, and see, but you'll not be able to move or speak. Next, you'll be injected with another chemical that'll stop your heart. And don't think you won't feel it. You will, and you'll be in terrible agony until you die. But you won't be able to flinch, or scream, or move, and the witnesses will see that agony in your eyes as the life drains out of you." Rossi and Callaghan saw fear in Mateo's eyes for the first time.

Mateo mumbled, "But I didn't kill anyone," then bent his head.

"It doesn't matter what you did or didn't do. It only matters what we can convince twelve people in a court of law. And we've got so much on you now that it'll be a slam dunk win for the D.A.," said Rossi, smiling.

Smythe looked at Mateo and slowly shook his head. "Then my client would like to make a deal. He would be willing to turn state's evidence and tell everything he knows for complete immunity and protection from those who may want to harm him."

"Ha! I bet he would. He'll get no free pass here," Rossi indignant.

"Then what about a reduced sentence, tried in state court rather than federal court, given probation, and given protection?"

Rossi was about to respond when Callaghan put his hand on Rossi's shoulder stopping him. "Wow!" said Callaghan. "You're asking for quite a bit."

"It's equivalent to what he knows," said Smythe. "And believe me, once you hear it, you'll realize he's just an honest employee, maybe somewhat naive, that was only trying to do the best job he could for his boss. And you'll be happy to give all of it to him."

"I don't know that we can do all that. Can we hear what he knows first, off the record?" asked Callaghan.

"No, you can't. But I'll allow him to explain to you about what he knows without names, dates, and any specifics. Off the record. After that, if you think what he knows is valuable, and you will, then we can move forward with a signed agreement. Once we have that, then he'll give you all the specifics so you can prosecute."

"Okay, go ahead," said Rossi.

"Turn off all your recording equipment first." Smythe was making sure he protected Mateo from any funny business that these officers may try to pull. "Take me to the next room so I can verify it's off."

Callaghan escorted Smythe to the viewing room while Rossi stayed with Mateo. The two men sat in an awkward silence until Callaghan and Smythe returned. When they opened the door to the viewing room Callaghan realized Sullivan and Martinez were gone. He reached over and turned off the recording equipment then they returned to the interview room. For the rest of their time interviewing Mr. Rivera, Callaghan wondered what happened to the two Riverside Officers that were supposed to be in the next room watching the interview.

Smythe instructed Mateo, "Mr. Rivera, the recording equipment is off so you may explain what information you have, but no names, places, times, or dates."

Mateo hesitated, then began, "First, I didn't kill anyone, but I know who did and why they did. I know this, not because I was there, and I wasn't, but because I was at the meeting when it was planned. Second, as far as cremating a dead body goes, I know who did it, but it wasn't me. I have no key to any crematory, and I don't know how to run any of that equipment. Third, any business The Factory does, is business my employer has set up. I'm only an employee following orders from my boss, but I do know who the customers are. They would include cartels, freedom fighters in South America, and even the CIA." Smythe smiled at

Mateo. He had done a good job explaining what he knew without giving away information that would be used to barter with.

"But in a court of law it would only be his word against someone else. Does he have any physical evidence?" asked Callaghan.

"He has some documents and pictures of other documents proving his story that include names, dates, amounts, and bank account numbers," replied Smythe. "They prove every single word."

Callaghan and Rossi looked at each other and smiled. "And just where are these documents and pictures?" asked Rossi.

Smythe stopped Mateo just as he was about to speak, "That's all you get, and it's the physical evidence that backs up his story. Anyone else's story is just that, a story, because there's no physical evidence to prove it. Now do we have a deal?"

"We'll need to verify a few things first, and we'll need to talk with our supervisor as well. So, this'll take some time," replied Callaghan. "And I think for the time being we should take custody of Mr. Rivera and move him to Riverside." Rossi and Callaghan picked up their paperwork and walked back into the viewing room.

"Where's Sullivan and Martinez?" asked Rossi.

"I don't know. They were gone when we turned off the recording equipment. I still think Mr. Rivera may be the shooter. All this other stuff may just be a red herring to sidetrack us from the murder."

"That's just what I was thinking," agreed Rossi.

"You go check with the clerk as to their whereabouts while I call the office to transfer Mr. Rivera," instructed Callaghan.

"The man's got enough information to blow this case wide open," said Rossi as he headed to the door.

"You know we may find all those documents when we search his house," said Callaghan as he scrolled his phone contacts to find the number of the FBI office in Riverside. "Then there would be no need to make a deal. And if he is the actual shooter, there'll be no deal for him."

"You're right," replied Rossi.

Five minutes later Rossi returned, "Those sons of bitches! They got a search warrant for Rivera's home. They're over there now."

"Shit!" roared Callaghan. This was the first time Rossi had seen Callaghan display any emotion other than patience, but Callaghan quickly regained his composure. "You wait here for the transfer order. I just called it in, and they'll be faxing it in a few minutes. I'll go to the home and collect anything they may have found." Callaghan quickly left the room and headed to the elevator. He needed to get to his car and out to DHS as soon as he could.

When Callaghan reached his car in the parking lot, he pulled out his cell phone and dialed a number that wasn't in his contacts list.

After three rings, "This is Jacobs." came a voice on the other end of the call.

"We just finished the interview and Rossi's waiting for the order to transfer Mr. Rivera to our facility in Riverside. But we have a small glitch that I'm addressing now."

"What's that?"

"First, Mr. Rivera says he has evidence to back his story, documents with names, dates, amounts, and account numbers."

"We always knew that might be an issue. That's why we developed a plan to handle it if it came up."

"But here's the glitch. Riverside Sheriffs are searching Mr. Rivera's home right now. They left while we were interviewing. I'm headed over there now to confiscate any information they may find, but I won't be able to plant any evidence since they're there now."

"Hmmm. That does present a small problem. Then we'll have to modify our plan a bit. Will Rossi be a problem to convince?"

"I don't anticipate any problems with Rossi. He's easily manipulated. He thought Goodman was the perp when we first arrived, but now he's thinking Rivera. Give me a few hours, and I'll have him thinking the president of the United States is the killer."

"Good. I'll have new instructions emailed to your personal account. I don't want any of this in the FBI's system. Get a warrant to search the reservation for Monday. That'll give our people the weekend to clean everything out. Update me if there are any issues."

"Will do," then Callaghan ended the call, got into his car and headed for Mr. Rivera's home.

******

Sullivan and Martinez sat in silence as they drove back to the Indio Detention Center. They had searched Mateo's home with three other deputy sheriffs. Callaghan had showed up just as they were finishing and was surprisingly supportive of their efforts. Both men trusted Callaghan and were glad the FBI had brought him in to work with Rossi. Callaghan seemed to understood their frustration and was compensating for the sake of team work. The search, however, had turned up nothing. No documents, no photos, no illegal weapons or ammunition.

Once they arrived at the Detention Center, they got the tape of the interview from the IT department and sat down in the computer lab to watch the full interview. They were surprised when the interview ended after Mr. Rivera was going to talk off the record. The tape was never turned back on so they didn't know what was said or what was the results of their 'off the record' conversation. This wasn't protocol.

"We need to reinterview Mr. Riveria," said Sullivan. "Can you have him brought back to the interview room while I call Rossi to find out what's going on?"

"Sure. I'll have him brought to interview room five."

Martinez left the computer lab and headed to the jail. Sullivan took his cell phone from his blazer pocket and looked up Rossi's cell number. The call went to voicemail after three rings so he left a message for Rossi to call him about the interview. As he left the computer lab and headed towards interview room five, he wished he'd gotten Callaghan's cell number earlier in the day. He made a mental note to get it next time he saw him. Then he called the main number for the FBI field office in Riverside.

"FBI field office. How may I direct your call," came a female voice after the second ring.

"Can you connect me with Special Agent Tony Rossi?"

"Just a moment," came her reply then soft elevator music began to play. Moments later, Sullivan heard ringing. After four rings, it went to voicemail so Sullivan left the same message as he did on Rossi's cell. Next, he redialed and asked for Callaghan when the operator picked up.

"I'm sorry, Sir, but I have no Special Agent Callaghan listed in our directory. Are you sure he's from our field office?"

"No, I guess I'm not sure that he is. What if he's on special assignment working out of your office but is from another office. Would you have a listing for someone doing that?"

"No, Sir. I wouldn't. You should contact the special agent who he's working with from our office."

Sullivan frustrated, "Okay, thank you," and hung up. Then he sat down in the viewing room for the number five interview room to wait for Martinez to bring in Rivera.

Fifteen minutes later, the viewing room door burst open and in walked Martinez, slightly out of breath.

"They took him!"

"What? What do you mean? Who took who?"

"Rossi and Callaghan. They took Rivera. He's at the FBI field office in Riverside."

It took several moments for Sullivan to comprehend what Martinez was saying, but became angry when he did.

"Those assholes! Callaghan played us when he showed up at Rivera's house. He wanted to make sure Rossi had gotten Rivera out of here before we got back."

"Son of a bitch. Let's call Rossi and find out what's going on."

"I tried. Straight to voicemail. And I called the field office number too. I'm afraid they may be planning to cut us out of the investigation, take the whole thing over."

As they left the Indio Detention Center, Martinez figured his special assignment was completed and would be back on patrol by Monday. He'd decided to start studying for the exam he'd need to pass in order to become a detective. He loved being a patrol officer, but this had given him a taste of something different.

******

It was just after 4 pm when Toni looked up from her desk to see a loud green Camaro pull into the parking lot and park in a stall across from the office door. A young man got out and tramped towards the office. He was tanned and wore sunglasses with a red ball cap over his scruffy brown hair. His red t-shirt and jeans were dirty and reminded her of Joe years ago when he came home from working construction covered in that white drywall dust that swirls around construction sites. The young man must have been six feet tall and still had that slim build from youth although muscle was forming on his arms, chest and shoulders.

Smiling, Toni stood as he entered the office and held out her hand. "Hi, I'm Toni Conti. May I help you?"

Mic removed his sun glasses and put the arm of the glasses in the collar of his t-shirt where they dangled below his chin. He took her hand, shook it, looked her straight in the eyes and said, "I'm Mic Montague. I'm here to apply for your open position."

"Fantastic," Toni, surprised. "My husband, Joe, will be excited to talk with you about it. So how did you hear about the position?"

"Ah, Connie told me about it." Not remembering Connie's last name.

Toni opened the bottom desk drawer and fumbled through the different paperwork until she found the employment applications. She attached one to a clipboard and handed it to Mic along with a pen. "Could you fill this out while I tell Joe you're here?"

Mic took the clipboard from Toni, looked at the application, and frowned.

"I know. Lots of questions to answer, right? Don't worry, I can help you with it if you like."

"No, it's not that. I just came from work, and I'm kinda tired. It's just gonna be hard to focus on all of this stuff."

"Well, sit down and I'll get you a water. Joe will be a few minutes so the application can keep you occupied while you're waiting." Toni handed Mic the water and went to the back to tell Joe.

Mic sat down in a lobby chair and started filling out the form: NAME, ADDRESS....

Moments later, Toni returned from the back. "Joe will be ready to talk with you in a few minutes. So, how do you know Connie?" she asked.

Mic hesitated. He remembered he shouldn't mention Sheldon. "I used to work at Witch's Brew, but I've been working in construction for a while now. She would come in to study."

"I know someone who works at Witch's Brew. His name is Sheldon Goodman. Do you know him?"

Mic thought for a moment. He didn't lie to people. He was always upfront and straight-forward. If he hadn't been asked directly, he would never have mentioned Sheldon. "Yup, I know Sheldon."

Mic spent the next few minutes writing and finished the application just before Joe burst through the door from the backroom. "Hi," said Joe as he reached out to shake Mic's hand. Mic stood and gave Joe's hand a firm shake looking him full in the face.

"I'm Mic Montague. Nice to meet you." Mic handed Joe the clipboard holding the completed application then both men sat down at the table, Joe on the end and Mic on the side next to Joe.

Joe perused the application paying close attention to the previous employment and the references section. "So, why are you applying for our position? You'd make a lot more money working in construction."

"Because I'm tired of working with a bunch of druggies. I don't do drugs and I'm tired of babysitting a bunch of addicts and redoing their work because they're too stoned to do it right."

Joe nodded. He had the same issue with the crews he ran when he was working construction. He didn't put up with poor quality work nor anyone on his crews that were impaired. That was a primary reason for him leaving construction and starting the business with Toni to build something they owned together.

"I see you know Sheldon Goodman." Mic had listed him as a reference because he had already told Toni he knew Sheldon.

"Yup, I know Sheldon," then he addressed the elephant in the room. "We were in a group home together, and we'd gotten pretty close back then. But I'm not Sheldon. I don't know what happened with him when he worked here, but don't judge me based on him. That just isn't fair. I'm honest, trustworthy, and I work hard. I'm someone you can count on. I've been successful everywhere I've gone. I was a crew supervisor at the coffee house, and, as young as I am, I've been supervising guys twice my age on the construction crews too. My work speaks for itself. Sheldon doesn't speak for me."

Joe studied the application again then looked up at Mic, "This business is unique. It's not for everybody. How do you feel about transporting bodies, operating the furnace, and handling some basic paperwork?"

"This business isn't unique. It's just plain weird. That's why I'm interested. I think I'd be a good fit for this kind of job, but I guess I won't know until I've done it."

"Well, would you like to give it a try starting Monday?"

Mic quickly inventoried what he would need to do in order to start Monday. He would need to call his boss and tell him he was taking a few days off beginning Monday. They wouldn't be pleased because of how much they had come to rely on him, but he didn't want to quit the job until he knew if this job with the crematory would work out.

"Yup, I can. What time?"

"I'd like you here by 8 am. The office opens at 9, but we'll start working at 8."

After several minutes of conversation with Joe and Toni, Mic headed to his car.

"I like him," said Toni.

"He's upfront with things," replied Joe. "And honest. You know what you get with him. That's so different from Sheldon, but he was direct about knowing him and not wanting to be judged by what happened with Sheldon. I was impressed with that."

"I wonder if he knows everything that happened with Sheldon when he was here, and the cremation?"

"I dunno, but I'm sure he'll tell us before too long."

Changing the subject, Toni said, "Connie's gonna take Sunday and Monday off. I think she's studying for a final so I told her, okay."

"Well, I'm glad Mic will be starting Monday then. I can start training him on doing transportation."

24

Saturday

It was 10 am when Mateo was brought from the detention area to an interview room at the FBI field office in Riverside. He was still wearing the orange jumper and white cloth slippers. Moments later Special Agent Cliff Callaghan walk through the door.

"Hello, Mr. Rivera. I apologize for the way you were treated in Indio. The Riverside Sheriff's Office isn't as organized as we are."

"My lawyer's not here. You know I'm not going to discuss anything without him. And I won't sign any agreement without him looking it over first." Mateo didn't trust Callaghan.

"Mr. Rivera, I don't think you'll need a lawyer for this. Hear what I have to say first, then you can decide. Is that all right?"

"Go ahead.?" Mateo sneered.

"Mr. Rivera, I don't want anything. I'm here to give you something."

"And what's that?"

"First, we've come to the conclusion you were not the shooter, and we're only interested in illegal activities that took place on the reservation, and the murders. That's why we are going to release you without bail. Charges will still be pending, for now. But if you cooperate with us, then they will be dismissed in the near future. I can't speak for Riverside County, but I'm sure they'll follow suit. Mr. Rivera, I'm giving you your freedom. Do you think you need your lawyer to agree to that?"

"Just what do you mean by cooperate with you? What do you want me to do?"

"We'll want you to testify at trial, and we'll require you to turn over your evidence to us. As of now, those are the only two requirements."

"As of now? You mean they could change?"

"We're not sure you have any real evidence. We've seen nothing at this point, and there was nothing found at your home. Without it, there is no deal. And because this is still an ongoing investigation, we may require you to do more for us as it continues to develop, but your agreement will keep you on the right side of this thing."

"Oh, I have the evidence safely tucked away. I guarantee you that."

"Good. Now do we have a deal?

"Yup, we have a deal. Now, when do I get out of here?"

A marshal escorted Mateo to be processed out. Everything that was taken from him in Indo, was given back to him except for his car. It remained in the Indio police impound lot. Before he left the building he called Charlotte. When she arrived, Mateo wasn't ready to talk so he just told her to drive, insisting they go to her apartment rather than his home.

Charlotte lived in a small complex of eight units at the top of Miracle Hill. The complex was walled and gated at each end of the parking lot that required a key card to enter. There was a pool and jacuzzi in the center of the complex that the units surrounded. The complex was exquisitely landscaped in desert plants and palm trees. As they walked from the parking lot, Mateo realized this place was quiet, peaceful, and tranquil. He felt safe there.

"Okay, we're here. Now please tell me what's going on," insisted Charlotte as they entered her apartment.

"Close those blinds," commanded Mateo thinking about Mulder. Was Mulder waiting hidden somewhere outside with a scope trained on those sliders, on him? He had no idea, and that scared him. Not knowing where a potential enemy was meant they could take you by surprise, by ambush.

Charlotte obeyed and closed the blinds. "Mateo, what's going on?"

"The fucking Riverside Sheriffs arrested me last night. They didn't know I was working with the FBI and took me to jail. The FBI got me out of the Indio jail and finally released me, but the sheriffs have my car, and they searched my house. Can you believe that! Those fuckers."

"They can't do that! Who do they think they are, anyways?"

"Well, they did, Charlotte. My FBI contacts told me they're planning to bring those Riverside cops up on charges. Those assholes! And I'll be the star witness."

"Well good for the FBI. They deserve to be arrested after what they did to you."

Mateo spent the next thirty minutes telling Charlotte about his experience being arrested, questioned, being in lockup then finally transported to Riverside and released. Charlotte listened intently, believing every word.

When Mateo had finally exhausted his story, he asked, "You still have all the documents I gave you, right?"

"Yup. I put them in my dresser in the other room."

"Great. I was so smart to let you hold them. These documents are the proof everyone needs, the FBI, the Riverside County Sheriffs, and ...." Mateo stopped mid-sentence. "Go get 'em, Baby."

Charlotte retrieved a file from the bedroom and laid it on the coffee table. Mateo pulled the papers out of the file began to reorganizing them As he worked with the papers the doorbell rang. Mateo froze and looked at the door then to Charlotte.

"You expecting anyone?" he asked, then looked back to the dining room table where he had left his holster and pistol.

"No," she replied then stood, walking to the door then peering through the peephole. "It's some man in a suit. I've never seen him before."

Next, came a loud banging. "Mr. Rivera, it's Special Agent Callaghan. Open the door."

Mateo was relieved. "Shit! Wait a second before you open it." Mateo quickly picked up the paperwork and stuffed it all back into the file then put it under the sofa cushion next to him. "Okay, go ahead."

Charlotte opened the door and stood back. As the door swung open, Special Agent Cliff Callaghan stepped into the apartment and closed the door behind him. "Good afternoon, Ms. Finney." Then he turned directly towards Mateo. "Mr. Rivera, I'm gonna need that paperwork you were just reviewing. Could you please hand it to me?"

"What the fuck? I wasn't looking at any paperwork."

Callaghan smiled as he scanned the room pausing at the dining room where Mateo's jacket and holster lay. "Ms. Finney, please sit down in the chair next to the sofa, slowly."

Callaghan didn't take his eyes off Mateo, but he did push back his blazer and pulled his pistol from its shoulder harness pointing it at Mateo.

Charlotte followed Callaghan's instructions and sat in the far chair.

"What's all this about?" asked Mateo, not sure what was happening. Callaghan had been so professional and polite when he was released, but now he held them captive. This guy had seemed to be on his side, but now he didn't know what to think.

"It's about that paperwork. Get it, now," Callaghan ordered.

Mateo cursed to himself that he hadn't gotten his pistol from the table before Charlotte opened the door. When his face flushed red, Callaghan became tense and raised his weapon to center mast. Mateo stared back at Callaghan as he began to reach under the sofa cushion.

"Slowly!" commanded Callaghan.

Mateo paused. "It's under the cushion."

"Okay. Then throw the cushion to the corner," pointing to the corner of the room with his pistol then quickly returning its aim to Mateo's chest. Mateo picked up the cushion and threw it to the corner of the living room exposing the hidden file.

"Now, stand and walk slowly to the other side of the chair and your girlfriend," demanded Callaghan.

Mateo did as instructed. She grabbed his hand and held it tight. Callaghan slowly moved to the sofa and picked up the file.

"Thank you, Mr. Rivera." Then he slowly backed out of the room through the front door, put his pistol back into its holster, turned a disappeared into the courtyard.

Charlotte released Mateo's hand then dropped her head to her hands struggling to catch her breath. Mateo walked to the front door, closed and locked it. "How the fuck did they know?"

"How did they know what?" she asked, still trembling.

"That we had the documents. This wasn't supposed to happen. I'm not sure what's going on now. And I may be fucked without them."

"Mateo," said Charlotte. "I don't think I've been that scared in all my life. I thought that guy was going to shoot us."

Mateo looked at Charlotte. She was still shaking and there were tears in her eyes. He stood, took her hand and led her to the sofa where they sat. Then he wrapped his arms around her and held her tight. At that moment every other thought vanished from his head except Charlotte and how scared she was. Doc, Mulder, last night's arrest and even Callaghan showing up, pointing a gun at them, and taking those documents meant nothing to him. He was only concerned for Charlotte. He wanted to make sure she was safe.

"It's okay, Baby. You're safe now. Nothing's gonna hurt you. I got you," trying to comfort her.

"Oh, Mateo," she sobbed. "Who was that guy?"

"I have no idea, Baby. I'm gonna call my contacts at the FBI to find out just what's going on. But I don't think I'll be able to reach them until Monday."

"He said he was a special agent. You think he was with the FBI?" asked Charlotte.

"I think he was lying, but he's got to have some fucking contacts with law enforcement because he knew I had evidence. He might be from the Riverside Sheriff's Office posing as an FBI agent." He surprised himself at his quick thinking to come up with this story. For the next few minutes Mateo sat and held Charlotte until she stopped shaking.

Mateo his sport jacket from the dining room and searched it. "Fuck! That's how they knew." He held up a small black electronic box he found in one of the pockets.

"What's that?"

"It's a bug, a listening device. Someone planted it in my jacket." Mateo dropped it on the floor and smashed it with his heel. "It was probably done while I was in Indio." But Mateo was sure it was the FBI, and Callaghan specifically. He realized he had misread Callaghan. He was the least trustworthy asshole he'd met since he'd been arrested.

He was sure Doc and Mulder may be after him, but now he figured Callaghan or maybe the whole FBI Riverside field office. He had no protection other than hiding out at Charlotte's, but the FBI knew he was there. Who else might know? He'd have to find a way to quickly protect himself and came up with a plan.

"Baby, I've gotta get my car. You'll have to drive me to Indio so I can pick it up."

"It's Saturday. Do you think they'll be open now?"

"Yup, the impound lot is open twenty-four, seven. They bring vehicles there all the time so they have to stay open." He replied, then getting back to his plan to leave, he said, "Get in your car and move it facing the road. Keep the engine running, but move to the passenger seat. And, keep an eye out for anything out of the ordinary, like anyone you don't know or doesn't belong hanging out or sitting in a parked car. Once you're in place, call me and I'll come out."

******

Mateo sat down on the bar chair that was part of the set in his kitchen and opened the can of beer he had just pulled from the refrigerator. He was tired after putting his house back together from the chaos the sheriff's had made when they searched the place. It had looked like a whirlwind had gone through every room in his house. Pictures were down, furniture was moved or tipped on its side. Drawers were pulled out or dumped on the floor. His mattresses were stripped and standing on one side in the hallway. He would need the rest of the weekend to clean the place up.

As he sat catching his breath, the two Dobermans he had picked up at Elite Canine Training jumped up and began to bark at the front door. On the way back from Indio, he had stopped at Elite and picked up the two dogs from Chandler Wilkinson, the owner and master trainer at Elite. Mateo often used Elite at the casino so he was happy to help Mateo out. He thought the dogs would be his first line of defense if anyone got into the house but would contact an alarm company on Monday to have a complete system installed.

"Sit!" commanded Mateo to the dogs as he quickly got up and hurried to the front door. The dogs stopped barking and sat at the door while he peered through the door's peephole. The dogs heard Charlotte's car long before Mateo did and that reassured him they were a good decision. Charlotte had a large plastic bag with her that read Pescado's as she walked to the door.

"Park it!" commanded Mateo to the two Dobermans, and they both turned and walked to their large pillows by the fireplace. They both lay down but kept their eye on the front door.

Mateo gave the command, "Stay!" just before he opened the door for Charlotte. After dinner, they completed their cleaning, became more familiar with the Dobermans, talked, and even laughed a bit making jokes about the search and how inept Mateo thought the Riverside Sheriff's Officers were. He was beginning to feel normal, more like himself.

25

Sunday

Connie walked through the church parking lot and entered the building through the front doors into a long vestibule decorated in purples and golds of various shades with green accents. The three crystal chandeliers hanging from the ceiling filled the room with muted light creating a warm and inviting ambiance. She heard muffled singing coming from the sanctuary to her left where services had started some time ago. There was one set of double doors leading into the sanctuary on the center wall of the vestibule and two single doors on each end of the vestibule wall. Tere were two couch tables pushed against the wall, each on opposite sides of the center double doors. Both had a beautiful flower arrangement in the center complimenting the deep purple carpet with its deep green foliage. They were twins, each being the exact replica of the other. To the right were several doors in metal door frames that led to long hallways connecting classrooms and offices to the vestibule. They reminded her of the metal door frames from high school except these doors looked like wood. This room was the heart of the building for its parishioners, connecting vital organs of the church to each other through the different arteries. The vestibule left the impression of a wealthy and regal church that was both luxurious and lavish.

She opened the first of the two double doors and walked into a large sanctuary room. She paused in the center aisle between rows of pews on each side. The pews were long, upholstered in purple, and extended from the middle aisle to the side aisle of the room. The carpet was deep purple and plush. She looked down the center aisle where she stood to the opposite wall. This aisle led to the center of the stage where music and worship leaders stood, eyes closed, hands raised, and singing with all their might as they led the congregation in song. Behind them were six large chairs all in golds and purples, centered on the stage. They resembled thrones and four of them were filled, but the two end chairs sat empty. Behind this was the back wall that held a stained-glass image of Christ on the cross. It stood the height of the wall, from floor to ceiling. The light from the setting sun still shone through the irregular pieces of glass making it twinkle. Connie thought it was breathtaking and began to question how a church so opulent and seemingly successful could be involved with anything illegal.

She sat her backpack on the last pew and took a seat next to it. An older man sitting on the far side opposite of her got up and walked to her. He smiled and handed her a piece of paper.

"Thank you. What's this?" she whispered.

"A bulletin," he said. "It has our service times and different ministries we offer," he replied, then turned and retook his seat.

Connie looked around the room and noticed it was maybe one fourth full and thought it was a small group for such a large room. Most people were sitting in the middle of the room or towards the front. She was the only one sitting in the back. She would stand out. There was a group of seven women, 3 pews from the front all sitting together. She thought they must be from the women's home. Across from them on the opposite side were a group of twelve men. They must be from the men's home.

She perceived people on the stage had already taken notice of her. The singers, musicians and even the ones on the purple thrones had given her subtle glances. Now all she needed to do was wait. They would come to her after the service and then the undercover operation would really begin. She felt the butterflies in her stomach again. They were savage when Sheldon dropped her off two blocks from the church, making her almost nauseous. The walk had calmed them and they had almost disappeared by the time she reached the parking lot, but now they were back. She thought if they made her sick, it would only help with her story.

******

As the service ended, people stood up and began to leave while others gathered about in small groups and talked, greeting each other with hugs. Connie sat at the far end of her pew and noticed an older heavy-set woman walking down the side aisle towards her. She had come from the group of women. She had shoulder length graying hair and wore a long gray dress that was conservative but stylish. Her bright rosy cheeks glowed as she smiled and held out her hand to Connie.

"Hello, Sister. I'm Sister Hortencia. Is this your first time here?" Connie stood to shake her hand, but Hortencia reached for her and gave her a firm hug.

Hortencia was stocky and several inches shorter than Connie, but she was strong. Connie looked away from Hortencia's eyes but still noticed they twinkled with a warmth that almost made her feel like she had known this woman all her life and could trust her.

"Yes, it's my first time here. I'm Connie." Connie looked down at her feet and only made fleeting glances at Hortencia's face.

Hortencia looked at Connie's body language, paused for several seconds, then took Connie's head in her hands and made Connie look her directly in the eye. "Connie, the Lord's revealed to me that you're in some turmoil, some trouble, a struggle you don't know what to do. That's why you're here tonight. It wasn't your decision to be here tonight. It was his." Connie pulled away, sat down, put her head in her hands. Now she had to perform the way she had practiced with Sheldon and Mic.

"Yes, you're right. I just don't know what to do!" She began to make sobbing sounds, keeping her head in her hands.

Hortencia sat down next to her, pulled out a tissue from her bra, and gave it to Connie. "Oh, Child, we'll figure this out together. It's gonna be alright."

Connie took the tissue without lifting her head and pretended to daub her eyes. She put some saliva on the tissue so it would be wet. After a few moments, Connie stopped sobbing and sat up.

"I don't know where to start," Connie flustered. "I guess I should tell you my parents kicked me out of the house."

Hortencia looked shocked, "Oh, Dear. Why did they do that?"

Connie began with her story, the scenario that Sheldon, Mic, and she had settled on. Her family had only just moved from Chicago where she had been dating a local gang member. Her mother and stepfather tried to break them up, but she loved the boy. Her stepfather was retired and wealthy so he moved the family to Palm Springs where they owned a second home. Once here she discovered she was pregnant. The parents insisted she get an abortion, but she refused. She was determined to have the baby, and she believed abortion was murder. That's when they kicked her out. Because she had just moved from Chicago, she had no friends here in the Coachella Valley and was all alone. She was two days on the streets when she heard the church had a women's home and that she might find help there.

Once Connie had finished her story, Hortencia sat thinking. "Oh, Child, I knew you were pregnant when I first saw you. You have that glow about you. We have a program for women who are in the same kind of situation as yours, homeless and needing help. But I'm afraid the program requires a two-year commitment. If you came into the program, we'd help with doctor's visits, the delivery, and help with raising and care of your beautiful baby for the next year while you finished the program. And we would provide everything you and your child needed while you're with us. This would be perfect for you, Connie. It gives you a family that will love you and helps you where your own family refused that responsibility. What a selfish decision they made! Your family here at New Life Empowerment Church won't be like that."

Connie looked up at Hortencia, "You'd do that for me?"

"Oh, of course, Dear. Now wait here while I talk with a few people to get it set up, and you'll be in your new home with your new sisters tonight." Hortencia stood, hugged Connie, then went to the front of the sanctuary and began talking with several other people.

While Connie waited, she thought what a wonderful person Hortencia seems to be, and she questioned again that the church, the women's home, and these people (if they were all like Hortencia) could be involved with any illegal activities like sex trafficking. But that's what she was here to find out. So far, she felt somewhat guilty about this undercover operation. Maybe things would be different once she was at the women's home.

A few minutes later, Hortencia returned with a man Connie recognized as the pastor.

"Good evening, Sister Connie. I'm Pastor Alfredo Eminis. Sister Hortencia tells me you're in trouble and seek refuge. Our church and ministry are open to help all of God's children. There's no shame in needing help. We all have been down at one time in our lives and have needed the help of our brothers and sisters. I was even in prison once before I found the help I needed to live a victorious life. And if God can do that for me, he certainly can do it for you. Now tell me what's happened."

Connie told Pastor Eminis the same story she told Hortencia.

Pastor Eminis asked, "You know that our program is a two-year program, don't you?"

"Yes, Sister Hortencia explained that to me," she answered, daubing her eyes.

Hortencia handed Pastor Eminis a clipboard with some forms attached to it and a pen. He looked at the paperwork and nodded then handed the clipboard to Connie.

"Connie, these are some forms we'll need you to fill out and sign. It covers the basic rules of our program, your two-year commitment, our expectations of you, and our commitment to you for the things we'll provide." Connie looked at the forms, but when she saw the last form wanted personal data including her social security number, her butterflies returned.

"Why do you need my social security number and all of this other personal information," she asked.

Pastor Freddie Eminis calmly replied, "We need it to put you on food stamps and to sign you up for any other community resources that may be available to you. In your condition, you'll get a significant amount of money each month from the state, and the state will cover all of your medical costs too. We'll save it all, and you'll get everything that wasn't spent supporting you. In two years, that'll be enough money to get your own apartment, buy your own car, even go back to Chicago if you like. It'll all be yours."

"I'm not feeling well," replied Connie. "Could I do this tomorrow? I'm not even sure if I have all this information. It may take me a while to get it."

"Pastor, maybe we could have her sign the other two forms now and I'll work with her to get the last one completed tomorrow," interjected Hortencia.

"That's fine, Sister Hortencia." Turning back to Connie, "Sister Connie, just sign these forms and you can complete the other one tomorrow when you feel better."

Connie looked at the two forms and questioned whether they obligated her legally for anything. She didn't think they would allow her in the women's home without signing them so she signed each form misspelling her last name and signing in such a way that it didn't resemble her normal signature at all. Once signed, Hortencia took the clipboard. The butterflies had settled for now.

******

Connie stepped out of the shower, toweled off, then slipped into pajamas that Hortencia had given her. Hortencia had explained on the van ride to the women's home that she was the den mother and responsible for all the girls at the home. One of the responsibilities was to ensure cleanliness including guarding against lice and flea infestations. This meant her belongings would need to be cleaned before entering the home. Hortencia was normally worried about drugs getting into the home since most residents were addicts trying to kick their addiction, but Connie gave her little worries about this. Before she left the bathroom, Connie booted up her cell phone and texted Sheldon saying, "I'm in. Going great," powering it down immediately after sending the text. Hortencia had taken the prepaid cell phone she had bought before Sheldon dropped her off and kept her personal phone hidden.

Connie also met the other women in the home and got familiar with them on the ride from the church. There was Sylvia and Monica. They were the youngest and had only been at the home for two months. Next was Vanessa and Esther. They had been at the home for six months and were more familiar with the people and the processes than Sylvia and Monica. All four of them slept in one bedroom. Connie would be bunking with Marisol and Sarah in the other bedroom. These two were older than the other girls and had been there for two years and ready to graduate from the program. Both planned to stay in the home and intern with the church for another year. That night Connie would learn Marisol and Sarah knew all the ins and outs of the program, how to manipulate Hortencia, how to smuggle in contraband, how to get out of chores, and even how to sneak out at night for a short trek into the surrounding barrios.

After all preparations were made in the home for the morning's activities, it was lights-out and all the girls went to bed, Den Mother Hortencia sleeping in her own room. Connie, Marisol, and Sarah stayed up half the night telling stories about their past, how they ended up in the home, and the things they got away with since they had been there. They giggled like teenagers but hoped they didn't wake up the other girls or Sister Hortencia.

When the stories lulled, Connie interjected, "Did either of you ever know of someone here at the home named Cindy?" Sarah had been laughing but stopped and looked at Marisol when Connie finished speaking. Marisol stared back at Sarah and gave her an ominous expression.

Marisol got up from her bottom bunk, pulled a small wooden box from under her mattress and walked to the window opening it full. Next, she took out a firmly rolled joint from the box, lit it, and inhaled deeply as she pressed the end of the joint between her lips. Sarah awkwardly rolled out of the top bunk and headed to the window. Marisol held her breath as she passed the joint to Sarah. Connie watched the tip glow bright orange as Sarah inhaled, taking the smoke deep into her lungs. Marisol began a slow exhale. The smoke from her lungs slowly billowed around her head then drifted out the open window.

Marisol kept her eyes fixed on the joint that Sarah held and replied, "Some things are just not talked about here."

Sarah passed the joint back to Marisol holding her breath as long as she could, then exhaled. She began to cough, once, twice, now three times. "Don't take such big hits," Marisol told Sarah as she held the joint between her thumb and forefinger and took a second hit. This time the tip not only glowed bright orange but wiggled down the length of the joint and towards Marisol's lips.

"But it's just us. No one's gonna hear," said Connie.

Marisol held her breath and licked her fingers, extinguishing the joint between them, then put everything back in its wooden box.

"Hey! I wanted another hit!" Sarah sounding offended.

"That's all you can handle, and it's all I've got until next week." Marisol walked to her bunk and put the box back in its place under her mattress.

"Cindy stayed in the storage room, but she left after a few weeks," Sarah continuing the conversation.

"Sarah! Shut your fucking mouth." Marisol clearly angered. Sarah didn't say anything more but climbed back into her bunk above Connie.

"We get away with almost anything, Connie, but talking about Cindy, or any other girl that disappeared from the back room could bring us trouble... big trouble," said Marisol as she lay down on her bunk. There was a seriousness in her voice that Connie had not heard before.

"But the person who told me about the church knew Cindy. That's how I knew about her."

"If you go talking about Cindy, people will think we told you about her. Then the shit's gonna hit the fan for us."

"I liked Cindy," Sarah interjected. "She got along well with everyone. I don't know why they... why she left."

"They took her didn't they," Connie finished Sarah's thought. "Where'd they take her?"

Marisol quickly interrupted angrily, "Sarah, I told you to shut the fuck up!".

"Sorry." Sarah sounded remorseful. It reminded Connie of a little girl who had just been reprimanded or a child that had just been scolded by her mother. But she wasn't done trying to get more information about Cindy.

"I won't say anything to anyone. I promise. I just want to know what happened to her," Connie pleaded in her most empathic voice.

Sarah kept quiet still feeling the pangs of Marisol's rebuke, but Marisol replied, "Look, Connie, anything we tell you has to be kept secret otherwise we're dead."

Connie thought Marisol was being overly melodramatic but agreed. "I won't say anything to anyone."

"Most girls that get put in the storage room are gone within a month, and the story is always the same. They couldn't obey the rules, they were caught using, they ran away, or they decided to move back with family. But we lived here with them and knew the story just didn't jive with what we knew."

Sarah added, "All their things are left in the room, and Hortencia has one of the girls clean it up. I keep what I want when I clean and give the other girls everything else. And the day they disappear there's always some excuse that she has to stay alone in the house while everyone else goes to the church for services or to clean or to some work detail the church will make money on. When we get back, they're gone."

"And it's Hortencia that does this?" asked Connie.

Marisol said, "No, not Hortencia. It comes from Pastor Eminis and from Brother Peter."

"Who's Peter?"

"He's one of the leaders of the homes. Hortensia and the men's home den father are under Brother Peter. He once took a girl out of the home by force because she kept asking questions about someone who had disappeared. He threatened us all to keep our mouths shut about girls leaving. Since then, no one talks."

"If you've been here for two years, how often do girls disappear?" asked Connie.

"Maybe every two months," replied Sarah who had been sitting quietly. "We thought they'd put you in the back room. You're young and attractive. I guess they thought you weren't a good candidate cuz you're pregnant."

"What do you mean, candidate, and just where do these girls go that disappear?"

Sarah was about to speak but Marisol stopped her. "Sarah, shut your fucking mouth!" To Connie, "We don't know."

"But you suspect," added Connie. Marisol and Sarah looked at each other.

Connie said, "I suspect the same thing. Sex trafficking."

Marisol's eyes opened wide, her mouth opened, and her chin quivered. "You need to keep your mouth shut about that, Connie. That's why Brother Peter took the other girl out of the home. They probably sold her into it too. Pregnant or not, you'll disappear just like the other girls if you start talking about it."

26

Monday

It was 8:30 am when Mateo walked out the front door of his house and to the unattached garage. He had gotten the Dobermans fed and relieved before he left. Feeding wasn't a hassle, but now he had dog poop around his pool in the planters. He had thought about Mulder and the possibility that he might be hidden somewhere with a scoped rifle somewhere in the hills but there was really no place to hide and still have a good shot. He decided not to take any chances and had Charlotte clean up after the dogs.

Charlotte had spent the weekend and had left earlier. He was in the middle of negotiations with Doc when he was arrested and needed to take care of that unfinished business, but he would start his day at The Factory. He still wondered if Doc was arrested too not knowing who had set him up.

When Mateo arrived at The Factory, he found there was a considerable amount of activity over the weekend. As he studied the security log entries, he discovered that Mike Riggs and Jim Coleman came with four other unnamed individuals and four box trucks. Doc had called before they arrived and instructed staff not to notify anyone, especially Mateo. Next, he inspected the facility and found all the offices had been stripped of paperwork. The computer lab still had tables and desks but all the computer equipment was missing. The computer room was the biggest surprise. The room had been cleared of all electronic equipment. There were no computers, no network switches, no terminals, no monitors, and no keyboards. The racks that once housed all this equipment were gone as well. The only remnants were a few wires that hung from conduit that ran along the tops of walls.

******

Mateo sat down behind his desk, picked up his IP phone and called Doc. Doc answered after three rings.

"Good morning, Mateo," said Doc in his normal cheery voice. Even in the middle of their conflict, Doc was the politician. It was his way. "I hope you're having a good morning."

"My morning's just fine," replied Mateo snidely. "Everything's gone from over here. The lab, the new offices, the computer room, even my office. What the fuck did you do?"

"I didn't do anything. You didn't think I was alone in all of this did you? Didn't you realize there are others I work with? The best advice I can give you right now is to just forget anything ever happened over there at The Factory. Don't alk about it to anyone, and that would include the Riverside Sheriff's Office, the FBI, or anyone you know. It would be dangerous if you did."

"Are you threatening me?" Mateo, now getting hot.

"No, I'm not. I'm just giving you some sage advice. Remember I'm not the only one that's involved, and there's no telling what they might do."

"Just who are these 'others' that you are so afraid of?"

"They're some influential people who'll make sure you go down for all of this, the gun running and the murders. Or they may just decide to have you disappear instead."

"You were the one that orchestrated selling guns to the cartels, and the murders. You'll be the one to burn for it. Not me!"

"Mateo, it's not who did what. It's what can be proven in court. You had the bloody vest, and your guy, Goodman, was the one that blew the whistle on you. Anything you said about me was hearsay and would never be used as evidence for anything. You've left yourself exposed, and those people you think I'm so afraid of will make you the scapegoat for all this. The FBI will bring federal charges against you, and you'll eventually be executed in Leavenworth, Kansas."

Doc's words brought back all the things FBI Special Agent Tony Rossi said when he was interviewed in Indio. Was it just a coincidence, or did Doc know something about that interview? Could he have a connection to the FBI, maybe the CIA, or could it even be the cartels that were orchestrating this and keeping Doc in the loop? He still had his trump card, the evidence.

"But I have evidence. It's not just my word against yours. Remember, you saw it at the bar."

Doc didn't flinch. He continued in his calm, easy-going manner, "Do you, Mateo? Do you still have all that evidence in your possession? You didn't lose it, did you?" Doc knew Callaghan had taken the information.

"You think that's my only copy? The FBI may have copies of it too. You never know." The documents Callaghan took were his only hard copies. Both he and Charlotte had deleted all the pictures after he downloaded them to a jump drive that held more files Mateo had gotten from his office.

Doc paused for a moment, "It would be in your best interest to destroy anything you might still have. It would be very dangerous for anyone to have that kind of information in their possession. Some very serious people would not be happy if you still had them, and if.... Hold on a second." Doc put Mateo on hold but came back on the line moments later. "The FBI just showed up with a search warrant. Tribal police are escorting them here to the Tribal Council building and to The Factory now."

Mateo felt his face get hot. "Shit! Doc, we need to work together to stop their investigation. It's to both of our advantages and keeps us both safe."

"We'll have to see how all this plays out, but right now, they're headed to The Factory."

"You said they're going to both buildings at the same time?"

"I was told there were two groups. They'll be searching here at the same time."

Mateo hung up the phone then called Charlotte. He didn't want to underestimate Doc. He knew Mulder had already been in his office. She picked up on the first ring.

"Charlotte, go to my office and look for anything that may not belong there, anything that may look incriminating. I'm afraid someone might have planted something there."

"I can't. The Tribal Police are already here and won't let anyone in the offices. They're escorting us down stairs to the conference room now. I gotta go." Charlotte hung up and Mateo stood at his desk, phone in hand bewildered. Just what should he do next?

******

Sheldon was busy helping with the morning rush at Witch's Brew. The team was working hard to keep up with the drink orders. He was just finishing up a caramel macchiato for a woman named Sherri. Her name was sharpied across the side of the cup at an angle in black cursive, and the 'I' was dotted with a heart. That's when his cell phone burred. He put the drink on the pickup counter and hollered 'caramel Macchiato for Sherri' then removed the cell from his back pocket and looked at the caller ID. It said blocked. Thinking it could be the police, he answered.

"Hello, this is Sheldon," in a half timid voice.

"Mr. Sheldon Goodman, correct?" came the voice from his cell phone.

"Yes, sir," he replied.

"I'm Special Agent Jacobs, and I've been working on the case you're involved in." Sheldon had never heard of a Special Agent Jacobs, but the call sounded official.

"We need you to come to the station right now. There are a few things we need cleared up," insisted Special Agent Jacobs.

Sheldon's heart began to race, "Well, I've been working with Officer Martinez and Detective Sullivan. Have you talked to them?"

"Mr. Goodman, this is not a request. Get in your car and get down here in the next five minutes or we will come there and arrest you."

"I don't get off until 2:30. Can I come then?"

"No, Mr. Goodman. Either you come on your own now, or we'll bring you in handcuffs."

"Okay, I'll leave right now," he replied, more fearful now than timid.

Sheldon's heart raced, as he notified Michelle, his manager that he had an emergency and needed to leave. He notified his crew then headed out the front door. He raced across the parking lot wondering why they were insisting he come immediately. He had done everything they had asked, and he had cooperated completely. He hadn't hidden anything from them, but still the officer on the phone said he would be arrested if he didn't leave immediately.

When Sheldon reached his driver door, he fished his car key from his pocket and inserted the key into the lock, and that's when it happened. Something, or someone, pushed him hard pinning him against his car knocking the air out of him. At the same time a heavy cloth was placed on his face covering his mouth, nose, and eyes. He took a deep breath to regain the air he had just lost but immediately felt light headed then dizzy. He reached toward his back pocket to grab for his cell thinking he might be able to call 911, but the cell slipped through his fingers and fell to the ground. As he lost consciousness, he could tell the cloth had a sweet minty odor to it.

******

Connie, Marisol, and Sarah were still asleep when Hortencia came to wake them. The three girls got up dressed and took turns using the bathroom. The other room would be cooking breakfast and they would clean up afterwards. As they cleaned up after breakfast, Connie thought this would be a good time to talk with Hortencia. She found her in the living room in front of an open bible.

Connie sat down next to Hortencia. "Hortencia. Could I ask you a question?"

"Yes, child. What is it?"

"The person that told me about the church and the home had a friend that came here. I was wondering if you could tell me what happened to her. I had promised to look her up."

"Really? Well, I'd be happy to. We've had so many success stories of women changing their lives around, finding a good man in the church, getting married, and becoming one of our church families. I'm sure it would be one of them. What's her name?"

"Cindy. Her name is Cindy. The friend told me she hasn't heard anything from her since coming to the home. Do you remember Cindy?"

Hortencia thought, then thought some more. Finally, she said, "Oh, Cindy had bigger problems than what we could help her with. She never finished the program."

"But what happened to her? I'm sure she didn't run away."

Hortencia became flustered and leaned away from Connie, then moved away from her on the couch. "You don't know about... anything about... Cindy. She DID run away."

"No, she didn't," Connie replied frankly. "She was sex trafficked wasn't she."

Hortencia gasped, "Goodness no, Connie. Where did you hear such a nasty rumor? It must have been Marisol... or Sarah?"

"I told you. I heard it from the person who told me about this place."

"I bet it was Sarah. She's such a gossip. Can't ever keep her mouth shut. Cindy's gone. Ran away. I don't know what happened to her after that."

Hortencia got up from the sofa and went to her bedroom. She closed and locked the door behind her. Minutes later the kitchen and dining room were clean from breakfast and everyone sat in the living room waiting for Hortencia to start morning devotions.

Hortencia finally appeared from her bedroom announcing, "Ladies, rather than have devotions here this morning, Pastor Eminis is going to hold a special devotional at the church. Brother Peter will be here to drive you there while Connie and I finish her paperwork. We'll join all of you there shortly."

All six ladies shot out of their chairs and beelined for their bedrooms. Connie stepped towards Hortencia saying, "Let me have the paperwork, and I'll get it filled out now."

"Connie, I don't have the paperwork. Peter is bringing it over."

Connie was certain Hortencia had the paperwork last night but didn't want to confront her again. She went to the bathroom, locked the door, turned on the faucet, then pulled her hidden cell phone and booted it up. She called Sheldon but there was no answer. She left a voicemail saying, "Emergency. Pick me up now at the home or the church, not sure where I'll be." Next, she texted him the same message before turning off her phone and heading back out to the living room.

Connie saw Marisol, Sarah, and Esther heading out the door while the two youngest, Sylvia and Monica, were still collecting items from their room. Both started towards the door as they finished. Peter had arrived and walked to the middle of the living room putting his arms around Vanessa. He was over six feet tall with long blonde hair. He wore an old straw cowboy hat that each side had been trained in a sharp curl. His sleeveless shirt exposed his brawny arms and revealed several tattoos; a marijuana leaf and a bare breasted woman were the two standouts. He must have gotten those before he had got religion, she thought.

"Vanessa, darlin', git yo self in the van, and I'll be there in two shakes," said Peter in his southern drawl. "Yes, sir," replied Vanessa then turned towards the door and the van that was parked in the driveway.

He spanked Vanessa on the butt as she turned, "Oh, Baby! I love dat ass."

Hortencia appeared from the kitchen. "Brother Peter, this is our newbie, Connie."

Peter reached out to shake Connie's hand, "Sista Connie. So glad y'all are here."

Connie reached out to shake his hand, but Peter grabbed her hand and pulled her to himself giving her a full-frontal hug. Connie was surprised and quickly pushed away.

Hortencia said, "Connie, I'm going to walk Peter out then I'll be back so we can get that paperwork filled out." Hortencia turned and walked out the door with Peter trailing behind her. Connie went to the couch and sat down hoping Sheldon had gotten her message and was on the way. When she heard the van start up and drive away, she breathed a sigh of relief knowing that Peter would be gone too. She didn't trust that guy. When she heard the front door close, Connie turned to see Peter standing in front of the door.

"Y'all wanna sit with me at the dining table so we can talk a bit," said Peter.

"I thought Hortencia was going to help me with the paperwork," Connie said, surprised. She didn't want to be left alone with this guy.

"Change of plans, Darlin'. Y'all come to the table now," he said as he moved towards the table but kept himself between the front door and Connie.

Connie got up from the sofa and moved cautiously towards the table and sat down facing the living room, the front door, and Peter. "Where's the paperwork?"

"Don't y'all mind 'bout dat paperwork, Darlin'," replied Peter. "Let's talk a bit."

"About what?" asked Connie, now feeling a bit nauseous. Last night's butterflies were nothing compared to what she was feeling now.

"What do y'all know 'bout Cindy, and why y'all askin' 'bout her?"

"I know she was here, and she disappeared." After she said this, she started to get angry. As she did, the butterflies settled and her head cleared. "I know she was sold for sex. I know the home, the church, and YOU are involved in sex trafficking!" Connie was angry now and felt determined. She stood up just as Peter stood. She stared him in the eye waiting for him to reply.

Peter's reply was a back hand to the side of her face. First, she saw white, but that quickly turned to black as she lost consciousness. Peter hit her so hard she was thrown back against her chair then to the floor sprawled out on the kitchen floor and the chair was sent crashing against the kitchen cabinets.

******

Joe met Mic at the front door to Desert Valley Cremations at 7:58 am.

"Morning Boss," greeted Mic.

"Good morning, Mic. Ready to learn the business?" replied Joe as he unlocked the door and walked into the office.

"Sure am."

For the next forty-five minutes, Joe oriented Mic to the business. As they were finishing up, Toni walked through the office door.

"Good morning, Mic. How's it going? Joe hasn't bored you to death yet, has he?"

"Hey! This is exciting stuff," said Joe. "He's on the edge of his seat right now." Mic smiled at Joe.

"You two gonna do the pick up at the hospital, right?"

"We're heading out now. You need anything while we're out?

"No, I don't think so. Mic, you started at the perfect time. Connie took a couple days off so that leaves us shorthanded."

"Great!" replied Mic.

"You know Connie's a very dedicated student, and sometimes she needs to take a day or two off for finals."

"Well good for her," said Mic, then cautiously, "but that's not why she's off."

"What do you mean?" she asked.

"Oh, maybe I wasn't supposed to say anything if she didn't already tell you."

Toni put her hands on her hips, stared at Mic, and said, "So, just what are you talking about? What do you think she's doing?"

"She's at the women's home doing undercover work," Mic stammered.

"Whaddaya mean, undercover work, and what women's home?"

"The church that runs the men's and women's homes are involved with sex trafficking, or so she think. Connie wanted to get proof of it then tell the police. She's pretending to be homeless and pregnant."

Joe looked from Mic to Toni, flabbergasted, but Toni roared, "You've gotta be kidding! What a stupid thing to do."

Joe, now realizing the potential peril, said, "If they're really trafficking then she could be in danger."

"But Sheldon's her contact. She's supposed to call him if anything happens."

"Sheldon! Whose idea was that?" Joe knew this was a bad idea.

Toni hurried back to the office and picked up her cell phone from the desk and tried to call Connie. Next, she tried to call Sheldon.

" Connie's phone is off. It went straight to voicemail. And Sheldon's phone went to voicemail after three rings."

"That's not right," said Mic. "Sheldon was supposed to be available all the time. He should pick up, but he's at work so maybe he didn't answer because you weren't Connie."

Joe knew they needed to act quickly and said. "Mic and I will go over to Witch's Brew and find Sheldon, then we'll go to the women's home and pick up Connie. Toni, you stay here, and we'll let you know what we find."

Toni disapproved of his plan and replied, "I don't think so, Joe. I'll lock up the office and be right behind you. And, Joe, it's a women's home, remember. Of the three of us, I'm the only one that's a woman, so I WILL be going."

Joe was not about to argue that point with Toni, and things might go more smoothly with Toni there. Joe and Mic jumped in the van and headed to Witch's Brew arriving just ahead of Toni. They pulled the van up next to Sheldon's car and got out. Joe headed for the front door of Witch's Brew, while Mic looked into Sheldon's car.

Joe returned from the coffee shop saying, "Sheldon's not there. He left a while ago on some emergency."

"Hey, Joe, come over here." Replied Mic as he stood with a cell phone in his hand. He held it up saying, "Look! It's Sheldon's cell. It was laying here on the ground."

"Are you sure it's his?"

"Let's see," said Mic as he pulled out his cell and called Sheldon. Sheldon's phone burred in Mic's hand. "Yup. It's Sheldon's."

They filled Toni in when she arrived then headed towards the women's home, Joe and Mic leading the way.

******

Connie became aware of her surroundings as regained consciousness. The right side of her face was swollen and throbbed in pain. The taste of metal was thick on her tongue and dried blood was on her cheek and lips. She licked at it trying to wash it off then opened her eyes to get her bearings. Her right eye wouldn't quite open from the swelling but she could see out of her left. She was in the storage room off the kitchen. The lamp was left on but the door was closed. Her wrists were cuffed to the bunk posts, each on opposite sides, and her ankles were tied to the bottom posts in a spread-eagle fashion. The duct tape over her mouth held in some kind of cloth keeping her from screaming or even breathing normally. The tape had been wrapped around her head and over the back of her hair. It pulled painfully on the stuck strands of hair when she turned her head. She could hear two voices coming from behind the closed door. It was Pastor Eminis and Peter.

"She's some kinda spy," accused Peter. "Look, I found this cell phone on her." Peter handed the cell to Freddie who examined it then handed it back to Peter.

"I've already set things up with Hector. He has room and will take her. But he's only paying us the minimum amount for her," said Freddie frowning.

"That asshole!" Peter was angry. "Y'all know anyone else we can sell her to?"

"Hector's our only option right now, Peter. We've gotta have her gone before the women return this afternoon."

"When's Mateo coming to pick her up?"

"I couldn't reach Mateo. You'll have to take her to Hector's place."

Peter scowled. The girl was trouble and there may be some repercussions from her just disappearing. But she knew too much. She had to go. "Now, I don't like this one iota, Freddie. Dat girl probably lied to y'all last night. People may come looking for her an dat would stir up a hornet's nest a trouble."

"But we've got to get rid of her now. We say she changed her mind and left. The women believe anything I tell them."

"Alright," replied Peter. "Y'all help me get her ready. Once she's out of it, we'll load her in the van."

"No, Peter. We can't have the church van anywhere near Hector's place. Let's get her ready, then you'll come back with your truck."

Peter grabbed his black Timberline backpack that had been laying by his feet, then they both went to the back room. Peter withdrew a hypodermic needle from the bag and laid it on the dresser. Next, he withdrew a vial containing heroine. He extracted the liquid using the hypodermic closely watching the liquid until it reached its mark then pushed out air from the needle until the clear liquid began to spirt from its hole.

Freddie held Connie while Peter took a small rubber hose from the backpack and wrapped it around Connie's arm. Once he found a vein, he said, "Now, Darlin, this won't hurt y'all one bit. Lie still for me 'til I finish."

She attempted to struggle, but Freddie held her fast. Peter stuck the needle in the vein and slowly pushed down on the plunger until all the liquid had been squeezed out of the needle and into Connie's arm. Connie went limp.

"Let's get going. I'll be at the church while you drop her off to Hector," said Freddie as he climbed off the bed.

******

When Joe, Mic, and Toni arrived at the women's home, the driveway was empty. Mic jumped out leading the way. Joe followed close behind while Toni pulled into the driveway and parked. Mic called out as he entered the house, but there was no answer. The house seemed empty.

"They're probably all at the church," said Mic. "Let's head on over there." Mic and Joe turned to go but Toni stopped them.

"No one's here," said Joe. "Mic says they'll be at the church."

"Did you check the house?" asked Toni.

"I called out," answered Mic, "but no one answered."

"Let's just check the house to be sure."

"You think she's bound and gagged in a closet somewhere?" Joe said.

"Let's just check," insisted Toni.

All three of them entered the house and started searching, looking in the bedrooms and bathrooms.

"Hey! Over here. I found her!" yelled Mic. When Joe and Toni got to the room, they found Mic kneeling over Connie. "They've drugged her. Probably getting ready to sell her to someone."

Mic motioned for Toni to come to him. "Take my place and try to keep her awake. We'll need to get her to the hospital as soon as we can get her free."

"Those sons of bitches!" said Joe. "I'd like to shoot 'em," as he began to untie her legs.

Toni replaced Mic and held Connie's head saying, "Baby, girl. Can you hear me?" Connie moaned. "Stay awake Connie. Stay with us. We'll have you free in a second." She tried to sound reassuring but fear for Connie overwhelmed her.

Joe had Connie's feet free and now he noticed the handcuffs. "Shit! How are we gonna get those cuffs off her?"

"No worries," replied Mic as he turned away from the dresser he's been searching. "I found a key."

******

As Peter got close to the women's home, he noticed a van and a car in the driveway. He drove his truck over the curb and parked in the yard blocking any passing neighbor's view of the front door. As he got out of his truck, he grabbed his black Colt Mustang .38 revolver that he kept under his seat. Peter held the pistol in his hand ready to use as he slowly and quietly opened the front door.

Joe and Toni had gotten Connie up and each put one of Connie's arms around their shoulders while they walked her out of the storage room and through the kitchen. She was groggy and her legs were rubbery, but with both of them on each side of her, Connie was able to maneuver with them as they led. Mic had left moments earlier to get a wet towel from the bathroom for Connie's face. Joe and Toni steered Connie through the kitchen and dining room but stopped in their tracks when they looked up towards the front door.

******

"What the fuck are y'all doin?" said the man in the straw cowboy hat as he pointed a pistol directly at them.

Peter moved to the middle of the living room with his Colt Mustang trained on Joe and Toni. The muscles in his forearm were taut and his index finger was threaded through the trigger guard and tensed on the trigger. Peter looked angry, and Joe and Toni froze. Peter took another step towards them

"Put her down," demanded Peter to Joe and Toni just as Mic stepped from the bedroom into the doorway with a wet hand towel. He stopped seeing Peter's back.

Peter heard Mic and quickly turned to see Mic staring at him. Mic lunged forward with all his might and grabbed the pistol with both hands as he dove. Peter fell backwards as Mic slammed into his body full force, cowboy hat flying across the room. They landed on the coffee table, Peter on his back and Mic on top of him, then onto the floor as the table exploded into a hundred wooden pieces and scattered around the room like a child's game of pickup sticks.

As they wrestled on the floor Joe and Toni stood frozen in their spots watching them; the gun nowhere to be seen. Then there was a loud pop that filled the room, and Mic rolled off Peter exposing the gun in Peter's hand. Mic held his stomach where blood was soaking his shirt and oozing between his fingers.

As Peter started to his feet, Joe let go of Connie and jumped over several pieces of wood that had only moments before been a coffee table. As he reached Peter, who was now standing, he grabbed the pistol and his hand with both hands and slipped his finger behind the trigger so it could not be pulled. Next, he moved Peter's gun hand up and away from Peter's body creating enough space to step between Peter's arm and body then around to Peter's back. He held on to Peter's hand and gun while he did this so Peter's arm followed Joe's path and ended up twisted behind Peter's own back. Peter let out a cry of pain as Joe twisted Peter's arm hard until he heard a snap. The pistol fell to the floor. Joe grabbed Peter's hair and pulled back while he kicked the back of Peter's knee which brought Peter immediately to the ground in a kneeling position. Finally, he slammed Peter's face into the carpet and held him there.

"Mic's shot," said Joe as he let Peter go. Peter rolled to his side holding the broken arm with one hand then curled up into a fetal position attempting to protect it. Joe picked up the wet hand towel that Mic had dropped, bent down to Mic, and put the towel over Mic's hands. "Here, Mic. Apply pressure to the wound and hold it."

Mic took the towel and held it tight against the wound. "Shit! This really hurts," he said through gritted teeth.

Joe turned to Peter, "Stay down. You hear me?" Peter moaned but didn't try to move.

"Toni, shoot the bastard if he tries to get up," as he handed the pistol to Toni who had by now helped Connie to a chair.

"I'll call the police," as she took the pistol from Joe's hand and trained it on Peter then dialed 911 on her cell phone.

Joe hurried to the van, got the gurney, loaded Mic onto it, and wheeled him back to the van. Next, he dragged Peter to the back room where they had found Connie and handcuffed him to the bunk.

"I'll drive Mic and Connie to the hospital," insisted Toni. "You stay here and talk to the police when they get here."

"That's what I was going to say," replied Joe. "I don't want you left alone with that guy."

27

Monday Afternoon

When Sheldon finally came to, he had no idea where he was or how long he had been out. It was like waking in the middle of a nightmare. Beads of sweat covered his face, and his shirt was soaked in perspiration.

His senses were muddled from the drug, and there was a fading pounding in the back of his head, but the fog cleared, and his eyes began to focus. Sheldon lay on a carpeted floor in room that looked like a study in a residential home. The blinds were drawn, but diffused light trickled through. He thought about Connie. Had she been caught and had Pastor Eminis instructed some of his men to kidnap him, and did he still have his phone? He rolled on his hips but couldn't feel the phone in his back pocket. It was gone. He tried to sit up but was held fast by clanging cuffs that were threaded through the iron framework of a desk. The desktop was made of a thick solid piece of glass and the whole desk weighed over five hundred pounds. The cuffs were tight around his wrists so he was unable to wiggle free.

Sheldon remembered when he and Mic were still in the men's home, and Mic had found a pair of handcuffs. He amazed everyone in the home by escaping from them. They would cuff his hands behind his back, and in just a few seconds, Mic was out of them. Everyone begged him to reveal the secret, but Mic said a true escape artist never reveals his secrets. One day, however, Mic decided to teach Sheldon his handcuff escape trick. He used a hidden paperclip to pick the lock. Sheldon, under Mic's instruction, tried for over an hour before he could get the cuffs to open. Sheldon got better with practice but was never been as good as Mic.

Sheldon reached to the desktop with his foot. Using the tip of his tennis shoe, he scooted a desk organizer to the edge then knocked it to the floor. Several pens, pencils, thumb tacks, staples, and paperclips fell across the floor. Next, he stretched out as far as he could moving his head towards the closest paperclip. He picked it up between his lips and moved back to where his hands were cuffed to the desk. He took the paperclip from his mouth with a cuffed hand and began working the clip into the shape he remembered Mic had taught him. Once he was satisfied the clip was in the correct shape, he inserted it in the lock and began to twist but no luck. He reshaped the clip and tried again, continuing to reshape the clip every few minutes. As he worked, he heard noises from the other side of the door. Others had come into the house. Now he worked franticly as he overheard their muffled conversation.

"Rossi and company will be here as soon as they finish at the reservation," Callaghan said as he sat down on the barstool at the island in the kitchen. Then he turned to Jacobs, "Have you heard from Martin?"

Jacobs was mid-forties, six feet tall and built like an athlete. His sandy blonde hair was cut conservatively but still long enough to wave over each ear. His blue eyes sparkled complimenting his pebbled chin. Jacobs carried a certain air about him that people naturally looked to as a leader. He came from money, and the males in his patriarchal family were leaders in business, and politics. Rules were directives that applied to others. And when laws got in the way of making money, they used their power to circumvent them. Jacobs learned early that he was intrinsically better than the rest of society. The family name represented wealth and power. But after graduating Harvard, he was approached by The Agency. Jacobs accepted their offer and spent the next five years traveling the world learning how to create human assets, organize, and run clandestine operations. After that, he moved to Langly, Virginia, and worked in the Central and South America Operations Departments. The youngest to attain such a high level at The Agency, Jacobs now managed those who did what he had been doing. This is where he met Doctor Reginald Martin who was working as an operative in South America and reported to Jacobs. Martin had left The Agency some time ago, but Jacobs couldn't resist getting involved with Martin's proposed operation at the reservation. He decided to run it "off books" which allowed him to take a significant cut in the profits for himself. Now he was here in the Coachella Valley personally terminating the fuck up that Martin had caused. He had to guarantee that any evidence trail would end here with Martin.

Callaghan and Jacobs wore gloves and coveralls were stuffed in a plastic garbage bag. Both men would don the coveralls later to ensure their clothes would stay evidence free.

"I did hear from Martin. He's on his way now. Mulder's with him," replied Jacobs then nodded to the door adjacent to the hallway. "Do you need to check on your little friend in the other room?"

"No. He should be out for a while, and he's handcuffed to that desk, so if he wakes up early, he won't be going anywhere. And we'd hear him moving around in there if he were awake."

Jacobs had been grooming Callaghan to become an Agency operative, mentoring him in their motive of operations which were quite different from the FBI. Satisfied with Callaghan's answer, Jacobs moved on with the termination details of the operation.

"Let's go over it one last time. What happens when Martin and Mulder get here? Tell me exactly as you understand it." Jacobs wanted to make sure Callaghan and he were on the same page, and the operation would go like clockwork.

"I have Martin move to the bar to examine the evidence we'll be planting to lead the investigation away from us. He can sit on a barstool or stand at the bar. Either is acceptable. Mulder will move to the hallway. Once they're in place, Mulder will get Martin's attention. When Martin turns, Mulder will shoot him with the weapon we will later plant on the kid. Next, you and I will put on our coveralls then get the kid from the other room. We bring him into the hallway and hold him. Mulder will shoot the kid using Martin's gun from where Martin's body is. Then Mulder puts the gun he used to shoot Martin into the kid's hand and makes two random shots towards the kitchen area. He'll put Martin's weapon into Martin's hand and take one random shot towards the hallway where the kid's body is. While Mulder's doing that, I clean up the study then we remove our coveralls, put them into the garbage bag, and give it to Mulder. You will also leave the house the same time as Mulder. Once he's gone, I call it in which will be just about the time Rossi and company arrive."

"Very good," Jacobs frowned, "but you forgot one thing? What is it?"

Callaghan thought. "I put the kid's fingerprints on the letter, wipe his spit on it, then put it in his pocket."

The letter was the evidence that would link the shooting to the motive. It was a hand written letter explaining that Doc Martin refused to hire Sheldon for the position Mateo had promised him. It was also written in Mateo's hand, not that Mateo had actually written it. Jacobs used The Agency's resources to get this letter written in what looked exactly like Mateo's own hand. It had been folded and crumpled to look like Sheldon had agonized over it for some time before coming to Doc's home and murdering him. Sheldon's saliva and prints would put his DNA on it giving more physical evidence to support this theory.

Jacobs thought for a moment then smiled. "Perfect! We follow the plan and it'll go off without a hitch."

Callaghan asked, "And Mulder's got the plan down?"

"Don't worry about Mulder. I've worked with him a number of times, and he's meticulous in his planning and execution. He'll be alright."

Callaghan furrowed his brow. He had another question but hesitated to ask.

"You know, I was just thinking about Martin and wondering if there was another option other than offing him. He was an accomplished agent in South America and distinguished among his peers. It just doesn't seem right to me. After all, Martin was part of The Agency."

Callaghan was an FBI special agent from the Chicago field office before Jacobs approached him to work clandestine operations on U.S. soil. Jacobs had taken a personal interest in him some time ago and had mentored him in the ways of the Agency which were quite different from the FBI. He even counseled him through his divorce. Jacobs was about the best friend he had in all the world, and he knew it would only be a matter of time before he moved from the FBI to the Agency. This, however, was the first time they were planning to kill someone. The moral and professional conflict tore at him but the mystery, glamour, and excitement of The Agency drew him like the Sirens of Anthemoessa calling to Odysseus.

Jacobs stared out the slider at the pool and lush yard that surrounded it as he thought. The view reminded him of the opulent lifestyle Martin was living because of his involvement with The Agency. He turned back towards Callaghan deciding to make this a learning opportunity.

"I know how you feel, Callaghan. I feel the same way too, but the number one priority is to protect The Agency at all costs. Operations on U.S. soil are no different than out of country operations. They must be clandestine and terminating an operation that's gone off the rails has to be done in such a way that nothing with lead back to us."

Jacobs paused for a few seconds then continued. "Martin is an asset, nothing more. When he retired, he got his pension and chose to go out to pasture. Then he got bored and wanted back in on the action and the money he'd make. If you look at it from his perspective, he only wants to use The Agency, and us, to serve himself. You know the routine. We use our assets to our benefit, and if we need to, cut them loose at the end of the operation."

Jacobs watched Callaghan as he spoke and thought he still needed more encouragement. "You know, Martin's the reason this whole operation went south. He's selling guns to the cartels and the local gangs. He's skimming money from our operations, and he thought we'd never find out. He knows exactly what happens to assets when they pull this shit. It'll be no surprise to him and guarantees nothing gets traced back to The Agency." Jacobs shook his head, "And he did much worse in South America when he worked for me down there. He was a cold-hearted motherfucker."

Now Jacobs spoke like a counselor to a client. "And how do you think Martin would want to go out anyway? Like an old man in a nursing home shitting in his diaper, not even able to remember his name, or in a blaze of glory, in the middle of an operation with guns blazing and explosives detonating that history will remember for generations? No, he'd want to end it like he lived it. I think we're giving him what he wants, what he asked for."

Jacobs studied Callaghan's eyes and his posture. He knew Callaghan had acquiesced. "Hey, go check on your kid."

Callaghan stood and crossed the white marble tile but stopped at the door to the study. Something seemed off. He opened the door then froze where he stood, "Shit! He's gone."

"What do you mean," emphasizing the next two words, "he's gone?" Jacobs' face turned red as he strode to the study door and stood next to Callaghan peering in. They saw the open handcuffs on the floor by the desk. One window shade was up, the window stood open, and the was screen cut.

Jacobs calmed himself. He knew that you don't get emotional when an operation ran into a complication. This, however, was a fucking disaster. He thought for a moment, then turned to Callaghan, "Go to my car and get a black leather case from the trunk. It'll be on the left side all the way in back." Callaghan didn't respond but turned and headed to the front door.

Jacobs took his cell phone from his pocket and texted Mulder. "Change of plans. We'll do Columbia Kingpin maneuver." Then he took the garbage bag from its hiding place and put on his coveralls, mask, shoe coverings, and hair net.

When Callaghan returned, he handed Jacobs the black leather case. He was surprised Jacobs was already dressed for the shooting. "What's happening?" he asked.

"Get into your things now," commanded Jacobs as he opened the case and took out its contents. "Do you know what 'Columbia Kingpin' is?"

"No. What is it?"

"It's our alternative termination. Martin actually developed it when I first started supervising the South American Department." Jacobs opened the black leather case and removed a small bottle of clear liquid then a syringe. He filled it with the liquid from the bottle and sat the syringe on the counter. Then he removed a rag and a larger bottle filled with another liquid. Callaghan immediately recognized it as chloroform. He had used the same stuff when he kidnapped Sheldon earlier.

Callaghan watched Jacobs as he filled the syringe. "What's in the syringe?"

"It's Potassium chloride. It's the best thing to use in this kind of situation because it's absorbed by the body, practically undetectable, and causes an instant heart attack. Unless a coroner's looking for it, it'll never be found."

"Mulder and Martin will come through the front door. You will be on the hinge side of the door, and I will be just behind you with this." He held up the rag and the larger bottle of liquid.

You will grab and restrain Martin on your side while Mulder does the same on the other side. I will hold this over his face until he's unconscious. Next, you'll remove his left shoe, remember, the left shoe, and sock. Then I'll inject him between the toes with the syringe. Mulder will monitor his heart rate until he's dead. After that, you'll put the sock and shoe back on his foot. Remembering to tie it facing away from the foot, not looking at it. The rest of it will be the same. By the way, that kid is a loose end that you'll need to take care of once we're done here. Now repeat it to me."

Jacobs and Callaghan rehearsed the mauver three times before Jacobs was confident it would go smoothly.

******

Sheldon ran fast on the hard flat sand of the flood control channel the city had installed years ago to protect the homes that were built by the San Jacinto mountains and ultimately the city of Palm Springs. His heart pounded in his head, and his chest heaved. His legs ached and knots were beginning to form in his muscles.

Sheldon had listened enough of the conversation to know the men on the other side of the door planned to kill him. When the handcuffs finally opened, he jumped out the window ran around the pool and down the south side of the property between the white brick wall and a long row of date trees. Once he reached the back of the property, he shimmied over the wall and dropped onto large boulders that lined the flood channel to protect the estates, from erosion. He gingerly climbed around and between these mammoth rocks until he was able to drop down on the flat channel. To his left, the boulders continued down the edge of the flood channel without a break. Behind the boulders was a solid cinderblock wall that marked the end of property lines of million-dollar estates.

Sheldon initially ran in the flood channel closest to the mountains, running through the ruts, climbing over branches and limbs. He chose the far side because there were plants that provided concealment, and if anyone was chasing him, there was cover where he could hide. Trying to escape on this side of the channel, however, was like running through an obstacle course. He fell several times, tripped on half buried limbs and dead palm trees that had been washed into the channel. He finally moved to the other side of the channel where the sand was flat and hard. There he could make time, but would be easily seen by anyone looking for him. The channel wound its way between the mountains and the estates until it reached downtown Palm Springs where it went underground. There would be exits the leading to the streets of the city.

He finally exited the channel at the Cactus to the Clouds Trailhead walking as quickly as he could through the downtown area and into the Welwood Murray Memorial Library, a historical building that was still part of the library system. Sheldon knew there would be computers and internet access where he could look up phone numbers, but who should he call? The only number he had memorized Connie's. He could call 911 or the sheriff's office, but just what would he say? He decided to get the number for the crematory, and call Toni. Then his mind went back to Connie. He was supposed to be her contact, her handler, her protection. Now he felt guilty. He had let her down. But what was the worst that could happen? After all they were church people and he had lived with then for 4 years.

He hurried through the front glass double doors and found his way to a computer terminal near the back. After looking up the phone number he went to the front counter and asked to use the phone. After three rings he heard Toni's voice. "Coachella Valley Cremations. This is Toni. How may I help you?"

"Toni, it's Sheldon."

******

Maria sat in the chair next to Connie's hospital bed and held her hand while caressing her arm with the other. Toni had called Maria after she arrived at Desert Regional Medical Center with Connie and Mic. Connie's arm was tethered to an IV that slowly dripped clear liquid into a clear collection bulb then traveled through the plastic tubing and into her arm. She was still groggy from the effects of the heroine did her best to tell Maria her tale. She had not realized there was a fight and Mic had been shot until her mom updated her.

Once Connie had finished, Maria said, "Oh, Mi Hija. Thank God you're safe. You could have been killed!" Maria stood and hugged her daughter like she was a little girl. "I don't know what's wrong with the police. It's their job, and they've done nothing! Thank God for good people like Toni and Joe, and Mic."

"Mom, but they didn't have any evidence to investigate. That's why I did it."

Maria sat upright and leaned forward in her chair, then corrected her daughter. "That's not so, Mi Hija. I talked with Officer Martinez, and he told me they were going to investigate, but he lied to me."

Connie, surprised, "What do you mean? When did you talk with him?"

"I talked to him last week right after you told me what happened. They did nothing, and you were almost killed!"

Now, frustrated, Connie replied, "And you didn't tell me? Why not?"

"The officer asked me not to say anything so I didn't. I shouldn't have trusted him. I should have reported it myself and told you too. Oh, Mi Hija, it's all gonna be okay now. You're safe, and the police had better do their job now, or I'll...." but stopped mid thought. She grabbed Connie's hand again and squeezed firmly while daubing a tear with her free hand. "Oh, Mi Hija, I could have lost you!"

******

Toni sat in a surgery waiting room chair but kept one eye on the hallway expecting to see Joe any moment. Sitting alone without Joe, Toni felt small and powerless. This was so opposite from how she normally felt, and she desperately wanted Joe to be there with her. As she pondered what might be happening with Joe, the surgery doors opened, and a doctor stepped into the waiting room.

"I'm Doctor Goldstein. Are you Toni Conti, the one who brought in Mr. Montague?"

"You mean, Mic, Mic Montague, right? He goes by Mic. I don't know anyone who calls him Mr. Montague. It's okay. You can call him Mic," said Toni, prattling on nervously.

"Yes, Mic Montague," replied Dr. Goldstein.

"Yes, I brought him in. How is he? Is he out of surgery now? Is he gonna be okay? He wasn't hurt too badly, was he? Is he being taken to a room, and when can I see him?" Toni sounded like an overly emotional teenager.

"I'm sorry," replied Dr. Goldstein in a slow and calm manner. "How do you know Mic?"

"Oh, Mic works for us. He was an orphan and has no family. We're the closest thing to family he has so you can talk to me just like you're talking with family. He's really a great kid. Now what's going on with him?" Toni, was anxious but realized she was chattering. She thought, Calm down girl. Act professional.

"Ms. Conti, Mic is a very lucky young man. The bullet passed through his abdomen piercing his intestine before exiting between his ribs. No bones were hit and no other major organs or arteries were damaged. We went in and repaired the intestine and sutured the entrance and exit wounds. He's in recovery right now and will be moved to a room in about a half hour. He'll need to stay here at the hospital for a day or two before he's ready to go home."

"Thank God," Toni said, with a sigh of relief. She felt more like herself.

"You should be able to check at the information booth down stairs in about thirty minutes to get his room number."

Toni grasped Dr. Goldstein's hand, shaking it vigorously, and said, "Thank you, Doctor. Thank you so much."

She paused, still holding the doctor's hand. After several moments she realized the doctor wanted to leave, and she released his hand, embarrassed. Toni's cell rang so she rummaged through her purse and found it. The caller ID said Murray Memorial Library.

******

When Toni answered the call, the voice on the other end said, "Toni, it's Sheldon."

"Sheldon! Where are you, and what happened to you?"

"It's a long story, but I'm okay now, I think I am anyway. I'm worried about Connie. Have you heard from her?"

"We know all about what you two planned. Just what were you thinking? No, you didn't think, and that was the problem. She's here at Desert Regional, and Mic's here too. The three of you had no business doing what you did."

Toni sounded like a mother scolding her adolescent son. The scolding made Sheldon begin to panic. Feelings of guilt began to envelop him, and the word, fuck-up, began to swim somewhere in his head.

"What are they doing there? What happened, and are they okay?" Then he said, "The hospital's not far. I'll be there in a few minutes."

"I'll fill you in when you get here. I'll be in Mic's room. Connie's mom's here and is with her."

28

Monday Afternoon & Evening

When Sheldon rushed into Mic's room, Toni sat in a chair by the bed. Mic was tethered to an IV that strung over the aluminum bed railing. There were several other wires that connected Mic to other electronic equipment that kept a steady rhythmic beat that mirrored green scales on output monitors mounted to the wall over the bed. Their sensor ends disappeared somewhere under Mic's gown. He was pale and breathed heavy as he slept under sedation, and bandages wrapped his stomach.

Sheldon froze, wide eyed from the shock of seeing Mic in this condition. Toni spent the next few minutes updating Sheldon about their rescue of Connie and how Mic was a hero. If it weren't for him, she and Joe might have been killed and who knows what would have become of Connie..

Finally, Toni fished out Sheldon's phone from her purse and handed it to him. "Now, Sheldon, just what happened to you?"

He took his phone and looked at the number of missed calls and text messages, not saying a word. Sheldon felt numb, his experience was only now beginning to affect his emotions. Everything became surreal, Mic lying in the hospital bed, Toni staring at him, even his kidnapping and escape. He wondered if all this was his fault because he wasn't there for Connie. He looked up at Toni, now feeling alone and afraid. He started to speak, but Officer Mando Martinez and Detective Bill Sullivan walked in through the open door. Officer Martinez closed it behind them.

Toni exclaimed, "Gentlemen. It's about time you showed up. Is Joe with you?"

"No, he's not," answered Detective Sullivan.

"Where is he? Is he on his way up?"

"No, Mrs. Conti. He's not. We need to ask you some questions about what happened."

"Okay, but let's wait for Joe to get here."

Detective Sullivan wrinkled his brow. "He won't be coming, and we want your statement. We already have his."

"What do you mean he's not coming? Where is he?" Toni, concerned.

"Toni, we have him down at the station right now. He'll be there while we sort this thing out," stated Mando, frankly.

"There's nothing to sort out! We came to rescue Connie, and some guy with a cowboy hat tried to stop us and shot Mic. I'm sure he's the one who drugged Connie too. They're running a sex trafficking ring out of that house. There's nothing to sort out!" Toni was adamant.

Detective Sullivan responded in a calm even voice. "This guy with the cowboy hat, Mr. Peter Anderson, says he's with the church. He says that all of you broke into the home, and he was just protecting the church's property. He says that Connie is a drug addict that moved in on Sunday, and she refused to go with the other women this morning so she could get high. He also stated that Mic had brought the gun, and was shot when he tried to wrestle it away from him. We're currently holding him and Mr. Conti at the police station while we figure out just what happened."

As Sheldon listened, he blamed himself for all of this trouble and wanted to crawl from the room.

Toni was appalled, "How could anyone believe a crazy story like that! No, The Cowboy brought the gun, and Mic was wrestling with him when he got shot. We were rescuing Connie, who is no drug addict, when The Cowboy stopped us with his gun. Mic saved our life." She paused then added, "And being a confidential informant should mean you'd believe us over him."

Officer Mando Martinez looked at Detective Bill Sullivan, but Sullivan didn't miss a beat, and responded, "You were a CI on a different case, and it was only limited for a short time. You do not have that status now."

Toni made a face at Detective Sullivan crinkling her nose and lowering her brow. "That's about the stupidest thing I've heard today, next to the crazy story The Cowboy told you."

Toni turned towards Officer Martinez acting like Detective Sullivan was not in the room, "Mando, you know I'm telling the truth. You know you can trust me, but your partner's acting like I'm a total stranger that has to prove my honesty and integrity. You know I've already done that, but he's gonna take the word of a sex trafficker over me? I'm not some convict or jailbird snitch. This is bullshit!"

Sullivan took a deep breath but kept quiet. Mando said, "Toni, we have to do a fair and impartial investigation. It's our job. Yes, we believe you, but we've also got to collect evidence that backs up your story. And we've got to do it in such a way that we're not accused of partiality. No one's been charged with anything yet. We're just keeping Joe and this cowboy out of the way while we do our job. We don't want either of them contacting anyone that might hurt the investigation. And since we're holding The Cowboy, we need to hold Joe."

Toni, beginning to calm, "For how long?"

Detective Sullivan answered, "As long as it takes to complete some initial interviews. After that, I think we'll be able to release him."

They spent the next hour interviewing Toni and Sheldon separately then talked with Mic who was finally awake. Neither officer was prepared for what Sheldon told them about the kidnapping and escape from a Las Palmas estate and through the flood channels. They a great many questions him, but he was only able to answer a few of them.

******

As Sheldon rode the elevator to Connie's floor, he blamed himself for all the trouble because he wasn't able to help Connie. If he had not been taken, then both Mic and Connie would be okay and definitely not in the hospital.

He found Connie's room and stopped at the door. If he went in, he would have to face his failure, and face it with someone he cared about, Connie. He had always found it easier to walk away when he screwed up. That's what he had done so many times in the past. The guilt made him feel so worthless that he had refused to face it. Maybe, if he went in and faced Connie, she might forgive him, and maybe he wouldn't feel quite so guilty about everything. But if he ran away, he could stuff all of the emotions and thoughts away, put them into his mind's closet that held all of his other failures. As long as that door stayed shut, he wouldn't need to deal with it. But the desire to see Connie was more powerful than the fear of her knowing he was the cause of all this trouble, so he slowly opened the door.

If Sheldon's experience had happened to anyone else, he would consider them not only brave, but some kind of a hero. And why not? Having been drugged and kidnapped then making a heroic escape just before being murdered and getting away in complete secrecy is the stuff that real heroes are made of. But what had he really done? Picked a lock on a pair of handcuffs, a parlor room trick. He had jumped out a window, climbed over a wall, and finally took a little run down a flood channel. All of them mundane, meaningless actions, and all while he was scared, scared shitless. Maybe he had misunderstood what was being discussed in the other side of that door. Maybe his life was not in any real danger. After all, he didn't know who those people were or why they might want to kill him, and he only heard snippets of the conversation. Maybe he had gotten everything confused, jumbled up in his head. Being scared shitless does that. Real heroes are brave. They don't get scared.

******

"What do you make of this kid's story, Bill?" asked Mando.

"I think he's telling the truth, as he understands it anyway. And I'll bet it has something to do with the murders and the reservation, not the sex trafficking."

"That's what I thought."

Sullivan pulled out his cell phone from his breast pocket. "I'm gonna give Special Agent Rossi a call. They're supposed to be searching the reservation today, so he may know something."

He found Rossi in his contacts list and pressed send putting it on speaker so both men could hear the conversation.

"Sullivan, what do you need?" said Rossi, sounding irritated when he answered the call.

"You in your car?"

"Yup, I've got you on speaker. Why did you call?"

"Did you finish searching at the reservation?" asked Sullivan.

"Yup, we did."

"Did you find anything important to the case?"

Rossi hesitated, "Ah... well Bill, we'll need some time to go through everything before we have any answers."

Mando mouthed to Bill, "He's stalling."

"You headed back to the office now?" Sullivan to Rossi.

"No, I'm actually headed to the Las Palmas area in Palm Springs."

Mando and Bill looked at each other, eyes wide. "What's happening there?" asked Sullivan as casually as he could.

"We're doing a search on Dr. Reginald Martin's home. I'm meeting Callaghan there."

"I see," replied Sullivan, then added, "Can you have Callaghan give me a call? I've got some information that may be relevant to your search of his home."

"Oh, yea. What's that?" Rossi's voice now aggressive.

"Just tell Callaghan to call me when you get there."

Rossi annoyed, "You can't give me the information now? What am I, chopped liver? I share everything with you, and you won't give me shit! Great job, Sullivan, making this a joint investigation."

"Just have Callaghan call me." Sullivan ended the call.

"I don't think we'll get anything else from the FBI, or at least from Rossi," Sullivan thinking out loud.

"I think it's coming from Callaghan. Rossi does whatever he says."

Bill lowered his eyebrows and clenched his jaw in frustration. "You may be right. Still, we have a triple homicide to solve and what looks like a sex trafficking ring to stop."

Mando looked at his notes, "We should finish up here then head over to the church. Connie Asghar is two floors down. You ready to go?"

Sullivan nodded towards the door. "Let's go."

******

Maria had been dozing and was startled when Sheldon appeared at the door of Connie's hospital room.

"Sheldon!" Maria sat up in her chair. She blamed the police for her daughter's situation, but was unsure about Sheldon. She finally said with some attitude, "Connie, Sheldon's here."

Connie opened her eyes and looked towards the door. Her auburn hair had been pulled back into a ponytail and held in place by a purple scrunchy. Her face was free of makeup and her normally dark complexion seemed more ashen, but her eyes sparkled when she saw Sheldon at the door.

"Sheldon, where you been? Are you okay?"

Sheldon stood at the door, shoulders stooped and rounded. He had heard the tone in Maria's voice. "Yea, I'm okay. I'm so sorry I wasn't there."

"It's okay, Sheldon." Connie sounded earnest. She was concerned for him.

"Come over here," Connie pointed to Maria's chair. "Talk to me."

Maria got up and started towards the door, and Sheldon. "You two talk. I'm gonna get something to eat in the cafeteria," and hurried out. Sheldon trudged to the empty chair and sat down. He sensed the warmth of Maria's body in the chair and felt like he was intruding, an outsider.

"Sheldon, give me your hand."

He raised his hand to the bed where Connie's outstretched arm waited through the metal railing. She took his hand and pulled it back through the railing, resting it on that side of her bed. Another wave of guilt swept through him, and he felt his eyes began to moisten.

"I'm sorry, Connie. It's all my fault for not being there for you. I really messed things up." He said, still looking down. He just couldn't look at her.

"Sheldon, look at me. It's not your fault. There wasn't enough time to get there after I texted you. It all happened so fast. I didn't have time to hardly think. Why are you feeling so guilty? What happened to you anyway?"

He told Connie his story starting with the phone call from the police and ending with his arrival at the hospital. Once he finished, he realized the guilt that had almost paralyzed him was gone. Connie sat and listened, squeezing his hand each time the story progressed to a new segment. Now, Connie shared her story with Sheldon. Then they both sat in silence gazing at each other, each amazed at the courageousness of the other, each in awe at what the other had faced, each having a new respect for the bravery the other had displayed. Sheldon couldn't quite comprehend it all, but knew this moment was magical in some sense, for him. He didn't know how far the impact of it all might change his life, but he knew it was life changing.

******

"Mr. Goodman, we meet again," came Officer Martinez's voice from the open door. Sheldon and Connie looked up, stirring from their shared reverie.

"We've come to get a statement from Ms. Asghar," Detective Sullivan stated as both men entered the room. "Mr. Goodman, we'll need you to leave while we interview her, but stay outside. We may want to ask you some questions once we're done."

Sheldon squeezed Connie's hand then exited the room.

As they were finishing up their interview, Maria walked through the door of Connie's room. "Well, it's about time the police showed up!" The two officers turned and saw Maria standing in the doorway.

"Maria, we're just finishing up our interview with your daughter," said Mando. "She's a very brave young lady."

"Yes, she is!" Maria's face began to redden. "And no thanks to any of you. Officer Martinez, I told you about this thing with the church over a week ago. And you promised the police would handle it. Now my daughter was almost killed because you did nothing about it at all!"

Officer Mando Martinez was surprised. He had filed the complaint, but it would take some time for it to be assigned to a detective and an investigation would need to be conducted before any arrests could be made. They couldn't do anything solely on her and her daughter's word.

"Mrs. Asghar, an investigation takes time. That's what we're doing now," replied Detective Sullivan. "We can't go out and arrest someone from you or your daughter's complaint. And what she did was very dangerous. She should have waited for us to investigate."

"Yes, it was dangerous!" Maria, now red faced. She put her finger on Officer Martinez's chest saying, "Because you did nothing about it! Your cars say that you serve and protect, but you did nothing to serve and protect my daughter."

"Mom!" Connie said. "They're doing their job. They're investigating. Let them do their job. It's okay. Calm down. Come sit by me and hold my hand."

Maria glared at the two officers with contempt. She said nothing more but walked to the chair, sat down, and grabbed her daughter's hand with one hand as she stroked her arm with her other. "Oh, Mi Hija. I'm just so worried about you."

******

Officer Martinez and Detective Sullivan walked out of the room and headed down the hall towards the elevator.

"We should go to the church next. We can interview the pastor and any of the women from the home," directed Bill.

Mando said, "And especially the den mother, Hortencia, and the two women she mentioned that were her roommates for the one night she was there. What were their names again?"

"Sarah and Marisol," replied Bill.

As they reached their car, Detective Sullivan's phone burred. He pulled it from his jacket pocket and looked at the caller ID. It was a blocked number. "Maybe this is Callaghan," to Martinez as he answered the call and put it on speaker.

"Detective Sullivan," he said, holding the phone in front of him.

"Bill, this is Cliff. Rossi tells me you have some information regarding our search of Dr. Martin's home here in the Las Palmas area."

"Well, we may have. It's just that we've come across a coincidence that may have a connection."

"Just what is it?" Callaghan asked.

"First, I wanted to know if you found anything from your search of the reservation."

"Bill, the whole search ended up being an exercise in futility. Everything had been cleaned out long before we got there. We're gonna go through some materials we confiscated but I'm not expecting to find much. I'll keep you posted on anything that may be of value to the case."

"Thanks, Cliff. I appreciate that."

"So, Bill, just what do you have for me?"

"You know that kid, Sheldon Goodman? He's been connected to this case from almost the beginning."

"Yup," replied Callaghan, "I've seen his name in the notes. What about him?"

"It seems he was kidnapped today and taken to an estate in the Las Palmas area. He says he heard some conversation about him being killed and used as a fall guy for a murder. He escaped and ended up at the local hospital. I'll have a detailed transcript of our interview by tomorrow afternoon, but that's the gist of his story."

"Hmmm, did he recognize any of the people?"

"He didn't actually see anyone but heard part of a conversation through the door of a room he was locked in."

"Well, Bill, then did he recognize any of the voices?"

"No, he said he didn't. Cliff, you don't have anyone murdered at Doctor Martin's home, do you?"

"How did the Goodman kid say they were supposed to be murdered?"

"He said they were supposed to be shot."

"No, no shooting victims here," replied Callaghan.

"Okay," Sullivan thought something wasn't quite right. "Any dead people there? Deceased by any means?"

"Well, Bill, since you ask, it seems Dr. Reginald Martin passed from what looks like a heart attack. We won't know for sure until an autopsy's done, but the man was under terrible stress, and he was in bad health. He was the CEO of the reservation's businesses and responsible for them. If anyone started illegal activities at the reservation like this Mateo Rivera security guy, he'd be ultimately responsible. He knew he could lose his job and maybe even his freedom. All the stress he was under from the murders and the investigation may simply have been more than he could take. And his heart just gave out."

Sullivan hesitated processing what Callaghan had just said then looked at Mando who was already looking back at Bill, disbelief in his eyes.

"Did you and Dr. Martin arrive together at the estate?"

"No, Bill. Once we started at the reservation, Dr. Martin left for the estate. I left before Rossi who was overseeing the search. When I got here, Dr. Martin had expired, lying in the middle of the entry. He must have just closed the front door, took four or five steps then collapsed and died right there on the floor. Hey, I may need to talk with that kid. Ah, Sheldon Goodman, right?"

"Yup, that's his name."

"Can you give me his address now? I don't want to go all the way back to the office in Riverside to find it."

Mando looked at Bill. It was a reasonable request from a law enforcement officer, from an FBI agent. It shouldn't be second guessed."

"Cliff, I don't have that information with me right now," said Bill, "and we're not going to be back to the office for some time."

There was a long pause before Callaghan spoke again, "That's okay, Bill. I probably won't need to see him anyway." Callaghan abruptly ended the call.

*****

Sheldon pulled into his trailer park and parked in his usual spot. It was evening and the sun had already set behind the San Gorgonio Mountain Range on the west side of the valley. The sky, however, was still illuminated by the red, orange, and violet hues that spilled over the tops of the range in its attempts to hide the setting sun. It had played peek-a-boo with him for the last half hour, peering between the tallest peaks as he rode with Toni back to Witch's Brew parking lot to retrieve his car. She told him Joe had been released, but they were still holding The Cowboy.

He was tired, but knowing Connie was safe and would be released tomorrow comforted him. He had stayed with Connie as long as he could until the nurses told him visiting hours were over and he'd have to go.

Sheldon unlocked his trailer, turned on the AC unit, grabbed a water bottle from his little refrigerator then went back outside with a small blanket laying it on the metal steps. He sat down, twisted the cap on the bottle until the plastic seal broke, then completely removed the cap and took a long refreshing drink from the bottle. Next, he held it to the side of his head. The cool water was refreshing as the condensation dripped down the side of his face.

As he sat, he noticed a man walking from the road into the alley of the park. He thought it strange the man was wearing a sport jacket over an open button-down shirt. As he came up the alley, the man looked directly at Sheldon.

"Hello," said the man as he extended a hand towards Sheldon. "I'm FBI Special Agent Cliff Callaghan. You are Mr. Sheldon Goodman, right?"

"Hi," said Sheldon apprehensive, but stood and reached out to shake the man's hand. Sheldon noticed beads of sweat on each side of the man's face. He must not have parked very close by.

"I wanted to talk with you about your experience today." Callaghan said, sounding calm, warm, and trusting.

"I already talked to the police. They have everything. Can't you get it from them?"

"I've already talked with them, but I've got a few more questions that they couldn't answer. Could we go inside for a few minutes? It won't take long."

"It's too hot in there right now. It'll be a half hour before it cools off enough to tolerate. Can we just talk out here?"

Callaghan hesitated. "Yes, I guess we can." He immediately proceeded to his questions. "Did you or do you know who abducted you today? Did you hear his voice or see him at all?'

"No, I didn't see anyone or hear anyone. All I know is someone came up behind me and held a cloth with something on it over my nose that knocked me out."

"Okay, that's good. Do you know who owned the home you were taken to or do you know its specific location?"

"I just know it was in the Las Palmas area. I might be able to find it if I walked back up the flood channel, but all the homes look the same so I'm not sure. Sorry."

"That's okay," Callaghan replied. "What about the two voices you heard through the door? Did you recognize them? Could you identify them if you ever heard them again?"

"No, I didn't recognize them, and I only heard parts of what they were saying. Everything was muffled cuz it was through a door. I couldn't really tell how they sounded. And I don't think I could recognize their voices if I ever heard them again. Sorry. I'm not very helpful, am I?" Sheldon had not recognized Callaghan's voice.

"No, you're doing fine. Hey, could I get a water from you? I'm not used to the heat out here in the desert."

"Sure," Sheldon turned and went back to the trailer door, and Callaghan followed close behind shutting the door behind him. He placed his right hand on the grip of his handgun that was nestled in its shoulder holster concealed underneath his sport coat. He clicked off the safety but held the weapon in place. He looked at Sheldon who had retrieved the water bottle from the refrigerator and had turned to hand him the water.

"See, I told you it was really hot in here. We should go back outside," said Sheldon, continuing to hold out the bottle waiting for the FBI Special Agent to take it from him.

Callaghan stood stationary, frozen for a moment, contemplating his next move. Then clicking the safety back on, he released his weapon, reached out and took the bottle. "Thank you. Yes, it is hot in here." He turned, opened the door and walked down the metal steps. Without looking back, said, "I'll be on my way. Good luck with everything."

Sheldon sat back down on the steps and watched the man walk away.

29

The Following Week

Mateo opened the slider and stepped out onto the cement deck that surrounded his pool. His two dogs followed him first peeing in the planters then sniffing around the pool before settling down on the dog beds he had placed on opposite sides of the slider.

The valley radiated a sense of sereneness as the night overtook the dusk that penetrated the very soul. Lights from businesses and residences shown on the valley floor breaking up the regular patterns of the city's street lights. The interstate was a long familiar snake of white and red splitting the valley between north and south. The all-seeing tram light on the top of the San Jacinto mountains surveyed the valley below, always watching but never revealing the secrets it learned.

The sky was a deep blue blanket as the stars twinkled in its foreground. Each one, as it twinkled, reminded Mateo of a life's blessing, an answered prayer, a moment in time where the gods smiled on him. He was about to close a deal with the Riverside County Sheriff's Office where he would turn state's evidence and eliminate the most serious charges, reducing his sentence to probation. Another reminded him of the guaranteed witness protection program for both him and Charlotte. The next reminded him of all the money he had in hidden bank accounts they would live on until it was safe to return. But the biggest star, the brightest one in the night sky, was the planet Venus. It reminded him of Charlotte.

Mateo took a deep breath. He could smell the aroma of the desert mesquite and sage in his lungs. It invigorated him just as the view from his pool invigorated him. But the thought of Charlotte was the thing that invigorated him most. He hadn't meant to fall in love with her. He had never imagined settling down with anyone. He had always seen himself as a confirmed bachelor. He'd told his family, coworkers, and friends that he'd never get married, But, now, he couldn't imagine life without Charlotte.

How had it happened? How had he come to feel this way about her was a mystery to him, but it had happened. Maybe it started when he began to trust her. Did the murders and consequential investigation push them together? Maybe it was only a catalyst for the inevitable.

His deal with the sheriffs was predicated on having the hard evidence to back up his story. That was his trump card, the one thing Callaghan didn't get, the jump drive. It was still hidden where he was sure no one would find it. After that, he and Charlotte would go into witness protection. In a few years, any danger would be gone, and they'd come back to the valley, the valley he was born in, grew up in, and would die in. The sand, the heat, and the wind were all in his blood, and he could never leave, or leave for very long. He could survive a few years outside the valley.

Charlotte would be back within the hour. He had cleared out a whole dresser for her and one of the two closets in the master bedroom while she gathered necessities from her apartment. She would let the lease go at the end of the month.

These were the thoughts Mateo had while he stood on his deck gazing at the infinity pool, the valley below, the San Jacinto Mountains, the dark blue sky with its twinkling stars pinned to its canvas. He was completely unaware of the scope trained on him. He didn't hear the bullet. It arrived before its high-pitched whistle and splattered red liquid on the deck and the lounge chairs. Mateo's body fell limp into the pool, as his life blood drained from him mixing with the water, the red pool grew resembling an oil spill. The dogs jumped to their feet, barked, and ran around the pool but quickly resettled in their beds.

******

Mulder rolled to his side. The skin around his eye mirrored the back of the sight that was mounted to his rifle. He had laid there for what felt like hours, eye pressed to the back of that sight. He knew it would take almost as long for the indentation it left around his eye to dissipate. He stood, picked up the rifle and disassembled it. He carefully put each piece back into its molded foam rubber cutout in the gun case. He closed the case and walked the two-mile hike back to his car.

This was the last assignment Jacobs had given him. Tomorrow, he would be on a plane headed back to Langley, Virginia. He trusted Jacobs because he had worked with him for several years, and Jacobs always made the right decisions. This was the first time he had questioned Jacobs, but not out loud, not to his face, and not in private. He had a nagging feeling about it. That was all. Maybe he was wrong, but he had always trusted his gut. It had kept him safe. It had made him successful in this business.

He wasn't sure about Callaghan. Callaghan was a trained FBI agent that Jacobs was grooming. He just didn't think Callaghan had the personality for this business. He wasn't ruthless. He was smart. He was tenacious, but he seemed to lack the killer mentality this job required. He fretted that Jacobs may send him back to the Coachella Valley to clean up something Callaghan couldn't or simply messed up. He didn't want to come back to the Coachella Valley, ever. He hated the sand. He hated the wind. He hated the heat, but most of all, he hated the people. The Coachella Valley was primarily Hispanic. Mulder was white. Why the United States allowed all these foreigners to come here was beyond his understanding. If the Coachella Valley dropped off the map tomorrow with all of its Venezuelans, Mexicans, Hondurans, Salvadorians, Costa Ricans, and the like, he would celebrate. America was white, and that's the way it should stay. Maybe he was wrong about Callaghan. Regardless, he would not mention it to Jacobs.

******

Twenty minutes later Charlotte walked through the front door with an armload of clothes, hangers dangling around her knees but suspended by various silk blouses, pants, and skirts. "Baby, can you give me a hand?" she called out. No answer, but the dogs ran to the slider and began barking. She left the front door open, shuffled to the couch, and piled the clothes on the cushions.

"Babe! Where you at?" calling again. Then she made her way to the slider and opened it.

"Shit!" she exclaimed and froze in the doorway gasping for air. Mateo's body floated face down in the pool. His flaxen hair spread out around his head, hands and feet in a spread-eagle position. Blood had mixed with the water and left a trail from his still body to the skimmer as the pump continued to suck in the diluted red liquid and pump it out through the returns.

Charlotte turned and ran back to the couch where she had dumped her clothes. Tears began to roll down her cheeks, and her hands shook as she fumbled to retrieve a jump drive that Mateo had left on the coffee table. She left the clothes lying on the couch but clutched the device in her hand as tightly as she could then ran out the door to her car. Both dogs trotted through the slider then out the open front door as Charlotte backed out of the driveway then peeled down the street.

******

Two Weeks Later

Bill Sullivan and Mando Martinez parked in the FBI Field Office parking lot in Riverside. The drive took almost an hour, and they talked about the triple murder case most of the drive, reviewing various theories and finally eliminating all but one. Mando's brand new detective badge was proudly displayed on his left side hip belt while his Glock 19 was holstered on the opposite side. He was still ecstatic that he had passed the detective's exam and had immediately received his promotion and assignment to the case, now officially working as a detective.

Stepping off the elevator, they walked down the hall until they found room 218, FBI Special Agent Tony Rossi's office. Rossi, dressed in a white short-sleeve shirt and loosened black tie, sat behind his desk but was leaning forward reading a document. His bifocal glasses sat on the end of his nose while he squinted to see the text clearly. There were two jumbled piles of paperwork made of files and loose papers on each side of his desk. A pack of cigarettes, lighter, and ash tray were half hidden by papers on his left and a phone sat to his right, also half covered by papers. His office was utilitarian. A computer desk and monitor sat behind him and to the side, and the only decorations were two pictures on opposite walls. The first was a picture of the president of the United States on the wall behind him. The second was a picture of the FBI director on the opposite wall behind visitor chairs. They could smell cigarette smoke in the air as they entered. Mando guessed the FBI didn't enforce no smoking regulations inside their building.

"Gentlemen, sit down," said Rossi when he looked up. He pushed his glasses back up on his nose and sat the document he had been studying square on his desk.

"Hello, Tony," said Bill as he and Mando pulled two chairs to the front of Rossi's desk. "I'm glad we're finally able to get together and share information. On the way here, Mando and I were reviewing our working theory of the murders."

Tony leaned back in his chair and squinted his eyes, "Really? Well, let's hear what you got."

Bill began, "The three murders were committed to cover up illegal activity at The Factory on the reservation. Doctor Reginald Martin and Mateo Rivera were heading up those operations. When Fred Asghar was elected to the tribal council, one of these two men had him murdered to cover up their operations. We believe he was killed somewhere other than his home and the two victims that were killed at his home knew what he had found out and were killed to keep them from talking. Mr. Asghar's body was cremated to hide evidence by Mr. Rivera and Mr. Goodman."

Mando continued, "Sheldon Goodman was only a naïve kid, manipulated by Mr. Rivera and possibly was to be set up as an escape goat, but their plan changed when he escaped from Dr. Martin's estate so they poisoned Dr. Martin making it look like a heart attack. We know they were selling weapons to South American organizations fighting for the overthrow of their governments."

Tony interrupted, "You mean Freedom Fighters?"

"Yup, they're sometimes called that," interjected Bill.

Mando said, "We also know they were selling to the cartels and to local gangs here in the Coachella Valley. We believe they were involved with some kind of bitcoin mining operation while not illegal, its profits were never declared nor taxed."

Bill added, "All this was done under the knowledge and protection of The Agency."

Rossi's eyebrows rose. "And just why would The Agency do that, Bill?"

"Because they were their silent partner taking most of the profits from the operations. And the death of Dr. Martin and Mr. Rivera created a dead end to that avenue of investigation, at least for us. The FBI has the resources, backing, and power available to further the investigation that Riverside can't."

Both Riverside detectives didn't know if Tony believed their theory to be true, but were sure the FBI would have found some evidence at the reservation verifying this scenario. They knew Callaghan was thorough and had taken charge of the FBI's investigation, but they didn't know he had taken all the evidence with him when he left. All they knew was that Callaghan had gone back to his assigned field office, and FBI Special Agent Tony Rossi was the point man for the. They had worked with Tony long enough to know he was looking forward to retirement, would only do the minimum requirement for any investigation, not make waves, and would ensure the FBI came out looking successful. If a case got dirty or would not be solvable, then it would be another agency's problem, like the Riverside County Sheriff's Department.

Rossi sneered then leaned forward in his chair. "Wow! That's the biggest bunch of bullshit I've heard in a long time." Rossi began to repeat the official FBI theory on the case that his supervisor insisted he repeat if anyone came around asking. "Fred Asghar shot the two victims at his home then went on the lam. He's probably in Mexico or somewhere in South America living off the grid. He murdered his girlfriend because it was a lover's quarrel that turned violent. The brother was killed protecting his sister. Mr. Mateo Rivera was murdered by a gang member because he stopped supplying guns while Doctor Reginald Martin, who died of natural causes, was completely unaware of Mr. Rivera's illegal activities. You know a gang banger was arrested down in Mecca just after Rivera's murder with the same armor piercing ammunition that was used to kill him, and kill the two victims at Asghar's home. The dumbass supplied gangbangers with the very weapons and ammunition that killed him. What a stupid dipshit!"

"The FBI does not acknowledge anyone was cremated illegally. There's no evidence, so it's only rumor and innuendo. As far as Mr. Goodman goes, there was never any evidence of a kidnapping at Doctor Martin's home. Goodman's most likely three bricks shy of a full load, and you two bought his whole story, hook, line, and sinker."

Rossi leaned back, crossed his arms and smiled a Cheshire Cat smile. Bill and Mando glanced at each other in disbelief, but Bill had worked with the FBI enough to know once they made up their minds on a scenario, they would stick to it and close ranks.

Bill said, "And what about the materials you confiscated at the reservation? You've had time to review them. Did you find anything?"

"No, Bill, we didn't. I've already told you that, and Callaghan took what we found."

"Mr. Rivera said he had evidence. We believe he did and thought it must be hidden somewhere on the reservation. Did you find anything like that?"

Rossi became agitated with this last question. "Mr. Rivera was a pathological liar! He'd say anything to save himself... and he manipulated the two of you into believing him. He got just what he deserved, a bullet in the brain."

Mando caught Bill's eye. He could hardly believe what spewed from Rossi's mouth. Yes, Mateo had broken the law. He was a criminal and subject to the law of the land. Justice for Mateo would have meant time in prison. The Riverside County DA wanted to make a deal with him, no prison time then witness protection. Mando didn't believe witsec would have been real justice. With everything he'd done, Mateo deserved some prison time. But the DA was looking at much bigger fish and was short on evidence. Mateo promised he could produce evidence to prove everything he said, but was murdered before he was able to hand anything over. They had searched everywhere after his murder hoping to find it, but had come up empty so they were convinced it must have been hidden on the reservation.

Rossi regained his composure and sounded more professional now. "Gentlemen, I'm working on a new case involving credit card fraud sweeping Riverside County. My supervisor instructed me to use all of my time to work on this fraud case. That's what I'm doing now."

Bill asked, "Well, who's working on our triple homicide case then? Has it been reassigned?"

Tony rolled his eyes, becoming irritated again. "No, Bill. It hasn't."

"Well, just what's happening with it then?"

Rossi narrowed his eyes and glared at Bill. "It's in good hands. You don't need to worry about what we're doing with it. And the joint operations have been closed, so there'll be no more sharing of information on this case."

Rossi sat up and relaxed. The muscles in his jaw, neck, and shoulders had been tight and tense but now were slack. "Now if you don't have any more for me, I've got to get back on this fraud case."

Rossi dug out the half buried red and white pack of Marlboros from under his paperwork and withdrew one of the round cylinders. He leaned back in his chair as he lit it and took a deep drag closing his eyes. He enjoyed the feel of the smoke filling his lungs. Rossi exhaled hard, and the second-hand smoke blew across the desk and into the two detectives' faces.

"Gentlemen," Rossi said, his eyes opening to look at both men then leaned forward, "not all cases get solved. This is probably one of them."

Rossi was done with the conversation, done with the case, and done with them. For reasons never communicated to them, the FBI was moving on and leaving it to be solved by another agency.

Rossi picked up the paper he had sat down on his desk when Sullivan and Martinez first entered his office, moved his glasses towards the end of his nose, and turned his attention to the small lettering on the paper as he took another drag from his cigarette.

Detective Sullivan was an expert with years of experience and he knew what this meant, but he wouldn't say anything on the trip back. Without the help of the FBI, the case might never be solved. It would become folklore for the reservation and the Tranquilo Band of Mission Indians.

30

One Month Later

Sheldon pulled into the parking stall at Witch's Brew parking lot and turned off the engine. Next, he retrieved his phone from the console to check the time. The phone had been sitting directly below the AC vent and was cold. He smiled as he felt the phone thankful for the working air conditioning. It was almost 5 pm. He got out of his car, locked it using his key fob, and hurried to the front door of Witch's Brew with his green backpack slung over his shoulder. He and Connie had agreed to meet at 5 to prepare for fall classes.

Last Saturday Connie, Mic, and he had gone to what seemed like every used car lot in the valley looking for just the right car. It had taken the whole day to find the best deal, and by midafternoon he realized that Mic and Connie would never agree on the same car. Mic liked muscle cars, fast and sleek machines that turned heads, but Connie liked smaller cars that looked cute. She agreed with his final decision even though the car "wasn't the cutest" as she put it. Mic just turned up his nose saying it was a car an old man would drive. But it got good gas mileage, had low miles, was an automatic, and had air conditioning. And with the money he had saved for a down payment, he qualified for the financing.

Sheldon hustled through the door and looked towards the back room. Connie was already there, sitting in a pillowed chair in the corner and a book in her hand. There was another empty chair, its twin, nestled in the conversation area. A small round table stood in front of them.

"Hey Connie," he said as he sat his backpack down on the table next to a half empty coffee cup then leaned over to give her a kiss. Connie sat up from reading her text book and kissed him back. "You been here long?"

"About a half hour. I wanted to spend some time with my book before you got here."

"I thought you worked until five today."

"I'm on call tonight with Mic so Toni let me go early."

"Mic?" Sheldon, surprised. "I thought you worked with Juan?"

"Juan's on vacation this week. Mic's filling in."

"Vacation? They give you vacation?"

"Yup. Paid vacation after you've been there for a year."

"Wow. I'm paid hourly here. No work, no pay."

Connie picked up her coffee cup to take a sip. "You should get something before we start."

Sheldon left his backpack and went to the counter greeting his coworkers then ordered a cup of ice coffee. He picked it up from the counter before going back to the conversation area where Connie sat. She had a highlighter in one hand, once again engrossed in her reading. He sat down in the empty chair then pulled a blue binder out of his backpack.

"Okay, what's the plan?" he asked.

Connie sat her book on the table and took the binder from Sheldon's hand, holding it up in the air between them. "The plan, Professor Sheldon Goodman, is to teach you how to use your binder we got you from the campus bookstore."

Sheldon laughed, "Professor? You sure you're talking to the right person? I'll be lucky not to flunk out my first semester."

"You're gonna do great, Sheldon. And that's why we got you all this stuff."

Sheldon noticed a familiar face and said, "Hey, look who just walked in," as he nodded towards the front door.

Connie turned. "It's Detective Martinez. I wonder what he's doing here."

"Hey, cops drink coffee too… and eat donuts," Sheldon said with a grin.

"Ha ha," she responded sarcastically. "I wanna see if he can give us any updates on everything."

Connie waited until Detective Martinez had picked up his coffee then called and waved, "Detective Martinez, hello."

Mando looked up, surprised that someone called him by name, then smiled when he saw Connie and Sheldon. "Hello Ms. Asghar and Mr. Goodman. It looks like you two are getting ready for fall classes."

"We are," replied Connie. "And I'm glad we ran into you because I wanted to know if you could update us on the investigation."

Mando hesitated, "I really can't tell you anything beyond what has already been published in the news. The murders are an ongoing investigation that the Sheriff's Department is actively working on. But for these kinds of cases, it may take a year or more before an arrest is made. I think the DA could give you more information than what I'm able to do."

Connie wrinkled her brow. Sheldon took her hand and squeezed it.

Connie said, "The DA hasn't told us anything other than we'll have to testify in court once that cowboy and the pastor go to trial. She wouldn't even tell us who else would be testifying or anything about the case. I've gotten more information from the news than her."

"Remember she has to protect the integrity of the case. I'm sure that's why she hasn't said more to you about it."

"As far as the sex trafficking case goes," continued Mando, "Mr. Peter Anderson and Pastor Alfredo Eminis are both being held without bail. Mr. Anderson is at county lockup in Riverside and Pastor Eminis is in the Indio jail."

"But what about the men's and women's homes the church runs, and the place out in Thousand Palms, the brothel?"

Mando sighed and tried to remember exactly what the news had reported before he spoke. "When the location was raided, we did find some evidence of illegal activity, but the fire left little for us to find.

They may have been notified before our officers showed up with their search warrant. Mr. Hector Alvarez, the registered owner of the property, is currently being sought by law enforcement but has not yet been located."

"That's as much as the news said," replied Connie as she squeezed Sheldon's hand.

Sheldon added, "And the two homes the church ran are now closed. They hired an interim pastor while they're waiting for Pastor Eminis to be released from jail." Sheldon still had a few contacts at the church.

"I can't believe they still want that guy as a pastor. Detective Martinez, isn't there some kind of law about that. You know like when a doctor loses his license, he can no longer practice medicine?"

"Unfortunately, there isn't. Doctors and pastors are completely different professions."

"Well, there should be," she insisted.

Connie's cell phone burred, and she dug it out from the bottom of her purse. Detective Martinez excused himself and left through the front door, coffee in hand. She read the caller ID. "It's Mic."

"Hey Mic, what's up?"

Sheldon could only hear her side of the conversation, but knew Mic was going to pick her up in the business van at the coffee shop.

"Where's your pick up?" he asked once Connie had ended the call.

"Riverside Hospital. Mic will be here in a few minutes so we should pack up."

Connie and Sheldon packed up their books and supplies then headed to the parking lot to meet Mic. As they reached their cars Mic pulled into the lot and stopped next to them. Sheldon gave Connie a quick good-bye kiss then walked to the driver's window as Mic rolled it down.

"Hey, Mic. How's it going?"

"Been great, Dude. And you?"

"Couldn't be better. You know I'm starting college this fall?"

Connie had entered the passenger side of the van, and said, "I told him, Sheldon, and we're going to be studying together."

"Ol' mother hen making sure you do your homework, right?" remarked Mic with a grin.

"No," replied Connie, "Good girlfriend supporting her boyfriend in the things he considers important."

"I'll take all the help I can get. I don't see you starting college."

"Now that you mention it, Toni's been talking to me about getting a funeral science degree. That way I could embalm people, you know, once they're dead." Mic smiled, joking.

"Yea, I think they frown on live embalming," Sheldon replied, almost laughing.

"Okay, boys. That's enough. No one embalms live people."

Mic rolled his eyes. "Okay, good girlfriend, you ready to go? We gotta go all the way to Riverside."

******

Seven hours earlier

Freddie Eminis lounged on his bunk reading his Bible. His orange jumpsuit hung loose on his body except for his waist. He didn't like that it showed how much weight he had gained in the past few years, how his stomach protruded over his belt or his love handles had grown. But that was before he was arrested and put in jail. In here there were no belts, no pants, no Tommy Bahama's shirts that hid his obtruding belly. Now everyone wore the same clothes, orange jumpsuits with the initials RCJ on the back, Riverside County Jail.

Freddie had already started a following in jail as he preached to the other inmates and was organizing a weekly Bible Study. Some of the other residents had taken to calling him "Preacher" after his second day in lockup. He liked that. He told them how he had been framed and was innocent, a martyr just like Jesus. But all the other jail occupants claimed they were innocent as well. Birds of a feather flock together, someone had said. But he was different from the rest of these jail birds. He had his reputation, he still had his congregation, and he still had complete control over his flock. They would believe anything he told them, and he would make sure Peter and Hector took the fall for this, not him.

Freddie, engrossed in his reading, was startled when the electronic buzzer sounded over the intercom, but the familiar voice calling his cellblock to lunch in the cafeteria made him smile. He was hungry. As he sat up and closed his Bible, the orange jumpsuit pulled on his stomach. Shit, he thought. I'm gonna cut out the dessert, soda, and any other sweets. Maybe I'll just eat a salad. He stood and slipped on his prison issued white canvas Velcro-strapped shoes then made his way into the hall.

The jail had three cellblocks designated by why someone was detained. Cellblock A was for the accused who had been arrested and were awaiting arraignment. Cellblock B was for inmates who had been arraigned and were awaiting trial. Cellblock C was for prisoners who were convicted and would serve their sentence in county lockup or were waiting to be transferred to a state or federal prison. Cellblock B held the most people, and it was the cellblock Freddie currently called home. There were almost fifty men living in Cellblock B mostly two to a cell. Freddie had a cellmate when he first got there, but he quickly rose to a position of power and influence utilizing his leadership skills, his Bible, and his manipulative abilities. Out of respect for Preacher's spiritual needs to seek the Lord uninterrupted, his cellmate moved to another cell.

Other men were leaving their cells and filling the hallway heading towards the cafeteria. Freddie greeted of them with a Christian greeting as he walked to the end of the hall. Once all the men were out of their cells and gathered where he now stood, the guards would open the gates leading to a much narrower hallway then finally into the cafeteria. As the barred gate opened, men spilled into the narrow hallway. Some hurried ahead of Freddie while others chose to wait until the hall was less congested before entering. Freddie passed the open gate and walked down the hall. Men jostled him on either side. Once he reached the cafeteria, there would be room for everyone, but the hallway always seemed like organized chaos to him.

Suddenly Freddie felt a sharp pain in his back. Then another, and another, each in quick succession, almost like a drummer starting a slow drum roll. He turned to see what was happening, but his knees began to buckle. The stabbing pain moved to this side then his stomach. As he fell to the floor there were more stabs to his chest. Now Freddie lay on the polished concrete floor. An object fell to the floor in front of his eyes. One end was wrapped with cloth tape. The other end was pointed metal and covered in blood. Men moved around him, away from his body, skirting the flow of bright red blood that spurted from his chest and turning his orange jumpsuit blood red. He knew the shiv had struck an artery and he was quickly bleeding out. He would be dead before they could get him to the infirmary, before the guards could clear the hall, and before they even knew he had been attacked. Freddie closed his eyes, the sounds of the men moving around him began to fade then echo. Before he lost consciousness an old hymn began to play in his head, almost angelic as he slowly drifted into sleep:

Nearer, my God, to thee,
Nearer to thee!
E'en though it be a cross
That raiseth me.
Still all my song shall be
Nearer, my God, to thee,
Nearer, my God, to thee,
Nearer to thee!

******

Edwardo dropped the shiv on the floor while men continued to shove and elbow their way towards the cafeteria. There was no reaction to what just happened. With all the activity, no one had seen anything beyond a sea of orange moving along in the flow, being swept towards the end of the hallway. And even if anyone did, no one in here were snitches. You would have to be crazy to snitch on someone who just killed another inmate. You would be dead before the next morning if you were to say anything.

Edwardo made his way towards the cafeteria. Freddie was at least twenty feet behind him now. There would be no way the guards could suspect him. Men who had spent time in prison know that those orange jumpsuits were great for keeping blood from splattering. They soaked it up and kept it on the guy that was shived. He double checked his hands. Good, no blood. He would give his jumpsuit a good look once he reached the cafeteria, but he also knew that if blood were to get any-where, it would be his hands. The quick stabbing motion and move-ment of the location with each strike kept blood off his hands and his jumpsuit.

He would make the phone call to Hector this afternoon and let him know it had been done. Hector didn't go into detail as to why he wanted this guy offed, but he didn't need to. Edwardo was part of the crew, and loyal to the end. He had done many things for Hector in the past, some would think even worse than what he had just done, and he would do it again if Hector asked him. Hector ran a big operation, and he had peo-ple everywhere. Edwardo was one of them.

31

The Next Day

Connie breezed in through the front door of Desert Valley Cremations that morning. Her hair was in a ponytail threaded through the back hole of her ball cap that sported the Desert Valley Cremations logo. Her eyes were bright and her face was lightly painted with makeup.

"Good morning, girl," greeted Toni. "You don't look like you were on call last night at all."

"What can I say? It was a slow night. Hey, is Mic here yet?"

"I haven't seen him," replied Toni. "He could be in back with Joe. They'll be busy all day with cremations."

The two women heard the door leading to the back open and close. Seconds later, Mic walked in smiling, his usual confident cheery self.

"Mornin' ladies. Where's the donuts?"

"No donuts today, Mic. Sorry." Toni had decided that she and Joe needed to go on a diet. The donuts didn't help them lose weight, and if she bought them only for the staff, Joe would end up eating most of them anyway. "Joe and I have started dieting, so no more donuts, for a while anyway."

"Hey," now pointing at Toni, "do you know who we picked up last night?" Mic looked excited, almost animated.

"Yup," replied Toni as she picked up the paperwork from the top basket and examined it. "A Mr. Alfredo Eminis."

Mic was puzzled for only a moment. Why didn't she recognize the name? "Pastor Alfredo Eminis of New Life Empowerment Church."

Toni, shocked, "No Sh...!" but stopped herself. She looked at the paperwork again. "Well, how about that." She picked up her cell phone from the desk and called Joe. "Joe, come in here right now!"

"What's wrong?" Joe sounded concerned.

"Just get in here. There's something you need to know."

"It's not about Mr. Robert Norman, is it? He's been in the furnace for a while now. There's no turning back with him."

"No, just come here, hurry."

Connie said to Toni, "Let me be the one to tell him." Then to Mic, "After all, Mic, you got to tell Toni."

"Sure, whatever," replied Mic.

Moments later, Joe hurried through the back door of the conference room then into the office area. "Okay, I'm here. What's so important that it can't wait until I get to a good stopping point?"

Connie grinned and looked at Toni then at Joe. Joe looked at the three of them and realized what was going to be said was going to come from Connie.

"Okay, Connie. What is it?"

"Do you know who Mic and I picked up last night at the Riverside Hospital morgue and is now resting peacefully in our reefer?"

"Who," Joe looked somewhat confused.

"Pastor Alfredo Eminis from the new something, something church," unable to remember the church's name.

Joe smiled, "You're kidding. Really?"

All three chimed in together, "Yup!"

"Well, karma's a bitch, ain't it," stated Joe as he smiled again. It wasn't a question.

******

The first day of college classes for the fall semester

Sheldon turned off Monterey Avenue into the Desert Valley Community College campus and looked for a parking spot. Connie and he had visited the campus several times during the summer to get books and explore the campus. The lots had few cars then, but today they were full. After driving around for several minutes, he found an empty stall under the shade of the solar panels that covered most of lot twenty-eight.

As he stepped out of his car and retrieved his green backpack from the front passenger seat, Sheldon checked his watch. It was 8:40 am on Wednesday, his day off from work, and his first day of college classes. He trekked across the parking lot towards the south annex.

Once Sheldon reached the campus sidewalk, he stopped to take in the view. The sky was blue, the air was crisp, and the sun shone through the green fronds of the palm trees that lined the sidewalk and were positioned around the buildings. There were fan palms, king palms, queen palms, and even date trees standing tall and stately all in straight formations. The grass, thick and dark, contrasted the large desert planters that held various shades of rocks and sands, all in desert colors. Mexican bird of paradise displayed their bright orange flowers with pride. Chuparosa, not to be outdone by their cousin, glowed in deep red and yellow. Bougainvillea with their purple flowering leaves dotted the landscape and called begging to take in their color and beauty while students hurried down sidewalks, disappeared into classrooms, or scurried down passageways, busy with all the demands a college student has on their first day of classes.

A sense of pride began to well up from somewhere inside him, a feeling he had rarely felt before. He realized his eyes were moist, a reaction from the feeling he was experiencing? He wasn't sure. What he was sure of though, was that he was grateful for where he was right now. This summer was the most bizarre summer he had ever experienced, and he wasn't sure how he had survived it all. But he had not just survived it, he had grown because of it. And now he is a college student. It felt right. In spite of everything, somehow, some way, this was his destiny... to be a college student. He wouldn't try to figure any more out, but just breathe in this moment, and relish in what he had, right here, right now. That's when he realized that the winds in his life, just like the desert winds had subsided. He existed in a calm that allowed him to not only have a plan for his life, but to follow it as well. Maybe he would become a nurse after all?

He thought of his mom. She would be so proud of him if she knew where he was today. Would he see her again someday? He hoped he would, and realized he no longer was angry that she had disappeared after they moved into the church's women's home. He still didn't know what happened to her, but he no longer believed she had abandoned him. He was sure Pastor Alfredo Eminis had lied to him so he still held on to that hope. Someday... someday.

Sheldon wiped the tears that had begun to track down his cheek with the sleeve of his t-shirt then slowly walked down the sidewalk that led to the south annex for his first day as a real college student.

Gregg Chesterman grew up in the northwest, and after serving four years in the Marine Corps, he settled in the Coachella Valley making it his home for the next forty years. He attended college earning a BA degree in General Ministries from Bethany University and settled into a career as an associate pastor as well as teaching and administrating in private education. Later he pursued a new career in secondary education earning an MS degree in Educational Guidance and Counseling from the University of California San Bernardino. He began working in the California community college system as an educational counselor and transfer center coordinator for the next twenty years.

After twenty years of a very successful career in community college counseling, Gregg retired from the California community college system and moved to Texas making his home in Wichita Falls. Next, he went to work for Midwestern State University then Vernon College before starting his own business writing and implementing murder mystery games at a local winery. Eventually he retired from secondary education and closed his murder mystery business to focus on his new project, Desert Winds, his first full novel.